Wh… …ded

ANNE M. CURTIS

cripperty
publishing

First published in 2019 by Cripperty Publishing

Cripperty Publishing
www.cripperty.com
Email: info@cripperty.com

ISBN: 978-1-9999967-1-0

Where Acorns Landed

For Molly

0

At this precise moment around the world, 14,732 planes are in the sky. One of those planes is flying over Lowell Watterson's house. Destination: Rennes. He can't hear the plane. He is listening to the radio. I have already told him how many planes are in the sky. He loves anything to do with numbers.

I can hear the plane. I can also hear my heart not beating.

I won't tell you much more. Waste of time. You'd only forget. Best I switch you to Lowell…

Chapter 1

Peel, Isle of Man

The radio was on. It had been on from the day his parents had disappeared and Lowell had been listening ever since.

His father had told him to stay by the radio. That was the last thing he said to him. But it had been one of those rare days on the island when the sea and sky are one big cotton-blue sheet, starched, wrinkles ironed away, just a crease in the middle for the horizon. Lowell had got distracted. His parents disappeared in the crease.

The desk lamp had also been left on, illuminating the radio. He never understood why. It had been a painfully bright day when they left. Sometimes, he wondered whether the radio itself had somehow managed to flick the lamp's switch. It was unlike any other radio; it had a mind of its own. There was no knob for tuning, no switch to change frequencies; the radio did all that for him. So Lowell just listened.

Work was out of the equation. He had stretched compassionate leave more than Curphey and Moore's books could take; with them being an accountancy firm it didn't take long to tot that one up. He looked like some mange-eaten stray now he'd ditched the pressed suits; there was something fake about all that preening, smoothing over the crumples, plastering over reality, denying the scrunching of water and limbs.

They still hadn't found his dad's legs.

Lowell had grown a beard; its curling ferocity surprised him. Even though the hair on his head nearly touched his shoulders these days, it remained lank and mousey. The beard was more appropriate; a prerequisite for a feral, wolf-man hermit abandoned to the deserted wilds of the lounge. That's how he saw himself anyway. His hair let him down, gave him the appearance of a homeless spaniel. Not that he spent much time in front of the mirror – there wasn't one in the lounge. He mostly only allowed himself to leave the lounge, the radio, for quick visits to the toilet and kept those to a minimum, rationing fluids and food. Tea intake was down to one and a half mugs a day; water, one mug at night (which also helped clean the mug, sort of). A pallet-load of mineral water stored under the sideboard kept the kettle (also in the lounge) stocked up. He ordered the water and the rest of his groceries online, got them delivered to the lounge window. He'd lived off cornflakes with minimal milk and pizzas in the early days, but then the original pizza delivery bloke had been replaced by Tim, from his old class at school, who'd turned up on the moped, all grins and questions. So the only pepperoni and three cheeses consumed these days were the variety he could heat up in a microwave. He had signed for the delivery of the microwave at the window too. His side of the window. The lounge side.

The internet made isolation so much more feasible; he could get on with life without all that moving of milieu. Google had helped pinpoint the cause of that pain in his side; well, it had given him a list of possibilities: cancer, appendicitis, trapped wind, or kidney stone. If he could choose, he would go for the blocked fart option; it had gone on too long for that though. As he always, since relocating to the lounge, saved going to the toilet until he was absolutely bursting, he'd started thinking he'd done himself some damage, overstretched his bladder, but he'd noticed what appeared to be sand or fine grit at the bottom of the toilet this morning. The most likely diagnosis now pointed to it being a kidney stone. The grit was just the drizzle before the storm. But he only noticed the pain when the radio set itself to untuned static. It chose to do that most of the time, so much so, the crepitating hiss of static had become almost part of the wallpaper. Static was what made home, *home*.

A small part of that hiss, picked up not just by his radio, but any untuned analogue radio or television, was actually the remnants of radiation going all the way back to the Big Bang. So if static was now part of the wallpaper, you could say the petals in the fleur-de-lys pattern were infused with the origins of the universe.

The radio only retuned when and where *it* wanted, and because of that Lowell mostly waited, afraid to leave the radio in case he missed something.

Sometimes the radio wandered to low frequencies, low enough to tune to the sounds of space, to the fizz of asteroids hitting the outer atmosphere, to the cacophonous screeches of solar storms entering the ionosphere. Whistlers. That's what the radio ham sites called them. For all their clambering din, the whistlers swept through Lowell like a choir of angels; inside the undulating gasps and gargles of the whistlers Lowell found his calm.

Then the radio would tune away from the whistlers. If he had his eyes open, which he rarely did after a session with the celestial symphony, he'd see the red vertical line moving behind the radio's tuning window. He'd given up watching that line months ago. The radio's exact frequency spectrum remained hidden; the tuning window had its own numerical reference points ranging from zero to seventy-nine. But the radio rarely tuned to the same place; there was absolutely no logic to the red line as far as he could tell. The radio usually chose static after the whistlers but occasionally it'd tune itself in such a way that the whistlers would flatten to a humming noise. The humming of bees. Such were the whimsical musings of the radio, acting the demented despot DJ, mixing in what it wanted when it wanted.

Those occasions, when the radio tuned to the hum, excited Lowell most. It meant Nell was on her way. It was sort of her signature tune; the radio's one predictability. Hers was the only voice that the radio had ever played. He had heard her the day the boat was found; that was the first time. Her voice had kept him listening. In the weeks and months to follow, his dad's bloated remains were found in the nets of a scallop dredger; his mum's body, mostly intact, though over-inflated and gnawed in places (ear, lower lip, fingers), was discovered by a dog walker on Fenella Beach. But still he listened. Nell's susurrant tones would make a spider sound heavy-footed; so diaphanous was the nature of her voice that it passed right though his skin and threaded a bow around his heart.

That same heavy-footed spider may as well be skipping on his scalp; it was itching that much. Three weeks he'd gone without washing his hair or rather dipping his hair under the shower head – that's what constituted hair-washing in the Lounge Age. He'd usually give himself a quick splash all over while he was at it. Just with water, mind; shampooing, soaping, rinsing took too long. The lounge had two resident washing-up bowls: one for dishes, the other for himself. There was a tide-line of grease around the yellow one. He never used that on himself. It had been in the family for years. His mum used to give it to him to be sick in whenever he had some bug or other as a kid and had still carried on using it for dishes right up until the day she left. The blue bowl, he'd had delivered to the lounge window. He christened it BOFO (Body Odour Feck Off) and filled it every morning with warm water from the kettle. The sponge, to wash his essential bits, made it into a sort of bed bath without the bed. He slept on the sofa. Not that that's where he washed himself. Too near the radio. He didn't want to splash that. He emptied BOFO via the lounge window. Mum would have been proud of him watering the flowers so regularly; she had loved her garden.

The twice-monthly shower visit was on hold. Lowell could always dip his head into BOFO if the itching got any worse. The radio had been tuning to Nell every day for the last week, several heaven-soaked minutes a day. He'd heard her more in the last week then in all the previous months combined. So, now more than ever, he couldn't tear himself away.

And he could speak to her too. He had discovered that last Friday. At first, when she answered, he thought he'd imagined it; he'd been with the radio for thirteen months and two weeks (409 days) and he had never even realised. The radio was not just a receiver but a transmitter as well. You wouldn't guess looking at it; there was no microphone to speak of, or to, for that matter, yet speak he did, and for the precious moments they had together, she listened and made everything better.

They hadn't worried before, his parents. He'd known them go out in a force six even a seven and not fret in the slightest. They'd had all the equipment they needed: the VHF radio to call the coastguard, the flares, and the mobile phone – they were all there onboard that old fishing (not that they ever did any fishing) trawler of theirs. So, when his dad had told him to stay by the radio, he hadn't taken it seriously. Why would he? Anyway, in all their years as proud owners of the trawler that was the first time Lowell had even seen the radio. And it wasn't as if it even bore any resemblance to a normal ship to shore radio; it was more like a prop from an old war movie. A radio that might have once blasted out Churchill's: *We shall fight on the beaches. We shall fight in the hills. We shall never surrender.* A radio shrouded in boxy Bakelite panels, the colour of stewed tea – concentrated tea: all the tea and caffeine of four servings in just one mug.

Something was coming through the static: bites of solid audio were emerging from the chaos. Lowell settled into the armchair especially reserved for such radio sessions. Why taint life's highlights being uncomfortable? It was like having pizza without the pineapple topping – he was going off pizza – or having Czech beer without the dry roasted peanuts – he had quit alcohol. Nell was the ultimate, the only highlight. He shuffled the armchair closer.

Humming. It had never gone straight to the humming before, the monotone hum. Nell's theme tune. She was on her way. He wiped the dandruff off his shoulders. The humming stopped abruptly; islets of static crackled and hissed.

'Nell,' he whispered. 'Are you there?'

'I am.'

Her voice was oxygen. He leaned forward, breathed her in.

'Candles,' she murmured.

He waited for her to elaborate. She didn't.

'What candles? Is there a power cut there? I guess not, otherwise how'd you be talking to me. Stupid of me. Batteries.' His words were as graceful as an elephant belly-flopping into BOFO.

'Candles,' she repeated. 'Three candles. The table is set.'

The red line shifted. Nell faded away.

Chapter 2

Brittany, Northern France

Brighid was off to see the Virgin Mary. That's what the kids had called her mother at the convent. They had also called Brighid, Jesus, on account of her being the Virgin Mary's kid. Brighid called her mother, Tessy. It was sort of short for Therese, and what Tessy herself seemed to prefer to be known as. Not that Brighid had ever asked her. She had only actually ever met her once that she remembered. Their first encounter, the bit at the maternity ward when Tessy brought her screaming into the world, she couldn't remember, so that didn't count. It was one of the strange things about the email, she'd called herself *mum*. Previous communications, her annual greetings didn't say *mum*. Any maternal reference was restricted to *mother* and that was always put in parenthesis, between brackets, separated from the rest of the words, like Tessy, separated from the rest of the world, isolated from everything else.

She never missed Brighid's birthday. There was always a birthday card. She always managed to get the address somehow. The early years had been easy; Tessy would have known where she lived. No, the mystery started when Brighid left the convent school dorms for her first flat in Liverpool, and deepened every birthday from then on in. Cards not only arrived to the house in Falmouth and the flat in Dun Laoghaire, but the addresses for Finsbury Park and Brixton were also spot on, and again this year, the birthday card from *(mother)*, envelope flushed pink all pleased with itself, had successfully landed on the porch floor of her Brighton apartment. She'd even got a card for her twenty-seventh to the poste restante in La Paz. Now Tessy had her email address, the unfathomable fell a few more fathoms. No-one could have told her. Tessy had been missing for years, ever since doing that runner from Ballybonkers. French stamps on card envelopes were the only clue to Tessy's whereabouts; there was never an address to write back to. Not until now.

The map had come first. In an email. Subject: *Map to House*. There was no message, no explanation, no cheers or regards with a name, just a link. She'd nearly trashed it, thinking it was junk or worse a virus, but the email address tesscbroceliande@hotmail.com got her thinking; she'd clicked the link. The zoomed-in map detailed an area in North-West France; a red triangle pinpointed the house's exact location. She had replied, asking if the sender (already sure it was Tessy) had forgotten to include their message. The response arrived just half an hour later. Brighid had read it so many times over the last couple of days that she remembered it word for word.

From: tesscbroceliande@hotmail.com
To: craftbrighid@gmail.com
Subject: It's me
Sent: October 14, 20:12

Brighid
This is urgent as in URGENT! I have to see you. Now you know where I live, get yourself here for 8:00 or thereabouts, Thursday night (French time). I'll have your room ready.
Lots of love

Mum
X
P.S. Your father sends his best wishes.
P.P.S. No need to bring sandwiches – I'll make tea.
P.P.P.S. This is the last time.

Her room was news. Brighid hadn't even known there was one. And where did this *Mum* come from? The birthday sign-ins were always the 'mother' in brackets thing – and never with a capital 'M' – always lower case – a subdued 'm' – an 'm' taking the backseat.

> *All my love*
> *Tessy (mother)*
> *X*

That's what she was used to.

She had debated not going, but the line about it being the last time (was that the number of postscripts or something more sinister?) had her baited and hooked. The channel crossing had squeezed out her credit card's dying breath.

Flashing lights dazzled the rear-view mirror. She edged her car closer to the ditch. The coach, practically touching her back-bumper since entering the Forêt de Paimpont, thanked her with a full-beam glare, then a whole heap of diesel exhaust as it passed. Fumes faded to the smells of autumn mulch, dank bark, the forest innards – glutinous darkness, clotted and congealed. She closed the windows. Tight. This, according to Arthurian legend, was the magical land of Brocéliande. If family legend was anything to go by – The Tales of Tessy handed down in oral tradition (from Nana, Granddad and Aunt Mary) – it was quite fitting that Tessy should end up here. She lived in her very own fantasy world after all. The fact she was still banging on about Brighid's father confirmed that.

She changed channels on the radio, switching from French rap to Johnny Hallyday. The car was shielding her from the outside, protecting her from the darkness, the shadows in the forest; it was her shining armour, hermetically sealing her in at 19.5 degrees. The air freshener triangle danced in the warm air blasting from the vents. The scent of vanilla. Tessy had offered her an ice cream that one (remembered) time they met. That had been vanilla too. She'd bought the air freshener the day before Tessy's emails. But it wasn't a sign; she didn't believe in signs. It was the only option available in the garage shop.

'Hey Brighid, I bought you an ice cream,' she'd said. Just like that, as if she'd always been there, as though Brighid was a kid on a family day out, mother just back from the ice cream kiosk, only away a couple of minutes. But Brighid had been fresh out of film school, was twenty-one years old. If Tessy had just slipped off to get her an ice cream, she must have been waiting several cow generations for the cream and queued all the way from Sydney to Cornwall. That's where Brighid was living then, Cornwall. Tessy had just turned up, completely out of the blue, handed her the ice cream. Brighid had only popped to the beach to get some fresh air; the edit suite had gotten too stuffy. She'd recognised her mother straightaway, having seen enough old photographs. Her mother had smiled, making the wrinkles around her eyes crisscross in exactly the same way as the lines on Nana's face had done. Yet she still looked much younger than the forty years she would have been then, even from Brighid's much younger perspective. At twenty-one she thought anyone over thirty was positively ancient; not her mother. Yes, she had those smile lines, but they were like premature wrinkles on a youthful skin, creased by too much happiness. Those lines annoyed Brighid.

More impatient headlights in the rear view mirror.

The forest was lapping up any remnants of twilight. She disliked driving in the dark at the best of times, so add in the unfamiliar road, a road flanked by deep ditches, she was going as fast as she could. Her reflection, all lit up, hinted at the same pattern of faint lines beneath her own tired eyes. The scent of warm vanilla was making her feel sick. She switched off the heater.

Brighid had taken the ice cream – it seemed only polite. When she looked up again, Tessy had gone. No explanations, no conversation, nothing. Tessy might as well have disappeared into the sea wall. Brighid would have thought she'd imagined it, dozed off, dreamed it, but for the cone of melting vanilla ice cream.

The forest thinned to the open space of a lake. This had to be the Étang de Comper, the Arthurian Lake of Vivian, the site Merlin supposedly chose to build his mythical crystal palace; the glamour of the lake was hiding it apparently. She'd been browsing tourist leaflets on her last double-espresso stop. So, if this was the lake, she was on the right road.

The pain in the ass coach again. Parked up ahead. Brighid signalled, then overtook. Spanish plates. Tourists sightseeing, perhaps. Lousy timing; it was almost eight o'clock on a rapidly darkening night. They would be lucky to even see the lake, let alone any crazy make-believe fairy turrets. Brighid's headlights brushed over the lake's surface. It shone back, rippling much like any other lake. Tessy would probably see Vivian waving from crystal ramparts, the glass drawbridge opening, the whole blinking fairy fan-fare.

She took the turn off for Folle Pensée. According to the

map, she was just a few kilometres away.

Back in dense forest, and more than a few kilometres of numerous steep climbs, descents and bends later, she was just starting to think she was driving around in circles then the sign appeared. A small rusted sign, partially hidden by foliage; a sign she may well have already passed during numerous circuits. She took a left, as instructed in the map and route planner. If this turned out to be the wrong turning, reversing would be a nightmare; it was more track than road with deep ditches again on either side. She was now, in theory, only two hundred metres away. Her heart was pounding so hard it felt as if an athletic hare was doing high-jump practice on her chest. Too many espressos, the imminent vis-à-vis with the long-lost Tessy, and wham, bang, double-whammy, a sumo-wrestler had broken into nerve-central, was stumbling upon her confidence and seizing its withering remains. The wrestler pounced, squashing, flattening.

Gateposts loomed into the reach of the headlights. She applied pressure to the brakes. A house name, chiselled into one of the posts, told her all she needed to know: *Hunvre.*

This was it.

The tall wrought-iron gates had been left open. Were they always open, or was this just for her?

Ancient trees laden with sumo fist knots lined the sweeping drive all the way up to the house. It was a big old house, a manor even. Shutters all closed; windows hidden.

She turned off the engine. Killed the lights. Tessy would have heard the car, was probably on her way out with a torch. And how was she supposed to act when Tessy came out with that torch? What happened then? Should she hug her?

With her eyes slowly readjusting to the tenebrous

shapes and forms outside, she could just about make out the front door and the steps leading up to it; there was a lantern on the top step, a candle-flame beacon barely showing her the way. She got out of the car, closed the door, clicked the key remote. The locks clunked in unison, sounding louder than normal. Her armour was off. She shoved the car key into the pocket of her overnight bag; the same pocket held a reassuring backup list of twenty-four hour check-in hotels.

No doorbell. Just a brass doorknocker. She used that.

'Door's open,' a woman's voice called out.

She couldn't remember how her mother's voice sounded (there was only that line about the ice cream to go on) but out here, all detached, disembodied from the rest of her, it sounded strange, disconcerting, as if she was hearing a recording of her own voice with a bit of reverb thrown in.

As there was no light in the hallway, Brighid grabbed the lantern and stepped into the fetid stink of damp, to the threadbare carpet choked in hairs, grit, soil, pieces of wallpaper. Beyond the corner of the L-shaped hall, was a door, half-open. A shimmering amber glow promised warmth and light. She set the lantern down onto a small telephone table that was missing the telephone.

'Look at you.' Tessy's voice seeped though the gap in the door. 'You're here.'

And Tessy was there. Her hair still blonde, or dyed blonde, all scooped up in a bun. And she'd gotten all dressed up for the occasion; her emerald silk evening gown was sheer debutante, dinner-ball, Hollywood premiere style. All glamour. No hint of madness. The red wellies were perhaps a bit of an eccentric choice, but then this was out in the sticks.

Brighid bustled past her, busying herself, securing

the over-night bag onto her shoulder, avoiding any unnecessary hugs. First hurdle accomplished, she scanned the room. The fire blazing in the inglenook hearth was the source of most of the light; candles supplied the rest. Between the candles on the mantelpiece there sat a framed photograph, of Brighid; a photo of her twenty-one year old self holding an ice cream, looking stunned, stunned and completely oblivious to the camera snapping away. She was just as dumbstruck *seeing* the photo. The dining table in the centre of the room didn't help; it was set for three. She had thought it was just going to be her and Tessy; now she feared her father was still very much present behind the scenes. There were candles on the table too. Three candles all in a row.

'Supper.' Tessy beamed. 'Our last supper.

Chapter 3

Peel, Isle of Man

'THE TABLE IS SET,' Nell had said.

What was that supposed to mean? Were he not so reliant on the radio, Lowell could have quite happily chucked it through the lounge window, it tuning away like that. But that was last night. Now, tonight, he was full of expectations, full of hopes. If the last week was anything to go by he'd be hearing from her again later.

It had gotten into his head, when he'd finally succumbed to the itching and had said head submerged in BOFO's tepid waters, that it was perhaps Nell's way of suggesting a date. She was contacting him daily, as though she couldn't go a night without him. Was that down to her or the radio's will? Maybe it was just that she was getting closer to the Isle of Man, and her signal was stronger. How close? Where? She was out at sea, that much he did know. It was the first question he'd asked her; the sound of the sea was always there in the background. Specifics such as location, the boat, what she was doing on it, were skirted over, pushed aside or forgotten. It was often that way; it was all part of her charm, her enigma. Anyway, her voice made him so dizzy that he often forgot what she said. They could talk for ten minutes, him mostly listening, and when he tried to remember, relish the conversation afterwards, he'd realise there were whole chunks he couldn't remember. Because of this, Lowell really didn't know too much about Nell. But he knew he loved her. He knew he would love her until his very last dying breath.

He had thought about writing down their conversations, recording them even, but that, he decided, would just take away the magic, snap the thread keeping them together. Besides, the one time he'd set up the microphone on his computer, placed it near the radio, the radio had gone berserk, spewing out deafening static; and with no volume button to turn it down, it'd driven him crazy for hours.

The bottoms of his jeans were wet again. Every night for the last five days it'd been the same. His socks were damp too and covered in sand. He hadn't been near the beach for months, so it was a complete mystery where all that sand was coming from. That wasn't all, he also had red marks around his belly button, like he'd been scratching too hard.

It wasn't as if Lowell was the forgetful type. His normally photographic memory had helped him sail through his A-Levels and bagged him the accountancy scholarship at Curphey and Moore's. No, amnesia was a feature characteristic of the Lounge Age, and in this epoch it was only found in isolated pockets: mostly the bits when Nell talked. That was frustrating, yet even more maddening was the persistent feeling he had that she'd told him some amazing things, mind-blowing things in fact, but he just couldn't remember. It was like the itch he got from not washing his hair; this itch, however, was on the underside of his brain, the dark side of the moon where the sun could never reach, where his fingernails couldn't scratch.

She had definitely mentioned something about a table. And candles too; that much he did remember. Had he got one of his dizzy spells between that and the radio fading?

He was fairly sure he hadn't. Not this time. So, candles on a table – what did she have in mind? A cosy candle-lit tête-à-tête? A restaurant perhaps? What about some metaphoric coffee afterwards? He peeled off his wet socks. He needed to get ready. A shower was out of the question, now more than ever. There was a packet of travel moist-wipes somewhere in the groceries box, bought to stall journeys to the bathroom; he'd already given himself the BOFO treatment, but that was hours ago, it wouldn't hurt to give his pits another going over; he could do with a dap between the toes too.

The cartons of UHT milk were just hampering his search, taking over the cardboard box. He snatched them up, plonked them in the fridge. He had dragged the fridge in from the kitchen shortly after giving up on the pizza deliveries; he had plugged the fridge into a timer so that it only went on during the hours allocated for sleep: 2 am to 6 am. The radio was mostly dormant then. It wasn't ideal; things still tended to go sour or a bit mouldy but that was better than having the fridge chunter on interfering with his listening pleasure.

The TV magazine was just plain in the way, taking up half the surface area of the cardboard box. He still watched television sometimes; sound muted, Teletext subtitles for the hard of hearing switched on. The travel wipes were poking out from the inside cover of the magazine. Kevin McCloud of *Grand Designs* was on the cover leaning against a perfect table, in a perfect lounge, in a perfect house.

Rubbing his armpit with the moist wipe Lowell scanned his own lounge. He couldn't bring her in here – wouldn't be a good first impression. There was a table in the kitchen; they could have dinner there, if that's what she wanted. He could order some candles online. And what about that double bed in his parents' room?

The radio hissed.

Had it heard his thoughts?

'Sorry,' Lowell mumbled. 'She'd be comfortable there, on her own. I'd take the sofa.' He needed to concentrate, block any images that could embarrass him in front of the radio.

The radio sighed and began shuffling through static. Then, it threw out its trump card. The supine hum commenced.

Nell was on her way.

'Lowell?' she whispered.

He was sorely tempted not to answer, just so he could hear her repeating his name. 'Yes.' He hated his own voice.

'Ahh, you're there.' The gush of the sea was still all around her.

He'd spent whole days trying to guess, imagine what she was: a deck hand, a captain, a stewardess, an adventurer, a mermaid, a sea angel – she'd been all of them. Maybe she'd already told him, maybe he already knew, but it was all tucked away in the dark side of the moon.

'I'm always here,' he said. 'We lost each other last night.'

'Did we?'

'The table – you were talking about a table. We got cut off.'

'Cut and set.'

'Sorry?'

'The place has been set.' She spoke slowly, as if talking to a child having difficulties catching on.

'Set? Where?'

The doorbell.

An image of Nell flashed in his head: at the front door, with captain's hat, life jacket, mermaid's tail (feet and legs included so she could stand and what not). He hadn't cooked anything. He was all out of food; delivery tomorrow. They could eat out; no need to stay in for the radio. But he stank, all his clothes were dirty. The sheets upstairs needed washing. The toilet needed scrubbing.

'Is that you?' he said finally, his voice wrung dry.

'How could it be me?'

He added a mobile radio unit to the image, slung it over her shoulder. 'Are you sure? It's definitely not you? It's not some surprise?'

'Lowell, it's not me.' Terse tone. She was losing patience.

The doorbell rang again. This time, longer, louder. Yes, definitely louder – as if the caller, intruder, was prodding the bell so hard it'd somehow upped in volume.

'Fuck.' The word just slipped out. He turned to the radio, muttered, 'Sorry.'

Without wasting another single moment, he dropped to his knees in one smooth motion and slid his arms, face, chest and stomach flat against the carpet, his beard joining the dust mites nuzzling in the weave. They had enjoyed full-board five-star accommodation, the dust mites, since he'd given up vacuuming – interfered with the radio.

'What are you doing?' Nell asked.

The intruder's footsteps clicked and then clacked off the doorstep. What were they doing out there? The bloody Riverdance? The tapping was getting louder, closer. They were at the window, prowling, trying to peer in. It had been so long since he'd had visitors, people hassling him to stop brooding – move on – get out more – that once they'd all gradually given up and gone away he'd gotten complacent, started leaving lights on. At least the curtains were drawn – one saving grace – he hadn't let standards slip to that extent.

'Someone's at the window,' Lowell whispered up to the radio.

A sudden loud knock at the window backed him up. The glass shuddered. Lowell shuddered. He held his breath, biting on a tuft of carpet.

'So why don't you let him in?' suggested Nell.

'Him?'

'It's a friend of mine.'

'What's he want?'

Nell's friend was drumming his heels away from the window, back to the front door. The door bell again. He wasn't giving up.

'Answer the door and find out.'

Had Nell not been listening, he'd have let him go on ringing the bell all night. But she was listening, listening and judging. He hauled himself up off the floor. He must have told Nell his address. How else would this friend know where to find him? He didn't have to invite him in. They could just talk on the doorstep. This friend could just say what he'd come to say and then go away. He would just get too comfortable if he came in, would want cups of tea and things. The kettle was in the lounge. He'd have to bring the tea out to him.

He paused in the hall, considered a retreat to the lounge. If he did that, though, Nell would know him for what he really was. Probably give their radio chats a miss. He strode forward with that thought and opened the door.

'At last!' Words shouted from a face concealed. Features eclipsed by a hood; and sunglasses. Huge sunglasses. The sort of sunglasses worn by skiers, muggers, assassins. But why sunglasses? It was dark out; the sun had gone. The man's face was as red as sunset – blood red – as if he'd just run too fast or drank too much. He was swaying, swaying in his all in-one skin-tight leathers, weaving his way past

Lowell and barging into the hall.

'Hector's the name,' he said, gazing around the hallway as if he was sizing up the joint. He had a camera strapped over his shoulder. Was that for logging valuables? Was this some sort of pre-heist jolly?

'I'm really busy. I'm sorry, I can't let you in.'

'Too late,' Hector pointed out, removing the camera. 'Someone's got to stop all that forgetfulness.'

0

THAT'S HECTOR, THE ETERNAL optimist. Lowell's already forgotten about the email he sent. *Il a oublié*. Is that how they say it in France?

Chapter 4

Brittany, France

'Never mind last supper, this is our first supper.'

Brighid hadn't meant it maliciously, yet it came out sounding that way. She had come all this way to finally meet Tessy, her mother, properly meet her, and Tessy was already snapping it away to be some last chance saloon. A log shifted in the fireplace, popping and sizzling, flames guzzling the dregs of sap and rainwater.

'Did you shut the gates?' Tessy asked, dextrously shifting subject.

'Not too keen on the dark.' The words tumbled out, all clipped tight.

Tessy rolled her eyes and sighed as though she'd spent a lifetime chasing her up on chores, then she glanced at the door and said, 'Can you do it? Can you manage?'

'If you've got a torch _'

'Why would you need a torch?'

'For the gate.'

Tessy grinned, emphasising those laughter lines under her eyes. 'Already taken care of.'

Brighid shivered. The draught from the hall. She wandered over to the fireplace, breathed in the smell of burning wood. The scent of vanilla from the car's air freshener still lingered in her nostrils.

'I was worried you wouldn't come.' Tessy's voice flickered like firelight.

'I couldn't not come. Are you ill or something?'

'Why would you think that?'

'The bit in the email about it being the last time.'

'Oh. Is that what it said?'

'You wrote it.'

'So you're here because you're worried about me.'

'You said it was urgent but you didn't give me a phone number, didn't reply to my other emails__'

'You've got things all back to front,' she said, gripping Brighid's wrist. 'It's me that's worried about you.'

'Why would you be worried about me?' She stepped back instinctively, freeing her arm. 'You don't know anything about me.' It came out all wrong. Words like bile.

'Oh but I do. More than you know.'

'Can you turn the lights on please?'

'He doesn't like electricity.' Tessy smiled, a sickly sweet smile. A too heavy on the treacle smile.

'Who doesn't?'

'Your father.'

So the invisible man was definitely still about. Her head was still frying in fantasy land.

'Your dad likes the old ways. Says the electricity keeps the magic out – interferes with his energy.'

Aunt Mary had told her all about the day Tessy's madness was introduced to the family. A nineteen-year old Tessy had come back from au-pairing in France, her belly swollen by six months of pregnancy. This hadn't exactly pleased Nana and Granddad but they were pacified by the news that there was to be a wedding. They wanted to meet their future son-in-law.

Nana made several platefuls of spam sandwiches, sliced diagonally, crusts cut off. Sandwiches were always sliced diagonally for guests. But Tessy turned up without the guest of honour. Seeing the sandwiches, Tessy told

Nana that she shouldn't have gone to so much effort, he didn't eat meat. That got Granddad started. He went off on one of his rants wanting to know what sort of man was it that didn't eat meat. Tessy answered that it was a very special man. That just wound Granddad up more. It was the high-blood pressure. When Brighid was a kid, she thought he had a Father Christmas face, and then he had the heart attack, had to lower his cholesterol – spam sandwiches were out, diagonal or otherwise – the Santa face lost its flush and paled.

But back in the time when Brighid was still growing in Tessy's belly, and there was a kitchen load of spam sandwiches (half of them marked for the bin thanks to their special future son-in-law) Granddad's cheeks were pumped full-throttle, red-alert. 'So where is he, this special fella?' Granddad asked. 'Already done a runner?'

Tessy had replied that he was there, right in front of him. That was when the penny dropped, all was not quite right. Granddad told her to stop playing funny buggers. Tessy retaliated by saying the only funny bugger there was Granddad, and that he was a lazy bugger at that. Granddad had been a grafter all his life so that comment went down like a lamb's tail at an abattoir. If he just made a bit more effort, Tessy had explained, he'd be able to see him. Granddad practically burst a blood vessel and tossed his spam sandwiches into the air. Tessy started screaming, shouting that he'd cut her fiancé's lip with the plate. Then she grabbed one of the serviettes, which Nana would have folded diagonally, started dabbing the air, whispering apologies for her dad's temper. A few days later, Tessy was sectioned with Brighid in her belly.

'So where is Dad?' It was probably best to play along; her mother was a sick woman after all.

'Why, he's right here.' She smiled wearily. 'You really

are silly sometimes, Brighid.'

Tessy needed help. It wasn't right that she was living on her own, not like this.

She was nodding now, nodding to the empty space that in Tessy's eyes contained Brighid's father. 'I know, I know,' she was muttering. 'But she needs to put her bag down first.'

The overnight bag was obviously causing Tessy some distress, so Brighid removed it from her shoulder and deposited it onto the floor. As this went unnoticed, she picked the bag back up again and dropped it.

It was enough to shut her up mid sentence, halfway through: 'Of course she still loves you. It's just…' Tessy stared at her for several awkward moments then hurried over to the table, set for three, and pulled out one of the chairs. 'Oh for goodness sake,' she snapped. 'Do as your father tells you and sit down.' The skin around her collarbone went all blotchy. She placed her hand there self-consciously. 'You're probably hungry after all,' she added, some warmth returning to her voice.

'Starving.' This wasn't entirely true. The only thing Brighid had managed to eat all day was the pain au chocolat on the boat over; unease over the big reunion made eating anything more substantial impossible. Her throat still felt tight and her stomach just as knotted as she sat down at the table.

'Vegetables and herbs,' Tessy announced brightly, lifting the lid off the casserole dish. 'All grown in our garden.' She ladled out the casserole of courgette, leek, broccoli and tomato.

'Delicious,' Brighid said, not humouring her.

Tessy was both an excellent cook and gardener: new facts about her mother.

Tessy cocked her head at the empty seat next to her.

'Thank your father. It's his recipe.'

She could play along, indulge Tessy and thank Fictional Dad or she could hit her with the reality, tell her she was delusional. Neither seemed a good option, so Brighid sipped her wine instead.

'Do you think I've changed – I mean since last time?' Tessy asked, shifting her focus away from the vacant chair, her blue eyes gleaming; no hint of mascara on her pale lashes.

'You look amazing.' Tessy was altogether quite beautiful, even without make-up. She hadn't realised that before.

Tessy winced, batting the compliment away with a wave of a hand; a hand of weathered skin, of broken fingernails, a hand that plodded the vegetable patch, chopped wood for the fire. 'He still looks the same as he did the day I met him, but when I look in the mirror I hate what I see. I look so old compared to him. He says I'm imagining it; I'm not. His eyes used to shine when he looked at me. Not anymore.'

'That's normal – happens in most relationships.' Brighid decided to humour her this time.

'But this isn't a normal relationship is it?'

'No,' Brighid said quietly.

'He says it's because his sparkle for everything is leaving him.'

Brighid studied her mother's features. She didn't look her fifty years. 'You look half your age.' She meant it. The laughter lines were no deeper than that day on the beach. Had she stopped laughing then?

'Time is funny in this house, in this part of the forest. It's slower. That's how we manage here.'

'Mum.' There she said it.

Tessy beamed, delighted at the word.

'Mum.' She said it again; she needed to pave the way. 'I'm worried about you. I think you need to see someone, a doctor. I could come with you if you want.'

'No, that's what they said the last time.'

'I don't mean going into a hospital.' She wasn't actually sure what she meant.

'You can't send me away. Your father needs me.'

'I'm not sending you anywhere.'

Tessy reached out to the empty chair beside her. 'You were right.' Her face creased up. She wiped her eyes. 'I know, I know,' she sniffed, 'but you wanted to see her as well. Anyway they approved it, gave it their blessing. Got her here.'

'Who's they?' Brighid said softly.

Tessy visibly flinched, then swung back round, wide-eyed, glistening with tears. 'I'm not crazy you know.'

'Maybe you just need medication. Not hospital. I mean, I think it's more community care these days isn't?' Was she saying the right thing?

'It's not me that's mad – it's the rest of them. They're all in denial.' Tessy snatched a serviette, diagonally folded just like Nana's, and blew her nose. 'You've got his eyes,' she said wistfully. 'Your father's eyes.'

The family, *she*, should have made more effort to find Tessy, checked up on her, made sure she was okay. Instead she had been disposed of, forgotten about. Become a legend, not a person.

That person, her own flesh and blood, plucked out some thyme that had trapped between her teeth, consigned it to the side of the plate. 'Your father's not able to eat these days,' Tessy said, now brushing the thyme away, making it fall from the edge of the plate. 'He doesn't have the energy.'

'So I see.' Fictional Dad's plate was empty. Tessy had

ignored it when serving up the casserole.

'You used to see him as well, you know.'

'I did?' She took another mouthful of wine, bracing herself for the next crazy installment.

'Magio, you called him.'

Magio: the imaginary friend she'd had when she was a kid. Nana had insisted it was just her imagination. But *imagination* had been far too much of a complicated word to say, so Brighid had just called him Magio instead.

'How would you know about Magio?'

Tessy smiled inwardly then turned to the chair next to her. 'Night, night. I'll be up in a bit.' She blew a kiss and slowly shifted her gaze to the door.

'Sorry to snap at you before,' Tessy whispered, shovelling up a forkful of squashed tomato and courgette. 'I can barely see him myself these days. I try to hide that from him – don't want to hurt his feelings. He's fading.'

Did this mean Tessy was getting better? Perhaps this was her way of holding on, clinging to the old delusions, telling herself they were still there – maybe it was easier than facing the truth, admitting that she'd lost the last three decades to madness, to the phantoms in her head.

'You just need help in coming to terms…' Brighid wasn't sure how to finish the sentence, so she left it hanging.

'Oh bog off. You're starting to sound like one of those bloody doctors. I know where you're going with that and you're not taking me there. Eat yer tea, it'll get cold.'

Brighid did as she was told. They ate the rest of the casserole in silence.

Plates cleared, Tessy offered her a refill of wine. Brighid nodded and as Tessy was pouring, Brighid decided to pose the question she had wanted to ask for years. 'That time in Cornwall – you just left. I only looked away a few seconds and you'd gone. Why didn't you stay longer? Stop and talk.'

'There was only time to give you the ice cream,' Tessy said, pouring herself a glass. She set the bottle back down next to the centre candle. 'And you wouldn't have accepted the ice cream from just anyone.'

'What was so important about the ice cream?'

'If you hadn't taken that ice cream you wouldn't be here now.'

'The ice cream's got nothing to do with me being here.'

'Oh, but it has.'

'I'm not even that keen on ice cream. I've got sensitive teeth.'

'Whether you like or don't like ice cream doesn't really matter. You didn't know it but you were at a crossroads on that beach. If you'd left one minute earlier you'd have walked straight under the wheels of a Ford Mondeo. Two minutes earlier and you'd have walked straight into the arms of the love of your life. Both would have been bad timing.' She ran her finger over the rim of her glass. 'Obviously you getting run over would have been more than just bad timing. I'd have been devastated.'

Brighid took another slug of wine.

'I need you to do something for me,' Tessy said, standing up. She waddled over (the wellies were a few sizes too big) to the fireplace (the fire was roaring) and removed something from the mantelpiece.

She returned to her chair and placed a small round tin on the table. There was no brand name on the label, just a delicately pencilled sketch of acorns. It was the sort of tin you'd expect to contain mints or pins; inside this tin, however, was a dollop of partially melted wax.

'Put your thumb in. Not too heavy, not too light.'

'Why would I want to do that?'

'Don't worry – it won't burn you. It's not that hot. Go on, before it sets again.'

'But why?'

'It's just something *they* need. Don't worry. I already know; they already know too, otherwise they wouldn't be going to all this trouble. But you know how it is, there's always some jobsworth who has to make sure every box is ticked. I wouldn't be at all surprised if they're just trying to make me look crazy.'

If she questioned the mythical *they* that would just start Tessy off again and she was way too tired to hear any more crazy tales of the world according to Tess. So to appease her, to shut her up she played along and pressed her thumb right on into the warm wax.

'Good girl. I'm so very proud of you.'

Chapter 5

Peel, Isle of Man

As it turned out Hector was neither an assassin nor a drunk. He had a problem with his balance when he first arrived to places. It took him a few moments to get his bearings, is how he explained it. Lowell had offered him a cup of tea. He'd been perfectly willing, well sort of willing, well sort of not willing to get the kettle out of the lounge, but Hector had wavered that offer. He was much too interested in the wallpaper at the end of the hall, so much so, he started picking at it with his fingers. Lowell tried to stop him, as anyone would if a stranger came into their house and started scratching their walls.

Hector simply raised his hand and said, 'Just give me a minute.'

If Hector was here to stop the amnesia, it was working. He remembered everything the man scratching his wall said and did so far. At least Hector was wearing gloves. Damage limitation. He also wore a necklace, a string of beads that dangled all the way down to his belly, beads that kept clipping the wall as he scratched.

Now, fifty-two seconds into that minute (Lowell was tracking the second hand on his watch) Hector made a curious whooping sound, started pulling a strip of wallpaper off the wall.

Lowell grabbed Hector's elbow to protest. Then he let go.

There was a door beneath the wallpaper.

Lowell had never known there was a door under the wallpaper and he'd been living in the house all his life, was even born in the house. And for as long as he could remember the hallway wallpaper had always been the same: red with pencil-thin green stripes. The décor in all the other rooms had periodically changed over the years, but the hall had always stayed the same.

'But, how did you know?' Lowell stammered.

Hector shrugged, freeing a piece of paper peel caught in his beads. 'I had an inkling the door would be there,' he said, returning to the wall/door. No need for any steamer or scraper; the wallpaper peeled away easily much like banana skin.

The door, he said. Not a door. *The* door; as though it was a door to somewhere important. How could he possibly know? There was no visible doorframe sticking out, poking its presence onto the paper. And no door handle either.

'We'll have to fix that,' Hector remarked. 'Can't have a door without a handle.'

The door did have a keyhole at least.

One minute thirty-seven seconds into the initial minute, the last chunk of wallpaper tumbled to the floor.

One minute thirty-nine seconds: Hector reached into the pocket on his hip. This was no easy task given the smallness of the pocket or the extra finger Lowell now noticed Hector had on each hand. He must have had the gloves tailored especially.

'Tra-la,' Hector said, all sardonic enthusiasm, pulling out a key.

'Where did you get that?'

'Pocket. Idiot.' He smiled. A smile to soften an insult, to soften the intrusion, then he unlocked the door.

The door was opened several inches, just enough for Hector and his big sunglasses to be able to peek in, to exclaim, 'Oops sorry.'

It was the sort of tone you would use if you'd just entered the wrong hotel room, or walked in on someone having a crap on the toilet, and with that he swiftly closed the door and locked it again, shoving the key back in his pocket.

'What're you doing?' Lowell protested. 'I want to see.'

'You can't,' Hector replied, outrage spilling in his voice, as though Lowell was some kind of Peeping Tom asking to see the female changing rooms.

'But it's my house. I want to see what's in there.'

Two minutes four seconds: Hector pulled down the leather hood. He had a mop of thick black hair, tied into a ponytail. A bigger ponytail than Lowell's would be if he ever had time to find an elastic band; there weren't any in the lounge, searching elsewhere in the house was out of the question.

'Do me a favour…' Hector sighed, both sets of five fingers now kneading his temples. 'Stop whining.'

'What? You've got some__'

And Hector really did have some nerve, loping down the hall, sweeping right into the lounge. 'Christ, man,' he yelled, 'this place stinks.'

Lowell scrambled in after him, but Hector had already thrown the quilt off the sofa, had plonked himself down, made himself comfortable.

'Well, well, well, what have we here?' The sunglasses were homing in on the radio. 'Now, that brings back memories. A crusty mate of mine from old Billingsgate fish market dragged an identical radio out from the Blitz. Who's to say it's not the very same radio?'

'It's my radio.'

'Yes, Lowell. I know it's your radio.'

Nell must have told him his name. What else had she told him? Any sentiment Nell's friend might be displaying (derision, curiosity, amicability, jealousy, probably not jealousy) was hidden by the huge sunglasses. So Lowell had only a few features to go on. There were the ears: nothing special there, they were just normal sized ears – they didn't stick out nor were they flat against his head – but his ears didn't twitch, not one bit, nor did his average sized nose, and there was no sign of movement, vertical or otherwise, from that thin, wide mouth; even without smiling its corners were a greater distance apart than any other mouth Lowell had ever seen. The ruddy complexion had paled to the same fawn hue as his all-in-one leathers, boots, and gloves. Still, that was a gradual change and had nothing to do with what Nell may, or may not have told Hector, nothing to do with Hector's take on that.

He was getting too relaxed on the sofa, reclining with his legs splayed, wiry arms stretching across the back rest. Lowell remained standing; to sit down would only encourage Hector to stay longer. The cornflakes box was still on the sideboard where he'd left it at breakfast. He picked it up. Best before was months away. Seven months.

'We need you to make a documentary,' Hector said.

'Sorry?'

He had never even owned a cine-camera or a video camera. His phone had a camera; he'd hardly ever used that, the phone or camera. He didn't know the first thing about making a home movie, let alone a documentary.

'But I'm an accountant.' Even that wasn't entirely true anymore.

'It's for a global audience.'

'You've got the wrong man.'

'Has she?' He sucked his impossibly wide lips,

producing a noise that threatened to siphon off Lowell's hopes and dreams.

Lowell clasped the cornflakes box tight against his chest. 'I did a Powerpoint presentation once, if that helps.'

Hector arched forward, clapped his knees: leather against leather sounding like the sough of wet leaves. 'So, you're interested?'

Lowell shifted his weight against the sideboard and nodded lamely. 'Possibly.'

'All you'd need to do is follow instructions; I'd provide step by step, clip by clip directives, bit like a flat pack, but I wouldn't be hanging around. I'd just bring in all the instructions, the footage, and that's that. The rest is up to you.'

'So I wouldn't have to leave the house?'

'Nope.'

'Are you sure?'

'It's a promise,' he said, wiping a bit of wallpaper from his beads.

'But I don't have any equipment, any software.'

'It would all be provided.' Hector thrust one leg forward, resting ankle on knee, scattering wallpaper shavings down the side of the sofa.

'The instructions,' Lowell said, still hugging the cornflakes, 'they'd need to be clear. I really don't have the first clue how__'

'Actually, that's a good thing, means the documentary will be less tainted.' The steel heel cap tapped the air as he spoke. 'The last thing this documentary needs is someone with ideas directing it.'

'Directing?' Lowell gasped. The cornflakes scrunched.

'Yes.' An impossibly wide smile. 'You're perfect. As I said, last thing this documentary needs is someone with ego, ambitions, someone trying to put in their own mark, bruising the footage with their stamp of auteur. No, it's better you don't have a fuckin' clue.'

'But if I'm following your directions…' Lowell hesitated, bit his lip. 'Then doesn't that make you the director? I'd just be director by proxy. Wouldn't I just be putting your creative mark on it?'

Three minutes fifty-one seconds.

'Stop looking at your bloody watch.'

Four minutes two seconds (Lowell was keeping count in his head): Hector rubbed a red bead between his thumb and fifth finger, then switched to a green bead and said, 'Good to see you're thinking, good to see some ideas up there, but for the sake of the foreseeable – try not doing that too much.'

'What's it about, the documentary?' Was that thinking too much? He had a right to know.

'It's a docudrama. A film within a film. A slice of a bigger picture. A bite-sized portion of the supersized sticky bun. That's all you need to know for now.'

'Sticky bun?'

'Just a metaphor.'

'But you have to tell me the subject.'

He let go of his beads. 'It's nothing dodgy, just the producers want everything kept hush-hush for now. So you in, or what?'

Even though Lowell sensed this probably signalled the end of the Lounge Age as cataclysmically as meteors and ice-melts marked the end of other ages, he heard himself say, 'Yes.' This whole thing with the lounge, hiding away from the outside world, had been mostly, and lately, all about being there for Nell. And if this was Nell's friend, he couldn't possibly say no, for without Nell he'd have nothing.

Four minutes forty-five seconds: Hector extracted

himself from the sofa and stood up.

'Could I have the key before you go?' Lowell asked.

Hector was inspecting the radio again, those damn beads rapping at the Bakelite. Tap. Rap. Tap. But not a single peep from the radio. It was only Lowell squealing, silently, painfully.

'It really is my door,' he reminded him, caring less and less about the key.

Hector was tilting the radio, examining the base. 'Ah, look, scratch marks. It must have been dragged along the ground at some point.'

'So really to be fair, if it's my door it would have to also be my key. I mean what's the good of a key without a door?'

'Or a door without a key?' Hector added, easing the radio back to its upright position, removing the plethora of pestering fingers from the radio, threading them around his beads, removing his beads. 'We'll let you have your key, but you have to set the wheels in motion before all that. Here,' he said, slipping the beads over Lowell's head. 'You're going to need these.'

Lowell wasn't a jewellery sort of guy, but as the necklace was a gift he just stood there, all polite grimace, wishing Hector would back off, quit adjusting the beads. Hector's breath stank of shellfish, of prawns gone bad.

Seven minutes four seconds: Hector took a step back and nodded. 'Perfect. Top dog.'

The key would have been a more useful gift. He opened the lounge door some more, trying to gee up Hector's exit.

'Anyway,' Hector said, stopping just short of the open door, 'it's way too early for you to have the key – we're not ready back there. We wouldn't want to spoil the surprise.'

'We?' Lowell asked hopefully.

'Nell amongst others.'

It was the first time her name had cropped up, although her name had been on the tip of Lowell's tongue the whole time.

'Is she in there, back there, behind the door in the hall?' He knew it was a ridiculous question the moment he put it out there. Still, he needed to know. It would drive him crazy if he didn't ask.

'You saying she's some kind of bleedin' magician? That she peeled the wallpaper off and on and just let herself in? You saying that she loves you so much she's been there all this time just waiting for you?'

'No.' He wasn't keen on the way this man had made him say it with such a tiny voice and in his own house, his own lounge. Why had he even agreed to do the documentary? Okay, he was doing it for Nell. There hadn't been any mention of salary.

Seven minutes forty-nine seconds.

'Fifty grand,' Hector said suddenly, as if he'd read his thoughts. 'Upfront. It'll be in your bank account as of tomorrow.'

Chapter 6

Brittany, France

A hole in the wall.

The hole was howling.

The wind was coming in, blowing the dust and render across the bare floorboards.

'Bedroom's perfect,' Brighid said, clutching the saucer with the candle, closing the door to Tessy.

She hurried over to the hole, set the saucer down away from the draught and knelt down on the shredded wallpaper, a bice green herringbone pattern strewn all over the floor. The hole was so big she was able to put her head inside – wasn't too dissimilar to sticking her face in an industrial sander, not that she'd ever done that before. Despite all the grit in the wind scratching her eyelids, scuffing her eyes, she was still able to make out a distinct absence of any stone or concrete that would have previously filled the hole. Seeing the filling had not lodged itself into any other cavity inside the wall she could think of only one other explanation – it had fallen out the other side. Lucky no-one was hurt. A stone the size of the hole would cause some damage. Blinking, she hastily removed her head from the sander and wiped the streaming dust from her eyes.

Something white, like porcelain, was protruding from the hole's perimeter. She pulled at it but it was stuck, embedded in the mortar. She leaned forward to get a closer look, to inspect whatever it was she was trying to extract.

A tooth.

Her own teeth bit her tongue in fright.

Looking again, she saw that it was actually part of a set of false teeth. Some old builder must have bent forward a bit too quickly when the place was being built, lost his false gnashers in the mix.

Noises entered the hole: ancient branches creaking outside, leaves rustling, the distant roar of a motorbike. She put her eye to the hole, but there was only darkness beyond the reach of the wall's aperture. Brushing the cement dust and wallpaper peelings from her face, she coughed up the grit catching the back of her throat and headed for bed.

Tessy was pacing the room upstairs, making the ceiling creak, making the candelabra hanging from the ceiling swing. Brighid was not entirely convinced that the candelabra was screwed in tightly enough to allow it to swing in such a way, in such a precarious way right above her face. She thought about getting out of bed, hauling the bed to one side, but it was an iron bed; it would make a load of noise and that could bring Tessy down investigating. She'd had more than enough of Tessy for one day.

A piece of plaster fell, just missing Brighid's bed. It wasn't that Tessy was particularly heavy footed, just that the house was particularly delicate. It was in that metamorphic state between being a house and a ruin. The house was a cocoon of a ruin, and every day it went without repair, its broken stone skeleton crept closer to the surface.

The candelabra marked the centre of the room. The bed was also in the centre, not against the wall but right out in the middle of the large yet otherwise empty room, like an abandoned boat: away from shore, adrift. She had placed the candle on the floor beside the bed, and in its flickering light the candelabra could almost be mistaken for an anchor.

The ceiling stopped shaking.

Tessy must have gone to bed.

The fly that had been buzzing aimlessly about the room was now taking a fancy to the candelabra, weaving over and under the faux gold branches. Over and under. Over and under. Brighid blew out the candle and curled herself into the belly of the bed, burrowing under the blankets, keeping out the fetid chill, keeping the fly from landing on her face, keeping the plaster out. The hum of the fly softened to a sound almost like waves; waves lapping against a boat: hoom, hish; hoom, hish; hoom, hish. Her breathing mingled with the rhythm and she fell asleep.

Soon she was dreaming. She was in a boat of some sort floating above the bed. Actually it wasn't a boat. She was in her old paddling pool, the one Nana had given her, the inflatable pink Barbie pool. She had always hated Barbie, so using a black felt-tip pen she'd given her fangs and spots. After that, every time the pool was filled and the water was too warm Brighid would end up a bit purple.

The fangs were still there and the spots. The Barbie pool was sweeping her away from the bed, through the glass of the window, outside to the darkness and shadows. In her dream the dark no longer bothered her, so Vampire Barbie and Brighid went sailing off, over the forest's rippling canopy, over Vivian's lake (still no sign of any crystal turrets), over hedges and fields, over precipitous rooftops, all the way to the coast and open sea.

Land ahoy! They followed its distant coastline. The sun rose all the way to its zenith and started to fall again. Finally, Vampire Barbie reached an island. Travelling on a cloud, up and over hills and valleys, they soon reached a lake, a pond. No, actually, the water appeared clogged; it was more a marsh or bog, with a throng of people around its banks. And as the cloud carrying the paddling pool passed overhead, many of the people shivered. The women gathered their shawls, the men their cloaks, wrapping them tighter, keeping the chill from coming in. That was the odd thing – Vampire Barbie pool aside – they were all dressed for another era, another time: the women in cumbersome skirts and petticoats, hemlines sopping; the men in jerkins, laced up and belted, shirt sleeves billowing, baggy breaches blooming, woollen stockings muddied.

And they were all watching the water, shouting at the water; their wind beaten hands clasping wide-brimmed floppy hats, flat caps, fedoras, bonnets and coifs.

Someone was under the water.

Vampire Barbie tipped Brighid overboard, leaving her to freefall. Using the gaze of the crowd as a slide, she slipped onto the surface of the marsh. No splash; she was weightless, devoid of all the material matter that made up her body. It was just her invisible dream-self cascading into the stagnant water, plummeting into the head of the drowning woman, stumbling into her drowning consciousness.

If I stay under water I can keep their words out, the drowning woman was thinking. Brighid could not only hear her thoughts, she felt all the pain, the cold, the pressure in her lungs, and the heaviness in her feet. Her shoes were sodden; she kicked them off. She could barely move her arms. Her wrists were tethered behind her back.

Crimson clouded the water. The drowning woman thought she was bleeding, wondered where from, then remembered: *Madder root, it's the madder root I used to colour my dress.* The downy undergrowth, the bed of the bog was soft, velvety soft. *I could lie down and just sleep awhile.* Brighid was losing the feeling in the woman's limbs. *So cold, so very cold.* The lichen and reeds shifted and curled into pillows and quilts; sleepy branches of bowing willow stroked her hair.

A woman above the water.

She was leaning over the surface, dress a churn of blue and black, and holding what looked like a large rock. She let go.

The surface wheezed and gulped, swallowing both the rock and the word *Murderer* with it. The rock tumbled through the water, its urgency dissolving as it sank, then it bounced gently off the drowning woman's shoulder and rolled into the murk. The half digested word bubbled in her ear and trickled out as mud.

As the rock shifted, bedding down into its final resting place, the water cleared going from a coffee (espresso no milk) colour to mushy pea green. The drowning woman blinked; her eyes stinging. There was someone next to her. His hollowed eyes stared back. Horns. He had horns: four, five, six of them, all coiled around a skeletal face. *A Loughtan sheep,* the drowning woman reassured herself. Its rotting corpse was all spongy, feathery tendrils. Threads of flesh and wool flinched as the silt settled, making the sheep look as if it had sighed.

She gagged and accidentally swallowed the water percolating through the putrid sheep carcass. Nauseous revulsion – Brighid wasn't sure whether it was her own or the drowning woman's – thrust her upwards; she burst through the water's surface.

The mob standing on the bank gasped collectively as though it was they that needed air.

Inside the not so drowning woman's head, Brighid

watched with the woman's eyes as she scanned the crowd.

Don't look. Don't let them see.

Silence. The crowd had taken in all the air they needed.

The woman in the blue and black dress, one front tooth missing, skin like sour butter, pointed at the not so drowning woman and shouted, 'She's alive! Nell is still alive!'

Chapter 7

Peel, Isle of Man

Five hours thirty-two minutes into the initial minute, into whatever transitory period came after the Lounge Age, Lowell still remembered everything Hector said. So, despite Hector being Nell's friend, there seemed to be no associated memory loss, that side of things anyway. Were the beads helping him remember? When he was at school, struggling to memorize his French vocabulary homework, trying to pin down the gender a definite article needed to be for a particular noun, he'd picture two rooms. One room for masculine *le* words, another room for feminine *la* words. It helped visualising *la glace* with *la bougie* and *la lune,* and *le pouce* with *le gant* and *le soleil.* As his French improved, the rooms in his head became a hoarder's paradise, so he added a hoarder to crawl and climb over the lexical pile up, to help locate whatever word he was after. The imaginary hoarder had a beard, rather like the one he himself sported these days.

If the necklace was to be memory assistant version 2.0, the tangibility of the beads provided the upgrade's definitive feature. A little bit of imagination transported everything Hector said to the interior of one of the glass beads. And to remember all Lowell had to do was rub that bead. That was the theory anyway.

Hector was down there – getting things ready. *Downstairs.* Hector had let that one slip. The word was now stored inside the second green bead down from the knot. There was a knot in the thread that held all the beads together; that knot was the reference point from which all the beads were defined. The second green bead down was Gr2. R3, the third red bead down, was reserved for Nell.

'I'll take these downstairs,' Hector had said, helping himself to a pint of milk and a packet of shortbread biscuits, taking them down to the basement, for that's what it was if there were stairs. Then he locked the basement door.

When Lowell had knocked demanding, more like asking, to see what he was doing down there, Hector had shouted through the door that he was just getting things ready. 'Tell Nell we'll have her suite ready in no time,' he had said.

Rubbing Gr2 bead really did seem to help; he remembered the whole one-liner, plus his own mute response. Hector already knew how to shut him up.

Suite.

Bedroom-en-suite. Bathroom-en-suite. It could only mean one thing. Nell was moving in. Okay, the normal thing would be for Lowell and Nell to have discussed it first (maybe they already had, surely he'd remember that?) but hey, if Nell had decided she wanted to move in, he would be only too ecstatic.

That banging and hammering was interfering with the radio, causing blips in the static, making it difficult to hear. Hector hadn't brought any tools in with him, just the camera. So how was it Lowell had even heard a power drill operating down there?

He'd have thought Hector would have left by now. It was impossible to relax knowing he was down there; Lowell hadn't banked on things changing quite so abruptly; as abruptly as the overpowering whirlwind of the all in one leathers kind now barging into the lounge.

There was a key in one of the kitchen drawers, he'd have to dig it out, start locking the lounge. Hector couldn't just waltz in whenever he wanted; a line had to be drawn somewhere.

'I'm still hungry,' Hector sniffed, waving the empty shortbread packet in Lowell's face.

Tesco's delivery wasn't until tomorrow. 'I could microwave a pepperoni pizza?' The thought of Hector eating the pizza he'd planned for himself made him hungry.

Hector shook his head. 'Vegetarian.'

'Like my parents.' Why was he making conversation? He didn't want this man in his lounge, and he certainly didn't want to start talking about his parents.

Thankfully Hector just grunted. Grunt now stored away in Gr2. Then Hector edged his sunglasses halfway down his nose and blinked. 'That's better,' he said, removing his sunglasses, rubbing his eyes. 'It was so bright before.'

'No it wasn't.'

He'd half-expected Hector's eyes to be cyborg or alien but they were just plain human eyes. Brown, heavy-lidded, and slightly red around the edges because of the rubbing. Unsure whether to be relieved or disappointed, Lowell opened the fridge, currently unplugged, interior light off. 'Cheese and pickle sandwich do you?'

Hector snatched up the sandwich, tore apart the packaging.

Lowell closed the fridge door. 'Shall I book a plumber?'

'Do what you want mate.'

'When do you need him?'

'I don't.'

Lowell scratched the itch in his belly button. 'I'd at least like some say in the choice of toilet and sink going in.'

Hector almost choked on his sandwich. Then, clearing his throat, he said, 'We've got another email you need to write.'

'What d'you mean, another?'

'A documentary needs an editor,' he replied, mouth full of pickle.

He had thought the deal was to grab the footage off Hector and then do the rest himself, by himself, following instructions flat pack style.

'And the editor needs a place to stay.' He wiped his mouth with his leather sleeve. 'This house for instance.'

Hector was throwing free accommodation into the package, opening Lowell's doors: *mi casa es tu casa* – or words to that effect. He wasn't even asking, just telling. Definitely, way beyond the job description – if he had a job description. Lowell was becoming the HR department and hotelier all rolled into one. Hector was taking over, taking over his house, his life, and he was just letting him, rolling over like a good dog, giving him his lead, taking his laptop out. Typing. Hector dictating.

'For fuck's sake, you can't type with those stupid gloves on.'

Lowell removed his gloves.

He had taken to wearing his gloves a lot lately; it stopped him biting his nails, well it was more the tips of his fingers, his thumbs to be exact. The thumb chewing had started after one particular conversation with Nell, the particulars of which remained a mystery, and had not stopped until he obtained the gloves, black leather gloves. He had gotten so used to the soft padding cushioning the flesh of his hands that he felt naked without the gloves now. And actually, yes he could type with them, often did; still, there didn't seem any point arguing with Hector, even if Hector hadn't even bothered removing his own gloves.

He didn't catch the name of the person he was emailing. He was too distracted. Lounge Age was being crushed just as effectively as the sandwich packaging between Hector's leather hands. Squashed. Scrunched. Crunched. Crackling.

Crackling.

Hissssss.

Hector nodded at the radio. 'You want to get that fixed.'

Hummmm.

Nell's calling signal.

He didn't want Hector here, listening in, sneering, spoiling the moment. 'Send,' he said, hoping it would also dispatch Hector out of the lounge.

'Okay, go to the send folder, and delete that email. We don't want you going back later, cyber stalking the editor, persuading them not to come.'

Delete.

Hummmm.

'Three's a crowd,' Hector sighed, depositing the sandwich crusts next to the laptop, closing the lounge door behind him.

'Your suite should be ready soon.' Lowell tried his best to keep the excitement from his voice, to keep some semblance of cool.

'Good. You'll need a place to work.'

'I thought...'

'What did you think? Watch that imagination. Imagine. Imagine. Imagine this is a regular documentary. That's what the editor must think. Wouldn't do to scare her.'

The conversation was over before he knew it.

She had probably said a whole lot more, but there was just the one line he remembered, *Good. You'll need a place to work.* That was the one line transfusing from R3 into his finger and thumb. He rubbed harder. Nothing. Maybe the beads weren't so great after all, not for Nell anyway; anything else, she might have said, remained securely locked up in the dark side of the unscratchable moon.

And there was he thinking he could do the documentary on his computer, in the lounge. An editing suite, a production facility, that's what Hector was building down there. Lowell hadn't even been consulted. Didn't he need to apply for planning permission for something like that?

But he wouldn't complain, and it wasn't just his overwhelming need to keep Nell happy that stopped him, or the hefty salary – Jesus, with that sort of money he could get away without working for two years, three years if he skimped. He'd checked his account online; the money was already there, as promised: crediting his account one second after midnight. No, it was something about the way Hector's voice had changed when he mentioned the bigger picture that even without asking, Lowell knew it was more than just a film. What Hector was talking about was something that transcended celluloid. He wasn't sure how he knew; it was a lot to assume just from the change of someone's voice, and it wasn't just because it was a knackered hackneyed phrase the media rolled out at every opportunity – no, it triggered something, somewhere in his brain, in the same place where all the forgotten stuff Nell had said was stored (dud R3 aside). There could be no gripes and grumbles, the big picture eclipsed all that; no questions asked.

Lowell had loads of questions he *wanted* to ask Hector about the production, about the big picture and about Nell, mostly about Nell, yet when he tried to voice them he immediately forgot what it was he was about to ask. Hector was supposed to be here to help him stop forgetting, well that was all going to plan when he was being told things Hector wanted to tell him, then Gr2 was fully functional, but when Lowell wanted to ask something vital, the question would just vanish clean out of his head, leave him just standing there humming and hawing. He was starting to seriously worry about the state of his head. He already knew he had a kidney stone, and he was getting more and more reminders of that, but maybe something else was wrong, a brain tumour or premature dementia. No set of beads could cure either of those. And why did he need the beads anyway? Shouldn't he be more than capable of remembering important bits of conversation?

Still, he was only forgetful with Hector, part-time (in the six hours four minutes fifty-three seconds he'd known him), and Nell, well, almost full-time; other than that, apart from the occasional wet ankles and sand between his toes, his memory was okay. Maybe, it was just nerves. Hector had this overwhelming presence, a confidence that highlighted Lowell's own inadequacies with a thick neon marker. Hector was like the perfect salesman; he could sell milk to lactating cows. And besides he was now sort of his boss.

And how had Hector known about that door? He had an *inkling* – what kind of answer was that? He might as well give up asking questions – didn't take him anywhere. He just needed to follow the instructions – no thinking involved.

But actually he did have a thought. An idea. A very good idea.

He knocked on the door to the edit suite-in-waiting.

'I'm busy,' Hector shouted.

'Sorry,' Lowell replied. Why was he saying sorry? 'I don't want the editor coming here.' There he'd said it.

'Does Nell know?' Hector's voice had an arctic chill.

'I don't know.' That was the truth.

'She won't be happy. Scuppers all our plans. Can't see Nell coming now. Not with that attitude.'

'I could do the editing myself. I mean if you gave me the instructions.'

'It's the editor or the project's kaput; finito; fin.'

'There're plenty of hotels nearby.'

'Don't be such a miserable bastard. You'll have to go the airport too, pick her up,'

'But you said I could stay in the house – you promised.' He didn't have to rub Gr2 to remember that.

'Can you hear yourself?'

'And what about the radio? I need to stay, to talk to Nell.'

'And what're you going to say? Are you going to tell her everything's off 'cos you can't even be bothered to go on a little trip to the airport? Can't see her being too impressed by that.'

'What's wrong with a taxi?'

Hector was walking down the stairs. Lowell could hear footsteps against stone. A stone stairway then.

'I'd pay. The taxi.'

Hector was no longer listening.

I don't want to do the documentary. He couldn't tell her that.

They would re-paper over the door and leave. The end. No love scene with Nell, no heroic saving of the day, no rolling credits; just end of transmission. Thank you and Goodbye. Actually, probably not even a thank you. Why would there be?

Back in the lounge, he heard the basement door open. Hector's voice.

'We can go out this way now.'

Who was he talking to? Why did he say *now*?

'Much more civilised,' someone with a deep, rumbling voice replied.

Apparently this was funny because they both laughed. Hector hadn't said anything about getting a friend or builder in. Had they both been laughing at him down there? Laughing at the pathetic owner of the house? If it was a friend and not a builder then why was *he* allowed to see the basement and not the pathetic owner? Lowell opened the door just a smidgeon; he wasn't, and never was these days, in the mood for introductions.

'Sorry about all the noise before,' Hector said, patting the man on the back.

The man wore a suit. A builder wouldn't wear a suit for work, but that didn't automatically make him a friend; he could be an architect, an interior designer. Everything about him was average: average suit, average height, average weight, average mid brown hair, and he had the sort of face you'd have to study just in case you bumped into him in town (not that Lowell went downtown much) so you could say hello and not look ignorant. Everything was average then, apart from the tortoise. He was cradling a tortoise beneath the crook of his arm. The tortoise turned its head wearily towards Lowell and stared.

Lowell swiftly and silently closed the door.

'Spectators always welcome,' said Hector, letting the man and tortoise out through the front door.

Hummmm.

Hummmm.

Hummmm.

'Lowell?' Nell's voice.

The voice that was his candle in the darkness: his light

in the ocean.

He didn't answer.

'I can hear you breathing.'

He picked up his credit card; he was a relatively rich man now. Hector was wrong; he could type with his gloves on. Quite easily, in fact. His parents' quilt wasn't available for guest editors; it was still on their bed, along with the imprint of his dad's toes and a stray hair.

'I can hear you tapping.'

A buy one get one half price offer on quilts.

'I'm here now.' He couldn't resist her.

'What's happening?'

'I'm just organising things.'

'Is there a problem? You sound…strained.'

'No, not really.'

'Go on.'

'Your friend Hector's inviting some editor to stay in my house.'

'And?' Her voice flickered: the threat of darkness – of the light going out.

'Just a thought. I'm sure if I can learn to direct, I could do the editing too.'

'You don't have the right thumbs. You know that.'

'Oh,' he said, instantly forgetting her reasoning.

'Don't forget the bigger picture,' she murmured.

There it was again, the all important bigger picture. Even sea angels spoke in clichés.

Static interference was rising.

'The tide's changing, I have to leave. I'll be with you soon, my love.'

The radio retuned. The chorus of the aurora took over. There were more whistlers than normal, more solar flares bombarding the outer atmosphere. The small choir had become a celestial orchestra; to Lowell it sounded like the greatest love song ever produced. This would be their tune: his and Nell's song.

She'd used the word, *love*: called him, *my love*.

He would do anything for her.

Chapter 8

BRIGHID SAT BOLT UPRIGHT.

Echoes in the darkness; her own voice bumping into the walls. She'd been shouting in her sleep, had woken herself up. The dream had been so vivid she could still smell the marsh, still feel the chill. She sank back down under the blankets – it was warm there at least – closed her eyes and quickly went back to sleep.

When she opened her eyes again, she was dreaming, falling from the sky, diving headfirst towards the summit of a hill. A hilltop thronging with people, the same crowd as before; they were gazing up at the sky, watching her fall.

A soldier, with cabasset helmet and breast plate like a steel doublet, was thrusting a barrel aloft, his puffed sleeves billowing, steering the cask from left to right and then left again, following the direction of her fall. The crowd cheered, egging him on.

The barrel interior homed in, its interior riddled with protruding nails, spike-side exposed.

She tumbled in headlong; nail teeth all around her: ready to bite.

It didn't hurt. That was the first surprise: the second was that her arms and legs hadn't come with her; they'd gotten lost in transit. Nothing of her was there, just her consciousness, and Nell. Nell was there, inside the barrel, and Brighid was back inside her head.

She tasted what Nell tasted, still spitting out the mud and grit from the banks of the bog, felt what Nell felt, a damp chill running all the way to her bones. And as the barrel was deposited onto the ground, and Nell raised her head out of the barrel, Brighid smelled the turf burning inside the cottages down the valley. She saw the gorse too, golden blossoms lit by the setting sun. And she heard the frantic whispers, only Nell (and Brighid) could hear, from beneath the twisted branches of the hawthorn tree.

Somebody pressed down on her head – hands like a psycho midwife's forceps forcing her back into the darkness, back into a foetal squat inside the spiked bellied barrel. The lid came down. Sepulchral darkness entered and reverberated above; they were hammering in more nails, securing the lid.

A stink of rotting fish. An old fish barrel; that's where she was: inside an old fish barrel. They hadn't even swilled it out beforehand – hadn't even given her that one little courtesy, graced her with that one tiny dignity.

Ankle-deep in scrunching fish scales; fish eyes squelching between her toes.

Fish eyes rolling up her calves.

She was losing her balance. Toppling.

Then it all went lopsided; she clenched feet and hands between and around the nails, preventing impalement; but when the cask was finally plonked on its side she almost slipped.

The first indication that the barrel was rolling down the hill came from the fish eyes tapping at her knees. Words pinged the barrel now: *Witch, murderer, sorceress, whore* – words slung like stones meaning to hurt. But Nell was concentrating, doing all she could to stop herself sliding into those nails.

Instead of picking up momentum – Brighid had seen the slope of the hill when she was falling from the sky, it was steep – the cask dawdled, lingering on every clod and groove.

Someone punched at the barrel. Nell slithered off the nails, cutting herself. But in the muddle of the bundled darkness and the scramble to retrieve a hold amongst the rolling spikes it was impossible to locate the pain. Just as she found a foothold in between the nails, someone kicked so hard their boot or clog nearly broke through the darkness. But it made no difference to the velocity. It was the wind – screaming through the tiny woodworm holes – the wind was clasping at the barrel, screeching on the brakes, slowing their descent right down.

'She's at it again,' someone shrieked.

The mob's fury dampened. The kicking and the pounding stopped.

'She'll kill us all,' someone else said; a someone who sounded like the woman who'd thrown the rock into the marsh, but her tone was all strangled, frightened, remorseful even. If she'd brought a wet cloth she'd be there trying to scrub out her spite, trying to rub out any earlier offence. *Didn't mean it, honestly – sorry*: it was that sort of tone.

The crowd's silence rolled in.

The barrel trundled to a halt and stayed like that for quite some time. Then, suddenly, without warning, everything moved to an upright position. A sword sawed a circle in the lid, a circle big enough to wrench Nell out by the hair; if Nell had still been there.

Someone shook the barrel, tentatively. And as the barrel shook, it rattled. So the bravest soul there, or perhaps the one with the most to lose if they chickened out, probably the soldier, tipped the barrel, emptied the contents: fish scales, fish eyes, four rusted nails, and a radio.

An old tabletop Bakelite box set radio – 1940's wartime state of the art – totally out of sync with a circa seventeenth century witch hunting scene, but this was a dream; random things were allowed to happen.

A woman made the sign of the cross and fainted.

◎ ◎ ◎

1...

Lowell rose out of the armchair and nodded at the radio. Counting.

2...

He opened the door to the lounge and entered the hallway.

3...

The sitting room was cold. The oil tank had run dry months ago. A bowl of mould on the coffee table. The remains of Dad's last muesli. Full fat milk. It always had to be full fat.

4...

He slipped in to Dad's parker. It was short on the sleeves, generous around the belly and chest. Zipping it up, he strode over to the fireplace. There were at least twenty acorns there now.

5...

All blown down the chimney.

They smelt of vanilla. He didn't know acorns smelt of vanilla.

6...

He reached into the hearth, snatched up one of the acorns and shoved it into his Dad's pocket.

He hesitated a moment, sniffed the throw and smelt the fabric conditioner Mum used to use.

Nostrils itching fleece fluff, orchard blossom and vanilla, he headed for the hall.

And then he continued counting all the way up to seventy-nine.

79...

He opened the front door.

◎ ◎ ◎

'How does it feel to be a day younger?'

Brighid was still sleeping, still dreaming, when the one-eyed seagull she was travelling with posed the question. They were riding on a gull-drawn carriage, the one-eyed seagull perched on the back of the seat, resting his wings. A ferry was crossing the waves in the sea below.

'Why? What time is it?' she asked.

The one-eyed seagull cocked his head to one side, giving the matter much thought. 'Are we talking days or hours?'

If she slept too long she'd miss her boat. Reality was threatening to break through. The seagulls flapped harder, their gargling shrieks sounding more like the thunder of a hundred stampeding hooves. A half moon flickered through holes in the clouds whipping luminance on the gulls' wings. Faster and faster they flew as the cold air sucked at her eyes – a plunger, pulling out tears, stirring a blurry soup of sea and sky. She smelt vanilla in the clouds. The gulls belched and swooped. She opened her eyes.

Still dreaming.

The one-eyed seagull let out a jubilant holler and the troupe slowed. Up ahead, below the billowing storm clouds, a castle loomed, its walls huge fronds of molten lava appeared to sprout from the sea. They edged nearer. She wiped her eyes; the lava solidified. It was the firelight inside the grounds that made the sandstone walls glow like an ember lantern – sandstone curtain walls that jutted up from a craggy isle, an islet stitched by sand spit to a larger island.

'Before you go remember this,' said the seagull.

'What do you mean before I go? Where am I going?'

'Red and green make yellow.'

'More like a muddy brown isn't it?'

The one eyed-seagull blinked, or winked, and said, '*Au revoir*,' then slammed his webbed foot down onto the back of the seat.

The chariot lost its equilibrium. She tumbled out. The gulls flapped on, leaving her plunging towards what looked like a church within the castle grounds. She hit one of its stained-glass windows, but it didn't break, didn't even crack; she just filtered on through the yellow in the glass: a saint's halo. And she kept on percolating, through the alter, through the flagstones, and into the room below. There, her consciousness snagged and dangled like an elastic band caught in the barrel vaulted ceiling. Windows. Windows shaped very much like the attic windows in the Amityville movies; only these didn't have glass, just bars. She was inside a jail then, a dungeon, hanging from the ceiling and, despite the freezing winds blasting in off the sea and through the bars, she was breathing in the stench of mould and piss.

A clicking sound; like hairdressers' scissors. Snip. Snip. Snip.

But there was no-one there.

Something moved on the earth floor, immediately below her elastic band self; a mound the size of an egg was visibly growing. Peeling.

Snip. Snip. Snip.

Soil scattered.

Two eyes on stalks. Snip. Snip. Snip.

A crab popped out, waved its pincers then abruptly fell sidelong back down the hole.

The elasticity, attaching Brighid to the ceiling, drooped and snapped, leaving her no other choice but to follow the crab into the hole.

And then out the other side of the hole, into a chamber; a chamber lined with crystallised golden resin that glowed like sunshine. Amber – that's what it looked like. Here: moth-like insects preserved. And there: a life belt hanging on the wall. A life belt? Why would anyone need a life belt in this place? Thousands of tiny bubbles littered the amber yet one bubble stood out – being much larger than the rest it was a bubble difficult to miss. It was more a goldfish bowl size of bubble, without the goldfish, and without the gold glow. There was no sunshine beyond the goldfish bowl bubble, only darkness. But, just before the darkness, within the twilight of the goldfish bubble, leaning back at an impossible angle was something she'd seen before; a whimsical something from the previous dream. The old Bakelite radio.

Someone was there, staring in at the radio.

'And who the hell are you anyway?' A voice asked. Nell's voice. Nell's voice emanating from the radio.

'Lord Barnacle,' the man at the goldfish bowl sized bubble replied, bowing to the radio, introducing himself, and now turning away from the bubble, absolutely delighted with himself, and judging from the smell of rum, extremely drunk himself. His round, rubicund face made him look more swine than human, like a man who'd eaten meat in such gluttonous amounts that he was starting to look like the animals he devoured. His wide lattice lace collar was like a bib on which his pig head lolled. His cloak, fur-lined cobalt velvet, was festooned in jewels that jingled as he pivoted back towards the bubble in the wall. Moaning, in what sounded very much like frustration, he continued the pivot returning to the radio like a dark, star strewn planet on a wobbly orbit.

'You have created quite a stir today, my dear,' he said, scratching his belly's equatorial regions.

He was so close to where Brighid now dangled she could smell the rotting meat trapped between his teeth – teeth that looked more like spent matches. And now as he hoisted his cloak, draping it over his left shoulder in a theatrical display, there was a distinct waft of stale sweat and semen: a putrid pottage seasoned with an abundance of lavender oil.

'It was all highly regrettable. As a man of the Lord, I abhor cruelty.' His small piggy eyes sneered at the Bakelite.

'Liar!' the radio spat (as much as a radio can spit). 'You started all this.'

He whipped out a handkerchief, embroidered with a coat of arms, appropriately two swines, and dabbed his face as though saliva actually was rolling down his cheek. 'I'll cut to the chase. You need to return.'

'When and how I come back will be my own choosing. You'll be long gone.'

'And what about your baby?' Barnacle gleamed triumphantly, as much as a row of burnt matchstick teeth could gleam.

'She's somewhere safe,' the radio announced confidently. 'Hidden from the madness. You won't find her. You will never find her.'

Barnacle returned to the big bubble, not quite prodding it with the sausage fingers. But then, something seized his attention. He started sniffing like a tormented hound.

Brighid swung her sleeping consciousness as far as the invisible thread holding her would allow. And then she saw – behind Barnacle's ridiculous collar, inside the goldfish bowl, scuttling along the base of the bubble, the crab was back. He came to a halt at the Bakelite, grabbing the radio, lifting it with his two front pincers. Radio onboard, he hastily escaped down a tunnel too small for Lord Barnacle to follow, even if he were able to burst through the big bubble. It was quite some feat for a crab to carry such a cumbersome radio, but this was a dream.

Now, as Lord Barnacle stood cursing at the big bubble, her sleeping consciousness was being tugged like a yoyo; her essence on a string was being winched out through the hole, up through the dungeon's ribbed arches, out through the cathedral's stained glass halo, and up through the night sky. All the way up to the scaly webbed foot.

'Fancy meeting you again,' said the seagull sardonically.

She settled herself back into the chariot.

'Before you get yourself too comfortable, there's something you missed in the last dream. Not the first time either – you're always missing things: like the cockroach on the dinner table – you missed that, like the woodworm in your flat, the crab on the Cornish beach. You didn't see him did you? But he saw you. Waste of ice-cream that, letting it just melt all over your hand. And you missed your father. Shame. He was hanging on for that candle-lit supper.'

The moon came out from behind the clouds.

'Which brings me back to your last dream. Did you spot the stone that rolled out of the barrel? No. I suppose, the radio's sudden appearance would have been somewhat of a distraction. Anyway, that stone reeled its way all the way down to the river. And there's the river,' he said, pointing downwards with his wing.

A river sparkled in the moonlight; it was really more an estuary being so close to open sea.

'We're a couple or so miles downstream from Slieau Whallian, the hill overlooking the bog where Nell didn't quite drown,' the seagull said, still pointing. 'And this is as far as the stone travelled, where fresh water meets salt. Then the tide went out and left the stone stranded.'

Without warning, the carriage nose-dived and started spinning; clouds, moon, castle, gorse, river, were wheeling so fast it was impossible to breathe, and then everything straightened, slotted back to where everything should be, just in time for the gulls to perform a perfect landing in the silt.

The one-eyed seagull leaped out and waddled purposefully down the bank. 'Your friend Nell,' he declared, his beak gesturing towards a triangular stone.

Brighid's essence adjusted itself in the chariot, trying to dispel its dizziness, waiting for the seagull to finish his sentence.

But the seagull just prodded the stone with his beak. Then, he peered back at Brighid's essence. 'Don't tell me,' he said finally, straightening up, crooking his wing tip to his hip. 'Don't tell me you thought Nell was the radio. Now that would be crazy.'

She didn't reply.

So he returned to the stone, kicked the stone with his scaly foot. The stone hopped, skipped and jumped away into the river.

'Bon voyage,' the seagull quipped. 'See you later.'

Brighid woke up leaving the stone to drift out to sea.

◎ ◎ ◎

Perhaps you could call this the Transitional Period. Approaching the outer fringes of the Lounge Age, momentary blips beyond the lounge might be quite normal. Theories that a wormhole was snatching him up and spitting him out onto some transcendental beach could be laid to rest; for the time being anyway, until Lowell was back in the lounge wondering why his socks were wet and sandy again. He had simply walked out the front door, strolled down the road and headed for Fenella beach. All completely unaided. No wormholes involved.

It made total sense to be standing here shoeless on the damp sand on a particularly cold October night. Just like the approaching tide, he had been drawn here. It was impossible to go against the power of gravity. Impossible to deny the itch in his belly button.

He removed his gloves, dropped them onto the sand, and unzipped his dad's parker. Then he scratched and scratched his naval. A car turned round in the car park above the beach; its lights warped his shadow, morphing his fingers and thumbs into long talons.

The moon was rising over Peel Castle.

The sea was creeping closer; the sand around his socks fizzed. He dipped his hands in the approaching waters. These very same hands had knocked back pint after pint. Didn't matter how much he scrubbed his hands, he would never be able to change things. He'd never be able to undo time. Never be able to go back kick his younger self's ass out of the pub, scream at him to listen to the radio. His hands would always be the same. His thumb prints would never change; the whorls would always remain the same pattern.

Those missed Mayday calls had entrenched themselves just as indelibly within his soul.

Further out, deeper into the bay, beyond the beach, between the castle and the faint shadows of the Mourne Mountains on the horizon, was a darkness that could wash away his thoughts forever. A fitting reunion with his parents: a maritime death.

The sea was pulling him in, embracing him.

He was waist deep: the cold, numb blankness was swallowing him.

A single wave, towering over the others, coiled and walloped him in the chest, toppling him, sending him somersaulting backwards. Instinctively, he grabbed something solid to get his bearings: a handful of shingle. The next wave pitched and rolled him back to the beach.

Slumped at the water's edge, shivering in his drenched clothes, Lowell clasped his arms around his knees and sobbed.

A crab scurrying across the sand paused briefly, its beady stalk eyes staring.

Catching his breath, Lowell peered down at his hands, realised the shingle he'd scooped up, when he was falling ass over tip along the sea bed, was still there, in the palm of his hand. A stone in the hodgepodge of grit and pebbles caught his eye. Jiggling his wrist, he filtered the shingle away between his fingers and then held the stone up to the moonlight. The stone was a perfect triangle.

As he rubbed his finger along one of the triangle's corners – something sparked between stone and epidermis, an energy, like the static charge of caressing a lusted for lover for the first time. Lowell stood up and smiled at the opalescent stone. The stone glittered in response, hues of moon and sea sparkle. He tightened his grip around the triangle and thought he felt a heartbeat. It might have been his own.

There it was again: a rhythm within his hand, within the stone. His feet seemed lighter as the beat pulsed through his limbs; he began to dance, skipping along the water's edge: no more grieving, no more despair. There was only the cadence of ecstatic joy and he was jumping to its drum.

Then suddenly and without wanting to, he curled his arm around himself, angling for a wide trajectory, and hurled the stone into the night sky. The stone whirled through the air and as it span it made a sound, a whisper: *Not yet my love, Not yet.*

It was Nell's voice.

The stone skimmed across the waves, hopped three times then plummeted back into the Irish Sea. Lowell fell to the sand, but this time it was not grief that rocked his body, but laughter. He had felt her. He had heard her. He had even seen her, in the blink of an eye, just as the stone was about to slap the surface of the water for the third and final time; she was there, sliding off the tips of the silver waves. The watery moonlight radiated off her naked body as she dissolved into the sea spray – her skin all luscious lunar iridescence, hair pearly velvet lustre – her feet whipping the surface into a frenzy of whizzing sparks and flashes. She was more achingly beautiful than he ever imagined.

How could he possibly forget a moment like this?

Chapter 9

Brittany, France

A letter on the kitchen table.

> *Brighid*
> *Had to go – our last day in the house. I've left a present in the drawer (of this table). I made it especially for you. Make sure you take it. You need it.*
> *You'll see again one day soon.*
> *All my love*
> *Tessy (mother)*
> *X*
> *P.S. We know you're a bit skint so have left you a little something. I'd say buy yourself an ice cream, but as you don't like ice cream, you best not. xxx*

You'll see again – had she missed out the word *me* – *you'll see me again*: is that what she had meant to say? Or was Tessy still barking on about her imaginary husband and co? She could have at least stayed and had breakfast with her, at least waved her off, said goodbye. And where the hell was she going? Brighid had assumed the house was Tessy's. Stupid really, how could Tessy afford to get into real estate? It was a rental, a squat even, and now Tessy was off on one, vacating the premises, and booting Brighid out in the process. How could she help her mother now? Just when she thought they had established a link, tenuous though it was, Tessy was off, deserting her. She wiped away a single hot tear and swallowed hard. She was being ridiculous. Tessy was not in her right mind. It was nothing personal. She pulled out the table drawer. Inside was a red coat with green cuffs, collars and hem. There wasn't anything else in the drawer, so Tessy's gift had to be the coat: the red and green coat.

Red and green make yellow: that little one-liner in the dream. Just coincidence. There was always the cold (and it certainly was cold here) light of day, always a perfectly logical explanation for everything. Last night's dreams were so vivid they almost felt real but they were just dreams, subconscious back-answers to the day before. The sea crossing bits in the dreams were self explanatory and the rest of it, well that was just her brain defragging the dizzying muddle of meeting Tessy, of witnessing her whirligig grounding in reality. There was always a rational answer to life's mysteries. Unlike Tessy, Brighid always sought logic.

Any fanciful leanings she might have possessed had been teased out of her at school. The bullying started the same week she had won the scholarship to board.

The opening line had come from Nuala Nicholls: 'You think you got the best marks in the exam don't you?'

That's what Brighid had been told so she nodded.

Nuala had another theory. 'I lost out on the scholarship because you don't have a real home.'

Brighid replied that her mother was busy doing more important things like helping Bob Geldoff in Ethiopia. 'She's a doctor.' She'd followed that with a quick sign of the cross apology under the desk, for God's eyes only. Lying was a sin.

The Live Aid concert had still been fresh in her mind. She'd watched an old recording at Aunt Mary's, the day after Granddad went to the old people's home, the day after she had moved into Aunt Mary's. She had gotten sick of beans, spam and boiled egg so was glad to move. That was all Granddad knew how to cook. Everything had fallen apart after Nana died. Granddad just went around stinking of whiskey and crying all the time.

'You got the scholarship because the sisters feel sorry for you,' Nuala said. Then she turned to the rest of the class to make the announcement. 'Brighid's mum isn't a doctor. She's a nutter. That's what Brighid's gonna be when she grows up – a nutter just like her mum. And she talks to herself. I've heard her.'

Brighid had been about to speak out in her own defence but was wise enough at eight to know that any mention of Magio, her imaginary friend, probably wasn't such a great idea.

'Brighid's mum thinks she's Our Lady, the Virgin Mary,' Nuala shouted. Everyone was already listening so she didn't really need to shout that loud.

'That would make you Jesus,' somebody else piped up as quick as a flash.

The whole class had laughed at that, and so for the two months that followed (seemed years at the time) she was mostly known as Jesus. Whenever the nuns mentioned Jesus during class, somebody would always snigger, turn round and look at Brighid. But then Nuala had to push things further. One swimming class she pushed Brighid under water. 'See if you can part the waters. Remember Galilee, Jesus.'

She had remained under water longer than she had thought possible, had observed the limbs of swimmers kicking past and the same limbs returning again completing another length. She still remembered the luminance from the overhead strip lighting refracting, trembling, bending like arms unable to reach. She in her own world: stranded, shut out. Her lungs had felt as though they'd solidified, become molten rock ready to burst. Seen through the stinging chlorine, her skin seemed to change colour, texture. Then there was the realisation, this could be it: if she stayed longer, this would be it, forever and ever, amen.

The lights above became a magnet, heaving her from the muffled darkness, and as she ascended she grabbed Nuala's ankles, pulled her down, punched at her through the water; not exactly the welterweight champion punch she had hoped, the water slowed her thrust so her fist barely stroked Nuala's cheek, but the look of terror on Nuala's face had been pure victory. That was the turning point, the point where she decided she was done with lurking in the shadows, done with being alone, apart. She still remembered the feeling of her blood quickening, of pure adrenalin pumping, knowing that the darkness was behind her, knowing that she would never let anyone put her there again. She emerged through the surface, to the noise and light, and was ignored by Nuala from then on. *Jesus* went away that day. And so did Magio.

Tessy was stuck in her own pool, separate, detached, unable to reach the surface. But hers wasn't a pool of water and chlorine but of crystallite distortions. There were moments when she was able to bore a hole though the prisms, a moment of clarity where she could truly be part of things, when reality didn't get all crooked and refracted, but those moments were perhaps rare and brief; the surface always ended up sealing itself, freezing Tessy back into her solitary confinement away from the world.

Brighid slipped her arms into the coat; a knee-length coat with a tailored waist that fitted Brighid's small midriff perfectly. And it was warm, sumptuously warm. There was something in the pocket.

A fifty euro note – more than just ice cream money. And a ferry ticket.

The ticket had Brighid's name on it, and the same port, Calais, and time of sailing as her own return journey, but with tomorrow's date. Why was Tessy encouraging her to stay another day when she wasn't even sticking around herself?

With Tessy gone there seemed little point in hanging around. The mouldy tomato slobbering its innards on the shelf was the only item left in the kitchen cupboards; the coffee she was craving would have to be found in a café. Nothing was brewing here.

She dashed upstairs, threw yesterday's clothes into her overnight bag. Glancing at the hole in the wall, she cleared her throat and spotted something on the floor, lying amongst the dust and wallpaper peelings.

Acorns. Three acorns. And a white feather.

They weren't there last night. She would have noticed. They must have blown in through the hole while she was sleeping. She rubbed the tickle in her nose. She could still smell vanilla. The scent from the car's air freshener had infused her clothes, her hair and even her dreams.

A small mirror was hanging on the wall, eye-height, above the hole. Her mascara had smudged; she licked her finger and rubbed out the mark. As she turned from her reflection, a sudden blur of colour streaked across the mirror. She swung back round, but there was no-one there, nothing there, just the bed still looking oddly marooned in the centre of this huge empty room. She peered back in the mirror; her own wide eyed reflection told her she had to get out of the house before she ended up as cuckoo as Tessy.

Daylight placed the decaying house under harsh spotlight highlighting the probable cause behind much of the interior damp. The outer render had peeled from the walls in chunks; slate from the roof had crash-landed onto the walnuts piled up on the drive; a recent fall which had not only smashed the tiles themselves but had proven an effective nutcracker for the various birds now feasting there. A wren, oblivious or full, perched on a branch of the walnut tree, erupted into bubbling whistles. The tree began swaying; there was no wind, not even a breeze. It was as if the wren's breath alone was stirring the bough, and as the branches seemed almost to sough in accompaniment they scratched more render off the walls. A house in need of total renovation, unfit for human habitation, condemned; not her problem or Tessy's now it seemed. The wren stopped singing, flew from the tree, over the gatepost and into the forest beyond. The wrought iron gates at the end of the driveway had been left wide open.

An abrupt rumble out in the road cracked the silence as effectively as roof tiles on walnuts. Vehicles had to be a rare event on this road (it was more dirt track than road) so Brighid went to the gates to investigate.

A coach, the same coach she had seen parked up at the Étang de Comper, Vivian's Lake. Somebody waved from the rear window, but because the glass was all misted up it was more the spectre of a hand. The hand wiped away the condensation from a section of the window. It was Tessy.

Tessy blew a kiss through the defogged glass and then to re-iterate drew an 'x' in the misted bit. As the coach pulled further away, Brighid searched for a clue to Tessy's next destination. Above the Spanish number plate, scrawled in bold lettering, were the words, *Picos de Europa.*

Brighid needed to find out exactly where Tessy was going, stop the coach somehow, get an address. There was no way she could organise the help Tessy needed without an address. She ran to her car, jumped in, turned the ignition; the engine kicked in, turning over its familiar murmur. All as it should be. The smell of vanilla: the smell of her own space.

The coach had departed out of sight, past the bend in the road, but it couldn't have gone far.

After driving for what seemed much longer than the five minutes indicated on the dashboard clock, she reached a junction, scanned left then right. No sign of the coach. Finding Tessy was now a 50:50 choice between left and right: odds on evens – she took the left, following the sign for Dinan. Her mobile, which had been unusually quiet since entering the house, began beeping. It beeped again as she drove past Lake of Comper, its glass-like stillness splintered as a stray breeze tickled its surface – still no sign of Merlin's Lady of the Lake. And still no sign of Tessy and the coach. She drove out of Brocéliande, leaving Tessy's world behind.

With the car parked in the shadow of the Chateau de Dinan, she headed for the tree lined Promenade des Petits-Fossés, following the flow of the medieval town walls. Pausing at the entrance of Le Jardin des Petits Diables, she checked her mobile. Five missed calls, two voice messages, three text messages, and one very low battery. She went to the text messages first, guessing they might use the least power. They were all from Kate.

Where are you?

What was she on about? She knew where she was.

You ok? Why aren't you back yet?

Because I'm in France. What was up with her?

Get in touch. Freakin worried.

Kate was one of life's worriers, but these texts were so over the top they risked altitude sickness. Something must have happened to have got her all stirred up like that. Brighid had gotten to the port way ahead of schedule, so they had let her board an earlier ferry. Had there been some kind of incident on the crossing she was booked on? That would explain Kate's concern.

A Wi-Fi zone wasn't much use; the battery in her mobile didn't have the energy for browsing, and stupidly, she'd forgotten to pack a three to two pin adaptor. Internet cafés were probably in short supply these days, but she needed to find one, find out what was happening in the world, find out what was happening with her hysterical friend.

A shunting wheeze behind her, getting nearer. She turned to see a middle-aged jogger; the florid flush and flailing flab flashed newbie status. An old man sitting on one of the benches that lined the way, leaned forward scrutinising the jogger's performance or the half price stickers on the soles of the jogger's trainers. Whichever it was, he quickly switched interest to something on the walkway of the ramparts. Brighid followed his gaze all the way up to the man just about visible, hood up, peeping over the wall, oversized sunglasses and camera concealing his face.

'Ici,' the old man hissed. Brighid realised he was talking to her.

'I'm sorry. *Parlez-vous Anglais*?'

The old man shrugged. 'Can you keep a secret?' he asked in broken English.

'Depends what the secret is.'

'Time is catching up with us,' he whispered.

The lines around his mouth crept up his skin as he

smiled. And as his age dulled eyes fixed upon her, a light seemed to shine within them, like torches in a mist, drawing her in. She pulled away from his focus and faced the dazzling light of the sun.

She was in urgent need of caffeine; the drowsy residues left behind by last night's dreams needed purging – she'd need her wits for the five or six hour drive to Calais, and the additional two hours to get from Dover to Brighton. An opening in the walls took her up the cobbled steps of Rue du Fossé and into the town centre. A boy, traversing the busy through-road, ripped the top off the baguette he was carrying and began munching. He wasn't the only one hungry. She stopped at a takeaway stall and bought a *galette,* a melted cheese *galette* that she devoured as she passed estate agents, hotels, bars, restaurants, and a comic shop window displaying vintage illustrations of the Invisible Man. The imposing granite houses of Place du Champ and Place du Guesclin gave way to the timber framed buildings of artisan shops, galleries, crêperies, and then she spotted a neon @ sign.

There were four new messages in her inbox. She opened the first one.

From: kat.mckate@gmail.com
To: craftbrighid@gmail.com
Subject: Bonjour
Sent: October 16, 15:25

Bonjour missus!!!
How you getting on with the Virgin Mary? (Sorry couldn't resist.☺)

The landlord turned up at my office just now – got a call from reception – can't believe he turned up like that. And he had a right head on him as well – shouting about your rent cheque bouncing. I've paid him for now – it was the only thing I could do to shut him up and get him to leave. Nosey cow on reception loved it.

Pretty brassick myself so can you pay me back as soon as? Sorry to hassle you. The boss is lurking.
Gotta go.
See you soon.
Kate
x

Delete.

Two other emails seemed to be responses to jobs she had applied for.

She opened the first.

From: hr@jallooder.com
To: craftbrighid@gmail.com
Subject: Digital Editor Vacancy
Sent: October 16, 18:50

Dear applicant
Thank you for your application re: our vacancy in the editing department. The standard of applicants was extremely high and I'm afraid you were not successful...

Delete. Next.

From: lowellwatterson@yahoo.com
To: craftbrighid@gmail.com
Subject: Editor Position
Sent: October 16, 23:03

Dear Brighid Craft
Thank you for your application regarding the temporary post of Digital Editor. I am pleased to inform you that your application has been successful.

The post commences on Monday, the 27th October at our Isle of Man base, but you would need to arrive the day before. I would also like to confirm, due to the temporary nature of this work, that accommodation will be supplied along with a very generous salary. Travel expenses will also be covered. Please could you confirm your acceptance for this position at your very earliest convenience.

If you have any queries at all please do not hesitate to contact me.
Kind regards
Lowell Watterson
Director
Aurora Productions (IOM) Ltd

She issued a small punch to the air, almost knocking over the cup and saucer holding her espresso. A row of faces turned from their monitors and stared momentarily.

She tried to remember the job details, tried to recall the job advert but drew a blank. She was pretty sure she hadn't even applied for any jobs on the Isle of Man but she had sent her C.V. to so many different places it was difficult to keep track. She hit reply. At last, there'd be some money coming in. Result.

She typed a resounding but formal YES to the job.

Send.

Next. Kate's other email.

From: kat.mckate@gmail.com
To: craftbrighid@gmail.com
Subject: Where are you???
Sent: October 18, 07:41

Brighid
Have called your mobile but keep getting some message in French. You were supposed to be off the ferry and back in Brighton hours ago. Have checked the sailing – it arrived on time. Guess you've just changed your booking – message must mean you're still on French network. Let me know what's happening – is all ok? Starting to worry you've broken down or had an accident or something.
Kate
x

Why did the email show tomorrow's date? Today was the seventeenth. She had booked to return tonight. Brighid rolled over the monitor's time display, a small pop up window popped up today's date: 18th Octobre.

A copy of Le Monde lay unattended on the next table. The date on the front page: 18th Octobre.

But that would mean she'd spent two nights at Tessy's house.

A new email.

From: hector@crabhq.com
To: craftbrighid@gmail.com
Subject: Rise and Shine
Sent: October 18, 11:03

Wakey wakey yer lazy cow :-O
Don't blame your mum – she didn't spike your casserole. We needed to fill you in on some background and where better to start than at Hunvre.
See you soon
Hector
x

She didn't know anyone called Hector.

Chapter 10

Isle of Man

'**What d'you mean** you've got a flight to catch?' Lowell exclaimed.

This was supposed to be *the* big day: the bloody editor was arriving in seven hours, twenty-five minutes, and Hector had suddenly decided now was the time to mention holiday plans.

'Two flights actually. Just a day-trip. I'll be back before you know it. So, if you can haul your ass off the crapper, don't forget Nell's special surprise. She wants to show her appreciation for all your hard work – 11pm – make sure you're in the backyard. No nocturnal wanderings to the beach.'

The toilet seat suddenly felt cold. 'Why would I go to the beach?'

His socks had remained dry and sand-free for over a week. Last time it happened he was ordering the groceries online one minute and the next thing he knew he was on the other side of the lounge completely drenched. Wearing Dad's parker.

'Just make sure you're in the yard, alright?'

Lowell wiped urgently and flushed. 'What's the surprise?'

Hector had already left.

◎ ◎ ◎

Brighid fastened her seat belt and pulled out an Isle of Man newspaper from the back pocket of the seat in front.

The last one onboard, with big jaunty strides, was a man dressed in brown leathers, raven black hair touching his shoulders. The air hostess glanced at his boarding pass and mumbled something inaudible: seat directions or welcome onboard or both; all delivered sourly. Unfazed, he smiled back, flicked his sunglasses up over his high wide forehead and brushed back his hair, accentuating cheekbones sharp enough to slice a lemon. A lemon dashed with mineral water.

She was thirsty. It had been one mad dash catching the Gatwick Express and locating the departure gate. The coat Tessy made had proven cumbersome to lug around with her suitcase, and with no space in the overhead locker, she was stuck with the coat, slung over her knees like a heavy blanket.

'14B. That's me,' the man in leathers said, sitting down beside her. No coat. No hand baggage. No issue with the overhead locker.

Vanilla. The smell of vanilla.

'Ice cream?' He said, proffering a tub of vanilla ice cream.

She hesitated, bit her lip.

'It was buy one get one free. Can't ignore a bargain.'

He pushed the tub closer. 'What's wrong? Sensitive teeth?'

'Actually, yes.'

He grinned. A wide grin. White teeth. Not too white. Slightly crooked.

The air hostess was bustling up the aisle, focus flickering from passenger to passenger. She halted to pass her sky blue eyes over the leathers in aisle seat 14B.

He reached for his seat belt before she had a chance

to speak. The air hostess nodded, but didn't smile. She returned to the cabin crew area, settled herself into her seat, fastened her own seat belt, then turned her head and gazed all the way up the aisle to row 14.

Brighid shifted uncomfortably in her seat, lowered her head to read an article on the aurora borealis. Unusual conditions and heightened solar activity meant the northern lights would be visible in latitudes as far south as the Isle of Man.

'Is it me or you she's glaring at?' The man in leathers whispered.

'I thought it was me being paranoid.'

'Hang on to that paranoia,' he advised, rather too dramatically. 'It's not a bad thing to have.'

Seeing them both looking back at her, discussing her, the air hostess's crimson lips took a nosedive; she even grabbed her seatbelt as though the shock of it would send her plummeting. Mouth back on terra firma she carefully studied her manicured nails.

Brighid was almost tempted to take the ice cream, she was that thirsty. He perched the second tub on the armrest between them, the plane now taxiing along the runway. Melted ice cream was accumulating around the lid, dribbling down the edges.

As the plane slowed, reaching the queue for the runway, he scraped out the last of his ice-cream with the small wooden spatula; then he shoved the sticky empty tub into the pocket of the seat in front, between the in-flight magazine and sick bag.

He wiped his lips with the back of his glove. The plane lunged forward dispatching the bargain ice cream from the armrest to bounce off the seat in front and land, lid-side down, right next to his leather boots. Same shade as the rest of his leathers. He undid his seat belt, leaned forward, and turned the tub over. Carpet fluff and the crumbs of airline biscuits lined the collapsed, soggy lid, rendering the ice cream inedible. So he left it there, on the floor, between them, vanilla ice cream rapidly melting.

He rubbed his knees, leather gloves against leather knees, and stretched his long legs without knocking the ice cream over. 'Holiday?' he asked, grabbing his seat belt again.

The plane lifted off the runway.

'I'm just over on a work contract.'

He clapped his seat belt together. 'What's your job?'

She cleared her throat. So dry and tickly. She was looking forward to the seat belt light being turned off, and the trolley rolling her way. 'I'll be editing a documentary.'

He smiled at this, his warm oak eyes shining, then sank back in his chair.

The air hostess was still examining her nails.

Brighid was already knocking back the last of her mineral water, the plane already commencing descent when he spoke again. Thankfully, the other air hostess had served her.

'What's the documentary?' he asked.

She turned away from her window in the sky. The clouds were failing to exhibit even the merest hint of the aurora borealis.

'No idea.'

He leaned forward. 'Didn't you ask?'

She shook her head. The plane was ploughing through the clouds, emerging on the other side, to the underbelly of the sky, to the runway lights below. She *had* actually asked in both emails. The replies had been full of logistics instead.

'Could be something dodgy,' he said, widening his

eyes in mock horror, clasping the chair in front. 'Best you have my mobile number just in case.'

She sucked her lips. What harm was there in having his number? She didn't have to call him, didn't have to give out her number.

'What's your name?' She said, pulling her mobile phone out from her coat pocket.

'Can't tell you.'

'Why not?' She curled a strand of hair around her ear, and smiled. 'Is it that embarrassing?' She didn't normally flirt with strangers on planes. She was almost doing just that.

He squeezed her arm mischievously. 'Wouldn't want to spoil things.'

◎ ◎ ◎

For Lowell, the very thought of Nell's special surprise, whatever it may be, made luminance ooze from every pore. That's what it felt like anyway. He had been tempted to wear sunglasses; it might already be dark, but for Lowell that scorching light was seeping out of every crevice, every corner. Everything was shining.

Now, having thumbed through the airport magazine several times, Lowell tried to read the article on the Island's multimillion pound sewage system but was not interested or able to focus on the words; he was too busy contemplating Nell's surprise, hoping it would be Nell herself, Nell in the flesh. First though, he had to collect Brighid Craft, bring her to the house, then the rest of the night was his own. She was coming in on the Gatwick flight at 19.15. Scanning the arrivals and departures screen again he saw the flight was still on schedule. He was grateful for that. He'd be even more grateful if Hector would just turn up on whatever flight he was on and meet her himself.

The airport was putting Lowell on edge, pushing away the light. The lustre that had been surrounding all things was starting to take itself off to its own departure lounge leaving nausea in its place; even the hope of what was awaiting in his backyard could not hold back the looming, stifling fog of in-your-face reality.

Iris. That was the name they had given the sewage project. A scheme that effectively shovelled shit, named after a flower. It was like the term *passed away*; Passed away: a euphemism hiding the shitty, choking, gnawing, bloated rawness of death. Passed away, they had said, as though his parents had simply sailed out of the harbour and faded into the horizon, a grey dot, calm waters all the way. They hadn't passed, they'd have thrashed, their lungs filling, battling with all their mites not to reach that big crease in the sky.

He rubbed his hands together trying to get rid of the urge to bite his nails. If it wasn't for his gloves, new rainbow-coloured woollen gloves, he'd have ripped his thumbs to threads by now. He'd lost his old leather gloves during one of his dizzy spells and had replaced them with the rainbow gloves. Movies always had the psycho wearing leather gloves.

The airport policeman had positioned himself beneath the flights status screen. He seemed to be looking for someone, someone specific. His radar gaze halted at Lowell. Something registered. Lowell was the beep on his radar; it didn't matter how dark it now felt, there was no escaping that radar. Out of all the people within the arrivals area, Lowell was the target; *the* someone specific the police had been searching for. The policeman was homing in, approaching. Lowell switched his gaze to the floor; any further eye contact and he may as well rip his ribcage open – expose his panicking galloping heart. What was it about the police? They always made you feel guilty even when you hadn't done anything wrong. But he had done something wrong. Maybe they could see into his thoughts, hear the guilt in his heartbeat, sniff the betrayal in his sweat. His hands were burning up inside his gloves, flushing blood-red if anyone could see them; hands that had been busy knocking back pint after pint when he should have been listening for Mayday calls.

'Lowell Watterson?' the policeman said.

They knew his name. A woman sitting nearby glanced up from a soap gossip magazine. He was more interesting than Coronation Street. This was his five minutes of fame. Next he'd be dragged out of the airport – on public display, everyone watching – to help with inquiries, interrogation, confession, jail.

Could he get locked up for not being by the radio? What did they call it?

Gross neglect.

Manslaughter.

'Yes, that's me.' A squelched pitch he had never heard in his own voice before.

'Thought so,' the policeman smiled.

Why was he smiling? Was that a smile police used to arrest a murderer? Didn't get too many of those on the Island. This was the pinnacle of his career – of course he was smiling. Lowell was the mouse; the policeman the cat – a cat with a bucket load of cream. The cat was clawing, toying with him. The final pounce was imminent.

'I think this is yours.'

The policeman licked his lips and extended his hand, padded, paw-like, all leather gloved (it wasn't just psychos and Hector; it was cops and psycho cops). Resting in that paw was something sheathed in laminate: Lowell's driving licence. He snapped up the licence from the outstretched paw, fearful any hesitation might summon the claws.

'Somebody found it in the car park and handed it in.'

Lowell thanked him willing the policeman to walk away, which he did.

With the driving licence safely inside his jacket pocket, jacket pocket zipped shut, Lowell sat down. The policeman was now at the other side of the terminal; detached, removed. The soap woman was leafing through her magazine; detached, removed. He pulled his hair into a tighter ponytail (clean hair) and inspected his jeans (clean). The washing machine had been busy this last week. There was no longer such a need to be tied to the lounge; everything he was doing he was doing for Nell and because of that she felt even closer. So he no longer had quite so many qualms about leaving the lounge to grab a quick shower, a very quick shower. He had moved the kettle and fridge back into the kitchen, had done all the cleaning and vacuuming Hector had told him to do. Not in the basement, he still wasn't allowed to see that until tomorrow. And with upstairs being so far from the radio, he had just given the bathroom and guest bedroom a swift once over, but in the sitting room and hall he not only cleaned but decorated. He wouldn't have gone for the colour scheme Hector had chosen, wouldn't have done any decorating at all, but with the paint already bought and opened, it would have been rather late in the day to complain. Red and green should never be seen, isn't that how the saying goes? Hector said it was sort of branding, for the production, for the bigger picture.

He used to be good with people, was able to stand up for himself, was able to make conversation, was able to make people laugh (with him not at him). He was someone people liked to be around, but that all got blocked up back there, and now he was just a constipated shit, festering in the bowels of his own inadequacy. He scanned the terminal. They were selling flowers in the shop. Should he buy some to greet Brighid? Would that be appropriate? He needed to keep things casual.

No flowers.

The driving licence was digging into his ribs, poking at the pocket's zip. If the zipper teeth split, the licence could fall out – could mean a rerun of the cop scene. He stood up and unzipped his pocket. The soap woman eyeballed him then returned her attention to the plot-spoilers. Licence retrieved – better to keep hold of it – he plonked himself back down.

Jacket: intact. Jeans: casual. Shoes: smart. Scarf: stupid.

Hector had given him the lairy scarf, the red and green scarf, seven hours and forty-seven minutes before Brighid's arrival. 'Good to put the corporate colours out there,' he'd said, tying the thing round his neck, insisting he wore it for the airport. 'Not too tight wouldn't want to drown you.'

Not *strangle*, but *drown*.

Lowell had never discussed his parents' death with Hector. But it was common knowledge, at least around Peel. It must have been a slip of the tongue. Even Hector's humour wasn't that cruel.

His palms were still tingling. His belly button itched. Resisting the urge to scratch, Lowell focused on the arrivals list. The Gatwick flight had landed.

The first of the arrivals emerged on the other side of the glass wall: a business woman – power suit, dagger heels – bypassed the luggage carousel and was first out through the swinging doors; an alligator woman who could eat Lowell alive. So many predators in the jungle. He suddenly longed for a retreat back to the Lounge Age.

The luggage collection area was filling: a young family; a group of men in suits; a man wearing an Arsenal football shirt, rosy faced, round-bellied; a loved-up couple holding hands, content, oblivious.

And then there she was – dark hair cropped urchin style. Brighid was smaller than he had imagined from the photograph. Her cream thick-knit knee-length jumper highlighted her flushed glow, her smallness, as did the coat draped over the crook of her arm, a red coat with green cuffs.

Red and green.

Maybe she was in on this. He had assumed she would be blissfully unaware, more in the dark than he was. It had all been set up as just a job, just a documentary. She was just an editor. Hector had set the scene like that. Maybe she already knew there was more to it. Lowell already knew there was more to it but he just didn't know what that *more* was.

Under the impression that the guise of it being *just a documentary* was to be maintained, that Brighid was to be effectively directed both inside and outside working hours, he'd declared himself (in his own head) the puppet master, ready to guide her around the pretence, to pull her strings. Perhaps it was the other way round, perhaps she with her red and green coat, all branded and glowing, was really puppet master. He couldn't ask her directly – the coat could just be coincidence. He would have to tread carefully, assume the role of string puller until otherwise instructed.

She was running her gaze over the glass wall, scanning the faces of those waiting alongside him. He raised his hand to wave. She waved back and smiled. A friendly smile. He hadn't expected that. The photograph she had sent, during the to-and-fro of emails finalising details, had been the typical passport sort: blue background curtain, skin tone smudged into the curtain's colour, features set in earnest formality. That cyan hue had suited his expectations, made him feel at ease; every aspect of his life had been tinged by that tone for months. This golden warmth was unnerving. It was a different light to the one that had carried him today; that was a pure white light that fused into his own, making everything brighter, magical even. Brighid's golden glow was another colour on the spectrum. If she got too close, the cyan, everything that felt safe, would change, turn into something else, get tainted, contaminated.

She was approaching the carousel. He prayed she had luggage to collect, to delay the vis-à-vis. What were they supposed to talk about? She stopped at the carousel. Still no sign of Hector. Which flight was he coming back on anyway?

Lowell was safe in his own blue glow for a precious few more moments. He had shut everyone out over the last year or so. Friends had persevered for weeks, some for months, but he upheld a strict regime, keeping curtains closed, doors locked, lighting to a minimum. If anyone came around unannounced (it was always unannounced because he never picked up the phone) he'd hide behind the sofa so as not to create any tell-tale silhouettes. Siobhan – to call her an ex-girlfriend would be stretching it, she was more a flash in the pan, a flash of pants, a pant of flesh – went on trying longer than most, probably guilt. It was because of her he'd lost track of time. She had distracted him the day his parents left; she was the reason he wasn't by the radio listening for any distress calls. But even Siobhan gave up on him eventually. And slowly grief's blackness warped into the cold blue light of isolation, ice-blue – an iceberg detached from the landmass – Ice Age, Lounge

Age; it was all the same thing.

Brighid had located her case. The glow was approaching, global warming quickening, sweat levels rising. He was suddenly afraid of what might happen once she got close. If he melted maybe there'd be nothing left.

Brighid rejected Lowell's offer to carry her case; he already looked too weighed down as he was, as though the ties of some unseen load were digging in his shoulders, drawing them in, crooking his back. A tic just to the side of his nose, above the undomesticated beard, shuddered as though the strain of carrying such a burden was chipping away at him. Being short, Brighid was used to people stooping over her – she was 5 foot 1′ in her bootless feet – but Lowell's was a different kind of stoop. Dark blue circles ringed his eyes; and his skin, but for the occasional patches of eczema, held the pallor of someone who didn't get outside much; this made the perspiration on his forehead look like sleet. He had a young face, she realised, without the wild beard, knackered eyes and done with life bearing – much younger than your average director.

'If we could just find a trolley__' Brighid suggested.

This seemed to please him. He walked away a lighter man.

Somebody tapped her on the shoulder.

The man in leathers she'd been sitting next to on the plane. Still smelling of vanilla.

'Don't forget. If your boss turns into a psycho, call me.'

He fired a crooked wide grin at her, then hurried away before she even had a chance to reply.

Despite the battered, old Ford Fiesta having a perfectly good boot to fit her suitcase, Lowell opened the passenger door, hauled her case in and wedged it between the front seat and dashboard. Brighid had no other choice but to sit in the back.

Waiting to reverse, waiting for the car behind to move, Lowell began drumming his knee with the car park ticket; it was an impatient relentless beat, something of an extension to his tic. He made no attempt at conversation, and she got the distinct impression that any effort she made in that direction would be decidedly unwelcome; he just kept on staring at the rear view mirror, shutting her out, blinking furiously, as if working on the principle that it would somehow tame his fidgety eyes. First impressions: he was either a stressed out workaholic or off his head on amphetamines. Or both.

No seat belt in the back.

Engine ticking over, the heater blasting, it was too warm inside the car to wear her coat, so she set it down on top of her case.

'Interesting coat,' Lowell said suddenly breaking the silence, still watching the other car reversing. 'Where d'you get it?'

'My mother made it.'

He turned, settled his gaze upon the coat, mulled the concept over; a concept, it seemed, that needed considerable consideration.

'Hmm,' he said eventually, looking at her via the rear view mirror. 'That would explain it.' Glimmers of plaque and tartar behind the beard hair. Were he a stray dog being assessed by a vet, his estimated age would have just increased. 'And you have to pretend you like it. Did she drop you off at Gatwick?'

'No. I do like it.'

'Oh.'

'Anyway, it matches your scarf.' She smiled to clarify the comment was banter not bitching.

He was too busy scowling at the car behind to notice. 'An unwanted gift too – I mean not that yours is, but I wouldn't choose red and green myself. It's a bit garden gnome isn't it? A bit __'

She finished the sentence for him, 'off with the fairies?'

The drumming stopped. He looked up from the coat, swung around (as much as his seat belt would allow), eyes ablaze. 'Did she, erm, have any particular reason to choose red and green?'

She shrugged. Lowell was already proving to be tiresome.

'Was it because you like the colours?' He blinked, extinguishing the burning scrutiny, switching his gaze to the other car now pulling out beside them.

'Well no, she wouldn't know.'

'Why wouldn't she know?' He did a cursory scan of Brighid's face, coat, and then returned to his vigil over the car park.

'Why would she? Look, it's not such a big deal, I just happen to like it. The coat. The colours. My mother just got it right, made a lucky guess on the combo.'

'That's all?'

'That's all.'

This finally appeared to satisfy Lowell. The drumming of ticket against knee kicked into a rhythm that could easily be mistaken for self-congratulatory applause. His tic slackened. 'You're just an editor,' he mumbled, more to himself, more to his chin hair than to her. 'Just an editor. Nothing more.'

She wasn't sure if he'd meant her to hear, but hear she did. And now she knew where she stood in the pecking order she would just have to nudge that bearded beak right off his high perch.

He breathed in, suddenly, sharply, yelped almost, as

though she really had just given him the slap to the back of his neck he deserved. 'At last.'

He released the handbrake and reversed out.

Chapter 11

Lowell was relieved to finally reach the house. Each time a car had passed on the unlit country roads, he'd spotted her eyes in the mirror. Staring. She wasn't watching him, she was looking at the road; he reminded himself over and over. Blue eyes, or maybe green, lighting up like roadside cat's eyes, then hiding again until the next car.

'*Chez-moi*,' Lowell said, regretting it instantly. He couldn't think of anything to say the whole journey back and now he'd finally found something to say, he had to go and say it in French. Where had that come from?

He opened the gate to the double fronted end-of-terrace house. Home, his home, Mum and Dad's home, no-one else home. A terraced house with a small garden at the front, red door, number thirteen, hanging baskets full of sleeping forget-me-nots.

'Oh,' Brighid said, plonking her case down on the pavement. 'I thought I'd be staying in a hotel, a B and B, or something.'

He had forgotten to mention accommodation came equipped with live-in boss, was just as happy about it as she was. He cleared his throat, clenched his hands. The door key was prodding through the wool and digging into his palm.

'Not to worry,' Brighid added all hollow cheer, picking up her suitcase. 'Lead on.'

The first thing to hit him was the smell of paint. He'd left the windows open for days, had thought the smell had faded; now, though, he realised the place still stank.

And his shoes made too much noise. Shiny shoes he'd probably polished too much; it was one chore that could be done beside the radio. His shiny shoes were hammering across the hall's wooden floor, floorboards the same shade of varnish as his father's half-empty coffin. Dad never liked anyone coming to the house either. Maybe he was more like his parents than he realised.

'The sitting room,' he announced, his voice reverberating as he opened the door. Acoustics had changed now Hector had cleared the room of all its contents. There was just the small sofa and armchair. And acorns.

The acorns had remained in the hearth. To accumulate. There was a whole pile of them now. They just kept blowing down the chimney. First time he remembered seeing them Hector was barking DIY orders at him.

'Vanilla,' Brighid said. 'Smells of vanilla here.'

'Yes,' he agreed. 'It's the acorns.'

Her brow furrowed. 'Acorns don't smell of vanilla.'

Lowell twiddled with the just-about-a-ponytail he had scraped and bound into an elastic band.

'For someone who doesn't like red and green, you've got an awful lot of it going on,' observed Brighid.

The walls were an alternating red and green; the ruby curtains and the green suite continued the theme.

'Company branding.'

'So the scarf's uniform?' she asked.

'Something like that.'

Lowell removed the scarf, only to reveal his red and green memory beads. He'd forgotten they were there. Then he folded, and folded, and folded the scarf until it was a tight roll, until it would fold no more.

There was a small television in the corner of the room (the main television was always in the lounge) but no rugs, cushions, ornaments, pictures, books. Just interfered with the theme, Hector had said. The Hospice Warehouse had been happy to take everything apart from the rug. The rug had a red wine stain; Mum and Dad only drank alcohol on Tuesday nights, sharing a bottle between them. Always a good Rioja. He never knew what was so special about Tuesdays. One Tuesday the beige rug supped a whole glass of Spain's finest. Salt never quite removed the stain.

Hector had hauled the rug off to the amenity site after the hospice van had left; the minging rug he'd called it.

'You got a dust allergy?' Brighid asked.

'No.' His tone came out all pinched, defensive, probably giving the distinct impression he would rather she were elsewhere.

'Just I've got a friend who's allergic. She keeps her place like this. Seems to help.' She turned to the door on the opposite side of the hall. 'What's in there?'

'My room.' He blocked her path to the lounge door, manoeuvring himself between the door and any intention Brighid might have to investigate, guarding the radio's realm, squeezing the scarf in his woollen gloved hands. Wool on wool.

She raised an eyebrow. 'Bet that's where you hide it.'

'What?'

'Your clutter.'

'Oh.'

He managed to steer her down the hall. 'The kitchen,' he muttered, another room for him to get out of the way. The kitchen had been left fallow during Lounge Age; last week he'd wiped a thick layer of dust off the yellowing Formica worktops and cleared the cupboards. The pasta had been six months out of date, but he couldn't see the point in throwing out the tins of Italian plum tomatoes; the big bag of plain flour was still okay until February next year. Hector, though, had insisted everything must go, mumbling something about temptation.

The kitchen still had the dated dark cherry cabinets of his childhood, the same terracotta wall tiles, the same old tired viridian lino. It had always been the warmest room in the house. Probably something to do with Dad and his obsessional baking – bread, cheese pasties, apple pies, filo parcels, vanilla pastries – but now even with the heating on, it seemed cold. The oil had been delivered last week, a full tank's worth.

Sandwiches. A plate of sandwiches, all sliced diagonally, doily beneath.

It wasn't like Hector to be so considerate; if he was back from his day trip he was staying mighty quiet down there. But it had to be Hector. Who else would have made them? Maybe the friend with the tortoise had let himself in.

Next to the plate was a sheet of A4 paper. He snatched it up.

'Help yourself if you're hungry,' he said, glancing over the sheet.

A list of rules.

'Starving,' Brighid replied, grabbing two sandwiches, placing them on the side plate provided.

'You can eat as much as you want tonight. You've probably eaten all sorts of junk travelling over, but tomorrow we start as day one with a clean slate.'

Brighid rolled her eyes. 'What's this Fat Camp?'

'The producers have issued strict dietary orders.' He slapped the paper onto the fridge door, securing it with a fish-shaped magnet.

PRODUCTION RULES

START DATE: MONDAY, 27 OCTOBER
PERSONS INCLUDED: BRIGHID
PERSONS EXCLUDED: LOWELL

1. NO SNACKING OUTSIDE OF MEALS. BREAKFAST IS AT 8:10AM. LUNCH 1PM. DINNER 7PM.
2. HYDRATION MUST BE MAINTAINED AT OPTIMUM LEVELS. HALF A LITRE OF WATER MUST BE CONSUMED ALONGSIDE LUNCH AND DINNER.
3. NO ALCOHOL.
4. NO MEAT.
5. NO FISH.
6. TWO COFFEES A DAY – NO SUGAR.
7. TWO TEAS A DAY – NO SUGAR.
8. SALT INTAKE MUST NOT EXCEED 6 GRAMMES PER DAY (ALL MEALS ARE PROVIDED WITH SALT ALREADY ADDED).
9. EAT SLOWLY. DON'T PLACE FOOD ON YOUR FORK/SPOON/HAND UNTIL YOU HAVE SWALLOWED YOUR PREVIOUS MOUTHFUL.

'So where can I ditch this?' She patted her case.

'Have you read the rules?' He asked dubiously.

She nodded.

'All the way, one to nine?'

'No snacks, watch the salt, don't eat with your mouth full – yep. Got it.' She said her mouth full of sandwich, wrinkling up her small freckled nose.

He narrowed his eyes. A flake of dandruff fell onto his eyelashes. 'What's in the case?'

Her hand gripped the case's handle.

'Any chocolate? Crisps? Booze?'

'What?'

She didn't have the figure of a secret gorger. Rules were rules though. If Hector had created them he could only assume it was with Nell's blessing. He wiped the flake of dead skin from his lashes. 'Could you open the case please?'

Brighid stiffened. 'No.' Her cheeks flushed as if she'd been slapped. 'I will not.'

This threw him. Short of snatching the case from Brighid's hand, there was very little he could do. And if he did do that, it was safe to say the production would be swiftly short of an editor, and perhaps a director; the look in Brighid's eyes, olive green eyes, was fierce.

'But how else can I be sure you don't have anything? If I don't check, I'm not doing my job properly.'

'Lowell,' she said firmly. 'I don't.'

He retreated into the hall, defeated. 'Your bedroom's up_'.

The phone was ringing.

Lowell froze.

'Aren't you going to get that?' Brighid asked.

The answering machine kicked in to the recording of his father's voice: *You have reached the Watterson household.*

We're not here to take your call, so we're probably out on the boat. Leave a message after the beep…

'Machine's second-hand. Should change the recording,' He muttered.

*BEEP….*the sound of someone breathing.

'But your surname's Watterson,' said Brighid.

The breathing continued.

'There's lots of Wattersons__.' His family life, now lack of, was not for her to judge. She had access to his house, what more did she want? He grabbed the phone. 'Hello?'

It's me, whispered Hector, barely audible.

'Where are you?'

Remember you don't know me. I'm not here.

Lowell quickly located the second green bead down on his necklace, Gr2, and rubbed it; if Hector had mentioned anything like that, surely it'd be stored there. Nothing. Lucky he hadn't brought Hector up in conversation. Probably helped she wasn't exactly chatty.

He directed her towards the stairs and followed her, still clutching the phone.

Quite some looker, isn't she?

'Who made the sandwiches?'

Shut the feck up. Don't want her thinking there's a lurker in the house.

Lowell threw open the door to the bathroom, to an overpowering smell of bleach. Taps and ceramic surfaces sparkled; no stains, no tide-marks. It certainly hadn't been anywhere near as clean when he'd left for the airport.

'Did you get someone in?' he hissed down the phone.

Stop shooting your gob off. You want to ruin everything? You're meant to be in control.

A shelf unit next to the sink, shelves labelled with their names. Towels were supplied bleached white, with Brighid's on the bottom shelf, Lowell's, the middle.

The top shelf had been left empty, unlabelled.

He ushered her to the door opposite the bathroom. His old bedroom. 'And this is your room.'

Again there was no getting away from the smell of paint, the smell of freshly painted crimson walls, and the smell of new carpet, brand new carpet the colour of grass. Bedspread and pillow case played with the same reds and greens.

Hector hadn't just arranged a cleaner but a whole squad of decorators and carpet fitters. Was it even possible to paint a room and lay a carpet that quickly? The clean lines along the skirting boards certainly didn't look a rush job. One coat paint. They must have used that. But who let them in? Hector was off on his day trip jolly.

Lowell had left for the airport allowing plenty of time for disasters. He'd half expected the car battery to be flat, being idle so long. A wise man would have checked beforehand, but that wise man didn't have a radio like his. And the last thing Lowell had wanted was to have to deal with mechanics. If the battery was flat he'd go by taxi. And as he hadn't wanted to start worrying about the inevitable conversations with the taxi driver, who would probably know all about his parents' drowning, leaving for the airport a little earlier than needed, leaving mode of transport up in the air, had seemed like the best plan. That way, he decided, he could tackle any nasty surprises head on. Worrying would just distract him from the radio.

The car had started first time, and still had half a tank of fuel left over from Pre-Lounge Age.

They must have turned up, Hector's team of miracle contractors, the moment his car revved away.

He shoved his hand over the phone's mouthpiece, hurled Brighid the sincerest smile possible; an attempt to butter up the staff. 'Goes with your coat. The décor.'

She glanced back unamused, dumped her case onto the floor.

'So, see you tomorrow,' he said. 'Ten past eight in the kitchen.'

He closed the door and heard her struggling with the sash window.

Pushing and heaving.

Pushing and heaving.

Finally, the lower window slid upwards letting the fresh air in, erasing the stink of paint from her room.

You already listening in on her? Bloody weirdo.

Case unpacked. Brighid edged her bedroom door open and peeped out, convinced she could still hear Lowell mooching about on the landing, scratching, the floor-boards creaking. Thankfully he was no longer there. Lowell's conversation was as minimalist as the décor, and almost anything he did say annoyed her. For someone who'd gone to all the effort of branding his home, dressing interiors with a commercial facade, a public face, he was extremely uncomfortable actually having people in seeing it. Downright rude in fact.

She headed downstairs, into the kitchen, grabbed another sandwich, and then opened the back door to a small backyard filled with potted plants. A couple of palm trees, an acer tree, thyme, hibiscus, fuchsia, some late blooming crimson roses, a mop bucket infused with a stink of bleach and a wheelie bin. The wheelie bin was perfect, as was the palm tree's huge ceramic pot. She stepped up onto the palm tree's top soil, hauled herself onto the bin lid, and clambered up the backyard wall, perching herself at the top for a better view of the sky, without the outhouse and carport getting in the way. Having read that article on the plane, she was determined to see the aurora borealis.

She wobbled momentarily. Her heart lunged, her fingers clasping at the wall, gaze hurtling 200 mph towards the concrete ground.

Balance restored. Heart still banging. She carefully shifted position, straddling the wall instead. Exhaustion had made her clumsy. Not a night had passed since leaving France without at least one of the three dreams. The series of three: the trinity of the bog, the barrel and the bubble.

Light flashed across the back yard. The back door was opening.

Lowell. She'd had enough of him for one day, so she lingered in the shadows, silent and motionless; meanwhile, Lowell just stood there looking at his watch. Some people pop out for a smoke; Lowell's guilty pleasure was to gaze longingly at his watch.

'At last,' Lowell muttered under his breath. 'A private moment. Together.'

Did he know she was there?

He was counting down now: '5-4-3-2-1.' Lowell gazed up at the sky, then emitted an almost silent whoop. 'Bang on time, bang on time,' he whispered.

The darkness overhead roiled as though a giant spoon had been dipped in; stirring, whisking, folding. Gauzy greens, nebulous reds swelled and billowed, splashing across the great big pan of sky.

'Oh I love you,' Lowell said.

Who on earth was he talking to?

Brighid pulled out her mobile. Switched it to mute. Tapped at the keys.

You were right. Boss = psycho.

He was in her directory as 14B. His seat number. SEND.

A new message. From 14B.

REALLY???

He's currently chatting to the sky.

OKAY...

Has given me a list of rules on diet.

YOU'RE KIDDING?

Nope.

She had searched for a glimmer within Lowell's features, some indication he was joking, but there was just that determined glower and the flake of dried skin falling onto his eyelashes.

BE CAREFUL. SOUNDS A NUT JOB.

A light drizzle, like sea spray, carried in the wind, dappled her face. She could hear the sea, smell the sea, taste its salt on her lips. Lowell would probably have issues with the salt, warn her about going over quota.

Think he's harmless enough.

HOPE SO. WANNA ESCAPE ALCATRAZ TOMORROW NIGHT? GIG AT MODDEY DHOO PUB. 8PM.

Okay :)

Now, the sweeping diaphanous reds and greens had dissolved into the darkness, now the cold was firmly in her bones, she willed Lowell to go back in. Her enthusiasm for the aurora borealis did not stretch to scouring the sky for residual spurts; she just wanted to go to bed, to be warm again.

'Fuck,' said Lowell eventually, looking at his watch. Then he went back into the house, released the latch, closed the door, locking Brighid out.

With no other choice, short of kipping in the cold backyard, there was only one thing she could do: knock on the back door.

The look on Lowell's face was as priceless as a Picasso portrait and just as disjointed. 'What're you doing?'

'Been looking at the aurora borealis.'

'In the backyard?'

Brighid nodded.

'How long have you been out there?'

'Long enough.'

Round one to Brighid in the red and green coat (her mother made it you know).

It wasn't his house anymore. Lowell couldn't even step out into his own backyard without people watching, eavesdropping. Nell's special surprise had arrived bang on eleven o'clock. So, it might not have been Nell in the flesh, but those lights in the sky had Nell written all over them; they were even the production colours: red and green. As if he needed more proof that there was a bigger picture. And it was all for him. It was her way of thanking him, of showing her appreciation for all his hard work. Brighid's voyeurism had tainted a perfect moment. *Aurora borealis*, her know-it-all-ass. She didn't have a clue.

He had been so taken with the moment he'd lost track of time (the last time that happened his parents had died), meant he ended up being late for the almanac. Seven minutes late. Input duties were meant to start at midnight, 00:00 hour, first day of production.

The almanac had involved tons of prepping; a monitoring system was all set up. Lowell had tweaked the floorboards before any carpets had arrived, replacing the nails with screws. Screws were easier to fine tune. The screws on the two floorboards to the right of Brighid's bed he had loosened two full turns (2x 360 degrees), the ones on the left: one full turn. As for the floorboards on either side of the door, he had twisted their screws half a turn and one and half turns respectively, and had followed the exact same procedure in various key locations around the house.

Hector had instructed him to record nearly everything Brighid did; every detail counted, he said. Of course it was difficult to document it all, so Lowell had negotiated it down to a list of crucial elements, sketching out tables and headers until Hector gave the final nod. This, Lowell then translated into a spreadsheet app on his smartphone. The term, *almanac*, had come to him during a brainstorm, and had amused Hector, who eventually agreed (after some prolonged laughter) that by charting the ebb and flow of Brighid's movements within the house it was indeed more-or-less like writing an almanac. Lowell had considered installing a hidden camera in her room but decided it was over-intrusive and ran the risk of being discovered which would in turn scupper everything. The floorboards had been his own idea too, and Hector, suitably impressed, had helped train his ear, by plodding around the house, so that Lowell was able to pick out the sound of each one.

He'd always been meticulous with accounts in his old job, was often accused of being too thorough, of taking too long, checking, double-checking, checking with the calculator, checking without just in case.

Brighid closed her bedroom door.

The almanac was open, ready. He checked his watch and entered 00:13 into the bedroom arrivals column. Blue font. Blue because of her passport photo, bloody misleading – too late to change the system now. The main bulk of the almanac contained tables charting entry and exit into and out of bed, bathroom, lounge, edit suite and the house itself. Another table had been produced to input data on interactions (column headers: start and end times, action, conversation), but Hector concurred that he could use his discretion on that one because if he went around recording everything, it would be too much of a distraction and nothing else would get done. A further table covered miscellaneous and anomalies.

The floorboard next to her door creaked, then the bedroom door opened. He tapped 00:14 into the bedroom departure column. The floorboard in the hallway sounded, confirming bedroom departure. This was followed swiftly by the rasp of the floorboard outside the bathroom. The bathroom door closed. Lowell checked his watch and inserted 00.14 into the entry column of the bathroom visits table.

If she was a like planetary object up there, then he was the terrestrial astronomer, tracking, observing. He should have used a red font; that would have suited her temperament more, red and fiery, the red planet – Mars, planet of war. She was already showing her true colours: snappy, snidey, confrontational, totally unprofessional. How could he have even thought she was one of them, one of the puppet masters? She was just the editor, another puppet, a lower level puppet at that – after all he had direct contact with the source. She didn't even know there were strings all around her.

Chapter 12

Lowell had set up a microphone in his bedroom/lounge to maintain vigilance throughout the night; now the almanac was up and running he needed to be resourceful. The mike was wired up to the headphones he'd be wearing for sleep from here on in and these were set at maximum volume, so should any floorboard-audio break the general room ambience he'd hear about it. The smartphone/almanac he kept next to the bed/sofa so he didn't have to get up should any data come in; he'd bought the phone a couple of aeons ago, just before the Lounge Age, had only ended up using it the once (prior to the almanac).

It wasn't, however, a floorboard overhead that woke him at 4am.

Voices.

Someone was shouting angrily, but it wasn't his new recruit talking in her sleep; it was a man's voice, and the words weren't English but another language, perhaps Arabic; he couldn't be certain. Where were they? Outside? Inside? Downstairs? Upstairs? The source was difficult to locate with the headphones on, so he removed them.

The shouting stopped.

Headphones back on, he rose from the sofa and grabbed the microphone. The lower he pointed the mike, the louder the voice.

The basement.

The shouting was coming from the basement. Hector was either watching a movie or had more company down there.

Figuring it was his house, therefore his business, Lowell sank to his knees, curled up a corner of the carpet, and set the mike onto the exposed, woodworm ridden, sanded and varnished floorboards of his childhood; the ultimate race-track surface for his Micro Machines car collection. Another memory was triggered, a memory of asking Mum who it was he could hear laughing under the floor; he had been sure he'd heard a woman wailing with laughter down there. She'd said it was nothing, had turned the television on to watch the horse racing. She wasn't into gambling or horse racing. The carpet arrived the next day (the same carpet he now clasped in his hand) with too much traction for car wheels to roll freely. The race-track switched to the kitchen after that, but that thick lino was nowhere near as good as the lounge floorboards. Had his parents known about the basement? Had a woman really been laughing down there?

Overloaded with paranoid thoughts he went back to bed/sofa. Hector could argue or watch movies all he liked down there; Lowell, on the other hand, needed his sleep.

Sleep, however, delivered no comfort.

His nightmare consciousness dumped him in a dog pound. Three dogs shared the kennel cell. A jack russell, a husky and another dog. Lowell was floating about inside the third dog's head, so wasn't quite sure what he looked like; judging from his paws he was a medium-sized dog, possibly a collie. The cell was only meant for two. There were just two beds. Two blue plastic beds, each bearing no blanket, just teeth and claw marks. The collie was sitting on the sticky piss-stained floor counting the breeze blocks that made up the wall.

Fifty seven.

Nell's voice woke him on the first morning of production. She didn't say much, just:

'Look under the radio.'

Then she was gone, lost to the static, before Lowell even had time to answer.

Beneath the radio was a large brown envelope. He tore it open. Heart thumping.

Inside was another envelope marked:

CONFIDENTIAL*. NOT TO BE OPENED BEFORE 08:30AM.*

There was also a key and a sheet of printed paper. Content on the paper was formatted in much the same way as the rules on diet, only this time the rules were instructions and marked for Lowell's sole attention.

PRODUCTION LAUNCH
LOWELL'S INSTRUCTIONS

1. THE KEY AS YOU MAY HAVE GUESSED IS FOR THE BASEMENT, OTHERWISE KNOWN AS THE EDIT SUITE.
2. DO NOT USE THE KEY BEFORE 8.30AM.
3. KEEP THE KEY SAFE. DO NOT GIVE IT TO ANYONE.
4. THE BASEMENT MUST REMAIN LOCKED AT ALL TIMES – WORKING HOURS INCLUDED.
5. THE ENVELOPE CONTAINS THE SHOT BY SHOT INSTRUCTIONS – YOUR FLAT PACK GUIDE ON 'HOW TO PUT TOGETHER A DOCUMENTARY WITHOUT LETTING ON YOU DON'T HAVE A FECKIN' CLUE' – FOR YOUR DIRECTORIAL DEBUT.
6. REMEMBER YOUR ROLE – YOU'RE A DIRECTOR – YOU MUST ACT THE PART.
7. DON'T TWITCH.
8. MAKE SURE BRIGHID FOLLOWS THE RULES ON DIET. YOU CAN EAT WHATEVER YOU WANT BAR TOMATOES. IT'S THE TOMATOES THAT HAVE GIVEN YOU THAT KIDNEY STONE – TOO MANY PIZZAS.
9. IT'S YOUR BASEMENT. DON'T ACT THE TOURIST. DON'T STOP AND GAWP. MAKE OUT YOU'VE SEEN IT ALL BEFORE.

WOULDN'T WANT TO BE YA
HECTOR

So, Hector was finally acknowledging just whose basement it really was; why then hadn't he allowed Lowell access all this time? If he was to make out he'd actually seen his own basement before, it would help if he actually had. Same applied to those diet rules Hector left in the kitchen. Why wasn't he given any warning, some pre-prep on what to say, do? Still, he had to admit to finding a little comfort in the vegetarian rule, reminded him of his childhood, even if he had ended up rebelling with those sneaky sausage baps at school lunchtimes.

A more paranoid person would think Hector was playing games. Lowell would be tempted, if the radio wasn't keeping its hidden beady little antennae on him, to open that other envelope, study the manual for the feckin' clueless beforehand; he could barely direct himself let alone another person; if that manual was anything other than elementary he was up shit street without a pair of wellies.

But no matter how good the manual, it could only be at best a bunch of cue sheets, a bundle of cues for action: *Brighid puppet edit this, Brighid puppet edit that.* It was still down to him to answer any awkward questions, to improvise. And whilst doing that, he was supposed to keep the almanac updated. Oh, and he was now food matron too. How was he expected to keep the almanac up to date if he had to supervise her mouth too? He might be in the bathroom, pissing sand, whilst Brighid was in the kitchen knocking back a third coffee. It was a logistic nightmare.

And how did Hector know about the kidney stone? Lowell hadn't told anyone about the kidney stone, unless, of course…Nell. He'd probably mentioned it to her (and forgotten about it) and Nell (who hadn't forgotten) had informed Hector. What else did they know? More importantly, how did the envelope even get into the room? He had got into the habit of locking it recently, mostly to block Hector from just strolling in whenever he wanted. Hector probably had a copy of that key too, had slipped in during the night. He had a key to the basement, and obviously the front door, so why not other keys? Perhaps the radio delivered the envelope – nothing would surprise him.

Having viewed enough spy movies to know the score with mission directives, he tore the instructions into unsalvageable pieces and was just debating whether it was also necessary to eat the paper shreds when he noticed the Post-it Note stuck on top of a set of clothes:

Wear these – H.

The suit jacket, jeans and battered old trainers were all his own. The T-shirt was a new addition he'd never seen before, and wouldn't have worn before – sporting, as it did, Hector's beloved combo of red and green. He put it on anyway, along with his jeans and then slipped on the jacket, the jacket he'd worn at his parents' funerals.

Brighid got out of bed at 07:32 and entered the bathroom at 07:35.

Lowell hadn't managed to get a proper look at the key before; it was always wrapped inside Hector's hand when he was locking and unlocking the door. Now that Lowell finally held the key himself, it sort of disappointed him. Although the keyhole didn't suggest it, he had imagined the key to be more substantial: cumbersome, rusted, its handle all ancient ostentation; for a key to a secret room that was the very least he expected, but it was just a standard Yale-type key, and judging by its rough edges, was just a key copied at the key-cutters. Hector, he suspected, had kept the original. He stashed the disappointing, but nonetheless much coveted key into his jacket pocket, and then fished it out again. Pockets were not a safe place for such a key; look what happened to his driving licence at the airport. His mother had left behind a ball of string in the cabinet drawer; it was one of the few things Hector hadn't insisted on giving to the Hospice Warehouse or the amenity site.

So, having cut himself a piece of adequate length, he then threaded it through the hole in the head of the key. Next, he tied a knot and placed the string with key around his neck.

08:09: Brighid closed the door to her bedroom (she'd finally left the bathroom at 07:49).

He entered the time into the appropriate column then placed the phone/almanac into his jacket pocket – he had no other choice – the rest would have to be done ad hoc.

He entered the kitchen behind her. Her hair was still wet around the nape. She smelt of mango, had obviously chosen her own shower gel over the allocated soap. Was that allowed?

'You've been busy,' she said.

It was said as a statement rather than a question, like a fact she had uncovered, like she'd just put two and two together. And she didn't need an accounts manager to work out the answer to that. And that's what he was an accountant; he didn't know the first thing about making films.

'The smell,' she added.

Her elaboration only served to confuse him more. Had he been that obvious sniffing about behind her?

'You've already made the coffee.'

She was right. There was a definite smell of coffee. But Lowell was not the coffee-maker. He brushed past her and made it to the kitchen first.

There was a coffee machine on the worktop, obviously brought in for the production because Lowell hadn't seen, used or drank from it before. He always drank instant; anything else was just a lot of unnecessary faffing. The coffee was already made; the jug was ready to pour. Its side marker indicated there was exactly one serving. None for him. And there was just the one dish, laid on the kitchen table, containing chopped fruit. A side plate of toast (one slice with a slither of butter topping) partnered the dish. Someone certainly had been busy. Hector was making himself right at home – access all areas. It was all very well Hector playing the perfect host in Lowell's house but where was he now? Why did he have to remain so elusive when he was needed most?

Lowell poured the single measure into Brighid's mug, emptying the jug, and instructed her to start without him. Then he went to the corner of the kitchen, behind the door, whipped out his mobile and updated the almanac with Brighid's most recent stats. He had a good head for figures; he might not remember much of what Nell said but he had no problem remembering numbers.

'Was quite some show last night,' she said, sipping her coffee.

He slipped his mobile back into his jacket pocket.

She was having a dig, had obviously seen his declarations of amour to the sky.

'The aurora borealis,' she insisted.

She needed to do less talking, more eating. The rules didn't actually say she had to eat everything but it was sort of implied; what with the way it went on about salt and hydration levels, it was pretty safe to assume the food had been weighed out in portions with all that in mind.

She hadn't touched the grapes yet. She might not like them. The juice inside the grapes could be segments in the hydration quota. She looked a fussy eater – skinny little thing. There was going to be trouble all the way with her; he just knew it.

Something tickled his hip. Different area from the kidney stone pain. Same kind of throb, but without the pain. Was something changing down there? Was the stone lodging itself somewhere else? This was no time for an emergency run to the hospital. Pocket. It was inside his jacket pocket. His mobile. Vibrating.

A text message.

STOP TWITCHING. ANY DISASTERS USE PHONE TO EMAIL hector@crabhq.com

A lifeline – he had been handed a lifeline. Brighid was eating the grapes now too. Things were looking up. Just five minutes to go. No time to stick the kettle on. And no time to make toast, besides Brighid might get a whiff, fancy another slice, form a revolt against the rules. He had his envelope, his phone and the key. The key's string necklace was too short. His face would end up squashed against the door while he was trying to unlock it; she'd know him for the phoney he really was. A cool, calm director wouldn't start the day like that, nose all squashed. He clasped the key necklace, began removing it, coolly and calmly. It jammed around his forehead, so he pulled. And as he pulled, he could feel it chafing, rubbing a red mark that might as well say LOSER right across his forehead. The squashed nose against the door would make him look less stupid, but now he'd started he had to keep on going. He turned to face the hallway in the infantile hope that if he couldn't see her, she couldn't see him, wincing and squirming. And off: up and over hairline and ears. Key necklace extracted. He swung round, began twirling the key string around his finger; indifference personified, or he would be, if his forehead didn't sting so much.

'Are you taking me?' Brighid bit into the last grape. Dish and side plate: empty.

She had caught him on alternating catch-up duties: clock watching – plate watching, monitoring strawberries, apples, grapes, toast; now all consumed. Her question confused him and that must have shown because, before he could add assimilating cryptic queries to the list of multi-tasking, she spoke again.

'To work? Are we going in together?' She knocked back a last glug of coffee then dumped the empty mug into the sink.

'Yes, but it's only downstairs.'

This seemed to surprise her. Risking appearing anal on timekeeping, he checked the clock again. The seconds hand was approaching twelve. The minute hand would be on the thirty in fourteen seconds.

'Let's go,' he said as calmly as he could, as if it was just the start of any other day in the office, edit suite – he had to remember to call it edit suite.

'I need to clean my teeth first,' she insisted.

'But it's 8:30.'

She was already running up the stairs.

At 8:31 she exited the bathroom. He entered the data into the almanac. He was supposed to be the boss. Director. He couldn't even direct Brighid out of a bathroom.

Now she waited and watched as he fumbled with the key. The gloves didn't help. She smelled of spearmint. His hands were trembling. The gloves hid that. The lock-mechanism made a promising click; the door opened.

Darkness.

He patted the wall for the light switch but there wasn't one.

'The main switch is further down.' It was all he could do, blag it, just as Hector had said, and hope for the best. The blessing in the darkness was she couldn't see him slapping at the walls as he descended, didn't see his hands flailing in the gloom.

Then his hand found something: string dangling. A light cord. He grabbed and pulled. Light flickered.

The blinking light made motion all disjointed, made everything seem like a scene in an old movie. In between the jumping frames of pulsating darkness, flash moments exposed the basement.

Darkness – light: the basement was much larger than he had expected, at least seventy square metres – larger than the house's actual footprint.

Darkness – light: a vaulted ceiling painted in brand colours.

Darkness – light: computer monitors (huge screen sizes).

Darkness – light: a door, thick oak, arched.

Darkness.

Light.

'Wow,' Brighid said from the top of the steps.

He had to keep such exclamations to himself.

Heat: surprisingly warm for a basement. Radiators: installed recently if the small mounds of powdered stone on the floor beneath were anything to go by. Kerching! He needed to stop speculating on the thousands Hector had added to the property value. It was distracting. At least ten thousand, maybe twenty. He breathed in, he needed to focus, stop gawping.

Smell: a cocktail mix of fresh paint and damp, dashed with the aroma of lavender. If the lavender perfume was there to hide the other odours it was proving as useful as a paper umbrella in a downpour.

Number four. It helped to remember the instructions by numbers, stitched things together in his brain, and in the bead. He marched back up the steps – stone steps, painted alternate red and green – passing the puppet making her way down.

Instruction number four completed. Edit suite door closed and locked.

'You planning on killing me down here?' Brighid quipped.

The echo in her voice bounded up the stairs, bounced back and forth off the stone walls as though it was looking for an exit, an escape route; none found, the echo carried on bouncing, eroding itself away, exhausting itself, becoming squashed, pulped, flattened until there was nothing left, a bit like his father's legs.

'For security purposes,' Lowell explained, making a point of skipping down the steps, keeping things light. 'We'll be working on some highly confidential material.'

Well, he supposed that was the reason; reason or not, it seemed to pacify her. Anyway the basement was winning her over, doing the talking for him.

'Bit of a cool place, isn't it,' she purred, stroking the surface of one of the desks.

They were like the Maserati of desks, all sweeping curves and high polish silver chrome. The larger of the two desks was equipped with two top-size monitors and a television screen. As there were also two chairs there, he guessed this was his and Brighid's edit hub; this was where they would get down to the editing nitty-gritty. He so wasn't looking forward to it. The second desk was presumably for admin, for when he needed space to check through instructions.

Like the tables, the chairs were more high-end design pieces than office furniture. Brighid was on her haunches giving them a closer inspection. He was about to do the same himself, but instruction number nine stopped him: this was his basement. He was supposed to be in character playing all jaded, seen-it-all-before.

So what if a few stealthy peeks dappled the performance? It couldn't be helped. Through the holes in his act he saw their craftsmanship; chairs designed as a pair, each following the same formula. A spinal network of twisting branches made up the outer frame; every single branch was entwined with an intricately carved network of winding tendrils festooned in gilded leaves. The inner support, with its emerald and scarlet velvet cushioning, was there to make things more comfortable. Would he get to keep the furniture when the production was over? Was that real gold on the leaves? Surely not.

To stop himself gawping, he turned his attention to the envelope. As it was after 08:30, he was allowed to open it. Four minutes and nineteen seconds after 8:30 to be precise.

The text gave little away. Flicking through the first couple of pages he was only able to glean a few specifics from the director's flat-pack manual:

1. That it only covered that day's edits (he guessed there would be subsequent daily envelope deliveries);
2. the name of the editing software he needed Brighid to open; and
3. what visual clip needed to be put with what audio clip (and the duration of each).

There was also a script. The main character was named Lowell. Lowell's dialogue consisted mostly of monologues filled with director-speak: 'Now put audio clip two onto audio track B,' and so on. But still no clues to the actual documentary script itself.

Completing the appraisal of the chair Brighid gave it a

light push. Wheels like solid silver balls spun across what Lowell suddenly realised was a marble floor.

He caught the chair. 'Must have cost a fortune,' she said, echoing Lowell's own thoughts. But the pound signs he saw were in the more permanent feature of that marble floor. They wouldn't be able to take that away.

He squatted down next to the editing desk and switched on the computer, grateful the 'on' button was immediately apparent. 'I took the initiative to import all the footage that's come in so far.'

This wasn't exactly true. Hector must have done that, he was just following what it said in the manual.

'What's behind the door?' she asked.

He had been so busy checking out the basement, concentrating on his role, act one: editing with Brighid, he hadn't even given any thought to what might be on the other side of the arched oak door. The door's strap hinges were a work of art, boasting an intricate network of twisting twigs and foliage, all handcrafted in silver. Same style as the chairs. The keypad code lock, however, just above the silver ball handle, was at complete odds with the rest of the door's craftsmanship.

'Good question,' he said playing for time. There had to be something in the manual.

There. On the last two pages:

HAD YOU PANICKING FOR A MOMENT DIDN'T I? HA HA! OKAY, SO SHE'S JUST ASKED THE INEVITABLE QUESTION: *WHAT'S BEHIND THE DOOR?* BEST WAY TO DEAL WITH A TRICKY QUESTION – THROW ANOTHER ONE BACK AT HER. ASK HER ABOUT THE DREAMS SHE'S BEEN HAVING LATELY. NO. ACTUALLY BEST NOT…LUCKY FOR US YOU'RE SO BLOODY THOROUGH AND STILL READING

THIS. SOME FOLKS WOULD HAVE JUST BLURTED IT OUT BEFORE THEY GOT TO THE END. HOWABOUT YOU TELL HER YOU'RE A FAILED ACCOUNTANT? NO. NOT A GOOD IDEA EITHER. JEEZ, SO MANY SECRETS.

LOWELL'S ACTUAL DIALOGUE TO BRIGHID: DOOR'S PRIVATE. OKAY, LET'S GET STARTED. (**CONFIDENTIAL ASIDE TO LOWELL:** AND FOR FECK'S SAKE STAY CALM…)

'Door's private.'

The wall containing the door extended beyond the area boundaries of the house. Puppet present, there was no way he could go over there, try the door, he'd just have to stick to guessing what was behind it: another cellar probably, belonging to the neighbour.

He checked his watch. 'I make it fifteen minutes into the working day, but there's not much work going on here.' That was off-script, him improvising, getting into the role of boss.

'You're the director. Direct me.' She said it flippantly, but there was a sting in her tone as if she was daring him, as if she didn't really believe he could direct.

He wasn't sure he believed it himself.

Brighid clicked the icon launching the editing software, and as it flashed through the progress of vital components: scanning, initialising, loading, Lowell sat next to her, thumbing though his notes. He had obviously given post-production some forethought, done quite a considerable amount of preparation.

'Okay,' Lowell said, rubbing his beard, still wearing his big woollen gloves. 'Go to the audio folder and insert audio clip one onto track A of the programme line. Once that's in we'll start adding the visuals.'

She inserted the audio clip as instructed and clicked play.

'More than three thousand years ago a hole appeared in the sky. It was a clear blue skied midday, but inside the hole it looked like night – there were stars. The Tuatha Dé Danann, for these are the people, the folk of the mother goddess Danu, this particular sky was hanging over, saw it as an omen. Many dropped to their knees in awe of the great hole.

Then it came.

A tree.

A tree thrown from the stars falling to Earth.

The tree landed near the Hill of Tara in what is now County Meath, Ireland.

Now, the Tuatha Dé Danann knew that this was no ordinary tree – trees generally lack the tendency to fall out of the sky – so the tree was immediately revered as a sacred icon.

But the tree began to wither.

The Tuatha Dé Danann, gathering all their green wisdom, tried planting it in the best forests of the land, watered it, stopped watering it, packed nutrients around its roots, talked to it, but still the crimson trunk peeled, the scarlet blush paled and the acorns and leaves departed, blowing away, one by one.

One of the ancient deities, older than even the Tuatha Dé Danann themselves, spotted the acorns and leaves blowing across his realm and came to the Tuatha to bestow his knowledge. And so Manannan Mac Lir, god of the seas, joined the Tuatha Dé Danann around the rotting tree. And together they pondered what could be done.

On the third day, the Tuatha Dé Danann's adopted god of light, young Lugh, true to his role, saw the light. The acorns were falling here and there, landing in random places, but the leaves were blowing as if in a determined swarm, not one leaf straying from its path. And so it was agreed there was only one thing left to do: they must follow the leaves.

Manannan, was not just a deity, but an excellent shape shifter – going about as a seagull was a particular speciality. That's how he chose to trail the leaves. And the Tuatha Dé Danann sailed behind. The leaves, unaffected by storms and winds, maintained a steadfast course heading south; it was as though an invisible line was pulling them, a force stronger than any wind could muster. The Tuatha Dé Danann, on the other hand, were forced to drain much of the magic reservoir of those onboard to keep the winds from knocking them from the trail.

Many sunsets later, they reached the northern coast of what is now Spain.

They continued to shadow the leaves by foot, in Manannan's case: wings. Then, finally the cluster of leaves they had followed for a thousand miles collapsed to the ground. But it was no casual resting place; the leaves had reunited with a much larger pile already gathered there. In fact, every single leaf of the sacred tree had congregated on the same mountain-side, a mountain that would later be revered as *the mountain where the season of autumn rests*.

Manannan settled his wings onto the ground and listened to the earth. And on the fifth day, the earth replied.'

'Okay,' said Lowell looking at his notes. 'Next, we need to bring in the footage, then, we'll cut and spread the audio accordingly.'

'So I'm guessing it's a documentary on mythology?' Brighid shifted in her chair, a chair more at home in a Wag bling house than an edit suite. If she sat the wrong angle, her sleeves would catch in the gilded leaves.

'It's much more than a documentary on mythology.' he replied enigmatically, scanning the paperwork, his finger urgently trying to find where they were up to. 'Bring in the clip labelled, *Arrival*.'

Lowell still wasn't giving much away. Any questions she'd asked in emails on subject matter had been equally skirted over, actually just plain ignored. She selected the clip from the folder displayed in the right-hand monitor, dragged and dropped it onto Track A of the programme line, then clicked play.

An aerial shot tracking hills and valleys. Pace slowed as a group of actors entered frame.

The extras agency must have scored some brownies having so many hipsters on their books, or perhaps it was the wig department that needed congratulating; the people pointing to the sky were all hair and beards.

'Go to the clip labelled, *Hole* and place it on the same track as the last. We're just going for a straight cut.'

Hole was a graphic overlay of the hole in the sky. A very realistic graphic overlay.

'Nice work on the hole,' she said. '3D design genius whoever did it.'

'Go to the clip called, *Tree* and place it on track A; it's another straight cut.'

'Happy with the first two shots?'

Lowell nodded, so she dropped the next clip in and pressed play.

The hole in the sky again. This time from a different angle; this time capturing the tree emerging from the hole, following the tree on its descent.

'Excellent,' Brighid said aloud; she couldn't help herself. Maybe Lowell was a whiz kid director after all.

He peered down at his notes. 'We need to do a slow-mo on this – needs to be three times slower than it is now.'

'Done.'

The tree was an incredible piece of animation: roots intricately twisted and gnarled; leaves delicately veined; stems writhing and shivering. Subtleties in movement, shape and shade revealed attention to microscopic detail. A little too much red in the bark, perhaps, and the greens were a touch too vivid on the leaves, but despite that, the tree was a dead ringer for reality, pure realism in a can.

'Do you think the colours are a bit strong?' she asked. 'I could play around with the levels.'

'No,' he barked. 'The colours have to stay the same. Don't alter anything.'

'Oop, what's that?' A flash frame. She shifted the timeline back, located the culprit in the second to last frame. A hand. A blurred, brown leathery hand waving against the blue of the sky.

'The ghostly hand of the cameraman,' she mused, offering up an answer to her own question. 'So you filmed the sky bits as background and laid the tree graphics over before importing it all in as a bundle, already merged,' she said, thinking out loud, deleting the last two frames.

'What did you just do?'

'Got rid of the hand.'

'You can't just go round deleting things like that. It might have been important.'

'Spoils a perfect clip.'

Lowell studied his notes. 'But it doesn't say anything

about it here.'

'You must have missed it.' He couldn't seriously be thinking of keeping the hand in.

'Every element is essential though.'

'Shame to spoil that clip.'

'Is it spoiling it though? Or is it important? We're telling a story here; isn't that hand part of the story?'

'Well, we can sit around philosophise aesthetics and cinéma vérité all day – you're paying so I don't mind.' She smiled to show she was joking, but he was too preoccupied to notice, lost to an internal debate over the illusion of the spectacle versus the mechanics of cinema versus how far to take realism versus whether that dodgy flash frame was taking things a step too far.

'Back in a minute.' He stood up, patted the jacket pocket, the pocket that held his phone, and marched off, still deep in thought. Then he swiftly returned, collected his notes, and dashed up the stairway. Having exited the basement, he locked the door.

She swivelled her chair round to face the other door, the arched door, and was just starting to imagine what she might find stored behind it, if she dared turn the door's silver ball handle – Lowell's Mum and Dad perhaps, when the keyhole at the top of the steps clicked. Lowell came in, locked the suite door and practically danced his way back down to his desk.

'I have the solution,' he almost sang, sitting back down in his chair.

'Delete it?' she prompted confidently.

'No, we're going to keep it. It's as important as everything else. The frame with the hand stays.'

'But it kills the shot.'

'Who's the director?'

Brighid didn't reply.

'*I'm* the director. You're the editor. You edit. I direct. End of.'

'Next clip then?' Her bank balance couldn't take it if she argued.

'Peeling,' he said tightly. 'Bring in the clip labelled, *Peeling*.'

Peeling began as a long shot of the valley, filmed from a hilltop. The camera zoomed in, closing in on the tree and the actors nearest to it. Quite some distance for the camera, but as the water poured onto the roots of the now rotting tree, there was no evident deterioration in image quality; focal centre remained as sharp as a lumberjack's axe.

Lustrous tree graphics were now replaced by an old tree trunk, presumably procured by the props department, if there was a props department. If not, the third assistant director or runner (she'd been both in the past) would have been sent out on a scouting mission to the nearest forest, between serving earl greys to the actors. Leaves tumbled and blew out of shot.

'Bring in the *Deities*,' Lowell said.

She dragged, dropped and played the clip.

Same valley scene. New actors. Action shot from a different angle. Camera perspective was now from a hill on the other side of the valley. She would have thought it better to have brought the camera or cameras up close, but then hey, she was only the editor.

Stroking the tree were two men. One of them, an old man, cascading torrent of a beard, hair the colour of surf, was kitted with a turquoise cloak which when he leaned from left to right, or when the cloak got caught in a gust of wind, made a sound like the sea running over shingle. He'd have to be wearing a radio mike for the camera to pick that up; that, or someone was stood on the top of the hill next to the camera rattling a bowl of shells.

The commentary continued over the footage.

'On the third day, the Tuatha Dé Danann's god of light, young Lugh, true to his role, saw the light.'

The camera panned to the other man nursing the tree. His blonde features melted as light saturated his image. The camera jolted and pulled away, as if the face was too bright for the one behind the lens, the one who had just gone and altered the iris settings to make everything that bright. The jerky camera motion was a bit of a cheap gimmick, ran the risk of being crass. It ended with another flash frame.

This time the flash frame was a figure in the distance, on the summit of the opposite hill. A smudge of brown clothing.

It could almost be 14B.

She needed to keep her emotions in check; if she was starting to think she was seeing him everywhere she was on dangerous ground.

'Let's delete that,' she said.

'No,' Lowell replied. 'He's essential.'

Chapter 13

Dinner had consisted of pasta, spinach and broccoli in a bland tomato sauce. When she had asked for salt, Lowell had reminded her that would be against rule eight, and had said that without even turning to look at the fridge door to check which number it was, had said it with a mouthful of steak. Steak and chips, that's what he had prepared for his own culinary delight; the rules didn't apply to him, and anyway he apparently had some sort of intolerance to tomatoes.

The pasta dish was prepared by outside caterers, already au fait with the menu rules, he'd explained whilst lashing a whole heap of salt onto his chips. The pasta, which had been left out on a plate, was barely warm, but Lowell had ruled out using the microwave to reheat it; *that* (he wagged his finger) would create steam, *that* (another wag of the finger) would make it lose moisture, and *that* (wag) would affect hydration levels. She had given up on the cold pasta two thirds in. This hadn't gone down well with Lowell, but short of funnelling it into her mouth, there was nothing he could do.

Had dinner not been such a fresh annoyance, she would have respected the rule on no alcohol, whatever number it was, but the miniature bottles of merlot lined up on the bar shelf were sort of cajoling her, not that she needed much cajoling.

14B was late.

She stepped aside for the old man who was dragging a stool noisily over the flagstone floor, only for him to go and steal prime location at the bar; he hobbled around the stool with his walking stick, did the full 360 degrees, and then eased himself up onto his front row seat, keeping his right leg outstretched.

'Pint of the usual, Archie?' prompted the barman.

Archie slipped his jacket to the back of the stool, craning his attention in the direction of a blackboard. Next to the skeleton sketch, a bit of seasonal marketing:

This Halloween
The skies are not so dark
See the dark, drink dark
Double dark rum – half price

'Aye, give me a rum chaser as well,' Archie said, resting his chin into his hand.

She couldn't help but overhear the conversation from the hen party, dressed as angels and fairies, standing next to her.

'Couple of small accidents,' said the hen fairy with the L-sign around her neck.

'Siobhan,' the barman hissed. 'We're busy here.'

'Her fiancé's a copper,' a hen angel was explaining to Siobhan. Siobhan was clutching empty pint glasses, trying to navigate her way past the angel's elbows; the angel was too busy untangling a strand of hair ensnared in the wire of her wings to notice Siobhan's glazed response.

'He had to cancel his stag night,' added the L-signed hen. 'Got called in last minute – was supposed to be doing a fancy dress pub crawl around Douglas. Still had his make-up on when he left. I didn't tell him. They'll be taking the piss something rotten at the station.'

'Must be more than a couple of small accidents for him to be called in,' the hen angel remarked.

'A few people got taken to A and E. Nothing major.'

Archie slipped his fingers around the stem of the brandy glass the rum had been served in and handed the barman a pocketful of twenty pence pieces.

'Merlot,' Brighid said, finally getting her order in. 'And a packet of those peanuts.'

'Loads of people ringing up the station, you said, reporting weird lights and noises.' The hen angel had now successfully freed her hair. 'Serves him right, organising our hen do for a Monday night.'

'The karaoke bus is cheaper on a Monday.'

'I wonder why that is,' the hen angel sniffed.

'We have to save every penny for the big day.'

Brighid grabbed her change, swung round, faced the hen angel. 'What was it? The weird lights and noises?'

'How should I know?' the L-signed hen growled, scowling at the angel. 'It's just people panicking over nothing,'

'I saw it,' said Archie, his back propped against the bar, warming the brandy glass with his palm, swirling the rum, coaxing the oaken bouquet, memoirs of the barrel; a blatant pause to inhale the attention of hen fairies and angels.

'You can't see anything without yer glasses,' the barman exclaimed.

Archie slammed his glass down onto the bar. 'If I can read your blackboard I can bloody well see the sparks I saw down on the quay. Scratched a couple of lampposts it did, bent some car aerials. Heard the whistling too.'

Brighid steered her glass, miniature bottle, and salted peanuts past the hen party, past the wings of twisted coat hanger and netting, and located a small table in the corner. She sat down and poured a generous measure of merlot into her glass.

'Cream of asparagus,' Siobhan announced. A listless tone, a tone screaming as soon as I find another job I'm out of here. Blowing her strawberry blonde fringe from her eyes, she delivered the bowl of steaming soup and plate with buttered bap to the crumple-skinned lady on the next table. The old lady was too busy to thank Siobhan, too busy brushing her citron tweed sleeve over the already clean tabletop. Shoving the bread back at Siobhan, she waved her away with her spindly arm then patted her slate grey hair; a perfunctory motion given that her hair was so fixed and flattened by lacquer. Plastered flat, more like a helmet than a hair style.

Brighid checked her watch. He was fifteen minutes late.

The door swung open.

She took a sip of wine.

A man with a baseball cap and white hair sauntered in. He peered up from beneath the peak of his baseball cap. There were lacerations all across his face. It looked as if someone had done him over with a knife.

The barman appeared reluctant to serve him. The baseball cap only partially covered the cuts; there were enough wounds on display to make the barman think he might be trouble. Slashed Man said something that pacified the barman. A pint of lager was poured, accompanied by an apologetic smile.

To Brighid's dismay, Slashed Man's destination proved to be the table right next to her. Helmet Head slurped toothlessly on the soup, glaring at him as he sat himself down opposite her. She lowered her spoon and said something in French, or what sounded French, the words sounding as solid as soup.

'I don't even know what she's saying,' said the man suddenly turning to Brighid, 'and I speak the fucking lingo.' The network of gaping lesions (fresh enough for scabby patches) ran from ear to ear, chin to cap and beyond. Something or someone had sliced this man up like a cake. One of them or both of them stank, an earthy, mouldy smell like musty walls. 'She left her teeth behind,' he added, cocking his scabby chin at Helmet Head.

Helmet Head growled spilling out more mashed sounds and spittle.

Brighid nodded politely. No matter how much she tried to block out his scrutiny, he was still there, right next to her, gaping gashes and all, gawping at her.

'Thank you,' said a voice booming across the room from somewhere in the vicinity of the flashing slot machines. A man with frazzled hair bowed to an invisible audience.

'We are the Spinwilders,' he declared in a deep, theatrical voice more suited to larger venues. 'And this evening we shall be spinwildering the living bejesus out of you. Enjoy.'

His garish scarlet suit possessed a cut, a tailoring, that would look more at home on a catwalk, if he'd had the face and height for it. He lifted his dumpy arm and snapped his fingers, gloves gagging any intended sound. Thick rubbery green gloves, the sort you'd wear in a garden to prune roses. His other hand clasped a bodhrán, and as he hauled himself down onto the stool, he whipped out a wooden tipper from his pocket and began drumming.

At the same table, another man rose to his feet, stooping as he did so to prevent knocking his head on the beam above. A very shiny head. A head not dissimilar to a polished apple. The polished apple nodded and then stared directly at Brighid. His small, deep-set eyes were like bugs; bugs that had carved their way to his core. Despite the dry weather outside, and central heating turned up to the max inside, he wore a pea green raincoat buttoned from chest to ankles; it was a wonder such a tall man could have found such an over-sized coat, yet somewhere on this planet, there obviously existed a shop catering for even taller clients. With no evidence of clothing beneath, it would seem he could very well be butt-naked, minus the mackintosh; he did at least have shoes, loafers as big as clown clogs.

Brighid grabbed a slug of wine.

Apple Man squatted down on his haunches, produced a fiddle from beneath the table. Then he sat down, slotted the fiddle beneath his chin and began playing. The first notes ricocheted off his pint glass, skittered across the table tops, jostled through the wings of the hen angels, and slipped in beneath Brighid's finger tips. She found herself tapping to the beat.

Even the mouldy couple's focus had shifted to the musicians: Helmet Head was still obsessing over the imaginary dust on her table, but the toothless snarls accompanying the intermittent rubbing of the table, were now targeting the bodhrán. Slashed Man was sinking back in his chair removing his glazed cuts from Brighid's periphery. Relieved to be removed from centre stage, Brighid scanned the room momentarily. Archie was getting himself another double rum.

Someone was shifting about on the stool between the scarlet suit and rain coat, hunched down, head beneath the table, slipping a mobile phone into a bag. Brown leather sleeves.

14B.

He straightened up, his hands clutching the flute he was now playing, eyes closed. The flute's melody was hurtling through the pulsing throb of the bodhrán, sweeping the room, tickling the air.

She suddenly felt stupid. She had thought they were meeting for drinks. But he'd sent that text inviting her to his gig. He had probably sent the same text to everyone else on his mobile's directory.

Slashed Man's hand grazed over his scabs and slipped to the back of his head. As he scratched his nape a small cloud of dust formed. Helmet Head scowled and rubbed the table some more.

Third track in, Brighid made a decision, pouring the remaining merlot into her glass. She'd finish her drink then leave. The Spinwilders were amazing musicians; she couldn't argue with the fact her feet were tapping the flagstones, but sitting in a pub on her own playing their number one fan wasn't quite what she had envisaged.

14B was nodding his head to the beat of the bodhrán. The oddity of a flautist wearing gloves made her look closer at his hands. The gloves must have been custom made to accommodate the extra finger she now noticed he possessed on each hand. Whether these (the gloves and the extra fingers) were a hindrance or a bonus when playing the flute she couldn't quite work out. The tempo of the current piece would suggest the latter.

Apple Man lowered his fiddle, inserted his forefinger into a gap in his raincoat and began rubbing his navel.

14B looked up, his eyes locked with hers.

She felt her ears flush.

He slid the flute from his lips and grinned at her.

She nodded back, sipped her wine.

Flute on the table, he squeezed past the bodhrán, now on solo softly pounding, and headed for the bar.

14B seemed to already know Archie because he patted Archie's back, then leaned forward to get the barman's attention. Archie knocked back the remains of his pint and gladly accepted the rum 14B had bought for him.

The drumming quickened.

'They can survive without me for the next one,' 14B beamed, setting his pint of Guinness down on to the table, handing her a miniature bottle of merlot.

The expression on the man playing the bodhrán said otherwise. He was positively incandescent, his cheeks the same shade as his scarlet suit. Apple Man was still happily prodding away at his belly button, oblivious to band feuds or anything else for that matter.

Vanilla.

A waft of vanilla as 14B sat down.

The scent of her dream. It was there in the clouds she rode through on the gull-drawn chariot every night, precipitation in suspension dripping eau de vanilla. The same smell as her car, and Lowell's sitting room. The scent of vanilla on the plane she'd put down to the ice cream tubs 14B had brought onboard. But it must be his aftershave, his deodorant.

She knocked back some more wine. Unscrewed the cap of the new bottle. Not because she was in any rush to top her glass, not because she was letting the bottle breathe; she wasn't even sure that worked with miniature bottles. It was something to do to stem the awkwardness.

He reached into his bag. A crossbody messenger bag of vermillion weave and verdant green lining. His only flash of vibrant colour. From the neck down to his boots it was the same stressed leather, the same shade of taupe, all creased and wrinkled like dried, dead leaves. Fishing out his mobile he crackled and scrunched like leaves on a busy pavement.

'So how's it going with that boss of yours?' he asked, quickly tapping something into his phone.

She poured herself a large glass of wine. 'Apart from him being a sociopath, you mean?'

He sipped his Guinness.

She shivered suddenly. The last one in or out had left the pub door ajar. 'D'you know what happens when I want to go to the toilet at work? He escorts me up the basement steps.'

He arched his eyebrow. 'Basement?'

'Yep, basement. He unlocks the door to let me out.'

'What? You work with him, locked up in a basement?'

She nodded. 'Creepy. Then when I'm back he checks his watch and jots something, presumably the time, into his mobile. Then he locks the basement door again. Would be petty to deduct toilet visits from my pay. But why else would he be doing it?'

'Sounds more like an accountant than a director.'

She took a slug of wine. 'Weirdest director I've ever come across.'

A cat slipped in through the open pub door. A black cat with no tail but enough stealth to weave around the legs of hen angels and slink across the room all the way to the Spinwilders' table without anyone but Brighid noticing. There, he settled for the space next to the clown clogs, curled himself into a ball, and promptly fell asleep.

14B cleared his throat, sank back some Guinness. 'What's the story with the house? Is it rented for the production?'

'No, it's his. I think it's his parents. Don't know if they're around anymore.'

He wiped his lips with the back of his gloved hand. 'He probably killed them.'

Her wine glass slipped from her fingers and rolled, emptying red wine all over the table, onto the floor and into the cracks between the flagstones.

For one split-second she had almost believed it.

14B caught the glass before it crashed to the floor. 'Sorry, I didn't mean it. Bad joke. Don't want you thinking you're living with a killer in your midst.' He placed the glass back on the table.

'Dead?' Siobhan appeared behind them. 'That dead?' she asked pointing at Brighid's empty glass. 'S'pose to put the wine in your mouth yer know.'

She tried to think of a witty retort; none came, so she fired back her coldest smile, pointed at the miniature bottle and held onto her glass.

'Freddy,' Siobhan yelled, 'throw us over the cloth.'

A towel was promptly hurled towards the table, dappling angel and fairy wings on its flight over.

'Lowell might be weird but he's not a psycho,' Brighid conceded, lifting her wine glass and miniature bottle for Siobhan to wipe the table.

'You wouldn't be talking about Lowell Watterson would you?' Siobhan asked, eyes widening.

Some of her blonde-ginger hair tumbled across her eyelashes, made her blink, which made her sweep it away, but didn't make her go away. Brighid had been caught slating the boss. Small town like this, everyone probably knew each other.

'No,' 14B said coming to the rescue. 'Different Lowell.'

Siobhan frowned, tapping the pint glass with her forefinger. 'Unusual name, Lowell. Are you sure it's not the same Lowell?'

'Lots of unusual stuff going on at the moment. Would make anyone think everything's connected,' he replied enigmatically.

Siobhan shook her head. Still in her early twenties, she was already a veteran at fielding nonsensical ramblings. It came with the job. 'The only Lowell I know is Lowell

Watterson, now he *is* strange. Not been right since his parents died.'

'Siobhan!' Freddy shouted from the bar. 'Customers need serving here.'

Siobhan sighed wearily and stomped back to the bar. Archie was retrieving his jacket from the back of his stool.

'Not everyone's how they seem,' 14B added, too busy keying something into his phone to look up. 'Take our man playing the fiddle. Looks like a flasher. But he's quite the chef, you know.'

She glanced at Helmet Head's empty soup bowl.

'Oh he doesn't cook for this place,' he said suddenly gazing up at her. 'He's more exclusive. Does a mean pasta.'

Apple Man smiled as if he'd heard what 14B had just said and was quietly digesting the compliment. The face of the bodhrán player, however, was now more scarlet than his suit. Their flute player had been missing for at least three or four tracks.

'Anyway,' 14B sighed, placing the phone on the table, leaning forward, his knees touching hers under the table. 'It's good to see you.' He grabbed her hands, squeezed them.

'Do you ever take your gloves off?' she asked, sounding more flirtatious than she'd intended, her knees tingling.

He smiled back at her, threading his fingers through hers, extra fingers included.

'I've missed you,' he murmured, so softly she wasn't quite sure if she'd heard him.

'But you don't know__'

Helmet Head began banging her spoon on the table, completely counter to the beat of the bodhrán.

14B immediately let go of her hands, removed the electric charge at her knees. The spoon banging stopped.

'Hello there fella.'

Brighid glanced up.

Archie, having staggered out of the gents, was talking to the cat who had obviously grown tired of the clown clogs and was now weaving, twirling his tailless body around Archie's ankles and stick. Archie was bending over the walking stick, was just about able to get low enough to run his fingertips over the cat's back.

'You look a bit like our Dhoo,' Archie remarked to the cat. 'He's not with us anymore. Expect you saw him round the neighbourhood, a black Manxie like yourself, but with white paws.'

Brighid rolled her eyes at 14B.

'Nothing wrong with that,' 14B replied. 'The cat will probably understand the bulk of what Archie is saying. He'd have picked up the name Dhoo, would have heard the name being called in the neighbourhood before Dhoo's demise. Archie will possess some of Dhoo's household scent, and as for the sadness with which he just said the dearly departed's name, this will have been noted and perhaps shared.'

Archie was still chatting away to the cat. 'You probably had a few run-ins with him. He was a jealous bugger, could get in a right temper – bit like the missus.'

14B grinned. 'Now, unless that cat has a particular strength in linguistics, a lot of that sentence would have gone right over his furry little head.'

Spotting their scrutiny, Archie hastily assembled some semblance of balance, propping himself against the neighbouring table, letting its pins share the burden. Helmet Head shooed him away.

'Anyway,' 14B said, leaning towards her, plucking a long white hair from her cardigan sleeve. "Looks to me like I'm preaching to the converted. You've got a dog haven't you?'

'No.'

She had always meant to get another dog, but somehow the time was never right. Not that she had chosen the one dog she'd had. He sort of chose her. He just turned up in Aunt Mary's garden one day, not long after the swimming pool incident. Thinking back, Algo probably replaced Magio. A collie was much more fun than an imaginary friend.

Through the pub window, she spotted Archie pause outside to gaze up at the sky, presumably looking for the aurora borealis. The motion of his head tilting up and back tipped his balance. He swayed then steadied himself on the pub railings; drunken logic apparently deducing that if he held onto the railings long enough he'd inherit sufficient amounts of its vertical rigidity to see him home. Balance refuelled, he stumbled away.

'The wife is calling,' 14B said rubbing his knee.

She cupped her hand over the top of her glass as a fly did several circuits over their heads and came into land on the table. 'I didn't know you were married,' she said brightly, concealing her disappointment.

The spatter of wine, bordering the base of her glass, turned out to be the fly's lights on the runway. A piece was missing from one of the fly's wings.

'I'm not. I never got the chance. I was talking about Archie.' He picked up his pint, gulped down more Guinness. The fly saw it as his exit call and took to the air, thrashing unsteadily towards the musicians. Setting his pint back down,14B kneaded his knee some more and stretched his long sinewy leg. He had done the same on the plane several times.

'Knee giving you gyp?' she asked.

'Force of habit. An old bike injury.'

'Your bike,' she sucked her lips. 'I'm guessing it's a

classic all the chrome on show Harley type.' Going by the retro leathers.

'Long gone. It was written off.'

'The same accident you hurt your knee?'

'It doesn't hurt.' His eyes clouded.

'Where was it? The accident.'

'Falmouth.'

She shifted her chair closer. 'I used to live in Falmouth. About ten years ago now. Is that where I've seen you? Sorry, just there's something vaguely familiar about you.' The more she had thought about him, the more she couldn't quite shake that niggling feeling they'd already met before their flight, someplace else, possibly years ago.

He shook his head mournfully. 'Fate must have got in the way.'

'Maybe we were neighbours.' She was sure she would have remembered. 'Maybe we shopped in the same supermarket, drank in the same pubs. Whereabouts did you live?'

'I was only there the day.' He shrugged. 'A boiling hot day. A vanilla ice-cream sort of a day.'

Old Helmet Head shot them a disdainful glare then hurled a finger to her mouth demanding hush. Glower still simmering, she turned away; shook her head.

He sprang to his feet. 'They're getting uncomfortable.'

'Who?'

Apple Man, having just completed his latest episode of navel poking, slapped his forefinger beneath his nose and sniffed. Lost in his own belly fluff heaven. The man in the scarlet suit, though, was staring at 14B, beating the bodhrán slow and hard.

Thrum.

Thrum.

Thrum.

14B stuffed his mobile in to his bag, snatched up his pint and in three mouthfuls drained the remaining stout. Flicking his hair from his eyes he squeezed her arm. 'Catch you next time.'

The bodhrán player hissed something at 14B as he sat himself back down. Both glanced across at Brighid then looked away. 14B keyed something quickly into his mobile then picked up his flute, hurling out a frenzied melody, a fusion of ice cream van sirens and flies buzzing. That's what it sounded like to her anyway. A daft part of her expected her mobile to chime. No message came.

'Freddy, turn the telly up,' a man's voice shouted over the music; a small crowd had gathered at the wide screen perched above the pool table.

Freddy pointed at the musicians. 'Sorry lads – band night – no football tonight.'

'Not football. Breaking news. Freddy, turn it up.'

She wasn't going to stay sitting here on her own, wine all over her clothes. She stood up, raised her hand at 14B to say goodbye. He was too busy looking at Freddy and now the television to notice.

◎ ◎ ◎

'What's that beeping noise?' Nell murmured.

Lowell reclined in his armchair, rubbed his beard. 'Just my phone. I can check later.'

'Sounds important to me.'

How could a text message possibly *sound* important? He carefully rose to his feet; he was always worried about accidently knocking the radio, skewing its positioning – every movement, every breath was oriented so as not to affect the aerial (just in case it had one, an internal one, that he couldn't see), so as not to affect tuning, not to risk losing Nell forever. Peeling his gaze from the radio, he grabbed his mobile from the table.

Four new messages. All from Hector.

BRIGHID'S IN THE PUB. TUT TUT.

Brighid had demanded the spare front door key. Just going for a walk to look for the aurora borealis, she'd said. Liar. Lowell hadn't had time to think, to ask Hector what to do, was totally caught off guard, basking in self-congratulatory glory over his first day as director, successfully completed. Hector's text spoiled all that.

The next text didn't exactly comfort him either.

OH DEAR. IS THAT RED WINE SHE'S KNOCKING BACK?

'Hector's at the pub with Brighid.'

'I know,' Nell purred. 'Stupid idiot.'

'No it's okay. He's keeping an eye on her.' Why did he feel this compulsion to defend him?

'Oh he'll be doing that alright. He can't resist. He got himself on the same flight as her too.'

'He did?'

WHO'S THE LUCKY LAD SHE'S FLIRTING WITH?

Gossip, he could do without. He sat back down into the armchair; all he wanted was to focus on Nell.

Nell sighed wearily. 'Hector has to stay away from her.'

'Why?'

'Safer.'

'What does that mean?'

'What does what mean Honey?'

'I don't know.' She had just explained Hector's back seat role in the production. To ask for a reminder would make him look stupid.

THE BARMAID. DIDN'T YOU HAVE A THING ABOUT HER?

Siobhan. So she was still working in the pub. She'd have been talking about him, laughing about him. He quickly keyed back.

It was a long time ago.

'What was a long time ago, honey?'

He hadn't even hit send yet, so he could dismiss any paranoia Nell was out boozing with them checking his replies. The phone was pointing away from the radio; even if she could somehow see through the radio, it would be impossible for her to read the message from her angle.

'Have you been keeping secrets from me?'

'It was before I even knew you.'

'Was it? Are you sure?'

'Of course I'm sure.'

'Could be your memory playing tricks again.'

He swallowed hard. Did she know something he didn't?

He could hear her breathing.

'What about the acorns?' she said.

Every hair on his body bristled. For a split second, the tiniest of split seconds, he remembered everything, not just their conversation just now, but everything, and then he promptly forgot.

By the time he no longer felt dizzy the radio had already switched to static.

Siobhan was Pre-Lounge. Had Nell questioned that?

He scratched his head, his heart still racing, and hit send. Hector's reply arrived almost immediately.

LEAVING PUB. WILL FOLLOW 2 MAKE SURE SAFE. H

Surely Brighid was big enough to walk back without Hector playing guardian angel. What was so special about her anyway?

SLOWLY, SLOWLY, WOULDN'T WANT HER TO SEE ME. LURKING IN THE SHADOWS. OH. THE WAY SHE WALKS. THE SAME AS ALWAYS.

The same as always?

JUST ME TEXTING ALOUD. SHE'S SUSSED A SHORTCUT. POOR LIGHTING IN THIS ALLEY. GOOD JOB I'M HERE.

The last thing he needed was Hector and Brighid getting together. She was too good-looking, that was the problem. Was it too late to add a new edict to the ones already on the fridge door? Probably no point; a rule forbidding fornication would probably receive the same two fingered salute as all the others. It would only encourage her, bring her crashing towards Hector. Speed up the inevitable. They'd make a cosy army, plotting strategies during pillow talk/ bitching. Lowell would be the common enemy in his own home.

And what could he do when she broke that new rule? He couldn't sack her, could he?

The front door closed quietly. The almanac was ready.

He noted the time in the arrivals column: 22.09: red font this time. Not blue. Red symbolised her Mars-like gravity pulling Hector in, dragging the whole project into oblivion. They'd probably fallen against the front door together, at the same time. Foreplay – pre-copulation – red for her fleshy Martian lips.

The sky had been red the evening his parents failed to come back. *Red sky at night, sailors delight.* How wrong could a saying be? *Red sky at night, parents in fright*; now that would be more appropriate; *Lowell's a shite, for not doing right.* He'd been too busy slobbering over Siobhan to hear any Mayday call.

'Did you forget me?'

Nell's voice.

He swung round faced the radio.

The radio. Why was he staring at the radio?

Floorboards on the stairs. He had to pay attention. Listen. Every detail counted for some reason. One set of footsteps. Hallelujah.

The floorboard creaked at the top of the stairs: 22.10 – red font.

Brighid's bedroom door opened. Actually, should he use blue or red? Perhaps the gravity on Mars was overrated.

Brighid was entering her bedroom alone. But she hadn't closed her door.

Now. 22.14. She was exiting the bedroom, weaving across the landing to the bathroom. She closed the door. Locked it.

She was emptying a very full bladder by the sounds of it. Just how much wine had she had? The toilet flushed: 22.15.

The tap was running upstairs. She'd be cleaning her teeth. Removing the red wine stains from her teeth, hiding the alcohol from her breath.

22.20: Bathroom door unlocked and opened.

A dull ringing sound. Someone calling her mobile.

She answered. The floorboards muffled the conversation, conversation slurred by alcohol. A suppressed giggle. He heard his own name through the cracks in the floorboards.

Her bedroom door closed.

She was walking towards the dressing table. There she stopped and switched on the small flat screen TV perched above the mirror.

She got into bed. The floorboard creaked left-side: 22:25.

He closed the almanac and texted Hector.

All cosy and safe. He had every right to be sarcastic.

STAY LISTENING, Hector replied. **KEEP JOTTING DOWN THOSE NUMBERS.**

Lowell didn't get to rest, didn't get time off; he had to carry on working, listening. What did she have that he didn't? Apart from Hector fancying her. Why should she get the whole five star treatment, meals prepared by outside caterers? He hadn't even met the caterers. How were they getting into the house? Had Hector given them keys? There was just the one plate on the table again this evening. He had to make his own dinner, had to run around keeping Blue/Red comfortable, track her movements as if she were some A-list celebrity. She even had her own in-house stalker: him. It was demeaning. He picked up the mobile and texted back.

Broken rules. Sack her.

He didn't have to wait long for Hector's response: **NO WAY.**

Rules 2 and 3 broken – hydration levels now AWOL. Alcohol consumed.

AND RULES 1 AND 8 – SALTED PEANUTS. ONE PACK. Hector added.

Sack Her!!!!!

NOPE. CAN UP HYDRATION LEVELS + LOWER SALT TOMORROW 2 FIX.

FIX WHAT? WHY?? It was easier to ask the questions that mattered in a text. So easy, he wasn't even forgetting the questions.

NOT YOUR CONCERN.

She's planning on heading out again. To get a kebab, Lowell lied.

BULLSHIT.

If you're so bothered about vegetarianism how come you wear so much leather?

THAT'S MY SKIN YOU CHEEKY BASTARD.

LOL. (He was in no mood for laughing out loud or any other sort of laughing. Besides, Hector's so-called jokes really weren't that funny.) **Whatever. Brighid's crap.**

NOPE. SPECIAL.

Why? He was working a lot harder than Brighid, so if she was getting special favours just because Hector wanted to hop into bed with her, that was just plain wrong, ethically and professionally.

N TOLD YOU. THUMBS.

Sometimes that was all that was needed to bring things back, the odd reference, a single word from Hector.

THAT'S WHY YOU WEAR THE GLOVES. NAIL BITING JUST SECONDARY. THEY COVER UP YOUR LACK, YOUR INADEQUACY: THE THUMBS.

'Thumbprint,' Nell had said. He remembered now. 'The proof is in her thumbprint.'

He suspected a whole heap more had been said on the subject, but it always came back as a snippet, and as Nell could talk in such riddles the bits he did recall often didn't make that much sense. Sense or nonsense, the essential bones of that morsel needed very little chewing over.

If Nell wanted proof, so be it. He removed his gloves and threw them to the floor. Brighid was already slobbing about in bed, dozing off in front of the television. He, on the other hand, was alert, sober, committed. And the gas fire would show just how fucking committed he was.

Down on his haunches, he unclipped the plastic hearth and cast it aside on the rug. Then, he turned the switch. The gas purred. He flicked the ignition, lighting the gas, rotating the dial all the way to five: maximum heat – ultimate dedication. Waiting: he didn't have to time his own actions; proof he was somewhat freer than the puppet upstairs – freer, liberated, at liberty to change things.

The flames were hot now. So, being free to stick his thumb into the fire, that's exactly what he did.

Nerve endings revolted in flinching spasms.

He clamped his elbow between his knees, clasped his wrist with his other hand. And as he held his thumbprint in the flames, the lines swelling up, the whorls melting, he began to count, not for the almanac, but for himself.

1-2-3-4……

When he was up to double figures, biting into his lip trying to distract from the searing agony, his thumb started smelling like grilled bacon.

A flat hissing noise.

He put it down to the blisters bursting, their serum sizzling, but it went on and on; the blisters would need to be the size of the radio.

The radio. Nell was coming through.

'Lowell?' she called. 'What are you doing?'

'Nothing.' He whipped his thumb out from the flame. His skin contracted in the colder air, hurting like hell.

'What's that smell?'

'How can you smell__?'

'A smell of burning. Flesh burning.'

'Nothing.' That's how she made him feel. He was nothing. She was everything.

'It doesn't smell of nothing.'

'Oh believe me it is. Nothing.'

'Hmmm…maudlin. I've entered on a bad moment. Talk.'

'Brighid,' he whispered her name in case she could hear. 'Is she really so special?'

'Is that a touch of the green eyed, cherub?'

She called him *cherub*; coming from anyone else he'd have cringed, but from Nell, with her breathy tones, that word was enough to make him forget the excruciating pain in his thumb; it was pure anaesthesia.

'She's not dedicated enough,' he explained.

'She still thinks of it as just a job, you haven't dropped

the mask?'

'What else is it though? What's behind the mask?'

'Patience love, patience.'

'She went out tonight.'

Nell sighed. 'And she didn't invite you?'

'That's not the point.'

'Isn't it?'

'I don't go to pubs. That's where she went. Was probably pissed out of her head. It's irresponsible.'

'Hector watched over her.'

'You know?'

'We already discussed this honey.'

'But what about rule three?'

'What are you talking about?'

'The rules. One: no snacking. Two: hydration must be maintained at optimum levels. Three: no alcohol. And so on to nine: eat slowly. Don't place food on your fork/spoon/hand until you have swallowed your previous mouthful.'

'Enough,' she said. There was a crinkle in her voice, a bubble in the smoothness, a squashed giggle. 'I didn't see that.'

'But how would you see it? You're not here.'

'Not in body perhaps.'

'But in spirit?'

'We've been through this ninety-seven times already.'

'You're counting?'

'That's what you need to do. Focus on the numbers.'

'The rules are one of Hector's wind ups aren't they?'

'There'll be some logic to the madness. Keep to those rules.'

'I'm not the one not keeping to them. Anyway they don't apply to me, just the puppet.'

'The what?'

'Nothing'

'I've been so distracted lately, I seem to be missing things. Is that what you call her?'

'Not to her face. Anyway she's broken rule three. Shouldn't there be some sort of punishment?'

'And what sort of punishment would that be? We could stick her in a barrel, roll her down a hill, give her a good flogging.'

'You're joking, right?'

'Yes Lowell. Don't deny her her last spoils.'

'Last?'

'Last time we'll be talking like this.'

'Does that mean?'

'Yes, I'll be there soon.'

'When?'

'So many questions today.'

'Sorry, it's just__'

'Your guest has made you tense. Hector will organise a special supper tomorrow. It's time __'

'What sort of special?'

'Sacrificial fish special. Goodnight Lowell.'

'Nell?'

'Yes?'

'I can remember everything you just said.'

The radio switched to static, but the red line kept on moving, scouring for other transmissions. It halted on a whistling sound, a whistling unlike any the radio had tuned to before. The whistle ascended, reached a peak, and then descended, and then it rose again and dipped again. On the third melodious roll, static returned.

◎ ◎ ◎

'Switch on the news,' Hector said.

Brighid's heart had skipped the smallest of beats when she'd first heard his voice down the phone.

'Why? What's happened?' she asked, staring up at the TV on her bedroom wall.

'Just watch and see,' he said. Then he hung up.

A special sport report. Then the weather.

Now.

Scrolling text revealed the breaking news across the screen.

REPORTS OF PHENOMENON IN NORTH WEST ENGLAND, SOUTH WEST SCOTLAND, IRISH REPUBLIC, NORTHERN IRELAND, ANGLESEY, NORTH WALES AND THE ISLE OF MAN.

> 'Eyewitnesses are reporting flashes of light and whistling noises.
>
> Okay, the footage you're seeing now was sent in by the brother of one of the passengers on that Belfast to Liverpool ferry. Gary Taylor's sister, Jane, filmed and sent the footage to her brother as events unfolded. It was shot on her mobile phone and is very grainy as you can see, but if you look to the right of the screen, it does seem to show ...it's difficult to tell but that looks like white flashes, sparks even. There's no audio and we must stress this is amateur footage and as yet has not been analysed or verified. But it does seem to corroborate eyewitness reports of the strange phenomenon that took place at 18:40 this evening.
>
> We have tried calling Jane Taylor, but have been unable to make contact. And, yes, that's the ferry we're looking at now, still stranded approximately five miles off the Cumbrian coast. Radio contact was

lost following the incident, but rescue teams are at the scene.

Our North West correspondent, Alex Turner, is at the ferry terminal in Liverpool. Alex, what's the latest?'

'Hello Samina, well, as you can imagine, there's some anxious people here behind me. Family and friends of passengers have gathered and now all they can do is wait.'

'Are we able to talk to anyone onboard at the moment?'

'No, I'm afraid not. This particular crossing is normally GSM enabled, but at the moment there does seem to be some problem with mobile phones onboard.'

'And no official announcements?'

'No. Port officials and police here are refusing to take any questions at the moment. They have confirmed that one gentleman onboard did suffer a minor heart attack. He's been airlifted to hospital and is currently in a stable condition. All other passengers are said to be safe and well. An emergency number has been issued, for anyone concerned about family onboard.'

'That number is now at the bottom of your screen.'

'This is Jerry Driscoll, his wife Maureen is on the ferry. You were talking to her via her mobile just as the incident was taking place. What did she say?'

'Well she was very shaken, very scared, you know. She didn't say much. Then she got cut off.'

'Jerry, what did Maureen say?'

'She said a row of flashing lights went right across the ferry. She was in the canteen – the lights, sparks she called them, bent her knife and fork.'

'Thanks Alex, we're going to have to leave it

there. We'll be straight back as soon as we have any further updates. We can now bring you to that press conference with the Irish Garda; Chief Superintendent Michael Walsh is about to make an announcement.'

'I'm Chief Superintendent Michael Walsh, I'll give you a quick update and then do a short questions and answers. Please understand, the priority is with the investigation, so if we can all keeps things brief. Okay. At 18.40 this evening, a number of accidents took place on some of the major routes into Dublin. On the M1 south of Drogheda, there were multiple pile ups on both northbound and southbound carriages. Similar incidents occurred, at the exact same time, on the N2 and M3. Over forty vehicles were involved in all. Miraculously no-one has been killed; seven people are in hospital, but there are no serious injuries.'

'Dermot Browne, the Irish Herald...Are you taking seriously the accounts of several eyewitnesses, the drivers and passengers themselves, that there were sparks and lights on the road, that some of the vehicles involved were actually damaged, scratched and the like, before any actual impact?'

'We are still in the process of going though witness statements. And we would like to appeal for any other witnesses to come forward. If you have seen anything at all please get in touch. The number will be coming up on your screen I believe, or call your local Garda station. All calls are confidential.'

'Fiona McSheffrey, RTÉ...And what about the other incidents? Dublin Airport is at a standstill, all aircraft grounded. Do you think there is any connection to the lights witnessed there, the damage to planes?'

'Any damage to aircraft recorded so far is extremely superficial and limited to planes parked up at the time.

No planes taxiing, in flight, taking off or landing were affected.'

'So far. But we won't know that for sure until all safety checks are completed. But Dublin Airport, the road accidents and other reported incidents – telephone lines going down, cars being scratched in driveways, the damage to mobile masts, car and house alarms going off – they're all within a horizontal line of each other, from Portmarnock on the coast to as far west as the M3 just North of Dunboyne.'

'That's correct.'

'But would you say there's a connection?'

'It's too early to jump to conclusions at this stage.'

'And all along that line, eye witnesses are blaming mysterious lights. Do the Garda have any idea on the cause of those lights?'

'At the moment. No.'

'And the accidents in the North, across County Antrim, do you think there's any link?'

'At present. No. And we have no reason to think there is.'

'Apart from them all occurring at exactly the same time, and all sets of witnesses reporting the same phenomenon. The whistling noises, the lights, the sparks are all being voiced by witnesses, not only in Ireland, but in England, Scotland, Wales, and now the ferry.'

'I really can't comment on separate investigations. I'm sorry I can't take any more questions at this time.'

Brighid popped the second pillow behind her back. It had to be some sort of natural phenomenon; a build up of too much electricity in the atmosphere, an electrical storm of some sort.

'We have just received some new footage. Again this has been sent in by a viewer so has yet to be verified. James Lynch from Manchester on holiday in North Wales filmed what looks like flashing lights coming in off the sea, approaching the resort of Rhos-on-Sea. Now, concentrate on the blue car parked up on the promenade. The lights are getting nearer. Now; what looks like orbs of light are bouncing off the car, and there goes one of its hub caps.'

'Jesus,' Brighid whispered.

'We'll play that again, this time with the audio.'

Man's voice off camera: *What's those lights, Heather?*

Woman's voice off camera: *What lights? Oh. They're like will-o'-the-wisps.*

Man's voice off camera: *Don't be daft. You only get those in marshes.*

Woman's voice off camera: *They're coming in.*

Man's voice off camera: *What's that noise?*

Woman's voice off camera: *Are you getting it? Turn the mike up.*

An abrupt muffled shuffling was replaced by a whistling melody; notes steadily climbing and then descending.

A text message. 14B. **NOTHING LIKE A BIT OF MUSIC TO LEAD THE WAY.**

She texted back: **What's your take on it?**

LET ME THROW THAT BACK AT YOU... IF YOU ONLY BELIEVE WHAT YOU CAN SEE – WHAT HAPPENS IF WHAT YOU SEE YOU CAN'T BELIEVE?

Too tired to deal with drunken musings, she switched her phone off.

◎ ◎ ◎

Closing his eyes was dangerous.

Sleep dragged him away from the radio.

Five minutes.

Five minutes or thereabouts.

When Lowell thought he opened his eyes again he found himself back in the dog pound. Standing over a metal bowl. Staring at his own dog reflection.

A white faced collie.

Sniffing chicken flavours sourced from China.

'I've been to China.' The dog was thinking aloud, for Lowell's benefit. 'I even know a bit of Mandarin. I've travelled the world over the years. I speak nine languages fluently and seven others at basic conversation level. Not bad for a dog.'

The dried food nuggets were aggravating his gingivitis, making his gums bleed. His throat felt tight; it was difficult to swallow. His stomach was in knots, worrying about the number five.

Something about the number five was tormenting him.

Chapter 14

Coming from anyone else, the bottle of mineral water on the desk would be a thoughtful gesture, but as this was from Lowell it just had to be another dig. He'd already had the proverbial shovel waiting at breakfast. Brighid would have happily skipped breakfast; a coffee was all she needed, but he'd swiftly pointed out that enough rules had already been broken.

'Let's play it,' Lowell said.

Audio lined up, Brighid went back a few seconds on the programme line, making sure there were no glitches between audio clips. It was clean. The new commentary commenced.

'Manannan settled his wings onto the ground and listened to the earth. And on the fifth day, the earth replied. Releasing the pulse beneath his feathers he ignited the rock inside the mountain. And so the spirit of the stone was extracted.

Tremors were felt as far afield as what is now Ireland, and it is back there that the Tuatha Dé Danann and Manannan returned, bringing the spirit of the stone with them.

Back on home shores, they were greeted with news of the tree's demise. The tree had rotted away;

there was barely anything left. But as the trunk had perished, its bark peeling, its sapwood putrefying, the tree's secret had become exposed.

A camera.

There was a camera inside the tree. And now almost all that remained of the tree was the camera.'

Brighid swung round in her chair, faced Lowell. 'So, it's not a documentary about Irish mythology at all; that's just the intro, a metaphor, a fantasy segment to set the scene?'

He was busy studying his notes. The film of perspiration glazing his face made it look as if he'd just been running, not sitting it out in the edit suite all morning. He was clinging to his side as well, like he had a stitch.

Question left unanswered, she threw another one out. 'Talking of fantasy, did you see the news last night?' She was making conversation, trying to snap the palpable tension hanging in the air since breakfast. If it wasn't for Lowell's beard, she was sure he would be showing his teeth, biting at the bit.

'No,' he said, practically snarling.

'Hope they've managed to get everyone off the ferry.'

She had been last minute for breakfast; even if it was only downstairs, a twenty or so stair commute, there had been no time to catch the news.

'What ferry?' Lowell asked, now stroking his chin, pushing any lingering growls back in behind the beard hair.

'You haven't seen the news?'

He shook his head.

'Head wrecker.' She rubbed her temples. Was she referring to the news or the wine. She hadn't drunk enough to get a hangover, but that's what she had right now thanks to the cheap plonk labelled up as something a bit more special.

'And it's not just the ferry, road accidents too, witnesses all reporting lights. And whistling.' Brighid eased the pressure on her temples; it was making the headache worse.

'What sort of whistling?' Lowell asked, his eyes like cyan bullets.

'Let's take a look shall we?'

The extra cable coming from the edit desk's TV monitor was the only clue needed; she flicked the button from PC to TV mode.

'Forty-seven separate traffic accidents across affected regions,' Brighid said, reading the scrolling news out loud.

Lowell leaned forward and upped the volume. The thumb on his right hand was bandaged. No gloves today; probably didn't fit with all that dressing.

'What happened?' she asked, pointing at his bandage.

'Nothing.' Lowell was too interested in the news to elaborate.

> 'Leading scientist Dr Damian Maher, interviewed on our News Hour last night, coined the phenomenon, *the UNDER*, an acronym for Unexplained Noise and Distortive Energy Release. It's a term taken up in many of this morning's papers. Incidents, all appearing to fit into the category of the UNDER have been reported in the Wirral; in Cumbria; in County Antrim, Ulster; in South West Scotland; in coastal areas of North Wales; in the Irish Republic and the Isle of Man.
>
> Sellafield's nuclear reprocessing plant narrowly missed the UNDER when the railway line serving Sellafield Station was damaged less than fifteen miles down the line from the plant. A controlled shut down

has taken place at Sellafield in response to the incident. More on that later.

In Merseyside, Liverpool John Lennon Airport will remain closed throughout much of the day whilst aircraft are checked. An airport spokesperson said that whilst the airport was not directly affected by the UNDER, its proximity to incidents across the Mersey in the Wirral was cause for concern. The grounding of planes was purely a precautionary measure as passenger safety had to be the upmost priority.

There are as yet no reports of any damage to any of the heavy industry stationed at Ellesmere Port, close to the airport.

Returning to Cumbria at 18:40 there were accidents on the A5093, A590 and A595. In South West Scotland at exactly the same time, collisions occurred on the coastal A747, the A75, the A74 near Lockerbie and A7. In Northern Ireland, also at 18:40, there was a minor accident involving three cars on the A2 coast road. And in Wales, at twenty to seven yesterday evening, simultaneous accidents occurred on the A5025 in Anglesey, the A546, the Conway Road, the A470, A547 and the A525 just outside of Rhyl. Back in the Wirral, a lorry jackknifed on the M53, again at 18:40. There have been no fatalities or serious injuries in any of these incidents. Emergency services at the scenes of the M53, A74 and A525 accidents say road works or heavy traffic helped minimise casualties, and for the majority of all other cases police are generally putting the lack of serious casualties down to sheer good fortune.

In Anglesey, the Celtic Gateway Bridge at Holyhead ferry terminal is closed as a precautionary measure; a number of cars in the terminal car park have minor cosmetic damage, but the terminal building appears to have escaped unscathed. Train and ferry services in and out of Holyhead remain unaffected. In County Antrim several buildings at a new business park have incurred what appears to be very minor structural damage. Engineers are on site surveying the extent of that.

These are just some of the higher-profile cases. Then there's the downing of several overhead cables – localised power cuts have been reported in small pockets of North Wales and Ayreshire; plus damage to mobile phone masts, hundreds of computers, cars, even cattle-grids. But again, no reports, so far, of any major injuries.

A viewer in the Isle of Man has sent in the following footage. Sarah Shimmin was filming her seven year old daughter's first Hop-tu-Naa, a Manx Halloween tradition similar to Trick or Treat. This was shot on the West of the Island, on Peel Promenade.'

Lowell leaned forward.

'I'm sure Sarah will understand if I say ignore her daughter and look to the right, to the bridge running across the causeway. The whistling within the audio is the same tune as other footage sent in by viewers.'

'I've heard that whistling before,' Lowell exclaimed. He had visibly paled; some feat for Lowell.

'When?'

Further details remained as firmly under wraps as his thumb.

> 'Get away from the bridge!' Sarah Shimmin shouted hysterically at her daughter. 'Come here. Get here now!'

The footbridge was visibly contorting as ephemeral lights streaked from one side to the other.

The footage abruptly switched to black.

'Lunch,' Lowell said, a remote control in his hand.

◎ ◎ ◎

That's what happened when he strayed from the script.

What was he thinking letting her switch to the news like that? It was the exact same whistling he'd heard on the radio. It was another signal from Nell. A warning to stay away from the TV. That little girl could have lost her life and he would have been responsible, just like the last time. How many times did he need to be told? Stick to the script. Radio. Documentary. Almanac. No distractions. That's how Mum and Dad died.

12:59. Kitchen. They were nearly late.

'Just popping upstairs,' Brighid said, all light and breezy, like rule one didn't matter.

'Just hang on a minute,' Lowell replied.

1pm. He pulled her chair out, nodded for her sit down.

Her face hardened.

He checked his watch, raised an eyebrow. Being a boss was probably a bit like being a father. Right now it was a battle of wills. Right now, she was huffing and sighing just as much as any petulant toddler.

Having plonked herself into her chair, she regained her composure, unpeeling the cling film from her sandwich.

'And what about you Lowell?' she said, a saccharine tone. 'Do you just eat when you want?'

Why couldn't the caterers whoever they were have made him a sandwich? It wouldn't have been that much extra effort.

She was eating too quickly.

If he reminded her rule nine stated she needed to swallow before biting into the sandwich again, she would probably just toss the rest of her lunch onto the floor, plate included. No, he had to settle for paltry mercies: at least she was actually eating the sandwich, and on time.

She glared back up at him.

He was making her uncomfortable, standing over her, watching her eat. He sat down, burrowed his hand into his jacket pocket, fished out his mobile.

A new message from Hector.

HOPE YOU'RE MAKING SURE BRIGHID'S NOT SNEAKING IN ANY EXTRA SALT. RULE 8. CHECK HER LIPS. HOW MANY GRAINS OF SALT THERE?

Three Possibly.

KEEP WATCHING.

He used to look forward to the lunch break in his old job. Thursdays was always grab a burger and chips day in the Rovers; a tradition he and Paul maintained for about two years, right up to the week the fishing boat went missing. Paul was another one who had pestered him with calls in the early Lounge Age. Every other work day, Pre-Lounge Age, Lowell had lunch alone at the café opposite the bus station. He always tried to grab the window seat. He got a better view that way. He didn't note the bus numbers and times down as the buses passed; there weren't enough of them to make it that interesting, but it gave him a certain pleasure to observe bus numbers 5, 1H and 4 running to schedule. If they had anything other than steam trains and electric trams on the Isle of Man, he'd have been right there on the platform scribbling down the numbers.

He had his own diesel train to track now.

14:00. Back in the edit suite. Blue font.

He had drawn a line with a pencil on the manual/ script marking where they were up to. 'Bring in audio clip sixty-two.'

'Of course this discovery of the camera inside the tree came thousands of years before cinema, before the Lumière brothers, Charlie Chaplin, Eisenstein and his revolutionary montage sequences. CNN, BBC and Al Jazeera were just figments of an untold future. But what if broadcast journalism had been around not just this century and last century, but for millennia? And what if in all that time cameras came in all shapes and sizes? Imagine a film crew that can camouflage themselves into any situation, observing, recording, without anyone ever knowing. Who would suspect a leaf flitting innocently in the wind, woodworm chomping away at the floorboards, a crab crawling along the seabed, a wing-bitten fly on the wall? Excuse the pun but perhaps it's not a pun.

Imagine if every historical, pivotal moment had been filmed, each unspeakable act of cruelty, suffering, and injustice. Imagine a leaf blowing over the sand and blood of the Roman Colosseum, a spider dangling from the corridor ceiling in Auschwitz, a butterfly

> flapping through the chains of slaves, woodworm gnawing on a cupboard during the French Revolution, a fly hovering over swollen famine-ridden bellies, a flea bouncing between the boots of the 34th Infantry Division in some muddy field in Somme; imagine leaves blowing above the waters of tsunamis, amongst the rubble of earthquakes, or over bin bags in a dog pound. Just imagine someone always watching, taking it all in: a cockroach scuttling over the blisters of an infant dying of smallpox, a crab crawling through the rubble of Hiroshima – amazing what a nuclear bomb can wash ashore. And imagine if it wasn't just mass injustices, agonies and tragedies being filmed, imagine if all the individual, personal moments of love and fury had been recorded too: the laughter under the floorboards, and all those supposedly mundane decisions that change lives.'

'Okay,' he said, rubbing his hands, reading from his notes, playing confident. 'Some of the footage that goes with this has its own audio, so we'll need to cut the commentary accordingly. Bring in the clip *Soundproofing* and play.'

Footage commenced on a street that was instantly recognisable; it was the same narrow, steep, winding incline, cars and vans parked up bumper to bumper, same sandstone houses, same old fish warehouse at the end. Shenn Varrinagh Street. His street. Home.

A lorry trundled into shot and then stopped in the middle of the road. The driver and another man leaped out, swung open the lorry's back doors, and hauled out a large roll of carpet. The camera zoomed in for a close-up. Beneath the plastic wrapping, the weave exhibited not just the same shade of red but also the exact same diamond pattern as the carpet in his lounge.

'Hmm,' said Brighid. 'I get the reference to the woodworm, but I was expecting something different.'

She wasn't the only one. How on earth had Hector gotten hold of an identical carpet? The carpet was about fifteen years old; it must be an old line by now and well out of stock.

She tapped her fingernail on the desk. Seven times. 'I suppose you didn't have far to go for filming doing it this way.'

'I guess not,' he replied, scratching his beard. A beard was a very useful device. Fifty percent of facial expressions remained mostly hidden. He just needed to concentrate on the upper half; steady his gaze, maintain calm. 'Next, the clip labelled *Sailors' Delight*.'

Imagery began in a blur then shifted into sharp focus. A close-up of a face.

His own mother's face.

Mum.

His lungs suddenly felt heavy, as though he'd been holding his breath for months.

She was in a kitchen. Their kitchen. The same old terracotta tiles with yellowing, flaking grout. Mum. Sitting at the Formica table, eating.

He could almost smell the chip shop chips she was eating.

Mum lowered the fork she was holding and swallowed.

'Here he is now,' she said quietly, same soft tone she always used.

Camera focus swooped to a hand, all thick and calloused. The hand was clasping a knife scooping mushy peas onto a chip laden fork. It was his father's hand.

Camera angle tilted back up to his mother; she was gazing at something off-screen, something in the direction of the kitchen door.

Mum's face abruptly blurred, and slipped out of shot as the camera panned across the kitchen.

Then he saw himself, standing at the kitchen doorway.

Brighid spun round in her chair, threw him a curious glance. 'Is that you?'

He felt too queasy to react.

How could they have possibly filmed this? He'd have noticed someone with a camera in their kitchen, especially as his parents absolutely never had guests. He'd remember someone filming in the kitchen. Wouldn't he?

Brighid tapped her finger on the desk. Three times. 'You look different without a beard.'

The Lowell slouching against the doorframe, hands in the pockets of his accountancy suit, bare chin scowling over a bag of chips, looked so much younger than his current self. He missed that younger version of himself. He missed his confidence, his easy laughter, his capacity to sulk just because his parents had eaten before him. That Lowell was as dead as his parents.

> 'Sorry love,' said Mum. 'I'd have got you some chips but I didn't know what time you were coming back.'
>
> 'We're heading out in the boat tomorrow,' Dad muttered with a mouthful of mushy peas.

The camera panned back to the kitchen door frame. His

younger self was no longer standing there. The audio registered heavy footsteps trudging up the stairs.

The camera swept back to Mum. Mum patting Dad's hand.

> 'Not to worry,' Mum said, 'you can tell him about the radio tomorrow.'

Brighid was staring at him waiting for his next instruction.

He'd lost his place in the director's manual. Page five. Page six. Pencil mark. There, just after *Sailors' Delight*. 'Audio clip *Bliss*,' he said, quietly, as quietly as his mother. 'Add *Bliss* to the timeline.'

> 'Talking of personal, let's go back to when our couple in the kitchen sealed their love. We won't go to the Irish honeymoon in hotel room number 220 – that would be intrusive; no, let's head to Marine Drive, where they're a couple all flushed by the nerves and excitement of their first date. He was showing off, taking the bends too fast. If that seagull hadn't swooped and frightened the living daylights out of the young Mister Whatever-his-name with his souped-up Mini, there would have been no bride and groom shimmying down the aisle.'

He set the manual down onto the desk, folded his arms. His hands were trembling. He needed to hide them.

> 'Second date, the morning after Marine Drive, they were already down the estate agents putting in an offer on a house with an unusually spacious basement.'

'This house?' Brighid asked.

'Yes.' He was just repeating what it said in the script.

(**CONFIDENTIAL ASIDE TO LOWELL:** REFERENCES TO THAT COUPLE IN THE KITCHEN AND UNUSUALLY SPACIOUS BASEMENT WILL HAVE HER DOING HER OWN SUMS. WHEN SHE TOTS UP THE INEVITABLE END RESULT = YOU BEING ONE OF THE TOPICS OF THIS DOCUMENTARY, JUST AGREE WITH HER.)

LOWELL'S DIALOGUE TO BRIGHID: Yes.

Chapter 15

The documentary had shifted from Irish mythology to something much more personal. Lowell's parents being dead and they, or someone playing them, appearing in a scene set in Lowell's own kitchen, now pointed to this all being some sort of tribute. An expensive epitaph. Expensive enough she hoped to cover her wages.

18:50. She was getting as bad as Lowell for checking the time. Hiding it out in her bedroom was a much better option than heading to the kitchen ten minutes early.

The internet was down, so the TV was the only way she had of catching up with the news. Messages to Kate, and other friends, trying to gauge their take on news events, had gone unanswered. In fact, the whole time Brighid had been on this island, the only messages she'd received were from 14B. And she still didn't know his real name.

The British Government were rolling out yet another junior minister she had never heard of to speak to the press. A time like this, she would have expected at least one familiar political figure. She had missed the start of the press conference, had been indulging in a long hot bath trying to get rid of the headache she'd had all day. So just why this particular minister was holding a tortoise in his arms was a complete mystery. He could at least pop the tortoise down on the desk, let it graze amongst the microphones; it wasn't exactly likely to run away.

A hand came into shot, vying for attention.

'Do you have any idea what actually caused the UNDER?' the voice behind the hand asked.

'As I said, some of our very best people have been assigned to this and are working around the clock.'

It sounded like a well rehearsed line; still, the tortoise did look suitably heavy lidded.

'So are you saying the Government has no idea?' another journalist shouted.

'We will get to the bottom of this. But as I'm sure you will all appreciate these are unprecedented events, so I do ask for your patience. We are utilising all available resources. Rest assured no stone will be left unturned.'

'Is there any reason to suppose that it might be terror related?' the same journalist asked.

The minister cleared his throat. 'As I say, we are keeping every avenue of investigation open.'

Brighid switched off the television. Hungry though she was, she was in no way looking forward to eating with Lowell. Closing the bedroom door behind her, she trod on a loose floorboard, and then reluctantly made her way down the stairs.

The red tablecloth and polished silver cutlery pointed to this being somewhat different from previous meals. Lowell's parents, or whoever that was in the documentary, had gone without the tablecloth for their chip supper. The rest of the kitchen, however, still looked exactly as it did when that scene was filmed.

Brighid's dinner, as always, had already been dished out. Lowell carried two plates over from the worktop. The same old Formica worktops as the documentary.

'What was that about the radio?' she asked sitting down.

Lowell just stood there, clasping the plates.

'The footage, this afternoon,' she elaborated. 'Was that your mum?'

He nodded absently, set the plates on the table and sat down opposite her. Lowell, it seemed, would be eating the same as her this evening: sweet potato (fried in paprika going by looks and smell), spinach, peas and salmon.

'I'd say any court would find you guilty,' she quipped, changing the subject. He obviously didn't want to talk about his mother.

'What d'you mean?' His tone was as spiky as a salmon's backbone.

'You going against food rules,' she explained, rolling up her sleeves. It was hot in the kitchen, yet Lowell was rubbing his hands as though they were cold.

'Oh.' He blinked and shifted his gaze towards the fridge door. 'You mean rule five: no fish.' The hand rubbing stopped 'No, but this doesn't count, it's a special salmon, a sacrificial fish.'

'Sacrificial fish? What are you on about?' she smirked. She was sick of his stupid rules. 'More like hypercritical fish.'

He grabbed the jug, poured water into her wine glass. 'Drink,' he barked. 'It'll fix rule two – hydration levels, fix that hangover – which is against rule three by the way.'

Place like this you only had to sneeze and the whole town knew about it.

'Exactly how much water am I allowed?'

He scanned her face for contraband scorn. None found, he skewered his salmon.

She picked up her knife and fork; the knife's handle was sticky. As serviettes had not come part of table dressing she was not going to risk riling Lowell any further by asking for one. She shoved some spinach into her mouth. Tasteless. It needed more salt; another thing she wouldn't be requesting.

'I was watching the news earlier.' The UNDER was proving a useful conversation piece. 'Everyone's off that ferry now. They were interviewing some of the passengers, showing close-ups of rings and necklaces scratched by the UNDER. One man was saying his Prince Albert had twisted.'

Lowell furrowed his brow. 'A Prince Albert. Isn't that a penis piercing?'

She nodded. 'Not a great place to have jewellery if there's some weird energy going about bending metal.' She scratched her head. 'No-one was really hurt apart from the guy with the heart attack – he's okay. And one woman had to have a piece of glass plucked out of her cheek. The UNDER twisted the frame of her glasses, broke one of her lenses. They were showing watches too, a lot of them stopped when it happened. Really bizarre. Did you see it?'

'No,' he said, shoulders noticeably stiffening.

She scraped up some peas and salmon onto her fork. 'Question is, what's causing it?' She was actually enjoying the conversation, even if it was with Lowell, even if it was mostly one-sided. She had to talk to someone. Kate wasn't picking up her phone. Aunt Mary was off sunning herself in California. 'What's the sparks and whistling all about? Do you think terrorists have got their hands on some sort of new technology? Someone's got to be behind it.'

'Someone,' Lowell agreed vaguely.

She grabbed a slug of water. 'Who though?'

He bit his lip. Hesitated. The skin on his forehead was so dry it was flaking; it made his eyebrows look as if they had dandruff. 'Maybe what they're *saying* is the aurora borealis is *actually* something quite different.' He said it so quietly and quickly she barely heard.

'Yeah, right,' she said, slamming her glass down onto the table. 'Jewellery repairs are a roaring trade in Lapland.'

His beard tightened.

She grabbed the hem of the tablecloth, dabbed the splashes she'd made when plonking down her glass. She had witnessed how much the aurora borealis meant to him the first night here when she'd been shivering on the backyard wall. 'Okay, let's say the aurora borealis *isn't* what everyone thinks it is,' she mused for Lowell's sake. 'Could the lights in the sky be some kind of alternative cosmic energy?'

'Exactly.' Lowell nodded, smiling, finally looking as if he was beginning to relax.

She tried the sweet potato. The paprika almost made up for the lack of salt. This was just like having a conversation with Tessy, she just had to play along with the fantasy. 'So you think it's some sort of alien visitation?'

The smile abruptly subsided. His knife screeched across the plate. 'You're taking the piss,' he growled, mouth full.

''Course not,' she lied, sliding a last forkful of salmon into her mouth. 'Jesus!' Something solid within the salmon; she spat it out onto her hand. 'A stone. It nearly broke my bloody tooth.'

He snatched the stone from her hand. 'You should have been more careful.'

'It's okay, no damage done, I'll live.'

He was too busy examining the stone to hear, wiping it with his bandaged thumb, wiping and rubbing what appeared to be a triangular stone.

As he turned the stone over and over in his hands, she tried to crane forward, shuffling herself into a better position to see it; when she got too close, he cupped his hands, blocking her view.

A tinny melody suddenly rang out across the kitchen.

Lowell visibly jumped.

'It's okay,' she said, more to herself than Lowell. 'It's not the UNDER.' She needed to change the ring tone on her phone.

He was already back on duty, peeking into his cupped hands, checking and checking the stone.

She fished the mobile from her pocket.

A message from 14B.

FORGOT TO ASK...DO YOU BELIEVE DREAMS CAN COME TRUE?

Chapter 16

Lowell unravelled the bandage from his thumb and plucked the loose fibres that had adhered to the raw, tumid flesh; flesh that reminded him of his father, his face all bloated and chewed, lying on the mortuary's stainless steel slab. Someone had put a sheet over the rest of him; the linen went flat where his legs should have been.

Had they filmed that too? Was that the next scene of the documentary? His parents hadn't told him they were being filmed that night in the kitchen, the night before they were lost at sea. Why were they filmed that night of all nights? He'd have remembered a cameraman in the kitchen; that was Pre-Lounge Age, so he didn't have any of the memory issues he had now. If the cameraman was hiding, why didn't his parents say anything? And why hadn't Hector said anything about it? Why hadn't Hector told him the documentary was going to be about his parents? Maybe he already had, but Lowell lacked even the faintest recollection of that little chat.

Holding his throbbing thumb to the air, he opened the sideboard and found the roll of cotton wool next to the bottle of his mother's nail varnish remover; blood red nail enamel had smudged into the label. Overlooked items; nearly everything else (apart from essential furniture like the sideboard and cabinet, beds, sofas and kitchen appliances) had been given away for someone else to enjoy. And so the house had switched from mausoleum to professional accommodation. Hector's description: said as he bundled out a bin bag full of Dad's shoes, slippers and boots.

And there was to be no more mawkish brooding; another humdinger of a lifestyle 'choice' (as though he had any choice) bestowed as Hector cleared the top of the sideboard of ornaments and photos: photos of grandparents – three dead before Lowell was even born. His grandfather, now dead ten years, his father's father, he'd only met a couple of times thanks to some big family fallout. Grandfather (not Granddad, Grandpa – he hadn't known him well enough for that) hadn't approved of his daughter-in-law, said Lowell's father had changed since meeting her: become cold, distant. He was probably right; his parents had doted on each other. So much so, they'd practically shut out the rest of the world, bar Lowell. He had been their little miracle, the baby they thought they could never have.

This had been their lounge, a place for entertaining guests if they'd had any. Lowell returned to the mahogany table that had never been set for a dinner party, and sat down in the same seat Mum used to sit to do her nails. He had already lit a candle and poured the antiseptic disinfectant into a saucer. The saucer was next to his phone. He'd sent Hector a message hours ago asking what his parents were doing in the documentary. But there was still no reply, not even a sarcastic one. Now, Lowell selected the smallest needle in the sewing kit (a freebie from a hotel in Brittany Hector had stayed in recently) and plunged it into the flame of the candle. Once the needle was so hot he could barely hold it, he whipped it out and dipped it into the disinfectant.

The magnifying glass was already in position; he had

inserted the handle in between two hardback books and gaffer taped them all together. The knife, Brighid had just used at dinner, was slotted into the same gap between the books, blade-side down, handle magnified. The magnifier and knife were able to stand unaided, freeing up his hands. The desk lamp was angled accordingly.

Now he thrust his burnt thumb into the lamp's spotlight, next to the knife handle, and with his good hand, picked the needle back up from the saucer. Through the magnifying glass he could see every ridge and whorl; last night's flames had successfully burned off much of the outer skin, but the print, though all turgid and as red as his mother's old nail varnish, remained the same. Biting his lip, he pierced the needle into the flesh that was all bloated like a drowned man; watery puss leaked out. He was doing it for her, getting ready for Nell. He would do anything for Nell.

Brighid's thumbprint was all over the knife handle. The light glaze of salmon oil he'd smeared over the handle, before she had entered the kitchen, had helped. An exact match or even a close match would be impossible to achieve, but if he could just push the lines in the same general direction as Brighid's, maybe it would be enough.

Using the point of the needle, he poked into the tiny folds of plumped tissue; a bead of sweat fell from his forehead, landed on the ball of his burnt thumb; the saline droplet streamed into the ravines of his scalded print, burning like lava. Barely able to breathe, he pushed the needle further, probing deeper into the valleys that had formed in his now dead mother's belly, foetal-formed folds that marked him, labelled him not so special.

The hand holding the needle as it punched at the lines, puncturing paths, burrowing new junctions, trembled like an alcoholic surgeon's; excruciating pain pierced every nerve in his body, a red hot poker pain, impaling, expanding, overwhelming every single part of him until he could take no more, until all he could do was throw the needle back onto the saucer.

He'd give himself five minutes. Five minutes and a carrot: the carrot, the temptation, he had been saving since entering the room. He reached into his pocket and whipped out the stone.

Hector's mysterious catering crew had prepared the supper, and laid the table using the tablecloth (having obviously rummaged through the kitchen drawers) and his parents' silver plated cutlery (previously reserved for Pre-Lounge Age birthdays and Christmas). All Lowell had to do was take the plates out of the oven. Hector had left a note with instructions.

Dinner tonight is hot. It's in the oven.
Two Plates. Yes there's one for you. No need to sulk.

But where did the stone come from? Had Hector stuffed it into the salmon, or was it one of the enigmatic caterers who did that? Maybe the stone had come with the salmon. Maybe the salmon had swallowed the stone?

He hadn't allowed himself to imagine, to dream, until this carrot time: anything else would have been premature, hasty, rude. Could this be the same stone? The same stone he had hurled into the sea? He remembered it now. The stone that had worked its magic, raised an illusion of Nell, all wet lustre, naked.

Couldn't be the same stone though – could it? It was so like the other stone, that magical triangular stone, the stone that had invoked a vision of Nell, but where that stone invoked, this stone ignited: ignited a memory, a memory of opaline skin, of iridescent wetness.

Tremors radiated and pumped through his body, sluicing out the pain whilst the stone warmed in his palm, melting almost; his tongue slipped across the triangular stone; slick, oiled, he gently sank his teeth in, gnawing, licking, chewing.

Then throwing his head back, panting, gasping, he dropped the stone onto the table.

Shivering.

Blinking.

Someone else in the room.

On the table. Fingers tapping the mahogany.

Naked woman. Cross-legged. Thighs apart: pale pelt, crimson inner flesh exposed.

She caught his gaze, closed her legs, shuffled her bottom off the table and stood up.

She was just how he imagined.

'Nell,' he stammered.

Suddenly painfully conscious of his wet beard, he shoved his hands over his mouth; a pathetic futile move – trying to cover up, trying to deny the undeniable. She was a witness; she, with her alabaster body, her very own ivory tower, had entered the room while he'd been drooling all over the stone. Humiliation: total, utter humiliation. Her large slate grey eyes scanned him up and down.

Their first meeting wasn't supposed to be like this.

She shook her head. 'So this is what you get up to when I'm not looking.'

The saliva was stinging his thumb. Should he show her his mutilation? Show her the extent of his commitment? Or would that be too sad, too desperate?

The voice that he had bathed in, been such a tonic through grief, swam in his ears, unfiltered by the radio, as mortification chewed at his hopes like a rabid hyena.

'I've been working really hard, around the clock,'

he said. A tremor in his voice let him down. A morbid inadequacy filled his head, making his neck wilt with the sudden weight of it, making his gaze fall and settle on the soft curling hair nestling between her thighs.

She crossed her arms folding ivory flesh. Did blood flow, did a heart beat under that porcelain doll skin? He longed to touch, to lick; she was just an arm's length away, trembling; she was trembling. Porcelain shaking. Alabaster doll in a quake – perhaps he should catch her, stop her from cracking, from breaking. She moved first, raised her hand and slapped him hard across the cheek.

'My gown,' she growled. 'Where is it?'

What was she talking about?

'BOFO,' she said.

How did she know about his old wash bowl from the Lounge Age? With his pride stinging more than his thumb, kidney, urinary tract, or cheek, Lowell stood up, or at least attempted to stand. It was more a jerky, clumsy elevation of limbs falling all over themselves, a marionette being jolted back into action. Sense of purpose returning, he scurried to the sideboard and dragged out the old BOFO bowl. A garment inside, all neatly folded; her gown he presumed. How it got there, he didn't know. Hector probably.

Nell snatched up the gown, an intricate weave of watery red and green, and plopped it over her head, threading her beautiful arms through the long fluid sleeves, pulling the gown down, over breasts, belly, crotch, thighs. It was a perfect fit. Then she scooped up her platinum hair, sweeping the veil-like mane from her face, exposing not only her finely chiselled bone structure, but also the red indentations on one side of her face, on temple and brow: two rows, like teeth marks.

'Now, if you are quite ready,' she said, looking towards

the radio. 'We have some urgent matters to attend to.'

◎ ◎ ◎

> 'A distinct pattern of the areas affected by last night's phenomenon has emerged.'

A map of the British Isles and Ireland popped up on Brighid's bedroom TV screen.

> 'Each dot represents an incident reporting the whistling, flashing lights and damage to metal structures characteristic of the UNDER. Now, if we join up those dots we can see the path of the UNDER. It's not an exact science, some dots are more spaced, others clustered, but there is a definite linear pattern emerging.'

Two horizontal lines appeared over the dots in the North and Republic of Ireland, traversed eastwards and ended at a vertical line that went straight down the middle of the Irish Sea starting in South West Scotland, crossing the Isle of Man, and finishing in Anglesey. Then, from that vertical line, at the top, middle, and base, three more lines protruded eastwards, joining up the rest of the dots, completing the linear pattern; a pattern that looked much like the upturned stick drawing of three candles on a table.

She changed channels. Another rookie news reader she hadn't seen before. More breaking news. Everything was breaking news at the moment. Still, the scrolling text that followed made her sit bolt-upright in her bed.

FIVE FEARED DEAD IN LIGHT AIRCRAFT CRASH ON THE ISLE OF MAN.

She upped the volume on the remote.

The camera panned across a promenade strewn with fairy-lights, and then settled focus upon the windswept reporter.

> 'The Isle of Man, an island already reeling from the UNDER, now has a plane crash to deal with. At around 10.30 this morning, air traffic control at Ronaldsway here on the Isle of Man received a Mayday call. Shortly afterwards, the plane that had made that Mayday call went down in a field several miles north of the island's capital. Five people were travelling on the small six seater aircraft; their ages range from sixteen to seventy-nine. Police say there is nothing so far to suggest this is in any way linked to the UNDER. An air accident investigation is now under way.'
>
> Visuals returned to the newsroom. 'More news on this when we get it.'

Brighid shuddered; her nerves were already jangled. That stone in the salmon had rendered her speechless. Now she'd had time to digest the stone's surprise appearance, she was able see things a little clearer. Okay, so it was triangular like the stone in her dreams, the stone that goes from barrel, gull foot to sea. But there had to be millions of stones boasting the same shape, formed from as many years erosion. As for 14B's cryptic text about dreams coming true, well she wouldn't bother replying. To think that enigmatic bravado had almost charmed her at first.

This was not the time either for paranoia about news

events being too local for comfort. The crash wasn't linked to the UNDER; right now, she'd just take their word for it. And a couple of Ibuprofen; with this headache, there'd be next to no chance of any rest. All she wanted was a good night's sleep, without dreams.

Despite her best efforts to tiptoe across her room, the wretched floorboards still creaked; it was the same on the stairs. Lowell would probably presume she was sneaking off to the pub. She just needed to break rule two, so she could slug back the ibuprofen, and would rather do that without Lowell's twitching scrutiny.

A slither of light: downstairs, beneath Lowell's door. He was talking, not talking, more whispering, loud urgent whispers. *Almanac*: the only word she could just about make out; the word, *almanac* flanked by panicked incoherent mumblings and a scratching, clawing sound. He was probably talking to himself, plotting more despot rules.

The plates had already been cleared away in the kitchen, tablecloth removed. She'd felt guilty about leaving the table like that, without even offering to wash the dishes, but at the time had been so thrown by that stone, and then 14B's ridiculous message she had just retreated to her room as quickly as possible. Not that Lowell had noticed her leaving, or the slice of sweet potato she'd left on her plate. He'd been so oddly obsessed by the stone himself, she'd presumed the dishes had gone amiss. She certainly hadn't heard any sounds from the kitchen suggesting the dishes were being cleared.

Clutching the glass of water, she headed down the hall practically tiptoeing. She preferred avoiding any arguments about rule two completely contradicting basic human rights.

Careful.

A voice.

Where did it come from?

Watch where you step.

The basement.

It wasn't Lowell. He was in his room. It was a man's voice though; a whiny tone as though mimicking someone.

She put her ear to the edit suite door.

Nothing. Just the thrum of her heart beating.

If Lowell was in his room, who was that in the basement?

Chapter 17

Up until today Brighid had thought Lowell couldn't look any more exhausted. Turns out he could. He'd barely said a word at breakfast. Now, having positioned the audio clip onto the programme line, she waited for Lowell's instruction. It didn't happen.

'Done,' she prompted. 'Want me to play it?'

His eyes flashed up at the monitor then down at his notes. He'd lost his place, forgotten where they were up to.

'Audio clip nine,' she reminded him. He was normally meticulously alert.

'Yes, play it.' He positioned his forefinger onto the appropriate line within his notes and held it there. A fresh bandage on his thumb today: chaotically wrapped and tied, as if it had been dressed in haste.

> 'Let's head back to the time shortly after the Irish gods discovered the camera, when the solar deity Lugh and the ancient sea god Manannan arrived with the camera through the mists to Manannan's Isle, now known as the Isle of Man. Having climbed the hill called Cronk ny Irree Laa they settled themselves down on its summit to contemplate the nature and function of the camera.'

'So this is for local TV?' Brighid asked.

'Sorry?' Lowell yawned, still keeping his finger on his notes.

'It mentions the Isle of Man.'

'Does it?'

'Are you okay?'

'More than okay,' Lowell said. Then he smiled, actually smiled.

She took it as a cue for some office banter. 'Have you unlocked the mystery of the stone yet?'

Lowell's knee hit the desk hard. 'How do you know about the stone?' His fingers were poised over his keyboard, halted mid-action.

'I was there, remember.'

He looked confused, fingers still hovering above the keyboard in suspended animation.

'When I bit into it last night – at dinner. Weird a stone that size turning up in the salmon.'

'Oh. Yes. Yes, it was odd.' His expression softened; his hands slumped to the edge of the desk, pushing his chair to pivot back and forth.

'I've checked my teeth; all intact, so there'll be no hefty law suits for you to worry about,' she said jovially.

Telling Lowell not to worry was normally like telling a dog not to pant in the desert, but he was grinning, be it somewhat wolfishly; he'd have been wagging his tail, if he had one. 'I'm not worried,' he replied.

'Good. What's next? Visuals or audio?'

'Audio clip ten,' he said, tracking his forefinger's position on the notes.

Brighid dragged and dropped the audio then clicked play.

'Although they had not yet worked out how to operate the camera, it was obvious to both Manannan and Lugh that the view through the eye piece was quite different from the view without the camera – a difference similar to cupping and uncupping your hands around your temples. If they kept both eyes open, they could see the world through the camera's eye and their own eye at the same time. Two realities. The camera could block out the periphery, zoom in on something specific; make the small large. And the large small. When Manannan looked at Lugh through the camera whilst keeping his other eye open, it made Lugh appear to be in two places at once. *Makes you look like a cúplood,* Manannan remarked.

A cúplood is someone who can be in two different places at the same time, but unlike Lugh who looked much the same both through the camera's eye and Manannan's eye, a cúplood's two selves can look very different. Completely different. And while we're on the subject of cúploods it's worth mentioning another interesting fact. A cúplood may have numerous incarnations; one self may die and be born again but the other self always remains the same. You could call both, or either, a projected self, but that isn't always an accurate description – that would imply something diaphanous, which is often not the case. Sometimes one's other entity is as solid as stone, as substantial as a dog licking a stone.'

'Audio twenty-two,' Lowell said hoarsely.

'Manannan studied the camera through humid

eyes, his gaze myriads of oceanic hues. Lugh's face alternated from a dazzling effulgence, enough to blind a mortal, to a subtle glow of amber radiance, cheeks burning with fiery sunset. When Lugh glowed with sunset embers, the two deities would seem to melt and become one. But it was whilst Lugh was at his brightest, that they both saw the projection of images within his rays: prophetic images of the future. When Lugh is unable to sleep and his luminous blankets are flapping in the skies above Manannan's Isle, it is not what is now called the aurora borealis we are witnessing, but the cracks in the big reality show.'

Brighid swung round, raised an eyebrow. 'That's not a reference to the UNDER is it?'

Lowell shrugged, too busy reading to look up.

'The UNDER only happened two days ago. And how long's filming been going on – weeks, months? We'd already started post-production before the UNDER had even happened. Are we twisting the script so it fits with current events?'

'Maybe the prophecy's being fulfilled,' he said, gazing at the monitor, his face deadly serious.

'I don't think any mainstream station is going to buy into that. Or are they?'

Lowell was the director. He had to have some of the answers, know where the documentary was heading, both in terms of theme and final airing.

'Why not? This is totally mainstream.' Lowell was not giving up. 'It's the big Zeitgeist. Weird things are happening – stuff that defies logic. People want answers.'

'The only weird thing going on, is you thinking your documentary is suddenly the great oracle.' She would not be divulging her dreams anytime soon.

'If there's anything my mother, taught me it's to have an open mind.'

This was the first time he'd mentioned his parents.

'Things don't always have to be neatly sorted into boxes, tied up with logic. Some things can't be boxed, can't be explained. Maybe that prophecy is one of them.'

'Well let's see what other gems you have in store then.' She grabbed his notes from the desk, then instantly regretted it. The conversation had made her uneasy; picking up the papers was a retort away from topic, a way of seizing control, but it was crass, way out of line.

He snatched the notes back from her.

'Sorry,' she said.

'You should be.'

'I just want to know what it is exactly we're working on. What's the angle? Who's it for?'

'Why do you feel everything has to be explained?' he glowered.

'It's not so outrageous to want to know. I am the editor after all. I have a right to know what I'm working on.'

The frown abruptly unfolded to a supercilious smile. 'Sometimes you have to just go with the flow, even if you can't see the bigger picture. Some things just can't be packed away in logical boxes.'

'Your mother...' she hesitated; that's who the documentary was about really, originally, before he started steering the script to a new agenda. It was a tribute to his dead parents who obviously had a thing about Irish mythology and other illogical unpackables. 'Is she no longer with us?' She already knew the answer. Maybe Lowell needed to talk about it. Bottling up grief was no good for anyone. Perhaps the documentary had started out with that in mind, as a cathartic assignment, as a way of coming to terms with his mother's death.

'And so into another box,' Lowell murmured vaguely, swinging in his chair, a faraway gaze into nowhere, lost to his own abstractions.

Normally, that brief trespass into the secret script would have sent Lowell into orbit. If he'd popped some extra-strong pain-killers for his thumb, it would have to be a horse tranquiliser to chill Lowell to this degree. Maybe his thumb had gone all septic and was affecting his brain. Something was affecting him. He was acting completely out of character.

'So if you can't say what channel or distributor this is headed for, I'm guessing there's been no agreements set up that side of things yet?'

Reclining in his chair, Lowell sighed. 'You always have to have your logical framework don't you?'

'What's wrong with that?'

'What are you so afraid of?'

'Nothing. Shall we move on to the next audio clip?'

'Okay, run it.'

'Which one?'

He sat forward, scanned his notes. 'I've lost my place.'

'The last audio was clip ten.'

'Fifteen. Bring in audio fifteen.'

Brighid selected, dragged and dropped it on to the timeline, then clicked play.

'It all began with the tree that landed to Earth; a tree that produced both apples and acorns: an apple-oak tree.

So as the leaves were blowing in the wind all the way to Spain, the acorns were tumbling hither and thither. And although some acorns never left Ireland, others crossed seas and oceans; in fact, acorns ended up falling in every land, on every continent. Eventually, trees sprouted from the acorns, and more trees sprouted from the acorns of those trees. It's said time behaves differently around such trees, in those magical places where acorns landed.

As for the abundant crop of apples, well that swiftly perished. Only one soul tasted that fruit; a dog made it over to the tree before anyone was able to stop him. He took a bite from one of the apples, and then stood up on his hind legs, turned to the people gathered there and spoke. It was just one word, *Delicious*, spoken in Ancient Primitive Irish (the forerunner to Primitive Irish and Old Irish), but it was enough to confirm, as if any further proof was needed, that this was indeed a very special tree. The dog ran away after that, still on his hind legs, and was rarely seen again.

But the apples, acorns, leaves, and camera aren't all that came with the tree. The tree had landed on Earth with a symbol already scratched into its bark. That marking eventually became known as the ceirtduir, symbol of the apple and oak hybrid. And this ceirtduir symbol would turn out to be the forerunner, the original first letter, the seed of what a thousand or so years later developed into the Ogham alphabet, the ancient tree alphabet of the Celts. But the original letter of the Ogham was so sacred that it was never etched onto stone. The ceirtduir letter was only ever written, inscribed on wood. All such inscriptions have long since perished. And so the ceirtduir became the lost, forgotten letter of the Ogham tree alphabet.

But who carved the ceirtduir symbol into the tree before the tree had even landed on Earth? Where were they when they carved it? And what did it mean? Now these are questions that would keep the Tuatha Dé

Danann debating for a very long time indeed.'

The clip accompanying the start of this commentary, a shot of an oak tree, with apple graphics already seamlessly overlaid, was followed by a number of incredible aerial views sweeping over rooftops, hills, open fields and sea, the occasional acorn slipping into shot.

Lunchtime arrived, 1pm on the dot. Tomato soup and a cheerless salad made of rocket leaves and more tomato. Lowell, as always, exuded the distinct impression he would prefer to be elsewhere. In between popping in and out of his bedroom and checking his mobile he mostly was. And once again he was opting for his own choice in lunch: a crisp sandwich, brown sauce slathered all over it. This he consumed in four rabid mouthfuls.

'The footage of the dog isn't ready yet, insert some black in there for now,' Lowell mumbled, brown sauce and crisp crumbs peppering his beard. Most of the afternoon had already passed editing in more aerial shots, breaking up the commentary, and adding music, Tchaikovsky's 'Waltz of the Flowers' from the Nutcracker Suite, to accompany the acorns' various voyages across the globe.

'Actually,' Lowell added, 'if you could shift the black filler a bit further up the timeline, we've missed something. Find clip title *Brocéliande* and slot that in beforehand.'

She scratched her wrist, turned to face him. 'Brocéliande? The Forêt de Paimpont, Brittany? I was there just a couple of weeks ago.'

Lowell released a small nod of disinterest.

Aerial footage swept forest tops, approached a clearing, a lake, the Étang de Comper, the Arthurian Lake of Vivian, and then a scattering of houses. Camera viewpoint descended on a road sign, Folle Pensée, then ascended again as the forest deepened. A dirt track, gateposts and ancient trees. The clip ended.

Her heart was pounding. 'Is there any more footage for that area?'

Filming had practically stopped on Tessy's driveway, she was sure of it.

'Next it's the clip labelled, *Letter*.' Lowell wiped his beard, ignored her question. 'It's a still-frame, twelve seconds duration; line it up with the commentary about the ceirtduir.'

The Forêt de Paimpont was famous for its connections with Celtic legends, so if they were going to film a forest, it was hardly a surprise one of those forests might be the Forest of Paimpont. Once this contract was over, and she had some money in the bank, she'd already decided to make finding Tessy, helping Tessy, a priority.

'Letter,' Lowell said.

Brighid dragged the clip onto the timeline: a close-up of the ceirtduir symbol that had apparently been carved into the tree that dropped from the sky.

Her heart missed a beat.

'That symbol,' she exclaimed. 'I've seen it before. It was on the news. It's the pattern, the path of the UNDER.'

Chapter 18

HOT CHOCOLATE.

Would it be such a crime? Probably.

It was more the lure of clutching a warm mug between her hands. The bedroom was cold. The wind was rattling the single glazed sash window. Brighid set her book down, a thriller about a stalker with an obsession for numbers she was too tired to read, and grabbed the TV remote control. News on, she shifted the pillow behind her so she could sit up and then bunched the quilt up all the way to her chin.

Her lips tightened.

The map showing the path of the UNDER was being broadcast again; there was no denying it was an exact match to the ceirtduir, an exact match to the original ceirtduir pattern engraved into the tree that fell to earth.

That was some co-incidence for the ceirtduir pattern to be in the documentary. But for the twitch above his beard, Lowell had remained completely unresponsive to any questions on the subject. Dinner had been conducted in complete silence and it was back to the usual vegetarian fare; this evening it was spinach and asparagus in a roasted red pepper. Lowell had oven chips. Seeing him scattering them across the baking tray, she had asked if there were any going spare. Rather than just saying no, he practically snarled. Turned out he didn't have much of an appetite. He ate barely half a plate full and threw the rest away.

She'd check the date on that ceirtduir clip next chance she got. It had to be a new shot; that was the only possible explanation. The ceirtduir, lost letter of the Ogham alphabet, was a fabrication, she was sure of it, hastily added into the documentary after the path of the UNDER was broadcast. They weren't just making a documentary, they were making a cake, a nut cake. Lowell was shopping for ingredients, for more nuts to add to the mix. It was obvious now: the documentary was part epitaph, part promo for a cult – Lowell was baking facts, stirring in news items to add credibility, trying to recruit more nutters into the mix. He was probably part of a large, lucrative cult set-up. That's where the money for the production had to be coming from: the swanky edit suite, her wages. If her bank balance could afford it, she'd be outraged.

And why was there no mention of the ceirtduir on the news? Where was the guest scholar who would have recognised the pattern as one of the original letters in the Ogham alphabet? If she could believe the documentary, the ceirtduir was long forgotten, if it ever existed at all. Maybe the ceirtduir was never even part of the Ogham.

Her mobile vibrated. She grabbed it off the bedside table.

A new message.

From Kate. At last.

You know that collie you broke your heart over as a kid? Algo. Wasn't that his name? Well, I know he must be long dead by now but there's a dog the spitting image in a pound in Ireland at the moment.

Kate had attached a screenshot image of a Facebook post.

The dog in the photo, peering mournfully through the bars of the pound, didn't just look like Algo, he was his absolute double. A white long-haired collie with a sweep of black across his chest like an open ended parenthesis. Just like Algo.

Like someone had painted a large left-hand bracket in black ink.

And he had one brown eye. One blue eye.

Just like Algo.

She scrolled down.

MALE COLLIE FOUND STRAYING. 5 DAYS RECLAIM TIME NOW ALMOST UP. NEEDS TO BE OUT OF THE POUND ASAP OR WILL BE PUT TO SLEEP. IF YOU HAVE A SPACE ON YOUR SOFA FOR THIS BOY PLEASE CONTACT THE POUND. DESCRIBED AS INTELLIGENT, INTUITIVE, AND A LITTLE OBSESSIVE. JUST NEEDS SOME TLC.

If she were in Ireland right now she'd be tempted. Actually, were she not tied to this contract she'd be looking up ferry times. Even though there was absolutely no way it could be Algo – Algo had disappeared around twenty years ago, she had torn the neighbourhood up looking for him – the thought of a dog so like Algo being on death row actually made her eyes sting.

There was just the one possible sighting, two months after he'd gone missing. She had a call from someone saying they'd spotted a couple leading a dog that looked just like Algo onto a yellow fishing boat docked up at Southport pier. She dodged school the next day pretending to have tonsillitis, took three buses across Merseyside, trying to track down that yellow fishing boat.

She tapped back.

If only. Hey, been trying to reach you. Where've you been?

Waiting for Kate's response her gaze wandered back to the TV.

'We're just going to show you some footage rapidly becoming a global internet sensation. Tom Dunne uploaded his video to YouTube two days ago and it's already accumulated over five million views. What you're seeing now is the UNDER as it crosses Tom's back garden in County Antrim. Tom is zooming in on the lights. Now, this is the bit that is the great bone of contention; the footage here has been put into slow motion, and is now fully zoomed in, so all we can see are the two golden lights, orbs of light, and inside each light there appears to be the faint outline of wings, a head, arms, legs. Now the lights merge, and those tiny diaphanous figures seem to embrace.

Tom's isn't the only video purporting to show some sort of life-form inside the lights of the UNDER. At least fifty other similar videos have since been uploaded onto YouTube. Many of today's papers are also running stories with photos seeming to show strange creatures inside the lights. On Twitter and forums all over the net, arguments are raging. On one side you have the sceptics – denouncing the videos and photos as an elaborate hoax – and on the other side you have the *believers*; the moniker they've given themselves speaks for itself. Hotels in regions affected by the UNDER are reporting a sudden surge in bookings in the last twenty four hours, thanks to what's been dubbed, *Fairy Tourism*. People from all around the world are flocking to see the UNDER and those disputed winged creatures for themselves.'

◎ ◎ ◎

'Faeries,' Nell said, shaking her head derisively.

Lowell darted over to the television and switched it off. He'd only turned it on to see the map of the UNDER, to see if it was, as Brighid said, anything like the ceirtduir. If it was, he was sure Nell would be impressed he'd made the connection. No need to mention Brighid's original input.

'Always the faeries.' The way she was sitting, all curled like that in the armchair, red gown tickling her ankles, she reminded him of a scarlet petal; a petal blown out from the space inside the radio. The radio was still gurgling and crackling away in the background. Now she was here, the hiss of the untuned radio was starting to get quite annoying. Not that she gave any impression of being irritated by it, quite the opposite. It was the only thing she was interested in; she wasn't just listening, there with her elbow leaning into the armchair's armrest, chin in hand, ear craned, she was transfixed.

He plonked his hand down on the dining table, attempted to lean casually. She didn't notice. He checked his phone. Still no messages from Hector.

'Faeries only have to sneeze and they grab all the attention.' She was mumbling into her hand, talking more to the radio than to him. 'Show the public a particular stone or a certain dog and they wouldn't even blink.'

Lowell felt his face flush, crimson suffusing from ear to ear. He knew exactly which stone she was talking about. It had fallen to the floor the moment she had first appeared. It was still there, one corner poking into the lounge carpet. Was that what she was complaining about? Should he pick the stone up now, or wait until she wasn't looking? Difficult to think, being so tired.

Exhaustion was making his cheek twitch. Coffee would be a bad idea. Caffeine would just make him twitch more. Besides, the kettle was in the kitchen now. He didn't want to leave Nell. It had been hard enough being stuck all day in the edit suite basement hoping she was still upstairs, hoping she'd still be there when he'd finished work. Each hour had felt like a year.

23.16. The bathroom door unlocked and opened.

He whipped the phone/almanac out from his pocket and entered the data.

Brighid was trying to tiptoe across the landing. She closed her bedroom door.

The floorboard creaked, left-side again (a creature of habit): 23:17. She got into bed.

He closed the almanac, slipped it back in his pocket. 'There's a bed upstairs if you need it,' he said.

He placed the emphasis on *you*; he didn't want her thinking he was suggesting anything, especially as she seemed so uninterested. He might have told her the same thing last night. He couldn't remember. He was sure he hadn't gone upstairs last night, made his parents' bed. Were there even any spare sheets since Hector's big clear out? She could have the sofa and quilt. He'd take the armchair.

'I'm okay,' she said, burrowing herself deeper into the armchair. Eyes, bright, alert, focussed only on the radio.

Did she ever sleep?

The lighting probably didn't help.

He turned on the lamp, headed for the main light switch next to the door. Then he hesitated; if he killed the main light, she might think he was setting the scene to make a pass.

'Light on or off?' He tried to sound ambivalent.

Nell stretched her thin arms, gown sleeves tumbling

past her small, sharp elbows. 'Off.'

In the dimmed light, her skin emitted a faint glow as though moon light seeped through her pores. He hadn't noticed last night, or didn't remember noticing. Maybe they'd kept the main light on. They had stayed up all night, as far as he recalled, just hanging out listening to the radio. The radio had mostly remained tuned to the whistlers, to the celestial choir of electromagnetic noise; it was like their very own personal concert. He'd gotten over initial embarrassments; even the tic had almost reached a standstill. Almost. Having Nell near him was pure heaven. Or would be pure heaven, if he could relax a bit more, if he could think of something witty that would make her laugh. Maybe then, she'd be less interested in the radio.

A new voice had come through on the radio last night.

He'd been racking his brains all day trying to remember who it was, what they said, but it was all just one big blank. That voice, and what Nell said after the voice, something about no-one ever really going away (virtually the only thing she said all night if his memory served him right) had mopped away every last blot of remorse and wretchedness. Almost. He was still none the wiser about his parents' guest appearance in the documentary. He didn't dare ask Nell. He might have already asked her and forgotten. Perhaps he'd already asked her at least twenty times already. That would explain why she seemed so bored of his company.

He needed to stop fretting, stop worrying about whether he should grab the stone up from the carpet or not. He sank down onto the sofa. The quilt was still folded, perched on the back cushion. To lie down would be rude. But he could tilt his head back, rest his heavy, stinging eyes.

So as far as he could tell, in the last twenty-four hours

Nell had barely moved from the armchair. She'd just been sitting there, listening to the radio all night and all day. That's what she was doing when he left this morning, *and* when he popped in after lunch. Before tea and after tea, she was still at it. Each time, he had wanted to throw himself on top of her; the relief she was still there was overwhelming. But each time he had managed to restrain himself. It wasn't just down to fear of rejection; every now and again, when the light changed, the sun came out through the clouds, Nell seemed to have a translucence about her. Sometimes he swore he saw the armchair shimmering through her. If he hugged her he might just slip right through her.

She wasn't interested in food. Her only demand was honey. Luckily, there was a jar in the kitchen. Hector must have bought it. She had a sore throat, made her voice all husky, as if it wasn't already sexy enough. She said it was the journey had made her throat all scratchy.

Beyond his leaden eyelashes, something moved.

Nell. She was leaning forward in the armchair, unscrewing the lid from the honey jar.

He sat bolt upright. 'Are you sure you don't want toast or chips or something with that?'

Her eyes met his.

'Chips with honey?'

It was difficult to think with his head inside this vast vat of numbness; that's what it was like, when Nell looked at him. His head was stuck inside a mammoth vat full of elephant strength gaga juice, but with peepholes so he could still see her eyes. He had gone and disappointed her again. 'But you haven't eaten. You must be hungry.'

She set the honey jar down next to the radio, uncurled her arm towards him, and then tickled his beard with her fingers.

There was no hiding the ferocity of his blush.

The hairs on his arms bristled like dog hair under a hairdryer.

This was the first time she'd touched him, as far as he could remember. Her fingers were softly pummelling and pulling his beard.

He licked his lips, turned to face her.

She was already releasing her celestial gaze, already returning her focus to the radio.

'Nell,' he whispered.

Nell's brow promptly creased.

Acute terrestrial rawness resumed.

'Sorry,' he muttered. She was trying to concentrate on the radio, she didn't want interruptions.

'Shut up,' Angel Lips snapped.

She might have napped in between, while he was at work, borrowed the keys from Hector, and sneaked out to the chippy. She didn't look like someone who ate a lot of chips. He closed his eyes, if he could just sleep half an hour that might be enough.

The faux leather on the armchair was rustling.

She was standing up.

Getting closer.

He didn't dare open his eyes. Was this the moment he'd been waiting for? She was standing over him, touching his arm, sliding down next him. Her breath was on his ear.

Then she whispered: 'Your mum wants to talk to you again.'

Chapter 19

Lowell was already in the kitchen, looking more tired than ever, hastily tapping something into his smartphone.

'Good to see you're on time,' he said, not looking up.

'As always.'

She wouldn't allow him to irritate her today. She poured her share (the last portion) from the coffee pot.

She had barely slept, and when she had, her subconscious had insisted on throwing her back under the castle. Staying up, watching the news might have been a better idea but her head had enough to deal with, without adding oddball headlines to the mix. It was all far too Tessy-esque. Wherever Tessy was right now, she'd be having a field day over the UNDER, but then she doubted Tessy watched the news.

'How's your thumb?' she asked, taking a much needed sip of coffee.

Lowell prodded the bandage, the same chaotic dressing as yesterday. 'Okay.'

A woman coughed. Muffled by a door, the cough had come from the direction of the hall, from the sitting room, or Lowell's bedroom.

Another cough. Source now confirmed: Lowell's room.

'Who's that?' she asked, without thinking.

'You heard her?' He sounded surprised.

'The woman coughing? Yes.' She couldn't help but

hear. It had been loud and phlegmy.

Without saying another word, he rushed out of the kitchen to join the mystery lady coughing her guts out in his room.

Lowell and the woman were talking. She had a husky voice, like someone who smoked sixty-a-day.

'And why shouldn't she hear me?' she rasped.

They were talking about her.

Lowell mumbled something inaudible.

'Your memory's getting better,' the woman said. 'Maybe I want her to hear me now. Maybe I'm tired of hiding.' She coughed again. 'Do you remember who you heard last night?'

'No,' he replied, sounding wary. 'Who?'

'All in good time.'

Lowell shuffled out from his bedroom, locked his door, and returned to the kitchen just as Brighid was savouring the last gulp of coffee, the last mouthful of kiwi fruit. She could only hope the woman had a key to get out, at the very least so she could buy herself some cough mixture. Why was she hiding anyway?

He checked the clock. 'Twenty-five seconds and then we start. Are you ready?'

If he were to whip out a starting pistol the moment the second hand hit twelve it really wouldn't surprise her.

'Do I have time to clean my teeth?'

'Nope.'

Side-stepping the imaginary starting blocks, she plonked her mug into the sink. Her teeth would have to wait until lunchtime, again. Lowell was back to his old miserable self.

Edit suite unlocked, Lowell opened the door, ushering her in. He remained on the top step, locking the door behind them.

As she descended the stairway her gaze fell upon a large blue plastic dog bed next to the arched door. She swung round, faced Lowell. 'I didn't know you had a dog.'

The light cord, dangling halfway down the stairway, struck Lowell's shoulder, and as it did, he seemed to hold his breath, to stop breathing. When the light cord hit him again, he blinked and gasped sharply as if he'd just resurfaced, been underwater.

'What the __?' he said, tone as flat as a deflated paddling pool.

The top lip of the bed had been chewed away. There was no blanket. No cushion.

'So where is he?' she asked.

He marched down the steps, ignoring her questions, ignoring the bed, switched on the computer, and sat down at the editing desk. Pen in hand, he started tapping against the side of the table, impatient drumming filling time, waiting for the computer to boot up.

Booted.

Sitting down, she double clicked on the icon to open the editing software. Lowell thumbed through his notes, puckering and sucking on his lips, emitting a pith-pith-pith sound like a paddling pool slowly releasing air.

'You don't need to come in this afternoon,' he said suddenly.

'Why?'

'Urgent maintenance.'

'What maintenance? Everything's working fine.'

'Bring in audio twenty-nine.'

She dragged, dropped and played.

'All will be revealed when the ancient Irish dog runs in meadows once more.'

'The visuals for that aren't quite ready yet. Insert some black for now on both tracks A and B. There's a lot to go in, so allow ten minutes on A. And put continuous black on track B.' He rose from his chair, picked up his notes. 'I'm just popping upstairs for a couple of minutes. Can I trust you?'

He stood there silently waiting for a response, his rose blossom cheeks turning deep crimson; finally realising the demeaning confirmation he was waiting for was not going to happen he hurried away, locking the door behind him.

She added both blank fillers as instructed, then seized a perfect opportunity to look up the date of the ceirtduir freeze-frame. It *had* to have been created *after* the news had broadcast the UNDER path.

Having located the folder of clips edited in the day before, she clicked to open. All she needed to do was find the right file, right click and get the properties.

A pop up window demanded a password. It was accompanied by a loud beep; loud enough for Lowell to hear just as he was opening the edit suite door.

He was back in his seat so quick that its support wheels span, bringing him into collision with the desk. The impact caused the monitors to vibrate, emphasising the trail of the cursor closing the folder window.

'Hey,' he snarled, 'that's confidential.'

'I was only trying to take a look at yesterday's clips – nothing I haven't seen before.'

'You only open what I tell you to open.' He tugged at a loose thread on his bandage.

'It was only old clips,' she repeated. Just how old, she was no closer to finding out.

'That's not the point __' A sudden whimper punctured his breath; he clasped his left-side.

'Are you okay?'

'Yes,' he grimaced.

'You don't look okay.'

His cheeks were so red they looked like two scarlet roses blooming out from bearded shrubbery. Perspiration shone like morning dew.

'It's just a stitch.'

'Are you sure?

'Do you want a medical certificate?'

Working with Lowell was as much fun as root canal treatment.

He sat down, stashed his notes back on the table, away from her legible reach. 'Let's return our focus to today's clips.' He cleared his throat. 'Okay, after the black filler on track A, insert the clip: *She falls into a deep slumber*.'

Brighid dragged, dropped and played.

A close up of water rippling.

The out of shot sounds of children squealing and giggling, laughter bouncing off unseen swimming pool walls.

An overhead artificial light shining on the water making it sparkle.

The camera panned to the water's edge, to the waves lapping against cracked duck-egg blue tiles.

'Let's run the commentary,' Lowell said. 'Audio one hundred and forty-two.'

> 'They say every time someone says they don't believe in faeries, a faerie dies. That's not strictly true; it's more a part of that person that dies, a piece of self that falls into a deep sleep. Sometimes, it reawakens in dreams and in madness, in our last hours and beyond. Those we drifted away from as a child have a knack of returning.'

She shivered. It suddenly felt cold down here.

'Audio ninety-seven.'

> 'Shudder. Co-incidents so co-incidental they're enough to make you shudder. Like ice cream on sensitive teeth.'

'Hang on,' Lowell interjected. 'Let's bring in the visuals, then we'll run the whole audio. Grab the clip labelled, *Ice cream*.'

She peered up at the door at the top of the stone stairs; if it came to it, could she push her weight through, force the door open?

She dragged, dropped and played. A frozen, dull feeling in the pit of her stomach.

A close up of a mouth wide open.

A dentist's chair.

A dentist's-eye-view on incisors, molars.

The stiffness in the back of her neck eased. She'd half expected to see Tessy handing her the ice cream. Exhaustion was squeezing her nerves like a mangle; the crazy dreams and subsequent insomnia were making her paranoid.

> 'How do you stop those shudders? Toughen the outer layer. Desensitise.'

A dull thrumming sound. Her mobile. In her cardigan pocket.

'Sorry,' she said, hitting pause on the timeline. She'd check for messages later, no use upsetting the boss anymore than she already had.

'It might be important. Might be someone worrying about you, you know because of the UNDER and that.'

Was this Lowell's sensitive side shining through? A rare event, she wouldn't waste. She fished out her mobile. A message from 14B. She opened it.

MEET ME ON 13:50 DOUGLAS 2 PORT ERIN STEAM TRAIN. H.

Talk about presumptuous, he didn't even ask. Lucky for him she had the afternoon free. But why H? Was 14B starting to unpeel his identity?

She slipped her mobile back into her pocket and ran the rest of the audio.

> 'A careful shuffle of the cards is all that's needed to reunite the king and queen of hearts. Throw an ace between them and you get bucket and spades. Ice cream interlude.'

'Are we missing something?' she asked. 'That doesn't make any sense.'

'Bring in the clip labelled, *Shuffle*.'

A panning shot of a shopping arcade: Wok Inn, Pizza Express, Palmer's Second-hand Book Emporium.

'That's Falmouth. Round the corner from where I used to work.'

She'd practically survived on noodles or pizza during tight deadlines. Palmers had only lasted one summer, had switched its business online, the same summer she was there. The camera halted, shifted focus to the Ford Mondeo waiting at the traffic lights. The lights switched to green. The clip ended.

'The dead sometimes choose to hang around awhile, unseen, watching over loved ones. But what's the point in lingering on the rooftops across the street if you always had the curtains drawn. They'd barely catch a glimpse of you, apart from pizza and Tesco deliveries. A mother who loves her garden so much would always be glad to see a son watering the plants, even if he was just using the washing-up bowl, even if it was only the flowers nearest the window, and even if the water was all dirty and soapy. Still, the soap helped keep the bugs away. Such a shame when pests start gnawing away at the blossoms.'

'Is that *you* the commentary's talking about?'

She had started to imagine the documentary was less the epitaph for Lowell's parents and more pointing a finger at her instead; so it was a relief the commentary was swinging back to more comfortable territory.

'Why would you ask that?'

She shrugged. 'Just thought it might be.'

'You look tired.' He said it without looking up. As though he was still reading from his notes. 'Nightmares aren't stopping you sleeping are they?'

'No,' she said numbly.

She hadn't told him about the dreams. He was guessing. And she did look tired. Two weeks of broken sleep did that.

He scratched his beard. 'Audio clip twelve.'

'Oops, hope we haven't hit any raw nerves.'

She stopped the audio. 'Who's this aimed at?'

'The target audience.'

'Yes. And who are they?'

He checked his notes again. 'Play audio twelve.'

> 'Let's change the subject. How about we go back to the Tuatha Dé Danann? Whatever happened to them? Well, the very same magic they had used to conjure the spirit of the stone out of the mountains, the Tuatha Dé Danann used on themselves, shape-shifting the hill innards into subterranean kingdoms. Many stories have been told about the people of these kingdoms; some true, some not so true, but eventually, over the years, the Tuatha Dé Danann have been relegated to mythical status. When you've lived inside the hills for so long, it's easy for people to dismiss you, to not recognise your aura rising out of the heather, riding in the clouds, hitching a ride on musical notes, surfing on a chip paper blowing up the street, or doing the commentary for this documentary.'

Bit of a capricious turn for a documentary to take, a bit of tongue in cheek bravado, but the bloke on commentary had the ideal voice to pull it off; his was a deep, powerful voice, a voice that wouldn't be out of sync on the lips of a Shakespearean actor, a voice that could run with any theatrical twist.

'Eighteen. Run audio clip eighteen.'

'Well, I know at least one person who'd love this,' she mumbled wryly, thinking aloud, answering her own question. Not just Tessy, so would a public now thirsty for anything remotely fairy. Target audience sorted.

'Run the audio.'

'Roll forward to 1605. Lord Barnes-Nicol, an aristocratic recluse, stepped out from the shadows, suddenly lit by a fire in his belly. Cobwebs in the manor's great dining hall were dusted away and its chairs filled by influential high society. Their chatter, when Lord Barnes-Nicol was out of earshot, was adorned with a tentative enthusiasm for this transformation in confidence and geniality. The largest mouths of those fortunate enough to get on the guest list remarked to the curious less fortunate that he was a most accommodating host: a great raconteur, philosopher and historian. One or two on the guest list found him to be somewhat coarse, perhaps a little too pushy. *One really had to make one's own opportunities,* was repeated as his chorus quote. He'd used the same line when he slapped the serving maid's backside, but such indiscretions didn't dent his popularity; he was, after all, by his own boastful admission, great friends with the king reigning in the lands across the water.'

'Clip eighteen was one minute fourteen seconds.' Lowell said, peering up from his notes. 'The next audio clip, clip forty-four, is two minutes fifteen seconds.'

Brighid dropped audio forty-four onto the programme line.

'Hang on, before you play it.' Lowell studied his paperwork. 'The footage to go with audio clips eighteen and forty-four is an exact fit. Let's slot that visual in now.'

'It's only a perfect fit if there're no glitches.' She wasn't sure why she even bothered saying it, Lowell would probably insist on keeping them in anyway.

'Let's run it. Bring in the clip labelled, *House Interior*.'

Brighid dragged, dropped and played.

Visuals commenced with a slow tracking shot through the corridors of a manor house. Hall tracking continued over the next piece of audio.

'Lord Barnes-Nicol's exuberant transformation occurred around the same time a terrible storm hit the island. Gales sent the sea in tumult for more than seven days. Many local fishermen lost their lives. Church bells tolled. Winds taunted widows' dresses. The entire island was in shock.

Lord Barnes-Nicol used this to his advantage. He pushed out the conspiracy that a certain woman living locally had created the tempest. Of course she had nothing to do with the storm. The only thing she was guilty of was persistently visiting Lord Barnes-Nicol in his dreams.

The first time a conscious Lord Barnes-Nicol set eyes upon her, standing on the steps of St Patrick's chapel, he very nearly tumbled headfirst into one of the new graves still awaiting their headstone. Gripping his chest, willing his heartbeat to return to normal, he decided there and then that he had found his scapegoat for the fishermen's tragedy, and that very same day hastily instigated the necessary legal proceedings. By doing this, he not only hoped it would put a stop to the dreams that had haunted him most of his adult life, but he would also gather favour with King James the First, otherwise known as James the Sixth of Scotland, who was fresh on the English throne just two years earlier. James was passionate about routing out sorcery in his kingdom.

But, a regal nod from across the sea was a passing insignificance; the trial, Lord Barnes-Nicol had prompted, also signalled the end of an era. For it was around this time millions of magical folk simultaneously vanished from the face of the earth; be it from under the gorse, or beneath the willow, any of them above ground and beyond the faerie mounds just simply disappeared. Or so it would seem. The Tuatha Dé Danann, still in their kingdoms under the hills were largely left unscathed.

One by one though, survivors began manifesting a strange, new disease: intangiblitis. Symptoms include depletion of magic abilities, abdominal itching and amnesia. It's a long, drawn out illness, many have succumbed to. Some species of the magical variety are more susceptible than others; the lesser winged diminutae have been particularly vulnerable, whereas the stonier varieties of the cúplood race boast just a handful of cases; a gritty lot, you never quite know where they'll turn up. One moment they're part of a supporting wall, next minute they're sitting on the next table to you slurping tea.

But then, that's just faerie stories, apparently. Or actually not; the lesser winged diminutae were momentarily *discovered* by renowned botanist Dr Jacques Trudeau in 1931. A lesser winged diminuta had flown in through Trudeau's lab window and landed right on his desk, allowing him ten minutes of observations and elation, but then the lesser winged diminuta had a dizzy spell and completely vanished. Poor Trudeau had been so excited about the transparent sacking dangling from the thorax of the lesser winged diminuta, he promptly assumed it to be the pinnacle of his career, but when he got to discover the really interesting stuff, he could no longer quite believe his eyes. The gramophone player played Clyde McCoy and his

> Orchestra's 'Sugar Blues', a sweet little accompaniment for Dr Trudeau whilst he hastily destroyed all manic notes and sketches on the subject. A six month sabbatical on the Riviera soon soothed any fears he was losing his mind.'

Camera viewpoint reached the end of the corridor and then entered the open doorway there.

> 'And here in the Great Hall is the very face of intolerance, a face that made many fear their own belief in magic, a face that caused so many to vanish, the portrait of Lord Barnes-Nicol, or Lord Barnacle as he liked to be called.'

Lord Barnacle. It was the same name, same face as her dream.

Chapter 20

Brighid was going against production orders, indulging in a quick caffeine fix before meeting 14B (or H as he was now calling himself), packed lunch already dumped in the nearest public bin; she didn't have the stomach for it. Anyway, how did the production caterers even know she'd need lunch-on-the-go? The café was full of lunchtime diners: life carrying on as normal, *there you go love*. She had heard that phrase over and over; it came from the woman behind the counter, words as knackered as the table's scratched laminate, yet the voice held a reassuring upbeat stoicism of business as usual, the cogs beating around the wheel regular as clockwork. She sipped her coffee, unfolded the newspaper someone had left behind. Headline: *MORE SPECTACULAR LIGHTS FORECAST.* She read on.

> *The aurora borealis, normally restricted to more northern latitudes, is predicted to light up Manx skies for more nights to come.*

A local weekly, headline decided pre-UNDER. Pre-UNDER, actually pre-visit-to-Tessy, pre-screwball-dreams, was a time when things, most things, tallied. Now there was so much that didn't make sense that even hiding beneath the Gobi desert wouldn't provide enough sand and gravel to bury all the head-fuck. And now Lord Barnacle had made an appearance outside her dreams, the odds against logic were stacking up as high as the Tower of Babel.

She knocked back some more coffee.

The ceirtduir clip *had* to have been created after the UNDER. Same as that blatant reference to the UNDER, those so-called cracks in the big reality show masquerading as the aurora borealis. Lowell was just riding on the back of news stories.

Another slug of coffee.

And maybe the other coincidences weren't so crazy either. With a bit of cogitation, the odds could start stacking in logic's favour. If the documentary was also documenting myth and legend then she might have heard or read the story before, or seen it in some cartoon adaptation as a kid. She had been worrying about money when she arrived in France, had just sent off so many job applications she'd forgotten the one she must have sent to the Isle of Man. That was one for her subconscious to remember, and remember it did, along with Lord Barnacle, a latent snapshot from something she must have read about the Isle of Man years earlier. Throw in the snippets of Brocéliande's Arthurian legend (coffee stop – tourist leaflets of the lady in the lake), mix in that illustrative reproduction of Lord Barnacle's portrait she must have seen before) and voila: the dream. Dream premiere at Tessy's, screening inside Brighid's head every night since. And what about the documentary filming the very neighbourhood she used to work? Coincidence. And the filming outside Tessy's house? Well, why not? Brocéliande was one of the prime locations for Celtic classics.

As for the UNDER itself, well, she'd leave that for the geeks to work out – conspiracy theories must be bouncing all over the place on the net. Then there were the so called fairies inside the lights of the UNDER, she was with the sceptics on that one. Tom Dunne, YouTube hoax extraordinaire, should be working for Lowell with those graphics skills.

Perhaps he was.

She checked her watch. 1.25pm. One last gulp of coffee.

Why was it the two times she'd actually got out and about on this island she ended up sitting next to same old lady? She was dressed in the same yellow-green herringbone tweed, hair still set and sprayed as solid as a helmet, skin like papyrus, slurping on her tea, lips pursed camel-like.

The old lady glanced sideways at Brighid. 'You alright?' she asked, curling her camel mouth, unveiling those toothless gums. Her strong French accent plus dental deficiency meant she was difficult to understand.

'I was miles away.'

'Desert,' Helmet Head replied.

'Sorry?'

'That's the problem,' she said loudly, shouting almost. 'You're looking for the desert.' She wasn't just speaking to Brighid, but to the whole café. Her growls pounded each table, reverberated off the counter. Everyone stopped what they were doing, turned to face her; the splutter of frying eggs punctuated the silence. 'Well it ain't here. Not anymore.' Her papyrus fist slammed the table.

Then, a sudden thud at the window.

The café's collective gaze switched from the old lady to the glob of blood now trickling down the window. A flutter of feathers spiralled to the ground. A sparrow lay dead on the pavement. As the café's clientele gawped and debated, another thud shook the window, another glob of blood: a second sparrow – life obliterated, its only sin, not recognising the invisible boundaries, believing everything was as it appeared; skull smashed by the realisation of glass, it fell on top of the other.

The old lady set her cup down onto the saucer and shook her helmet head. 'Blinded by the sand, blinded by milieu.'

Pursing her camel mouth, she stood up, heaved her camel coat from the back of her chair. She was inserting her stick arms into the coat when the waitress marched over.

'What's this about no desserts? We've got ice-creams, cakes, knickerbocker glories.'

'*Desert,* you silly cow, *desert.*'

Once outside, Helmet Head shooed away the shoppers that had gathered around the dead birds. Propping her hand onto the window, she bent down, scooped up one of the dead birds, kissed the sticky plumed chest and stuffed the bird in her camel coat pocket. Still stooped, leaning against the window, she grabbed the second bird, kissed its mashed head and shoved that bird into the other pocket.

Brighid asked the waitress for directions to the train station; they were swiftly delivered, all sour and curdled.

Now, having exited the café, turning right as instructed, Brighid stepped on gummy feathers. A fly, with a piece missing from its wing, was already at the scene, its siren buzzing to the call of blood. Gruesome voyeurism made her pause to look at the fatal spillage on the window, at the wing-bitten fly already wading in the slowly congealing blood.

Following the directions for Lord Street, she quickened her pace. The station might well be only ten minutes away, but she still needed to buy a ticket. Helmet Head was up ahead, pockets bulging with the dead birds, a wing poking out of each pocket.

On the opposite pavement, outside Clague's Knives and Pegs, stood the man with the facial scabs the old lady had sat with in the pub. He removed his baseball cap and waved it at Helmet Head. Helmet Head and dead birds crossed the road to join him. Once there, she kissed him on both scarred cheeks; Cordial greetings completed, Helmet Head snatched the cap and slapped him across the arm with it, knocking the camera strapped over his shoulder. Camera caught and saved, the man nursed the lens, and as he did, the old lady plonked the cap back onto his head. The baseball cap hid some of the wounds.

With no sign of 14B outside the copper domed, red-bricked Victorian station, Brighid headed inside, but he wasn't in the waiting area either. The 13:50 was due to leave in five minutes. Her mobile vibrated. 14B. She opened the text.

GET ON TRAIN. H

Despite his infuriating messages, her heart was racing. Ticket in hand, she ran to the platform. A sign on the white picket fencing warned: *YOU ARE BEING WATCHED.* She scanned each carriage; all were full (probably those fairy tourists), but 14B was nowhere to be seen. She just had the last one, the front carriage, to check when the station master signalled. She either boarded or missed the train. She closed the wooden door behind her, and sat down. She had the one remaining empty carriage and as she had the place to herself, she stretched out.

The carriage door opened. An elderly man smiled, clocked the empty seats, turned and shouted, 'Marge over here!' Scrambling hands, elbows, shoulders onto the doorframe, he hauled himself into the carriage, his walking stick walloping her leg.

'Oh, I'm sorry,' he said breathlessly.

She had seen him somewhere before. 'Didn't hurt,' she lied.

'Really, Archie, you're so clumsy,' said a voice from the platform.

Brighid rubbed her leg. 'Weren't you in the pub the other night?' she asked. He was the old man who'd knocked back too many rums.

Archie's eyes widened, he slapped his finger to his mouth.

A lady of bulky build, white perm and orange makeup, was next up, hauling herself in, handbag, plastic shopping bag and all.

She stood awhile, inspected the carriage. 'I can't sit there,' she exclaimed, swinging round to look at Archie, her handbag very nearly swiping Brighid in the face. 'I'll be sick. You know I can't travel backwards.'

'You can sit next to me,' Brighid offered. 'Seat's not taken.'

The locomotive's whistle screamed.

'Won't be the same,' Marge shouted over the whistle. 'It's mine and Archibald's special day.'

Hissing steam billowed from the engine.

With the train shunting into motion, Brighid got up, changed seats with Archie (Archibald, whatever his name was).

Satisfied, Marge plumped down next to Archie, patted him on the hand. 'Our son Stuart's got a private pilot's licence, yer know.'

Brighid nodded vaguely.

'He was supposed to fly us to Scotland. Hotel was booked and everything.'

Archie shrugged and rolled his eyes. 'We're still here.'

'Always a reason for everything,' Marge sighed, patting

his hand again. 'So Archibald said, why don't we get the train to Ballasalla instead? Not the same I know, but we haven't been on the train for years. It's our wedding anniversary you know. Forty years.' Marge widened her eyes and paused.

This was the bit Brighid was supposed to express disbelief, tell her she didn't look old enough, etcetera, etcetera, yadda, yadda, yadda. In no mood for such social niceties, she simply nodded again. The slightest encouragement now, could see the next hour doomed to small talk. She preferred to look out the window, to the outskirts of Douglas, to the small industrial estate, cottages all in a row, barrels stacked outside a brewery, more cottages in a row.

'Forty years,' Marge repeated, leaning forward, still ferreting.

Trapped. 'Congratulations.' She had to say something.

Marge whipped the plastic bag from the floor and brandished it aloft. 'A treat for the anniversary,' she announced proudly.

There it was, she knew it, one word of encouragement was all it took.

'Lamb,' Archie elaborated.

'I'm making a stew tonight. Our anniversary meal.' The bag of lamb was lowered to nestle on Marge's lap. 'You married?'

Brighid shook her head.

'Ahhhh, never mind. Maybe one day.' She caressed her perm and smiled sympathetically, her scarlet lipstick bleeding into peripheral lines.

The backward motion of the train was starting to make Brighid feel slightly nauseous.

'Aye, a Bobbie Dazzler like her,' Archie piped up.

Marge linked her arm tightly into Archie's. 'When's

your stop?'

'Last stop,' Brighid replied, enjoying the irritation it caused.

'Is that where you live, Port Erin?' Archie was treading dangerous ground; Marge's scarlet nails were pressing into the sleeve of his blazer, tent pins claiming domain.

Brighid shook her head.

The tent pins dug down. Conversation stopped.

Light rain, soot black, flitted through the open window. Brighid rose to her feet, swaying with the rocking motion of the train, pushed the window shut. Sitting back down, she grabbed her mobile, keyed a text.

Where are you?
B

Send.

Steam wafted past the window, a thick mist, swirling, spiralling, dissolving into nothing. Sheep clambered over a collapsed section of dry stone wall, pioneering a new field for the herd. The train continued panting and hissing further up the track: psss – hah; pss – hah; pss – hah.

A stench of decomposing lamb meat. Marge must have smelled it too because she promptly removed the plastic bag from her lap, shifted it onto the seat beside her, and twisted the bag's handles into a knot.

The train's whistle screeched like a banshee.

First stop: Port Soderick. A couple of doors slammed further down the train. Brighid pressed her cheek against the glass, peering for a view of 14B, just in case he happened to be on the train, just in case he'd decided to catch up with the train at Port Soderick.

'You can see them can't you?' Marge whispered eagerly, any former grievances cast aside. She prodded at the window, pointing at a section of platform vacant of people. 'Themselves, the little folk.'

A cloud of insects hung in the air outside. 'The midgies?'

'Faeries,' Archie interjected with conviction. 'Any Manx man worth his salt believes in them.'

'Don't waste your breath,' Marge snarled.

The whistle shrieked and they were off again. Brighid kept the same vigilance at the next station, Santon, but there was still no sign of 14B, still no reply to her text message, and thankfully no more talk of fairies from her fellow passengers.

The clouds parted. A dash of warmth. Sunlight dappled fallen leaves, wreathing them in honey hues. She stretched her legs, sat back. A thread of smoky vapour stitched a line in the gap between clouds: a plane passing overhead. She closed her eyes, resting, but avoiding sleep, avoiding dreams. She thought back to Helmet Head, to the man with her, to his scars – the full extent of damage was only evident once the baseball cap had been whipped away – scars that crossed from cheek to cheek, temple to temple, running right down the centre of his face, tracking widow's peak, nose and chin. They had formed a pattern, the outline of which itched at her eyelids, tickled her consciousness.

And then it dawned.

The searing realisation stung her eyes. It was the shape of the ceirtduir; his scars were the same shape as the UNDER path.

New scars they may be, but those scabby wounds had bled, dried and started to seal before the UNDER had even happened.

◎ ◎ ◎

14:35. Lowell knocked on the edit suite door. 'Nell.'

'I thought I told you to stay in the lounge.' Her voice sounded a long way away. Further away than the edit suite desk.

'What are you doing down there?'

'Maintenance.'

'I can help.'

'No.' She sighed wearily. 'Go and listen to the radio.'

◎ ◎ ◎

End of the line for Archie and Marge: Ballasalla station, and a fresh swipe at Brighid's ankle.

'Sorry love,' said Marge cheerily, handing the walking stick back to Archie.

He had notched up forty years with Marge, experience enough to gag any farewells. He shut the door behind them, peered in at Brighid and winked.

Switching to the opposite seat, Brighid was glad to at last have the carriage to herself. She rubbed her ankle, dear old Marge had given it a hammering. She rolled up the hem of her jeans, pulled down her sock, checked for injuries. A red mark; it'd probably bruise but then fade. No lasting damage, unlike the scars that etched the map of the UNDER all over that man's face. Had they been fresh marks the explanation would be straightforward enough – he'd be just some nutter (or victim of said nutter) who'd got a bit carried away revelling in current affairs, but those crumbling scabs were definitely pre-UNDER, at least a couple of weeks pre-UNDER.

She must have imagined it. Exhaustion was playing tricks with her eyes, morphing the man's scabs, implanting the shape playing so much on her mind.

It was the only possible explanation.

The train huffed and chugged out of the station, entering a level crossing. Amongst the cars waiting behind the freshly painted red and white gates, a driver at the front of the queue, on Brighid's side, clasped her steering wheel so tight her knuckles were bone-white. Being caught in a standstill, sitting surrounded by metal, probably made people feel vulnerable post- UNDER. The train carriage was of wooden construction (bar the nuts and bolts and braces holding it all together) with a vaulted ceiling, barrel-vaulted, like the castle jail. Like the barrel they rolled Nell in. The train's wheels would be metal. And the track. Either warping would send the train hop, skipping and jumping over the sidings and into whatever solid object happened to be available.

But there were no signs of any more UNDERs, and the train, at least now as it passed through the level crossing, was doing a comforting snail's pace. Outside, a man set his heavy looking suitcase down onto the pavement next to the gates and waited, parker hood up, head down against the drizzle. He hadn't bothered zipping the coat, had left it open to the elements, open for a good scratch of his belly. As Archie and Marge shuffled up beside him, joining the queue to cross, he abruptly stopped scratching and turned to look at them; the motion caused his hood to fall onto his shoulders, unveiling a flash of golden corkscrew curls. The tan across his flawless profile had not been achieved in these chilly climes. He was Model Man: airbrushed perfection. Too perfect. Suddenly aware of Model Man's intense scrutiny, Archie glanced across at the man beside him and then squinted as though he was looking directly at the sun. Turning away, he nodded. Model Man smiled broadly back, displaying a dazzling set of teeth as white as the fencing holding back the cars.

The locomotive whistle screamed.

What was 14B playing at? Why had he insisted on getting her on this train? Why hadn't he replied to her text?

Steam gushed, rolling, fraying over fields of sheep.

Ballabeg, Colby, Port St Mary, and then Port Erin station. End of the line.

The cold air hit her as soon as she stepped onto the platform, her cotton coat offering little protection. She blamed the deceptive warmth of the autumn sun shining in through her bedroom window as she'd gotten ready. She blamed her own vanity: this coat suited her more than Tessy's coat, aesthetics over comfort for the day out with 14B. Date. If she was to be totally honest with herself, that's what she'd thought of it as, a date. And it was that fizz: first date jitters (how stupid) and sunshine that had supplied the metaphoric sand to bury the babel. As irritating as he might be, that message this morning had her running around like some dumb love-struck idiot. Desperate. She wasn't. This was the last time she'd ever agree to meet up with him again.

Cold wind: that was the only thing greeting her on the platform. And the grit and cinders carried with it. Cinders in the breeze. Cinders on the platform. But no 14B.

She reached for her mobile.

In Port Erin. Where are you?
B

Send.

She plonked herself down on the nearest bench and waited for 14B, or 14B's reply, or the next train back, whichever came first.

Two lads, Goths, approached.

'Anyone sat here?' asked the one with long black hair. Skateboard released from under his arm, he flipped it so one end rested on the ground, flicking his hair, as he did so, revealing blonde roots the colour of his skin.

She moved up the bench giving them space.

'They know more than they're letting on,' he said, talking to his defiantly ginger friend and depositing himself on the end of the bench.

Ginger Goth swiftly stamped on his own skateboard, flipping it into a vertical position, and sat down, next to Brighid, wedging into what little space his friend's sprawling, outstretched limbs had left for him. 'I read on some forum that scientists reckon it's the end of the world but they're not telling us 'cos they don't want mass panic.' He raised his hands to the air, coat sleeves pre-ripped to display arms boasting a myriad of bangles, jangling his arms in mock panic.

Blonde roots scratched his head with a skull-ringed finger and narrowed his kohl-edged eyes. 'Apocalyptic hysteria.'

Her mobile vibrated.

MISSED YOU. H

No apologies. No sorry for sending you on a wild goose chase. No sorry for making you a cold damp muppet on a bench waiting for nothing. No sorry I can't even tell you my full bloody name. No sorry for the constant CAPS LOCK; it was every message, like he was shouting.

She left the Goths and made her way over to the man in uniform, the station master or the ticket collector, warming his hands around a mug of steaming tea.

'Is there a train to Peel from here?' she asked.

'Christ, no. You'd have to get the train into Douglas and then bus it.' He took a slurp of tea. 'There's only the one last train back, and we just got word that's been cancelled.'

'Your bosses worrying there might be another UNDER?'

'Sorry?'

'I'm surprised you're even running at all. Could be dangerous if the UNDER comes along again and damages the tracks.'

He scratched an itch under his cap. 'I don't know what__'

Someone grabbed her arm. Ginger Goth. 'Taxi's waiting for you.'

'I haven't ordered any taxi.'

Ginger Goth pointed at the taxi parked up opposite the station 'Taxi driver says you have.'

She marched across the road. Why couldn't the taxi driver just haul himself out the taxi, instead of getting everyone else running around looking for his fare?

'Peel?' the driver asked, rolling down the window.

It was 14B.

'Where've you been?' she asked.

'Hop in,' he said, already rolling the window back up.

'No. Not until you tell me what you're playing at.'

The window rolled back down. 'I'm not playing at anything.'

'So why did you get me to go on that bloody train when you had absolutely no intention of meeting me.'

'Careful,' he exclaimed.

She pressed herself against the taxi as a double-decker bus swept past her.

She stepped back, dug her hands into her pockets, and turned away. She'd grab a taxi but not this one.

'I wanted to see you,' he said.

She swung back round. 'Well you have a funny way of going about it.'

'Please,' he urged. 'Get in.'

She opened the rear door, sat down on the backseat.

Turning his head, checking the road before pulling out, his dark hair flopped over his shoulder; his gloved fingers drummed on the steering wheel as a car passed.

A gap in the traffic.

He steered the taxi out onto the road and radioed base. 'Just leaving Port Erin. Heading for Peel.'

The response came back as static.

'What made you think I'd have the afternoon off?'

'You did, didn't you?'

'Yes, but__'

His eyes met hers in the mirror. 'Wasn't there some urgent maintenance needed doing?'

'How do you know?'

'I know one of the tech guys.'

'Small island,' she smiled.

'I have to grab any chance I can. I keep getting called away.'

'That sounds like a man with a girlfriend,' she replied warily. She kept getting the distinct impression he was hiding something.

'No. Nothing like that.'

'I didn't know you were a taxi driver,' she said, changing the subject.

Wiping away the condensation she peered out of the window. The moisture smudged her view, smearing the lines between hedgerow and pavement. The wipers were scraping the windscreen, screeching and gnawing, screeching and gnawing.

'I'm full of surprises,' he said eventually. 'You don't even know the half of it yet.'

Screeching and gnawing.

'What d'you mean?'

The taxi radio hissed static.

'For fuck's sake,' he breathed. 'There's no getting away from them.'

The rain fell harder, heavier. The screeching stopped; the windscreen wipers pushed on, lubricated.

There's been another UNDER,' he said suddenly.

'When?'

'Not so long after your train passed. UNDER twisted the railway lines somewhere between Ballabeg and Colby stations.'

'Jesus. How d'you know?'

'I'm a taxi driver, I know everything. Lucky for you the UNDER wasn't earlier.'

Red light. He stopped at the traffic lights.

'Are they saying what's behind it yet?' Who *they* were, she wasn't exactly sure: the government, the military, scientists, the media, the pope, taxi headquarters, any of them, all of them.

Green. He released the handbrake. 'I've heard all sorts of theories driving this cab. Had one fella in earlier, totally convinced it was UFOs.'

'UFOs? And why not.'

Was that really her saying that? She didn't believe in UFOs. She was the bastion of grounded logic. But what happens to the grounded, when that ground, reason, shifts? What do they recommend during an earthquake? Stay away from windows, brace yourself, shield yourself from falling debris. The chaos was falling thick and fast, she was anchoring down as best she could, but parts of the rope kept fraying.

'Had another one there in the back, thought it was the CIA. Reckoned it was some new covert weapon they were using to scare the masses into submission. The Americans would come to the rescue. All hail the leaders of the free world. That or some terrorist group were doing it. Politics of Fear.'

Science and politics: now this was more comfortable territory – a theory clobbering the absurd. A man-made threat that could be explained, possibly fixed. Order resumed, anchored down.

'Then there was the priest. I asked him what he thought. At first he didn't give anything away, just sat there doing the rosary. But then, when he was getting out of the taxi, he suddenly turned to me, said he'd seen them. Angels, he called them. I guess some of them are.'

'Probably as confused as the rest of us.'

14B shifted into fifth gear, looked at her in the mirror. 'I'm not confused.'

'You think it's some sort of new weapon as well?'

'It's not that,' he replied confidently. 'It's the faeries, the little folk, the magical folk, the sidhe, gods, angels, ghosts, call them what you will. It's funny, they've been going on about faerie tourism in the news – they don't know how right they are. But it's not just the faerie seekers who have come from all over, so have the faeries, the magical folk, in all their various forms.' He rubbed his nose with the back of his hand. 'Most of them were taken – years ago – they just vanished one day__'

'I've heard this before. What is it, a local fairy story?'

'I suppose you could call it that. Now they've returned. It's one great big magical reunion. The sparks and metal bending are just down to plain old transdimensional differences. Then there're the whoops of joy. I'd say most of the flashes of light come from that.'

'Nice one. But, seriously, what do you really think?'

'Question is, what do you think? Where do you think they've been all this time? Were they buried so deep you didn't even know they were there?'

She shook her head. 'How should I know?'

He grinned at her in the mirror. 'No-one's getting hurt by the UNDER, not really hurt. Sure there're a few scratches and bruises here and there, but that's just people getting in the way, jerking their heads forward at the last minute, craning their necks to look at the lights. And who do you think just phoned Manx National Transport HQ telling them their rail tracks are knackered? You see, they're not here to cause harm.'

He picked up the radio. Static bludgeoning debate. 'Approaching Peel. What font colour do you use? Blue; that's it. Get blue font ready for the arrivals column.'

The radio spat back static.

A truck lumbered out from the entrance of a quarry. 14B flicked the indicator, glanced into the mirror and overtook.

He'd probably told the same yarn to every customer since the UNDER, now UNDER in plural. He was just spilling out the same old spiel. Had forgotten this rendition of the spiel hadn't finished spieling, hadn't wound up revealing the wind up that it was. The final punch line was left untold.

That wasn't the only thing that had been left untold. 'Harry, Henry, Hannibal which one is it?'

'Sorry?'

'Your name.'

'Oh, that would just be rushing things.' He grinned into the mirror.

She scanned the front of the taxi. No ID card. Ordinarily that would worry her.

'Anyway,' he murmured. 'Remember in the pub, you mentioned there was something vaguely familiar about me?'

'Yes?'

He breathed in, as though he was about to say

something important.

The radio hissed.

'Go on,' she prompted, as soon as the radio had calmed.

He simply shook his head.

The taxi entered the thirty mph zone of Peel, turned several corners, trundled down the road and stopped halfway down the hill, right outside Lowell's house.

She got out of the cab, leaned towards the driver's open window. 'Well, thanks for the lift. You go through some roundabout ways to pick up a customer.'

He smiled at that, his oak brown gaze meeting hers. He licked his lips, one pulsing second. 'I'd kiss you if I wasn't on duty.'

The radio screeched.

With that he sighed, wound the window up, pulled off the kerb and drove down the rest of the hill.

She was just fishing the front door key from her pocket when something dawned on her. She stopped what she was doing, peered back down the hill; the taxi was already at the junction at the bottom of the road. He'd dropped her off right outside Lowell's house, yet she hadn't even told him the address.

◎ ◎ ◎

Moments of genius have a knack of grabbing you just when you least expect them.

Lowell had left the basement this morning for a bit of private space, a place to writhe in agony, to bite his hand and stop the screams. He couldn't do it in the edit suite in front of Brighid, and he couldn't do it in his lounge/bedroom on account of Nell, so he had locked himself in the bathroom, and whilst there, awaiting the kidney stone's next excruciating instalment, he'd used the opportunity to take a piss. It was while he was pissing blood and sand that the idea of the text came. Zipped up, hands washed (careful not to wet his bandage), he had fished his fingers into his pocket and found not just his own smartphone. Hector's phone was there too.

With absolutely no recollection on just how Hector's phone had found its way into his pocket, Lowell concluded that he had probably found it lying around during one of his more hazy moments and had therefore put it in his pocket for safekeeping. Whatever the reason, it was the perfect tool for the brains behind the scene. Act number whatever – Brighid Gets Stood Up.

H for Hector and also for handler, for the handler pulling her strings, controlling her movements with the prod of his fingers. H the handler, or puppet master, had got her out of the way, under control, boxed in – on the slow train, on the straight and narrow so to speak.

But then Hector, not H the handler, the other H, Hector, had come through on the radio.

'I'm driving a bloody taxi aren't I'.

'Where d'you get the taxi from?' Lowell had asked.

'It's called improvisation. You'd know all about that now wouldn't you?'

Hector had sounded annoyed; so annoyed, Lowell had forgotten to ask him how and why he'd filmed his parents. Hector obviously didn't like it when *he* was the one being played. Anyway wasn't Lowell just making sure everything went to script?

GIVE HER THE AFTERNOON OFF – BASEMENT WILL BE OUT OF BOUNDS. TELL HER URGENT MAINTENANCE.

That's what it said in the manual this morning. Access

limited to authorised personnel – Brighid not included. So what better way to get her out of the way, then booting her out after the morning shift, sending her on a fruitless excursion?

Now, afternoon was slipping towards early evening, Nell was still down there in the basement. Yes, she'd ordered him to stay in the lounge but surely, he was allowed to use the bathroom? That's where he was now, taping a note to the toilet lid.

Brighid
You'll be eating alone tonight. Still no excuse for letting standards slip, so please make sure you're on time – 7pm. Don't be late. Don't wait. Eat everything on your plate. But remember – eat slowly. You should know the rules by now – chew and swallow before putting the next lot of food onto your fork or spoon. The saltcellar stays in the cupboard – already sufficient salt in your meal. Drink the glass of water provided, but don't go to the tap for more. And stay away from the kettle – and the pub.
Regards
Lowell

He'd nearly signed it *H* – force of habit after the texts he'd sent. That note replaced babysitting duties, she was old enough to eat alone. He wasn't ignoring Hector's stupid rules, just trusting the staff more.

The dietary rules could still be an elaborate wind up courtesy of Hector, written to make him look like an uptight idiot, but as this had neither been confirmed nor denied (he'd forgotten to ask), it was his job to make sure the rules were followed. Sort of.

For the first time in ages, since way back in Pre-Lounge Age, his old self was very nearly shining through. *No-one really goes,* that's what Nell had said (a gem of a phrase, both bead and brain had retained and treasured). He'd rubbed and rubbed every single bead just in case specifics to that mystery voice had slipped down string of Gr2 and R3. It was a complete waste of time; he couldn't even remember whether they were male or female; let alone who it was and what they'd actually said.

They were dead though.

That much he did remember.

Was it too much to hope it might be Mum? Or Dad? If no-one really goes, if the dead can talk via the radio, then his parents had to still be about somewhere.

Was that what Nell was doing down there, liaising with the dead?

The toilet lid. Best place for the note. He couldn't risk putting it in Brighid's bedroom. She might not go there until later; she might choose to hang out in the sitting room instead; but if he put the note in the sitting room, she might just go to her bedroom, bypass the sitting room altogether. With all that traipsing around looking for H and all that cold air, she'd need a wee. The bathroom would be the one place she'd definitely go.

A taxi was pulling up outside.

Lowell ran downstairs to the lounge, closed the door. The almanac was out ready, next to the radio. The front door was opening.

Time noted: blue font.

Brighid charged upstairs, coming to a standstill on the loose floorboard outside the bathroom. She knocked. No answer (obviously). Then she opened the door, sighed loudly, muttered something along the lines of, *for fuck's sake,* and slammed the toilet lid up against the cistern. She released the contents of her full, cold bladder then flushed the toilet. Hands washed. Bathroom exited. She walked across the landing.

Good little puppet – now run along - shoo.

16:47, she entered her bedroom and closed the door.

Marionette show over. Surely now he'd be allowed into the basement?

Chapter 21

Lowell's little note was not just infuriating, but downright insulting. Brighid rubbed herself dry as she paced her bedroom. The long, hot shower hadn't calmed her down at all, she was still livid. Bedroom curtains drawn, she draped the towel on to the radiator beneath and switched the television on.

On-screen graphics flashed Breaking News: NEW UNDER HITS UK AND IRELAND. Brighid upped the volume.

> '...these incidents, or reported incidents, we must stress many of them are yet to be substantiated, although not in the exact same locations do appear to follow the same pattern as the first UNDER, affecting the same linear areas of Northern England, Scotland, Wales, Northern Ireland, the Irish Republic, and the Isle of Man. Social media, viewers' emails, and reports coming in from our own correspondents, all record the second UNDER taking place at twenty-five past three this afternoon.'

Her coat was still on the bed where she'd thrown it. She reached into the pocket, snatched up her mobile and texted 14B/H.

How did you know my address?

Dropping her phone onto the bed, she shivered. The cold from all that waiting around on the train platform was still there in her bones, despite the hot shower. She had half-expected Lowell to start clawing at the door, demanding to know if she was swallowing any shower water.

The draught from the large single-glazed sash window was making the curtains billow. Her allocated bleach white towel was stifling any barely warm air from the radiator.

She marched across the room to the chest of drawers, treading on at least one loose floorboard, and tugged at the faux antique handles of the largest drawer, the bottom one; it glided open with the unease of a cheap flat pack; a flat pack with walnut stained façade. She whipped out her jumper, slid the thick Aran knit over her head. It was too big for her, went all the way down past her thighs, touched her knees almost. Rolling and folding up the sleeves, another 'Breaking News' graphic flashed up on screen.

ISLE OF MAN LIGHT AIRCRAFT CRASH: FIVE CONFIRMED DEAD. FOUR OF THE VICTIMS OF TUESDAY'S CRASH WERE FROM THE SAME FAMILY.

Still no reply from 14B, she headed downstairs.

Lowell was there.

He was standing outside the edit suite with his ear pressed against the door.

He visibly jumped when he saw her, then slunk away from the door.

'I got your note,' she said coldly. 'I have absolutely no intention of going to the pub, but I fancy a cup of tea with my meal, so I'll be putting the kettle on.'

Lowell blinked. Clenched and unclenched, then scratched his hands.

'Okay,' he mouthed silently.

'What are you listening for? Is someone down there?'

'No,' he muttered. 'I wasn't listening to anything.'

'Are they still there?'

His cheek twitched. 'Who?'

'The techies. Whoever's doing the maintenance.'

14B's techie friend. Of course. That's how he'd known her address. His friend must have told him. And there was she, stewing in the shower imagining all sorts, worrying 14B had followed her back from the pub that night.

Lowell checked his watch, glared back up at her. 'It's ten past seven.'

She sighed wearily and sauntered off to the kitchen.

◎ ◎ ◎

The waiting was driving him crazy. So crazy, the almanac had missed a few basic planetary movements. Brighid's hair was damp as she waltzed downstairs for dinner. Bare legs and bare feet. Toenails painted blue. Looking too comfortable. At home. She wouldn't walk around the reception of a hotel like that. Data for bathroom entry, he had successfully inputted, but she'd been that long in the shower, the numbers for the bathroom exit had gotten lost between his ear and whatever Nell was doing behind the door, so too had the fact Mars had failed to enter the kitchen at 19:00.

22:40 The floorboard next to Brighid's bed creaked.

22:41 Nell was still down in the basement.

He was tempted to pull up a corner of the carpet, point the microphone at the floorboards, but the last time he did that, he was being watched.

23:10 He could take no more.

This time he didn't knock, just slipped his key into the edit suite door, and silently let himself in.

He had been speculating about the arched door in the basement ever since the edit suite had first opened for business; he'd assumed it was either the door to a neighbour's cellar, or the entrance to an old smuggler's tunnel, passageway to a cave further up the coast. The latter was his favourite option.

This was the first time he'd seen the arched door open.

Nell was at its threshold, stretching every fibre of her being trying to peer in; she was so focussed on whatever it was beyond the door that she didn't notice Lowell sneaking into the basement, creeping down the steps. Once at the bottom, he ensconced himself to the obscured area next to the stairway and squatted down.

The dog bed was still there. Same dog bed as his dreams. Nell must have pushed it to one side when she'd opened the door.

His eyes were starting to adjust to the darkness beyond Tessy's luminous hair. What lay there, beyond her beautiful, sunshine hair, was something quite different to anything he'd imagined.

That darkness wasn't contained in any passageway, or cellar; that would be like comparing a glass of water to an ocean, several oceans – no, the darkness had a density, a volume of endless dimensions. Lowell had space in his basement.

Literally.

Actual space.

The intergalactic variety.

She was drifting away from space, sniffing the air now, tiptoeing around the basement, sweeping the air with her exquisite nose. He had showers every morning these days so the creases forming on her brow couldn't be down to him; he quickly sniffed his armpits just in case. Beyond the deodorant, there was perhaps a hint of onion, but it had been an especially stressing day.

He scratched the itch in his belly button.

'You,' she breathed, swinging round, hurtling her gaze directly at him.

He rose to his feet, barely able to breathe.

'I thought I told you to stay in the lounge.'

Despite his ears prickling as though they were being dragged back flat against his head, despite the almost overwhelming dizziness, he mustered enough breath to ask: 'Where does the door lead to?'

The rage fogging her eyes cleared. 'If I told you I'd only have to make you forget again.'

'Tell me.' He swallowed hard, clasping the memory beads. 'Please tell me.'

'Drop,' she said.

'What?'

She raised an eyebrow, shook her head. 'The beads.'

He let go, slammed his hands to his sides.

'Good boy.'

Was that how she saw him? Sure, she was probably a few years older than him but__

'The garden.'

'Sorry what?' he stammered.

'The Garden.' This time she said it with such absolute veneration that if she were to write it down, he was sure it would be with a capital G.

'What Garden?'

'The Garden where dreams grow and nothing perishes.'

Lowell rubbed his head. 'But where does the door lead

to?'

Nell sighed. 'The garden.'

'I don't have a garden, apart from the patch at the front, but that's not really a garden, and the backyard.'

Her face softened; her eyes, slate grey pools, sparkled. She stepped closer, her hand brushed his cheek, tugging playfully at his beard. He was in Nirvana, Valhalla, whatever paradise was called, he was there.

'I forget sometimes you don't know who you are.' Her fingers were weaving through his chin hair. Her thumb touched his lips.

Then she let go of his beard, furrowed her brow; eyes clouding, she turned away.

A shooting pain whipped through his bladder. He clutched his side. *Look at me. Look at me.* He needed her balm to numb it all away.

Her eyes met his. He was back in paradise.

'You were there for Brighid when she needed you most,' she murmured.

'I was?' It was difficult to concentrate, to understand anything she was saying; her words had the substance of honey dribbling over his ears. He was adrift. Pain-free. Those eyes, those celestial eyes. He was in Heaven. No need to scratch his hands or belly button anymore. Locks could go unlocked. Almanacs could go unwritten. Grief could be forgotten. He could stay here forever just bathing in her eyes.

Nell was trembling; she actually seemed nervous.

He had never seen her look so gorgeous. This vulnerability made her seem smaller, less intimidating…

…irresistible…

He scooped her shoulders into his hands, cradling her sunshine and moonlight hair, threw his tongue on to her cheek.

He was flying through paradise at a million miles per hour. He closed his eyes savouring it.

Paradise shook.

Lowell tottered.

A razor-sharp pain blasted through his urinary tract.

The kidney stone.

He toppled forwards, hands grasping the air wildly for something to hold on to. And then he found the floor.

When he looked up, Nell was no longer there.

◎ ◎ ◎

Up until now the dream was always the same. This time, however, what Brighid saw after tumbling from her vampire Barbie carriage, was not the muddy, reed-choked pond, but a swimming pool.

A huge Olympic-size swimming pool.

Light strummed at ripples on the water's surface.

Fluorescent light strips, illuminating the pool, dangled from the domed ceiling she was floating through; the middle strip pulsed on and off, making a faint buzzing sound which the dome amplified, making it sound like an electric snore, rattling in and out. The dome's green paint was frayed and peeling like a huge nostril caked in dried snot; that's how she saw it, used to see it. A laminated poster, next to the life belt, on the once familiar mustard yellow tiled wall, declared there was to be *Strictly No Petting.*

O'Shea's Aquadrome: the site of many a dreaded swimming class the nuns had made them go to every week. It was here she'd turned away from the imaginary Magio, and the bullying that went along with him.

All the dream regulars had gathered around the tiled pool side, cracked duck-egg blue tiles: the women with their bonnets, coifs and shawls, the men in their breeches and woollen stockings. All still purporting to be from a time centuries before. Now though, each and everyone seemed somehow more vivid, tangible. Scanning their faces for a clue to their essence, she found no Perspex transparency. Skin was not semi-flesh, half-skin, half the air and tiles behind; it was wind battered, knackered, fresh, plump, spotted, flushed – not fuzzy, features sketched in, dream-like, but alive. Chlorine merged with that melange of dead Loughtan sheep and peat smoke aromas.

Plunging into the pool, she registered no splashing sound, no wetness of skin, no dragging of clothes, no cessation of air; she opened her mouth, but it was not water that flooded past her parted lips, but vanilla laden oxygen. As she plummeted further and further into the depths of the pool the lights above faded, dwindling to darkness. She waited for the floor to hit her feet, or where she imagined her feet to be, but its tiles remained elusive: there was nothing to halt her, to bounce her out of descent. There was no bottom to this pool. Impulses to swim against the force, to fight the descending current remained mere twinges in her limbs, ineffectual pulses as productive as sparked matches underwater.

Then, just as she thought she'd be sinking forever, the tide shifted.

Wallop.

Contractions in the darkness.

Wallop. Light.

Nell was there, drifting about underwater, with that same look of torment.

Something was pulling Brighid, dragging her upwards and away at such a speed that first Nell and then the crowd abruptly blurred into ruffles of red and green. Red and green morphed into the aurora borealis.

The aurora borealis shifted, sharpened and solidified into a coat.

Brighid saw herself wearing that coat, her red and green coat.

She was standing next to O'Shea's no petting poster, lingering amongst the crowd. Drawing closer, zooming in, it was as if she was looking at herself through a well-lit mirror; her features were that clear, even down to the open pores around her nose, the stray hair missed last time she'd plucked her eyebrows, the faint scar she'd gotten as a kid falling from her bike during the cycling proficiency test.

Her mirror-self turned its head and as it did, an invisible current, as strong as the one in the pool, hurled Brighid to her doppelganger's ear and thrust her down the aural canal.

Ear needed syringing.

With that thought and the mental note to make an appointment with the surgery nurse she realised she was now inside her own head, or her own mirror image, thinking and seeing inside her own mirror-self.

Someone pinched her elbow.

'Sorry about that, you stepped into shot,' he said, flicking his oversized fringe.

14B. He was holding what looked like a professional broadcast type of camera.

'Word of advice, don't be so hard on Lowell.'

'You know him?'

'He's sweating it back there, worrying, always worrying. He thinks you hate him. He just wants to be loved. He's just a puppy really.'

A girl, skin all pasty pallor, who'd been slipping though the crowd, halted suddenly at the pool side, stiffening in fright.

Then the girl screamed.

More shouts followed, not from the girl – she was now all doughy silence.

The crowd was thinning; people were fleeing to the EXIT, splashing through the footbath, heading for the changing rooms, in noticeable terror. The few remaining, regrouped and huddled, forming a yawning gap, bestowing Brighid's consciousness, and 14B's lens, with an uninterrupted view of the pool.

As she stared into the water, as 14B gripped the camera zooming in on the swimming pool, another smell infused her nostrils, purging the stinging chlorine. Vanilla: its essence so salient she could almost see it rising out from the water as steam, like candle smoke, reaching towards her, its nebulous arms hugging her, anaesthetising fears in a vanilla embrace.

'Nuts,' 14B whispered.

'Acorns,' she replied.

The woman in the pool crashed through the water's surface gasping for air.

She stared directly at Brighid. Her face reddened by the slap of oxygen. The bags and lines beneath her eyes seemed more pronounced.

But it wasn't Nell.

It was Tessy.

14B pressed the camera's stop button, and the dream went black.

◎ ◎ ◎

Lowell curled into a ball lowered his chin into his chest and wished he'd never been born. It was a long fall from heaven to despair, and he had fallen fast and heavy.

Air from intergalactic space, or whatever it was back there, wafted from the open doorway, drifting across the basement, and as it slid up Lowell's legs, curling around him in a furtive caress, he breathed in the draught, thirsty for one last scent of Nell.

But the only smell he could detect was that of dank stone. Then the draught slipped away, dissolved into the cracks in the wall at the far side of the basement, leaving him all alone.

Alone with his pain.

Alone to feel the pounding spasms in his urinary tract erupt into applauding fists.

Now that Nell was gone, there was no longer any need to hide the agony ripping through his insides; no longer any reason for him not to writhe and thrash in a hopeless battle against the arrowhead kidney stone digging, impaling and slicing down the shaft of his penis. And as his hands slammed the marble ground in a desperate bid to counterbalance all that barbed thrumming, the earth answered back in cold silence.

He suddenly needed to piss.

The bathroom upstairs was out of the question. Too many steps and stairs to crawl. Brighid and her blue toenails would be out like a shot, asking too many questions, wanting to call an ambulance.

He gripped the third step instead, hauled himself up, unzipped his trousers and urinated.

Blood in his urine.

Deep red like a fine port.

POP!

Like a cork, the stone shot out, unblocking the neck of his penis, releasing a torrent of backed up vintage.

The stone bobbed in effervescence.

Emptied, Lowell tucked his penis back into his trousers, squatted down onto his haunches and fished out the kidney stone. Tiny though it was, its razor-sharp curved edges were testaments of torture.

It had a shape similar to a parenthesis, a closing bracket, a bracket signalling the end of something. Well, it was certainly that. He tossed the stone to the floor.

It was the kidney stone's fault. If it hadn't chosen *that* moment; if he hadn't been so distracted holding in the agony he might not have been so clumsy. What was he thinking, licking her face like that?

He twitched his nose. Now without the agonising distraction, he could smell something.

Sniffing urgently, sounding like a basset hound on a trail but feeling more like the fox caught in a snare, he circumnavigated the edit suite, then stepping backwards trying to gauge scent levels, he bashed into the edit suite desk. Actually, it was easier to pin down the smell if he stood still. His nostrils registered traces of burning wood, turf, smoke, vanilla acorns.

And chlorine.

It was stinging his eyes. He blinked. Hot tears streamed down his face. As he wiped his eyes and squinted at the open doorway, the darkness beyond shifted; delicate luminance smeared, thickened, to an outline. In the darkest realms of space, shadows were billowing.

Clasping the desk, he blinked again. The darkness blurred like breath on a lens.

A mist rose, thickening into what could almost be described as sea fog. The fog entered the edit suite, billowing around the computer monitors, the keyboard, and around Lowell. And then the fog giggled. Actually giggled. It felt warm as well. Warm and damp like a thousand breaths.

And out of the thousand breaths came orbs of light. Hissing. Wheezing. One of the orbs sneezed. The nearest orb. The orb with fragments of gauzy movement inside.

The outline of a wing; sheer as a cobweb.

The delicate tracing of a tiny arm; as translucent as rain.

Eyes with no face.

Eyes with no face that stared.

Lowell froze.

The eyes with no face tired of him, diverted its gaze, and slipped back into the fog. The fog and eyes were retreating through the door, back into space.

Was that where Nell had gone?

Maybe all he needed to do was follow her.

He approached the door with caution, wary of any gravitational forces that might suck him out from the edit suite and send him tumbling into the deepest realms of space. Heart thumping, he finally reached the threshold. He could barely breathe. Standing on the brink of space was like standing on the tallest cliff on a moonless, windless night. There were no stars. No planets. Just this excruciating awareness that if he fell off the edge of the room he could carry on falling forever. His toes curled around what felt like a cliff so high that if he were a beacon he could reach out for miles, draw any fishing boat back to shore, his parents' bright yellow trawler included.

The burn on his thumb was throbbing to the rhythmic beat of a lighthouse light. It was as though his thumb needed to be out there in the darkness. A lighthouse light thrives in darkness. So, holding his thumb out to the dark, he lifted his whole hand into space. The prickle in his palm vanished, the pain in his thumb washed away. He craned his body forward, raised his other arm to join its counterpart in space, spreading them like wings; the frayed edges on his bandaged thumb fluttered like downy feathers in flight.

Something threaded through his fingers. Whatever

it was bristled like electrostatic; it was as though he was prodding a television screen, but without the solid section of glass. Sliding his hand back and forth delicate wisps of light bubbled through his fingertips, fizzing.

Hissing.

Like the radio.

He'd always assumed the untuned bits in-between weren't important.

But everything is important.

Everyone is important.

Dogs included.

He knew that now.

Shifting forward, reaching his hands out again, he heard a voice.

'What the feck are you doing here?'

A new shadow was sifting the darkness.

Hector.

'Leave,' Hector said, the way you'd order a dog to stop chewing something he wasn't supposed to.

Lowell whipped his hand back from space.

The fiery pulse in his thumb resumed. Rubbing the burn, he found a certain pleasure in the pain; it fed the lure of soporific bliss.

Hector fell upon him, seized his arm and hauled him away from space. 'Don't even bloody think about it,' he growled, kicking the door shut behind him.

Lowell jerked his arm free.

'You're not ready,' said Hector. 'Not yet.'

Hector was cradling a TV camera under his arm; its lens was fogged with moisture. Hector's hair was wet; water was dripping onto the camera and marble floor. And he had a pair of swimming goggles around his neck. 'Stinks!' Hector snarled. 'You been pissing yourself?'

Lowell stuffed his hands into his trouser pockets. 'I'm

not taking any more footage. I'm done.'

Hector plonked the camera down onto the editing desk. 'What's up with you?' he asked, circumventing the piss and blood next to the stairway. 'You got your period or something?'

'She's gone,' he whispered. Any louder and it might make it more true.

Hector's eyes darkened. 'Who's gone?'

'Nell.'

'Maybe you stopped believing.'

'I'll never stop believing.'

'Well someone has. That or intangiblitis got her.' Hector sat down on the desk next to the camera. 'Same thing really. One's the cause, the other's the outcome. When people started fearing believing, what they once believed in didn't vanish so much, it went elsewhere. Could be she's only visible on another track now, or perhaps, perhaps, you can't see her unless you're dead yourself.'

Lowell's heart plummeted. 'Are you saying she's d__'

Hector leaned back, nearly knocking into the monitor, and rolled out a wry smile. 'So many possibilities. Which do you prefer? Stone? Faerie? Spirit? Angel?'

'I just want her back.'

Hector sighed wearily. 'Now that's a line nearly everyone says at some point in their lives, about someone they love.'

Lowell edged closer, knitting his fingers into knots. 'Where is she?'

'You already know. You just can't remember.'

'Did you see her?' Lowell nodded at the arched door.

Hector folded his arms. 'Why would you think she's gone that way?'

'I didn't see her go up the steps.'

'Did you see her go through the door?'

'No.'

'Where's the door lead to?'

'How should I know? Door's always shut,' he replied truthfully.

He could only guess what was beyond the door; could only guess what Nell had been doing down here all that time. If she was watching the documentary when he'd sneaked in, he had no recollection. He remembered creeping down the steps, remembered licking her face, remembered pissing out the kidney stone, but that was all he remembered. If Nell had slipped out through a smuggler's tunnel, he had absolutely no recollection. He would have remembered if she'd opened the door. Nell had either vanished into thin air or had crept out the same way Hector came in; via the basement steps.

'So you don't know what's behind the door?'

'How could I? I don't have the key code.'

Hector picked up the camera, began wiping it with his leather sleeve.

'Where did she go?'

Hector glanced back up. 'You're asking for help? From *me*?'

Lowell bit at his fingernail, tasted fried fuse box, apple and vanilla acorns. 'Yes.'

His voice sounded tiny.

Hector arched his eyebrow. 'Funny that.' He set the camera back down on the desk. 'Where's my mobile?'

Lowell fished Hector's mobile from his pocket and handed it to him. 'I was improvising, that's all.'

Hector slammed the mobile down on the desk. 'You have to be the one shuffling the cards to improvise.'

'What?'

'Nell told you to do it.'

'No she didn't. It was my idea, the train.'

'No, it wasn't.' Hector smiled. 'She just let you think it was.'

'But I sent the text telling Brighid to get on the train. No-one told me to do that.'

'Didn't she?' Hector rubbed his knee. 'Who'd do you think put my phone into your pocket in the first place?'

Lowell stared back blankly.

'So you thought it was all your own idea, sending those texts pretending to be H, using my phone to pretend to be me?' He shook his head. 'Cheers bud.'

'Anyway.' Lowell's fists tightened. Hector had some nerve sitting there claiming the moral high ground. 'What were you doing filming my mum and dad?' There. He'd said it.

Hector cocked his head. 'Why do you think it was me that filmed them?'

'It's your project.'

'Where do you get that idea?'

Lowell shrugged. 'You turned up at the house, remember?' He couldn't conceal the sarcasm from his voice. 'Told me I was making a documentary.' His heart was racing.

Hector tutted derisively. 'Your poxy documentary's just a film within a film; a small film at that, a drop in the ocean.'

'Why have I gone to all this trouble if it's so unimportant?'

'Will you listen to yourself? You've only been director five minutes and you're already throwing hissy fits. I didn't say it wasn't important; it got Brighid here didn't it? Kept you informed. Kept all the cards in place.'

'So we're the target audience?'

'Target audience?' He rolled his eyes. 'You been listening to Brighid too much. Remember the bloke with the tortoise?'

A stranger waltzing through his hall, tortoise nuzzling in his arm, wasn't the sort of thing Lowell was likely to forget. But then he'd forgotten plenty of stranger things he was sure.

Lowell nodded.

'Tortoise spotted you spying on them.'

'It's my house,' he exclaimed indignantly.

'They were here for a viewing.'

'What viewing? We hadn't even started the editing then.'

'Not the documentary. The big picture – the piece he and the tortoise needed to see.'

The big picture, there it was again. In the big picture he was supposed to be saving the universe hand in hand with Nell. That's how he'd imagined it.

'Oh, and you know that other time when you pulled up a corner of your lounge carpet to listen in on one of the screenings?'

'The man shouting in Arabic? That was in the big picture?'

Hector nodded. 'Woodworm spotted you putting the mike to the floorboards. The voyeur watching the voyeur.'

'Woodworm my ass. Is there a secret camera in my room?'

'It was Quechua by the way. Not Arabic, you muppet. The bit you heard was a family argument in Cochabamba, Bolivia; a family dispute that ended up getting right out of hand.'

Lowell plonked himself down on one of the chairs. 'Why were they watching?'

'They don't watch. They consume. They soak it up through their pores, scales, fur, feathers, whatever they happen to be sitting in at the time. But I'm not just talking imagery and audio here; they take it all in, all the emotions, all that unbearable, crushing awareness of the here and now, all its dreadful aftermath. Screenings have been going on for thousands of years. Your basement is just one of the latest many in a long line of auditoriums. Twenty three years we've been in your basement.'

Lowell shifted uncomfortably in his chair. 'But you only peeled the wallpaper off the door a couple of weeks ago.'

Hector grunted, a half snort that didn't even make it out as a half snort. 'There's more ways to get into a mango without creating a sticky mess. You know your next door neighbour, number fifteen?'

'Yes.'

He was saying yes but he didn't really know him, apart from the odd nod between neighbours passing on the street, and what with the Lounge Age there hadn't even been the odd nod for quite some time. He worked for the Water Board, that much he knew (from his van), would be approaching retirement age. He'd lived next door for as long as Lowell could remember.

'He lets us in via a few loose stones in the basement wall.'

Twenty three years, Lowell's whole lifetime, the bloke from the Water Board had been letting strangers in downstairs. From cradle to Lounge Age.

'And remember the woman you heard laughing? Another screening. How old were you then? Seven? Eight? You were playing with one of your Micro Machines cars, rolling it along the bare floorboards.'

'How could you possibly know about that?' His voice was all choked whisper.

'Let's see, if we can work out the date your parents bought the lounge carpet__'

'Why did they buy the carpet?'

Hector shrugged. 'They liked the pattern? I dunno.'

'Why was it in the documentary? Fifteen years ago the carpet was laid. Fifteen years ago, but somehow your crew were there filming its arrival.'

'They're not my crew.'

If his parents had been in on it, surely there wouldn't have been any need for Hector's lot to sneak in via next door. Unless. Unless his parents had been hiding it from him. Lowell twiddled his toes, trying to glean some comfort recalling the carpet's soft pile, Lounge Age padding. 'They were just sitting in the kitchen eating their chips like nothing was happening. Why didn't they tell me they were being filmed, that there was a film crew in the house?'

'Maybe they didn't know.' Hector tugged at his goggles; the water inside sloshed from left to right. Right to left. 'Camouflage. Have you not been watching your own documentary? Have you not listened to a word I've just said?'

'It was the night before they died.' Lowell swallowed hard. 'Did you know they were going to die?'

'What am I the shipping forecast?'

'I never told you they died at sea.'

'Didn't you?' Hector shook his wet head, spattering the monitors and desk. 'Common knowledge isn't it?'

He always knew there was something more to it. The calm sea they had capsized in. The desk lamp left on to illuminate the radio on an already bright day. The extra groceries Mum had bought before leaving, as though she'd known there'd be no trip to the Co-op the following Saturday. He breathed in sharply. 'Did they kill themselves?'

''Course they didn't. Now you're being paranoid.'

He was no longer sure about anything. 'Bit odd, a film crew were here that night of all nights.'

'Oh, they'd have been here a lot more than that.' Hector grinned. 'Woodworm's a right bugger to get rid of. You think you've got rid of one infestation, and bang there's another hole.'

Hector was not going to riddle his way out of this. 'But why did they choose that night for filming?'

'It's called editing.' Hector scratched his head. 'Like you calling her Nell.'

'That's her name.'

''Course it's not. Just Nell sounds more like a proper name than the original name you had for her, Nil. That's what she was to you when she first came through on the radio, the number zero. The position of the red line in the tuning window. Nothing. Nil. It took months for her to convince you otherwise.'

'No it didn't.'

Hector leaned forward and glared at him. 'Are you sure?'

'Please. Where is she?'

Hector's frown softened. 'What happened last time you couldn't see her?'

Lowell threw himself at the steps and headed for the lounge.

Chapter 22

THE DREAM HAD SEEMED so real, so vivid, Brighid had found it impossible to get back to sleep. 7.15 am, that's all it was, yet the table was already laid (catering crew already clocked in, clocked out). Set for one: one plate with a boiled egg (still with shell) and bread and butter; one glass of grapefruit juice.

As there was a chance Lowell might have heard her get up (good chance with those dam floorboards), and as it was way too pre-caffeine to put up with Lowell's food monitor routine, she quickly poured herself a measure of coffee – jug allocated with just enough for one – grabbed the tray next to the bread bin and carried her breakfast into the sitting room. She could catch up on the news; even that was more palatable than having breakfast with Lowell watching every mouthful.

Television: on, she sank down onto the sofa (resisted the urge to stretch out, rest her eyes), took a sip of coffee, and began peeling the egg. The shell already had a small fracture; bits of egg had bubbled out and congealed: inside coming out.

> 'In other news…a number of leading scientists are claiming that heightened solar activity is to blame for the erratic behaviour of some bird and insect

> life. Certain species are particularly sensitive to the increase in electromagnetism caused by the solar storms. Many birds relying on electromagnetic fields for their navigation are, says Helena Osborne of the Royal Botanical Society, quite literally going astray.'

The tangy edge of the grapefruit juice had been muted, sweetened with honey – made it very drinkable. She set the glass down on the table, dipped the bread into the yolk. The catering crew had changed colour palette. All other meals had followed a red and green theme, or hues thereof. Today was a yellow day. Even the bread was yellow. And the egg white. Or the not so egg white, more boiled in turmeric soup egg off-white.

> 'And now we just want to bring you yet another curious item…French media are covering a story about a coach found abandoned in a remote forest area.'

Visuals cut to the forest. The camera panned to a cordoned off area holding a coach, then cut to a close-up of the coach's rear. The number plate displayed an 'E' for España. Above that were the words: *Picos de Europa.*

Brighid chewed on her egg. Tessy had boarded a coach with the exact same wording.

> 'The coach, parked up in the depths of the Forest of Paimpont for the last two weeks, is thought to have been carrying French and Spanish nationals, but there has been no sign of the driver or any of the passengers.
>
> French police have as yet been unable to identify those thought to be travelling onboard; they're

currently sifting all missing persons' cases that could hold any possible connection. Around forty or so rucksacks and cases were left on the coach. They contained clothes and toiletries bought in France and Spain and also numerous novels in French or Spanish.

But it's the note left taped to the coach's rear window that has the whole of France speculating. Written in French, on an A4 sheet, it said: *Don't look for us.*'

The camera tilted up to the rear window. The note had already been taken away for forensic analysis, so the camera zoomed in and focused on a faded 'x' marking the glass.

She nearly choked on her egg.

Tessy's kiss.

Tessy had drawn an 'x' into the condensation – on the coach in France – to demonstrate a kiss – a kiss goodbye.

She felt dizzy.

The victims were Spanish and French nationals. Would Tessy be classed French? She had lived there for years. Brighid's birthday envelopes always had a French stamp. She'd have bought all her clothes in France, probably read novels in French.

Brighid switched on the light in the hall. There was little point standing around speculating, panicking, she'd call the police.

She picked up the phone.

The line was dead.

She'd left the television on, the lounge door open.

'So let's go back to our main headline: the second UNDER. Our science correspondent is here in the studio. Dermot, scientists have come up with the term the UNDER, but do they really know what's going on?'

'In a word: no.'

Brighid lowered the phone onto her shoulder.

'And that light aircraft crash in the Isle of Man, killing five people?'

'Air accident investigators are working around the clock to find out the cause of the crash. Nothing so far suggests any link to the UNDER. The accident did occur during poor visibility…'

Upstairs. She grabbed her mobile from the bedside table.

No network.

She'd just have to go to the police station in person.

She needed to get ready.

Bathroom. She splashed cold water on her face.

Maybe she was panicking, getting things out of perspective. Tessy had gotten on the coach, but how far had she gone? She might have just been hitching a ride up the road.

She dried her face with her allotted towel, stared into the mirror at the dark shadows under her eyes, the faint scar on her forehead, and she carried on staring until her breath misted up the reflection, then placing her finger onto the condensation, she drew an 'x'.

Brighid knocked on Lowell's bedroom door. No answer. She'd leave a note instead, but how to word it? *Sorry can't work, had to pop into Douglas – think my mother might be dead.* To the point, but crass.

The letter box clapped once. Post. One letter – window envelope, red: a Manx Telecom bill reminder (didn't bode well for the wages) addressed to Mrs Watterson – Lowell's mother presumably: Lowell's dead mother. If Brighid had been a believer in signs, this wouldn't be a good one.

Why was she being so morbid? She had no real reason to think Tessy might be dead. She had simply reverted to norm: being unreachable. She swallowed hard pushing back the rising panic; this emotion surprised her. She barely knew Tessy.

She needed something to write with, but there was no note pad and pen by the dead phone. Given the circumstances even Lowell couldn't be too annoyed if she used the back of the envelope to scribble the message.

The television was still on in the sitting room.

A woman with an explosion of glossy curls was talking to a reporter, her voice breaking with emotion.

> 'He always said he'd find a way to get in touch, you know when he's gone. You see, it's not just faeries showing up, it's also the dead.'

People were becoming hysterical, herself included; fancy going on television talking such absolute nonsense. Some people would do anything for five minutes of fame.

She switched the television off.

Entering the kitchen in the hunt for a pen she heard a door close in the hallway.

She swung back round expecting to see Lowell checking his watch. But there was no one there.

Somebody coughed.

A woman's cough. In Lowell's room.

Brighid marched towards his door.

And knocked.

◎ ◎ ◎

The door swung open almost immediately.

Tessy.

Tessy was standing there. In Lowell's room.

'What are you doing here?' Brighid gasped.

'Oh, just sneaking about.' Tessy grinned, glancing over her shoulder.

Brighid didn't know whether to slap her or hug her. She plunged her hands into her coat pockets instead. The pockets Tessy had made for her.

Lowell was sitting in his armchair, elbow on armrest. Hand in chin. Sleeping.

Brighid's head felt as if it was orbiting the earth faster than the speed of light. One minute Tessy was in France: missing presumed dead; next minute, she was here, right smack bang in front of her, lurking about in her boss's bedroom. All inane smiles.

'Does he know you're here?' she hissed at Tessy.

'No.'

'What are you playing at?'

Tessy shrugged. 'Nothing.'

There was a mark on the side of Tessy's forehead, two elongated bruises, the shape of a mouth, as though someone had bitten her.

'You can't just break into my boss's house.'

'He doesn't mind.'

'He will when he wakes up.'

Tessy stared back impassively. She was wearing a gown the same 'classical' colour combo as Brighid's coat.

She gripped Tessy's wrist. 'I was starting to think you were dead.'

Her vacant smile abruptly subsided. 'What would you rather?'

She dropped her mother's wrist. 'Don't be ridiculous.'

Suddenly coughing, Tessy covered her mouth. 'Sorry,' she spluttered. 'All this moving about has irritated my throat.'

'That coach you were on in France, it's just been on the news.'

The smile was back. 'We wondered how long it would take them.'

'What?'

'To jump to conclusions.'

Tessy's hair was clinging to her head like wet reeds, as though she'd gone two weeks without washing it; that or she was fresh from a plunge in a pool.

'Doesn't matter. You need to speak to the police. Tell them what you know.'

Tessy stepped back. 'Why would I do that?'

'Then, we need to get you sorted.' Whatever sorted meant. Mental health services? Emergency accommodation? She'd meant to Google it when she got back from France, find out exactly what avenues were available, but she'd put all that to the back of her mind. Without an address to even reach Tessy, it had seemed a pointless task.

'Nope, she's still not got it,' Tessy murmured absently, glancing towards the sideboard.

Brighid pushed past her mother. 'Who're you talking to?'

There was no-one else there. Just the sideboard with a washing-up bowl on top. Lowell was still sleeping in the armchair.

'I wish we could be a proper family,' Tessy sighed, releasing a long, husky grunt that sounded like ice being crushed.

'We still can be,' Brighid conceded.

Tessy's gaze floated back to Brighid; she blinked as though she was trying to see under water, as though a miry murk was stinging her eyes. 'A proper family,' she repeated. 'One that can sit round a table and all see each other.'

She was still harping on about Imaginary Dad. She had retreated back to that island in the mire where hallucinations could get so shiny and sharp around the edges they became real: all high contrast, high-definition, Technicolor brightness, real. She was hanging out with her husband again. Reality was lost beyond the fog with all the other bits. Nodding at the empty space next to her, Tessy truly believed she was gazing at her husband across some vivid yellow meadow, colours all turned up like a Tim Burton film.

'Imagine,' Tessy said wistfully, 'imagine seeing each other all at the same time. Dog included.'

'What dog?'

Tessy blinked again. The mist appeared to clear. She was marching towards Lowell.

Brighid followed, hot on her heels. 'Don't wake him.' The situation was complicated enough without involving Lowell.

It was the first time she'd seen inside Lowell's room. It looked more like another lounge than a bedroom. In fact, there wasn't any bed at all, just a three-seat sofa with a quilt folded over the back rest. Plus a dining table, a bureau or drinks cabinet (the former probably) and over on the far wall, a gas fire with poorly fitted plastic coal-effect.

Tessy was sidling right on up to Lowell, her sheer gown revealing faint bubbles of cellulite, small folds of belly fat; she was leaning over Lowell, craning her face up to his. Then she glanced back up at Brighid and grinned broadly. 'He's not asleep.'

She was right; his eyes were open, his brow creased in deep concentration. He was all hunched up, chin slumped in his hand, and that focussed he didn't even seem to notice they were there. Saliva drivelled from the corner of his mouth, trailing down his beard. He was wearing the same clothes as yesterday, as though he'd slept in them; if he'd slept at all – those weren't bags under his eyes, they were freight baggage.

Brighid touched his shoulder. 'Lowell?'

For a moment he lifted his head, turned wearily around, but his eyes seem to look right through her. It was as though he couldn't even see her. Then his exhausted gaze fell back to the table next to him.

To the radio.

The radio.

The very same radio that appeared in her dreams.

Or a radio that looked very much like it.

Brighid edged nearer, barely able to breathe.

Close up, it was identical to the radio the crab dragged around in the castle dream; it even had the same faint scratches around the edges, the exact spot those crab claws clasped every night. And like the radio in her dream it offered no immediately apparent knobs or switches, just a thin vertical red line in the tuning window that was now twitching silently on zero without any help from Lowell.

'Don't touch it,' Tessy warned. 'He'll go into meltdown.'

Brighid pressed down on his shoulder. 'Lowell. We're late for work.' Quite what she was going to do with Tessy while she worked, she hadn't worked out.

'Oh, don't worry about work,' twilled Tessy.

'Ignore her.'

'Plenty of chance of that. He's too busy in his own world now.'

'Lowell?' She sank to her haunches.

His glazed, heavy eyes remained fixed on the radio.

'Poor Lowell,' Tessy mumbled. 'Looks like a knackered old sea dog.'

Brighid tugged at his sleeve. No response.

'There'll be no more documentary,' Tessy remarked.

Brighid swung round. 'Who even told you we were making a documentary?'

Tessy threaded her fingers through her hair. 'Doesn't matter; the important bits are in; it's served its purpose.'

'How would you know?'

Tessy raised the eyebrow nearest to the bite mark, furrowing the bite mark, making it look like lips puckering. 'You're not the only one involved in the broadcast industry.'

She rose to her feet. 'Oh, c'mon. You don't know the first thing about __.'

'Don't I?'

'You've got a Luddite's love of technology. You even tape up your plug sockets.'

Tessy narrowed her eyes. 'You think you have all the answers don't you?' She suddenly leaned forward and blew on Lowell's face.

Lowell didn't even blink.

The radio's tuning line however, immediately twitched from zero to five. Instead of a frequency range, the tuning window displayed round numbers from zero to seventy-nine. Now, as the red line flicked back to zero, the radio fired into life with a hiss of untuned noise.

'See.' Tessy grinned triumphantly. 'The radio just comes on whenever I want. Who needs technology?'

Lowell suddenly yelped, scrambling elbows and chin onto the armrest. Beard nestling on the backs of his hands, he was staring at the radio in much the same way a dog lost in the desert would eye a bowl of water.

'Lowell?' Brighid pressed.

'Stop worrying.' Tessy squeezed Brighid's palm with cold and clammy fingers.

Brighid instinctively jerked her hand away.

'That's your problem,' Tessy sighed, marching over to the dining table. 'You're always worrying.'

'You don't even know me.' She hadn't meant to use such a harsh tone.

Tessy leaned back against the dining table, curling her hands around the edge. 'I know you better than you know yourself,' she said, scooting her backside up onto the table, sitting forward, crossing her legs. She glimpsed over her shoulder, snatched up two books that had been taped together, scanned their titles, both made references to maritime navigation, and then placed them back down on the table next to the half consumed candle. 'I'm surprised you still can't see your father though,' she said, glancing up at her. 'You can see me, can't you?'

''Course I can.'

Tessy shook her head. 'You're a funny mix.'

Brighid started buttoning her coat up. She needed to find a phone that worked. She wasn't sure who needed medical attention first. Tessy or Lowell. Lowell was practically catatonic.

'I haven't got a fever,' Tessy said, fanning her face with her hand. 'So why would I need a doctor?'

'I didn't say__'

Brighid swung back round. Lowell was shifting about in the armchair, sniffing the air.

'Nothing wrong with Lowell either,' Tessy added, swinging her arms from side to side. 'A waft of my armpits soon wakes him up.'

Lowell was gazing at the table, eyes agog, eyeballs practically straining on the lead. His bizarre fugue was lifting.

'Meet my mother,' Brighid said, smiling lamely. 'I tried to wake you but__'

'He can't hear you,' Tessy declared, lowering her arms. 'He can't even see you. Or me for that matter.'

Now Tessy had stopped flapping her arms, Lowell's face promptly went all limp. Furrowing his brow, eyes flashing desolation, he sank back in his chair and sighed mournfully. The radio was still stuck between stations, its untuned crackling sounding like a dog clawing at plastic.

'Terrible thing when we doubt our own senses,' muttered Tessy, snapping the candle from its saucer. 'But anyway, let's get back to me and you.'

Brighid folded her arms.

'The shape of the ceirtduir.'

'You know about the ceirtduir?' She'd assumed the ceirtduir was something the documentary had made up.

''Course I do.'

'It's the same pattern as the UNDER,' Brighid said, trying to beat Tessy to it.

Lowell was rolling his head, as if he was in a yoga class, as if he was trying to ease a stiff neck.

'That's not all,' Tessy beamed. 'The flat where you were living in Finsbury Park, your bedroom wallpaper had the exact same pattern.'

'No it didn't.' If it did, she couldn't possibly remember. She couldn't even remember what colour the walls were. Tessy was bluffing.

Tessy was also yawning. A belter of a yawn. A yawn wide enough to swallow the earth. 'Sorry,' she said, placing her hand over her mouth. 'I'm absolutely shattered; being in a few places at once really takes it out of you. She shook her head, trying to dispel the tiredness. 'You used to light a candle and listen to the BBC World Service when you went to bed in that flat. Drifting off to the shipping forecast reminded you of your travels in South America; you know, when you lit a candle next to your handy travel-sized short wave radio. Pretty basic some of those hotels you stayed in. There was no bedside lamp, just the light switch by the door, not the bed; the candle next to your bed made you feel safer.'

Tessy was guessing. Simply guessing. The fact she was right, didn't prove anything. That Tessy somehow knew of her travels and both addresses in London was a well-established mystery. Tessy's birthday cards always somehow managed to find her, even in South America. If Tessy felt better trying to make out she'd not only visited the flat in Finsbury Park but had been there in Peru, Colombia, Ecuador, Bolivia and Argentina backpacking alongside her, then so be it.

Tessy cleared some phlegm from her throat. She either had a throat infection or smoked a lot. Like the woman, Brighid had heard Lowell talking to, the morning before.

'Just how long have you been here? In this house?' Brighid asked.

Tessy threw her a small smile. 'That was the only time you really looked at the wallpaper in Finsbury Park,' she said, ignoring her question. 'When you turned the light off and lit the candle. Sometimes you even traced the pattern with your finger tips. The candlelight made the pattern look different. Made it look more like stickmen on a horse.'

The horses. She called it her gaucho room. She winced. Was she really that pretentious back then? 'What were you doing in my room?'

'I'm your mother.'

'Cut the crap. Seriously. What were you doing in my room?'

She shrugged, picking at the wax on the candle 'I often

watch you.'

'I thought you were living in France?'

Tessy lifted her head, opened her mouth to reply and then stopped. Following Tessy's gaze, Brighid guessed Imaginary Dad was apparently crossing the room. Destination: sofa. Whilst he supposedly settled himself between the cushions, his wife cast the candle to one side, slid her backside off the table and briskly sat down on the sofa's armrest. Lowell gasped audibly and began sniffing the air, eyes reeling in the backdraught of Tessy's sudden movement.

Caught in that breeze, Brighid stood uneasily between Lowell and Tessy. She plunged her hands into her coat pockets, squeezed the house key. She'd need the key to let the doctor in. Who was the priority? Her mother, now zoning in on the empty sofa, or Lowell blindly clawing at the armchair, nostrils sweeping the vicinity?

Chlorine.

Tessy smelt of chlorine.

Brighid breathed in, the key digging into her palm.

No. She was imagining it. She *had* to be imagining it. She needed to watch that. Dangerous cocktail: insomnia and crazy dreams. She sucked on her lips, trying to imbibe some sense of reality, and turned to face Tessy. 'Why are you here?' she asked, shifting from one foot to the other. 'How did you even know I was here?'

Tessy hefted her gaze away from the male fantasy she had sprawled amongst the cushions and peered up at Brighid. Her eyes were more limestone grey than blue.

'You need me,' she said.

'No I don't.' The words just slid from Brighid's mouth.

Tessy turned back to the sofa. 'You've gone and upset him.'

'I'm sorry,' she mumbled. It was the first time she'd

apologised to a sofa.

'He says it's completely out of place, your cynicism.' Her gaze settled on Brighid. 'Haven't the dreams taught you anything?'

'What dreams?' She hadn't mentioned the dreams to anyone. Not even her closest friends.

Tessy swatted her question away. 'If you could try not talking over him.' She cocked her head to one side, nodding intently. 'Anyway,' she said, peering back up at Brighid. 'Your father's right – there were a lot more than just forty folk on that coach. A lot more. Those lights you assumed to be reflections in the coach windows, reflections of sunlight. Think again.'

She was making it up as she went along, adding ingredients to her very own nut cake. A nut cake that could sit proudly on the shelf next to Lowell's nut cake documentary. Only a sprinkling of logic kneaded the World Service and travelling into the same bowl. It was probably Lowell's radio had given Tessy the idea. Mix in a dollop of nutty additives about the coach. And bake for fifty minutes or however long it took to burn Brighid's brain. Her mother would only be satisfied once she'd achieved that goal.

'So what were they, the lights?' she asked sourly. Sour enough to curdle any cake mix.

Tessy turned her gaze back towards the sofa, as though the answer was just loafing about on the cushions, for all to see. An excruciating silence followed within which Brighid pondered the depths of her mother's madness. The constant cackle and hiss of the untuned radio was enough to drive anyone crazy. She was half tempted to switch the damn thing off. Finally, Tessy nodded and peered up at her. 'They were the same lights that stopped you drowning in the swimming pool when you were at the convent.'

Brighid felt her jaw slacken.

'He's good isn't she?' She grinned. 'Freaks me out every time, the details he remembers. Intangiblitis stole his memory for a while.'

'How do you know about intangiblitis?' The only place she'd heard it mentioned before was in the documentary.

'How do I know? Are you for real? I've been living alongside it for years.' Her stony gaze skimmed Brighid up and down. 'Your father had completely faded away, but now he's dead, his recall is back stronger than ever.'

'He's dead?' This was a breakthrough. Perhaps, now Tessy was slowly coming to terms with the fact the husband she thought she'd been living with all those years didn't actually exist.

Tessy's mouth slackened. 'Oh, I'm so sorry Love. You didn't know did you?' Lowering her gaze, her face brightened. 'Not to worry, I reckon he knows everything now. Hang on,' she said, cocking her ear towards the sofa.

'What else is he saying?' Brighid was playing along. It was the easiest way to communicate with her mother. The only invisible man around here was sitting on the sofa inside Tessy's head.

'He's not saying anything. It's the radio. Listen. Something's coming through.'

Amongst the interference and crackling, there was a whistling sound.

Lowell squealed in his armchair.

'Lowell thinks they're whistlers. And yes, solar activity is quite intense at the moment and when solar flares hit our atmosphere at very low frequencies it is possible to pick them up. That's the scientific explanation anyway. But these aren't whistlers.'

Tessy was a constant surprise. This capacity to speak techno-babble was completely unexpected. She was right though. This was no random sound from space. It had a definite pattern, a tune Brighid had heard before.

Eyes widening, Lowell sank his beard back down onto his armrest. His ears were twitching, his mouth drooling.

'Shame isn't it?' Tessy said.

'What is?'

'All that talent crushed.'

'Who are you talking about?'

'If it wasn't for that Ford Mondeo who knows how things would have turned out. Trashed his motorbike and that's not all.'

'Who's motorbike?'

Tessy arched an eyebrow. 'The leathers don't give you a clue?'

14B.

He had played the exact same melody in the pub.

'Is he okay?'

'Happened a long time ago.'

He'd mentioned a bike accident. But apart from his knee, she didn't know of any other injury, let alone any that hindered his playing. Was that why he wore gloves? Were his hands scarred? It didn't seem to affect his playing though. 'Do you know him?'

Tessy shook her head. 'What is it about us, we just can't get a normal boyfriend? One with a pulse. One that's not dead.'

A chill ran right through her.

Tessy grinned. 'You just shivered.' She turned to Lowell still hunched over the radio, oblivious. 'She just shivered.'

'I didn't.'

Tessy leaned forward, clasping her knees in her hands. 'Things haven't been quite right lately have they?'

Brighid plunged her clenched hands back into the deep pockets Tessy had provided.

'You're a popular girl, why haven't your friends replied to any of your messages?'

Her gaze locked on Brighid. 'It's almost like you've disappeared off the planet completely.'

Had Brighid not felt so fixed and rooted to the spot, as though marshland was now sucking her in, she'd have recoiled from this scrutiny. Tessy's eyes weren't just grey, there were also flecks of amber and copper thrown in. And something else was there, colour in motion: faint hues of red and green flickering like an internalised aurora borealis.

14B was still playing on the radio. The melody was changing; notes soaring and dipping and rising again.

Soaring and dipping and rising again.

Soaring and dipping and rising again.

The whistling noise of the UNDER.

'It helped, you know,' Tessy suddenly said, talking over the noise of the UNDER, 'having you there in my darkest moments.'

14B wasn't just playing the melody of the UNDER, it was the exact same tone. The exact same instrument playing it.

'What darkest moments?' She breathed, managing to step out from the marsh. Heart thumping.

'I think you already know.'

'No. I don't.'

'Are you sure?'

'Of course I'm bloody sure.' She bit her lip.

Tessy smiled a saccharine smile. 'Have you been swimming lately?'

Chapter 23

Brighid had no idea how she'd ended up here. She had just needed some air. Making a sharp exit from Lowell's house, escaping Tessy's crazy ramblings, escaping Lowell, escaping the radio, she had kept on running, everything a blur. Now catching her breath, sitting down on the promenade bench, shivering, she fastened the top button of her coat, the coat Tessy had made, and scanned the full length of the promenade.

Her heart lunged.

It wasn't the twisted bridge that startled her. She'd already seen that on the news. Looming in the background, beyond the bridge, was a castle. The roofs and much of the walls were no longer there, but still, it reminded her of the castle she had dreamed of every single night since France. For a moment, one crazy second, she had actually thought it might be the same castle. It was the first time she'd seen Peel Castle, and the last thing she wanted to see right now.

She turned away from the castle, gazed out to sea, breathed in slowly.

What was that smell?

She hadn't noticed before. Her nose had been numb to it – sense of smell squashed by the absurd. Tessy and the nonsensical were eternal bed-mates but Tess suddenly turning up making out she somehow knew all about her personal and work life, *and* her dreams, was like wheeling the bed right into the padded cell dragging Brighid along kicking and screaming.

Why would 14B play the sound of the UNDER?

It didn't make a gram of sense.

Not yet.

She just needed to work it out.

She breathed in deeply. The hairs inside her nostrils tickled. She sneezed.

What was Tessy doing in Lowell's room? Just how long had she been there? Was that Tessy she'd heard Lowell talking to the morning before? What was she doing hanging around in Lowell's room at breakfast time? Why was she hiding? Why hadn't she come out and spoken to her there and then? Had Tessy stayed the night? Both nights? With Lowell? That didn't bear thinking about.

She cradled her forehead in her hands, got her nose to follow the smell.

Vanilla. The aroma was so intense, so concentrated; it was almost unrecognisable.

A solitary seagull stood perched on a lamppost watching the sea, silent, reverent almost, as though the scent of vanilla was locking him into a trance. Do seagulls even have a sense of smell? She wasn't sure of anything anymore. She got up from the bench. Other people must have noticed the stench but where were they? Manx flags lined Peel promenade, but its citizens were nowhere to be seen. It was just her and the Zen master seagull.

And her mobile phone.

She fished it out from her pocket.

No signal.

She glanced back down the promenade.

A phone box. She dashed over, swung open the door to the booth. A stink of stale piss. She possessed neither coins nor phone card. 999 was free. If Tess had vital information for the police then they needed to know. Mother or no mother, around forty people were missing from that coach in France: this was way too serious for Tessy to keep anything to herself. Could she ask for an ambulance too? Tessy needed psychiatric help for sure, but Lowell's dazed state could well require urgent medical attention.

She dialled 999, glimpsed at the castle through the booth windows.

The same dead tone.

She took the nearest side road off the promenade and entered a labyrinth of sloping streets and lanes, of old fisherman's cottages huddled in twisting rows. But the journey through Peel remained a solitary one.

Increasingly desperate to see someone else, to find out just what the hell was happening with the phones, just why the streets were suddenly so empty, she started peering in through windows. Subtle sideway glances were quickly relinquished – this was no time for etiquette – she began to stare in, blatantly cupping her hands on window panes, to gawk at lounges, dining rooms, kitchens, at televisions that had been left on, untuned, without a digital signal, stuck on white noise. But not one single soul picked up the remote, banged on their telly. She hammered on windows, rang every doorbell on a terrace of houses, yet still every single door stayed shut.

Then, up ahead, outside the pub on the left, she spotted a brewery wagon, its engine ticking over, smoke pulsing from the exhaust. Just because the driver's seat was vacant, it didn't mean the driver wasn't about somewhere – somewhere inside *The Oak and Apple* (head already full to capacity processing coincidences she let any significance to the pub's name pass right over). The driver would be in there, delivering, collecting empty barrels, gossiping with the bar staff about how bloody quiet Peel was today. Brighid tried the door. It was open.

The kipper baps on the tray at the bar were on special offer, but there was no-one exactly queuing for them.

She shouted, 'Hello.' Her voice sounded as squashed as the kippers flattened between bread wrapped in cling film.

No response.

A beer tap, left on, had run dry. The pint glass below, as full with beer as her brain was with preposterous absurdities, had overflowed into the spills tray, which in turn had overflowed into a large puddle behind the bar. She reached forward, flicked off the tap. There was little point turning off a tap that was no longer running, stemming the flow on something not flowing, but she did it on impulse: it just felt the right thing to do.

The area behind the bar presented a door marked *staff only*. If there was a brewery delivery then there would be someone about behind the scenes, down the cellar, rolling the barrels. She knocked, then entered. Past the kitchen area, and the plate of half eaten Marmite on toast, and the open fridge door (she closed it), was a flight of steps. Someone had dropped a mug of tea – mugs of tea. That was two handles amongst the smashed crockery on the top steps, two mugs of spilt tea, broken and discarded. A chunk of ceramic declared one of the drinkers as *The World's Greatest*, but whatever he or she was the greatest at was all smashed up, obliterated.

She called out again: 'Is anyone there?' Her voice quivered.

The World's Greatest and their tea buddy remained silent.

A text message. 14B. At last.

IS IT YOU OR THEM?

She swiftly tapped back.

Where are you?

Her mobile beeped back. The message had failed to send.

Up on Michael Street, Peel's shopping centre, there were no shoppers. As the door of the Co-op was wide open, Brighid stumbled right on in, hurrying past the ketchup, mushy peas, sweet corn. A carton of eggs had fallen to the lino. Yolk oozed from cardboard sides that said, *Free-range – freedom to wander*. The hens weren't the only ones: the whole of Peel had gone free-range. Behind the counter, whisky, vodka, gin, and cigarettes were all left unsupervised: a looters' paradise, if there had been anyone about to do the looting. The drawer of the cash till was open, notes and coins still stacked, untouched.

Another message. 14B.

YOU DIDN'T HALF SCARE THE LIVING BEJESUS OUTTA THE BARSTAFF BACK THERE. x

She glanced up, half expecting to see 14B. But there was just the buy-one-get-one-free offer on toilet rolls. If he was in the pub at the same time as her, why didn't he say something? Surely, he must have noticed how stressed she was. She called him back. Dead tone. Then she tried Jo in Belfast. Dead tone. Brian in Liverpool. Dead tone. Kate in Brighton. Dead tone. She tried 999 again. Dead.

YOU'RE STUCK WITH ME.

'But where are you?' she muttered through gritted teeth.

Another message.

BEHIND YOU.

She swung round. Fair Trade coffee was half price for a limited period only.

YOU NEED MORE THAN COFFEE.

'Okay, you can stop now,' she sighed wearily, her gaze darting up one aisle then the other. There was still no sign of him. 'Where are you?' This time she yelled it out loud.

No response.

It was as though he was deliberately pushing and prodding her, trying to push her over the edge.

Back on Michael Street, a chip wrapper romping in the wind wrapped itself around her ankle like a lecherous phantom. She kicked it away and trudged on in the direction the chip paper had forced her foot.

Before long, one house in particular caught her eye. It was the rusted hanging basket chain (without hanging basket) hanging suspended from the house that did it – a fishing rod fishing in air catching nothing but the wind, casting shadows onto the sash window below. The chain squeaked as it swung; an unoiled, abandoned sound. Behind the glass of the window, light flickered; a television stuck on untuned white noise like the rest. This time though, someone was there. A man was sitting on the sofa in front of the set. She tapped on the window. He didn't respond. Something moved behind the sofa, but the nets blocked definition.

The front door was sticky with fresh paint: red

framework, green panels. Red and Green. Maybe it was that had drawn her to the house, not the hanging basket chain. She pressed down on the handle. The door opened.

'Close the door after you,' a woman's voice called from the same direction as the hiss of static.

That done, she immediately felt boxed in within the small and gloomy hallway, so wasted no time in opening the door to her left, the door where the light from the untuned TV seemed to flicker around the edges, as though the door was the only thing holding the static back.

Instead of greeting her, instead of demanding to know what the hell she was doing, standing all wide-eyed and breathless in his lounge, the man on the sofa didn't even turn to look; the tufts, gelled and sculptured into his hair and flattened by the cushion cradling his head, simply lolled on regardless; viewing the frenzied pixel dance on TV was apparently much more important.

'Don't mind him,' the woman's voice said over the gush of white noise. The words were right next to her.

'I'm down here.' The voice said.

Brighid lowered her gaze. A young woman, she couldn't be more than twenty years, peered out from an opening, a trapdoor in the floor. The carpet had been rolled back to the far wall, exposing the room's floorboards: each board had been painted alternating red and green.

'You been outside? Stupid question. Sorry.' She smiled a limp smile then lifted her elbows off the floorboards, tugged at her blonde ponytail, tightening it. 'I must look a right mess.' She had been crying; black mascara trails stained her cheeks.

'Where is everyone?' Brighid asked. 'The whole town's gone AWOL.'

The woman prodded a pink frosted fingernail into the floor. 'I know. I saw them go.'

A piece of green paint peeled and curled under the woman's nail. She scraped it out, rubbed it between her fingers. 'We'd run out of bread. I've got to have me brekka in the morning – I'm a right bitch if I don't. Post-brekka Breeshey, Tim says, is an altogether much nicer person.' She nodded in the direction of the sofa. 'I only wanted some toast.' A single tear cleared a channel through the mascara stain. 'It was horrible. I'd only got halfway up our road,' she sniffed, 'when I saw it. Like a tornado it was, yer know, like you see on the telly, but this tornado didn't have wind and it didn't take houses – it took people – all of them. Has to be the UNDER they've been going on about. Funny though, there wasn't any whistling. On the news there's always a whistling noise. All I heard was the screech of brakes. My neighbour, Mrs Crosby, she was at the top of the street, talking to some woman – slaggin' someone probably; miserable ole skeet. Anyway, this tornado thing, the UNDER, whatever it was, came along, swallowed Mrs Crosby *and* the woman she was with. They just vanished. There one second, and then, whoosh, fucking whoosh, they're gone.'

Her mobile vibrated. 14B.

TALK ABOUT DELUSIONAL.

She blinked. Message still there. She wasn't imagining it. He was definitely sending messages, messages so uncannily relevant, he had to be following her. She had entered the house alone, but even if he was standing outside the house right now, there was no way he could listen in. He'd have to have his ear firmly pressed against the window for that. Her gaze shot towards the window. No sign of him.

Breeshey was gazing at the bit of paint peel she had

now annihilated between her fingers. 'There was a young lad just hanging around in the lane opposite, kickin' a ball against the wall. UNDER got him as well. Couldn't do anything to help him – he just vanished.' She flicked the paint peel into the air. 'UNDER didn't take his ball though – left that behind. It's not interested in things, just people, oh and animals. It took a cat. There was this small tabby running across the road – I thought it was going to get run over – that car was racin' down the road towards us, was inches away from the cat; but it just missed the cat, then the cat vanished. The car just kept on. Brakes screeching.'

'Did you notice the smell?' Brighid felt uncomfortably tall (something she wasn't used to) looking down at Breeshey in her cellar, so she knelt down. Her legs, she realised, were trembling: knees rebelling against brain's rebuttal of Breeshey's story. 'There's a really strong smell__.' She restrained her voice from slipping into high velocity. 'On the prom. A smell of vanilla.'

Breeshey eyed her nervously. 'Are you sure? You might have imagined it.'

Brighid plunged her hands into her pockets. 'Of course I'm sure, but your neighbours vanishing? Actually vanishing? C'mon.'

'What do you think they're doing, playing hide and seek?'

Brighid shrugged.

'You think the whole town's got nothing else better to do than shut down its businesses, stop the traffic, hide in their houses, just to play some elaborate hoax on you?' Breeshey's face flushed with anger. 'That's some ego.'

'I'm not saying I don't believe you.' She was trying desperately to not believe, telling herself this woman was a liar, a lunatic, but she kept coming back to the same conclusion, somehow trusting Breeshey more than herself.

Outrageous though it was, everything she had seen in Peel backed up Breeshey's version of events. 'Just, it's a lot to take in.'

'I'm not saying it isn't.'

'Do you have a phone I can use?'

'You've got a mobile haven't you?'

'Yep, but for some reason I can't make outgoing calls.'

'Same here. Land line's dead too.'

'What about a car?'

Breeshey licked her finger tips, rubbed the area under her eyes, smudging the mascara stains. 'I must look like a bloody panda.'

'You look fine.' It was better than the obvious: *who's going to see you?* She needed Breeshey on her side. 'Where's your car keys?'

Breeshey scowled. 'We don't have a car.'

Had this been a movie they'd just hotwire a car, but she had no idea how to do that. 'We could just walk round together 'til we find someone, anyone, with some answers.'

'What walk across the island? Expose ourselves to the big invisible liquidiser? Are you mad?'

'Quite possibly. If it runs in the family, yes.'

'I thought Tim had gone mad, was having a breakdown or something, that, or he was on the wacky-backy. Used to be a right idle bastard, then he started all this decorating and crying all the time.' Sighing, she slid her fingers over the floor. 'What d'you think of his artwork?'

Brighid arched her eyebrow. 'Colourful.'

So colourful, the floorboards were the same colour scheme as Lowell's house. Lowell had said it was company branding. *Red and green make yellow* – that was the line in her dream.

'I hate it. We'd only just bought the carpet a few months ago – cost a fortune as well. Why he had to start ripping it up and painting the floorboards I don't know. He was up before it was even light this morning, painting the front door. I mean that's not even logical is it? What's the point in painting in the dark?'

Tim was too busy gawping at the untuned TV to even twitch a finger at the critical panning.

She pursed her lips in exasperation. 'Anyway, when I came back before, *legged* it back, and told him what I'd seen, he was as shocked as I was, but do you know what he said?'

Brighid looked over to the sofa. Tim, it seemed, would not elaborate.

'He said he couldn't stand the itching anymore.'

'What itching?'

Breeshey slammed her hand down onto the floorboards. She was wearing a ring, looked like an engagement ring. 'He couldn't handle it.' Her voice suddenly sounded scratched, a diamond scraping across glass, grinding at syllables. 'He should have stayed, looked after me.'

Brighid rose to her feet, approached the sofa, unease stirring the pit of her stomach.

A face the colour of printing paper. Eyes complete blanks. Tim wasn't watching television. He was dead.

His shirt had been ripped wide open, exposing a torso drenched in blood, a chasm instead of a navel, a belly button gorged out. The knife had fallen to the floorboards, its blood dashing Tim's artistry. The red boards had turned a corroded vermillion; the green had gone brown. Shitty brown.

Brighid gagged. 'Have you called an ambulance?' It was way too late for that.

'Even if the phones were working, who'd answer?' She began to sob.

Brighid rushed back to the trapdoor, fell to her

haunches and draped an arm around Breeshey's shoulders, shoulders convulsing in grief and shock. 'Might be best if we get you out of here,' she said gently.

Breeshey rubbed her eyes with her fists. 'I'm not leaving.'

'You can't stay here.'

'I wouldn't leave Peel. Might be worse.' She swallowed hard, fighting back more tears. 'At least it's stopped here. For now anyway. We might have just got the passing storm. It could have stuck around in St Johns, Glen Vine, Douglas. You go walking around there and you could get sucked up by the big fat Hoover in the sky.'

This was a possibility Brighid hadn't even considered. Peel could be the best of it, the only place vacuumed and left. Peel could be that awkward corner under the sofa, a quick sweep with the nozzle and that was it. Anywhere else might be stuck on permanent vacuum mode. She had been safe here so far.

A new text.

SERIOUSLY? ARE YOU BUYING THIS SHIT?

Breeshey's eyes narrowed. 'Who's sending the messages?'

She shook her head. 'Just my mobile playing up.' She slipped her phone into her coat pocket. 'Okay. We'll stay in Peel but we need to find help.'

'Where is there to go?' Breeshey sniffed.

'The police. There must be some local bobbies about in Peel.' Even if they didn't know what was going on, even if they were stuck incommunicado, they might at least have some kind of emergency exit plan.

'The UNDER's got them,' Breeshey said confidently.

'You don't know that.'

'Can you hear sirens? No.'

She released her arm from Breeshey's shoulders. 'It's like I said we're bang in the centre of a no-go-zone. Health and Safety will be stopping them going anywhere.'

'I'm staying here. With Tim.' She lingered a moment, bit her lip, her eyes glazing with hopeless tears; then she gripped the trap door, lowered herself into the cellar, and promptly slammed the door down. Shut.

She had two choices: stay festering with the dead fiancé or go find help.

Brighid rose to her feet. 'Where's the nearest police station?'

Sirens or no sirens, it was worth trying at least.

The road leading up to Peel Police Station was unchartered territory. If there was an enormous virtual vacuum cleaner right in front her, stuck on permanent 'on', stuck on sucking the living daylights from anything that moved, except Breeshey and that solitary seagull, she wouldn't know until she walked right into it, would be the last thing she'd ever know.

And what about Tessy and Lowell?

Brighid had stumbled out of the house onto the deserted pavements; it had taken her just a few seconds. Was that when the vacuum had passed? Was it the same time she was unbolting the front door? Was it the same exact moment she'd turned her back on Tessy, that exact moment she told herself not to turn around, not to tell her to wait, not to tell her to stay? The exact moment she had wanted Tessy to just vanish.

At the cop shop, no-one was attending enquiries. The sign said to ring the bell for attention, but that attention was not forthcoming. She pushed on the bell, long and hard this time. Still nobody came.

There was a door next to the glass partition; unauthorised entry was strictly forbidden. She ignored the sign and entered an office absent of police and admin staff. Restraining the panic threatening to take hold, she picked up the phone on the nearest desk.

The line was dead.

Her mobile shuddered.

A message from 14B.

DO YOU BELIEVE IN COPS?

'Why are you doing this?' she asked out loud.

BECAUSE I LOVE YOU.

She drew a deep breath, slumped herself down into the cop's chair. She just needed to ignore the messages. Concentrate on the situation in front of her. So the phones were down. She already knew that. The desktop monitor was in screen saver mode: a looped animation of a fat cartoon cop trying to catch a sheriff's badge repeatedly tumbling from the sky. The badge looked like a shooting star and vanished whenever the cop got near. She grabbed the mouse, waking the screen into active mode and then clicked the internet symbol, opening the browser.

The server could not be found.

Seeing the notebook on the desk, she sat up. Every single *i* was methodically dotted; every *a* and *o* sealed into full circumferences. She leafed through previous pages but found no emergency instruction, no note telling her to head to a big building over the hill protected by barbed wire and top military personnel. But then, this was no zombie movie. If it was, she'd end up over that hill grateful for the food in their institutional canteen, grateful for the crisp white sheets on her foldable camp bed, grateful for the steaming hot water in the showers, and then she'd start detecting an ominous, ulterior agenda lurking beneath the façade. She'd be the character lured into the lab to be experimented upon.

Telling herself she was relieved she didn't have to face such dilemmas, she picked up the silver framed photograph from the back corner of the desk. A studio shot of the absent cop's family; the soft focus provided extra saccharine topping. A plump woman, with an abundance of hairspray, eye shadow and cleavage, grinned stiffly, her arms curled around her young daughter and son. Brighid normally knocked such syrupy portraitures, classing them synthetic, plastic fluff, but now she set the photo back down as if it were a priceless work of art.

◎ ◎ ◎

The promenade was still deserted. Above the empty pavements, the seagull maintained his silent vigil. The stench of vanilla was so pungent now it was making her eyes water.

There was no particular reason for Brighid to return to this place, bar the fact she'd been here before, so it felt safer than leaving town. As reasons go that was a tricky one to pin any sense to; she'd already explored most of Peel, any street in Peel had the same safety value. Reason had vanished much like the people of Peel, and for that reason and that reason alone she returned to the same bench and sat back down.

Procrastination; that's what it was.

She was putting off the inevitable. Sooner or later she'd have to return to Lowell's house. Tessy had spent Brighid's whole lifetime hiding, so if she was already gone by the time Brighid went back to the house, she'd just be doing what she does best. There would be no way of knowing if she'd vanished like everyone else. And what if they were still there? How long could she stand being cooked up in the same house as Tessy, Tessy reeling out unnerving personal snippets of things impossible for her to know, without going completely crazy herself? For the time being at least, sitting it out on this bench waiting for normality to come flooding back was probably a slightly better option.

Despite feeling lonelier than she'd ever been in all her life, the idea that perhaps she wasn't alone, not really alone, kept haunting her. Perhaps, the vanished hadn't vanished at all, not completely, but had just shifted out of visibility's spectrum. Physicality, and the ability to move things, to exert their presence upon an object may well have deserted them, but they, their crucial essence, might still exist. A whole mob could be standing right in front of her, spooks in their own land.

Dark clouds blocked any silhouettes of Ireland on the horizon. Had the ceirtduir, the latest UNDER and its devastating new sideline, opened there too? How far had it spread? Had it crossed the earth and swallowed everyone up?

Her pocket vibrated. She fished out her mobile.

MAYBE EVERYTHING'S ALL IN YOUR HEAD. AND WE'RE INSIDE THERE, TAPPING AWAY, KNOCKING AT THE DOOR.

Ignore. She just had to ignore his messages. Stuffing her phone into her pocket, she glanced back out to the horizon. The sun slid behind the clouds lining the slate grey cumulous with a fiery radiance. She shivered. It reminded her of an antique oil painting she had once seen, a seascape with war torn galleon. The dark oils used for the storm clouds suggested war, the end of an era, death; the golden hues that had dappled the edges of the clouds, the curling tips of waves, hinted at divinity, hope, a new dawning. She breathed in the stench of vanilla. If this was an oil painting depicting war and hope, who was the enemy? And where was the hope?

'I know you,' a man's voice declared.

She had been so lost to her thoughts she hadn't noticed the man just metres away, an old man resting up on his walking stick. Eye contact made, he plodded into motion, shortening the distance between stick and bench, each bow-legged step deepening the lines on his face. She leaped up to help him, and as he plonked himself wearily down onto the bench, she clasping his elbow, she realised they had met before. He was the old man from the steam train, the old drunk from the pub.

'I don't know where she is,' he said breathlessly. His eyes were red raw as though he'd been crying.

'Who?'

'My wife.' More tears threatened.

The sun came out fleetingly, shone on a glob of blood on his nearside eyebrow, making it glisten.

'What happened?' She motioned to the glob that no longer glistened, to the glob that sat darkly brooding amongst errant hairs.

He hastily wiped the eyebrow with the back of his hand, smudging the blood onto his forehead. 'Marge is missing. I've looked everywhere.' His face crumpled. He broke into sobs, nuzzling his head on her shoulder.

The wife's name triggered her memory: Marge whining his name. Marge and Archie. Archie – that was his name.

He gazed up at her, his chin digging into her shoulder.

'She was jealous of you, yer know.' His wet cheek slithered onto her neck.

She edged away.

Archie sat up, brushed imaginary dust or hairs off his trouser legs. 'I let her down,' he mumbled wretchedly. 'I should have saved her from this.' He brandished his stick at the beach and gasped in a way that sounded as though the wind had caught his breath, rolled it up, thrown it back into his mouth. 'What's that smell?'

'Vanilla,' she said, opting not to give him a reassuring pat on the knee, keeping her distance. 'Marge will come back – they all will, I'm sure.' She was not in the least bit sure.

He shook his head. 'Stupid argument. It was a stupid row. About the weather of all things. She was worried about the fog.'

'What fog?'

Archie shrugged mournfully.

'Maybe she's just gone off somewhere – she's probably just letting off steam. I mean she might be back home now fretting about you, the same way you are about her.'

With both hands gripping the crook of his stick he leaned forward, staring blankly at the ground. 'Everyone's vanished'. He sighed. 'The neighbours – Mrs Quiggin and her kids, Jimmy – my old mate Jimmy, the Shimmins.'

'Is it just in Peel?'

He glanced back up at her. 'I don't live in Peel, love.'

'How did you get here?'

'Might have a stick but I've got wheels too, yer know.'

She could come out from under the sofa. Peel wasn't the only place free of the big cleaner in the sky. The UNDER had done its damage and passed. Full stop. For now.

'Can you give me a lift?

His bloodied brow furrowed.

'I can drive if you're not up to it.'

He sat upright. 'Of course I'm up to it.' Then he lowered his head, prodded the ground with his stick. 'But there's no point, unless you're after a bit of sightseeing. The whole island's been taken, what I've seen of it.'

The sun came out, removing the gilt edging around the clouds, making the sand sparkle, making the seaweed shine.

'Is it just the Isle of Man? Has it happened anywhere else?'

A population of eighty thousand plus had just been zapped into thin air all around her, but all she could think about were the people she knew elsewhere, the hope that life would be going on as normal back home, and in the millions of other homes around the world.

'How would I know?' His finger probed his ear.

'Car radio,' she suggested.

'Won't tune to anything.' Finger out, ear fluff onboard, he wafted it under his nose and inhaled.

'Might be your aerial. Probably got bent with the UNDER.'

Rubbing wax onto his trousers, he shook his head. 'Nothing wrong with my aerial; it's everything else that's wrong.'

The seagull swooped down from the lamppost, landed on the railings.

Inside her pockets, her nails dug into her palms so much they hurt.

Archie's gaze slipped to something behind her, his eyes widening. 'Do you know what? I think I might know where Marge is.'

Brighid turned to see what he was looking at.

'The castle. She sometimes goes there when we've had a row. Don't know why I didn't think of it before.'

'Well, there's your answer.'

He struggled to his feet. 'You have to come with me.'

'To the castle?'

'Aye.' Archie grinned.

The seagull shuffled into a more comfortable position.

She hadn't even dared look at the castle, not properly. 'I can't.'

'I can't go on my own! I need someone to help me on the steps.'

Brighid was the only *someone* available.

'She'll be there. I know it,' he pleaded.

'Leave her there then. She'll come home when she's good and ready.' Ready was something Brighid was not, not in terms of the castle. It was the last thing she wanted to see up close.

'What, and leave her there for the UNDER, to be taken to God knows where?' The old man's eyes were welling up again.

Guilt kicked her off the bench. 'Grab my arm.'

Her unease about entering the castle was still there as they crouched beneath the police tape, ignoring warnings not to cross the buckled bridge over the causeway, and was still there as they ascended the castle's ancient steps but it had smudged and faded much like the blood on Archie's brow. There were bigger issues at stake – the island's population had just gone down to single figures (global statistics would stay seven billion plus until she knew otherwise) and this old man would probably never see his wife again. Her paranoia over a dumb dream, her shameful hesitation to help, was pathetic.

With no-one around to take the admission fee – no surprise there – Archie steered the route into the castle grounds, up the grass bank towards an ecclesiastical ruin, signposted, St German's Cathedral.

She had been here before. Every single night for the last two weeks.

Much of the building had crumbled, but it was undeniably the same place. The very same church she tumbled through after being hurled from the gull-drawn carriage.

She wasn't going to panic.

Peel Castle; stunning castle ruins, prime location, an islet at the end of a sweeping bay. Now that must have featured in many a 'Come to the Isle of Man' advert. Her brain had simply filed it away and thrown it back up in her dreams.

They entered through one of the open archways, passing a cluster of centuries old gravestones. Grit rained down as a seagull fidgeted atop roofless walls.

'She'll be down there,' Archie said, removing his hand from her arm, pointing to a doorway. 'Will you take a look?'

The doorway led to a narrow unlit flight of steps. Archie's hand was on the small of her back, coaxing her forward.

'It's where she always goes.'

Holding onto the dank walls hemming her in on either side, she began the descent into darkness. Archie was still behind her.

'It's too steep for you Archie. Stay there.'

The shambling and rasping refused to quit.

'Go back Archie.'

The steps went round a sharp bend. Concentrating, not wanting to lose her footing, she glimpsed an iron gate at the bottom. Spurred on, she sprung down the final steps, and entered the room beyond. A chill hit her.

The windows, bars, view to the bay, barrel-vaulted roof – they were all there – the exact same as the dream.

A thunderous clang tore through the déjà-vu.

The prison gate slammed shut.

Archie was chamber-side in, blocking her exit. 'Sorry,' he smirked. 'It's part of the contract.'

Chapter 24

Lowell was relieved there had been no sign of Brighid this morning. He'd expected her to hammer on the lounge door, demanding to know why he hadn't opened the edit suite. But she'd been unusually quiet. Totally silent, in fact.

No bathroom visits.

Not even a creak of a floorboard.

Not that he'd been listening.

His ears were too busy homing in on the radio. When he'd first started listening properly again last night there'd just been the odd intermittent islands of static hiss amongst tortuous stretches of silence. But this morning, around the time Brighid should have been eating her breakfast, something else came through. Not just the whistlers, but the noise of the UNDER. Last time the radio played that, Nell had turned up the very next day. He wiped his beard.

It had to be well after lunchtime by now. Not that he was hungry. Not that he was looking at his watch. And there was still no sign of Brighid. Not yet anyway. He was still director, so he just needed to direct one more scene. After that, the poxy documentary would have to find itself a new director. He was returning to his old role: keeping watch over the radio. Without distractions. To achieve that, it was vital the next scene involved a letter. He'd leave it up to the woodworm to get the best angle.

Paper and pen in hand, he pulled out a chair and sat

down at the table, the table where Nell first appeared, naked and cross-legged; the same table Mum used to do her nails every Wednesday 8pm. Maybe it was Mum's rigid timekeeping, her tendency to count even the baked beans on her plate, that first got him interested in numbers.

Five. Seventy-nine. Zero. The red line had darted sporadically between them this morning, but had remained on zero since.

Zero. Nil. Nell.

Hector was right; when Nell's voice had first come through on the radio, he had placed a lot of significance on the position of the red tuning line. He was sure she had said her name was Nell. Perhaps he imagined it. But she'd never corrected him when he'd called her that. Not that he could remember anyway.

Subsequent chats they'd had, the red line often tuned to other numbers. He had jotted down the numbers in case they followed a pattern, but after much deliberation he had concluded the numbers were in all probability completely random. Her voice could turn up on any number. Nil lost its significance, but Nell stayed.

Until now.

Now he needed to find her.

He'd already scoured the carpet, had gone down on his hands and knees, scrutinised every fibre. But the triangular stone was no longer there. It had vanished just like Nell.

He'd use black ink for the letter. Not blue. Not red. Almanac colour coding was a thing of the past.

Dear Brighid

It is with regret I must inform you that your contract with Aurora Productions is terminated with immediate effect. Once the internet connection is restored, I shall transfer all

money owed into your account. Please vacate the premises as soon as possible. Leave the key in the kitchen. I am no longer available for comment.
Regards
Lowell

He had absolutely no regrets at all. It was a mere formality. He regretted licking Nell on the face. That was why she disappeared. He was sure of it.

He scooped up the letter, folded it so the crease was exactly in the middle, and then his nose twitched.

There. Nell's smell again.

The table and one of the arms of the sofa, he'd already discovered this morning, possessed a concentrated clump of the same lingering scent he could smell all around the room. He treated himself to a sniff of the table again and then sniffed again; short, sharp sniffs, devouring every particle. Nose hairs basking. He flared his nostrils, shivered. Craned his nose closer. Burrowed his cheek onto the mahogany. Breathed in. Honey. It was as though she were there, lying on the table beside him.

He closed his eyes.

His head felt as though it were resting on the softest pillow, a pillow plumped with essence of Nell. He was floating in honey. Vanilla. Chlorine. Honey. Vanilla. Chlorine.

Honey.

Chicken flavouring sourced from China.

Bleach.

Piss.

Dog.

He was back in the dog pound. Back inside the kennel cell.

This time, though, Lowell was no longer inside the

dog's mind, but leaning against the breeze blocks, without limbs or torso. He peered down; no sign of any beard hairs; it was safe to assume then, his head was also absent. Despite all that he could still see.

A collie with the same white face and paws of previous dreams, raised his head from his plastic bed and stared right back up at where Lowell would be if he were really there.

One blue eye. One brown eye.

'Time I introduced myself,' said the dog, heaving himself up into a sitting position. He was a long haired collie, completely white, apart from a patch of black on his chest

'Algo,' he said offering his paw. 'One of many names I've had over the years, you can call me that. The pound call me 4274. I'm just another mutt.' He scratched his ear with his back leg. 'Sorry. Itch. Not exactly five-star accommodation here.'

The black on his chest followed a definite pattern, a curve not dissimilar to a parenthesis. Not dissimilar to the shape of the kidney stone. The kidney stone was a mirror opposite, a right-hand bracket. Algo's black patch was more an opening bracket.

'Do you know what day it is?' asked the dog.

'I've no idea,' Lowell heard himself reply.

'Day five.'

Algo straightened up wearily and shook himself. 'Five days they give you to be reclaimed. No-one's looking for me. Not anymore. And as for a new home, I'm just not pretty or young enough. Sure, folks stare in from time to time. Sometimes alone. Sometimes with children. I've tried my best to get their attention; I've even thrown myself against the bars, howled at them, but that just pushes them away. They see the stiffness in my bones. The centuries

I've roamed the earth it's no surprise I've gathered a spot of arthritis along the way.'

Algo rubbed his chin along the rim of the plastic bed, all chewed and scratched from previous tenants. 'Seventy-nine,' he murmured.

'What?'

'Seventy-nine scratches on this bed.'

'Oh. Okay.'

'I used to be an accountant.'

'But you're a dog.'

Algo's ears flicked back, flat against his head. 'He's here.'

Chapter 25

Archie locked the dungeon gate.

Brighid was motionless: stunned – stun gun shot between the eyes and hauled into the abattoir type of stunned. Her head was reeling, absorbing dungeon dream scenery. Ribs of sandstone supported the vaulted roof. Just like the dream.

'What contract? What are you talking about Archie?'

He leaned back against the gate, stuffed the key into his jacket pocket. 'More a gentleman's agreement.'

'No gentleman locks a girl in a cell.'

'Your boyfriend gave me twenty quid.' He rubbed his chin. 'Plus a couple of tickets on the train to keep you company.'

'What boyfriend?'

He shifted his weight back upon the stick. 'Nice chap. Probably wants to propose or something. Biker fella. Wears leathers.'

'Unlock the door, Archie.'

He wagged his finger at her. Then swayed.

This wasn't ideal terrain for a walking stick; the earth and stone floor sloped all the way down to the outer wall of the castle where four arched openings provided the cell's only illumination. Just like the dream. Each opening, or window, possessed bars impossible to squeeze through, cold air blasting in from vanilla bay.

A second doorway.

Smack bang opposite the one they'd entered.

'Hector. That's the chap's name.'

She swung round, faced Archie.

'See, nothing wrong with my memory.' He grinned.

The same name had cropped up in an email, when she was in France. *Wakey wakey…We needed to fill you in on some background… where better to start than at Hunvre. See you soon, Hector.* Or words to that effect.

Her head was spinning. Hip throbbing. Phone. Her mobile was vibrating.

She plunged her hand into her pocket, grabbed her mobile.

OOPS. LOOKS LIKE I'M RUMBLED X

Peering up from her phone, she glared at Archie. 'Is this some sort of elaborate hoax?'

He shrugged, his grin subsiding.

'Where is he?' she demanded.

Was that 14B's real name? Hector? He couldn't have sent that email. She hadn't even met him at that point. Why would he send that email? What was he doing on the same flight as her? Why was he sending these text messages?

Another message.

WAKEY WAKEY.

Even the most sophisticated of hoaxes couldn't plunder her subconscious and come up with this location. She needed to distract Archie, make for that other gate and run for it.

'Hector's not my boyfriend.' A discreet step backwards. 'So it's a bit creepy, actually illegal, to hold me hostage here.' A little step to the side.

'The other gate's locked.'

The old guy didn't miss a trick. Not about to take his word for it, she made straight for her exit plan.

'It's locked.'

There was no way he could know; the crack in his voice highlighted that.

She pulled and pushed at the gate.

Archie's bluff was bang on; he'd got it right and didn't he just know it, smiling from ear to ear like that. He was demented, traumatised; events had kicked the marbles right out of his head.

She needed to talk him round, talk some sense into him. She already knew his Achilles heel. 'Imagine what Marge would say if she found us here – you locking yourself up with another woman.'

He swallowed a generous gulp of air. His eyes welled up. He pulled a handkerchief out from his jacket pocket and dabbed his face. 'What's this? Bereavement counselling?'

'She'd have to be dead for that.'

He stared back blankly.

A loud scream.

But it was not her own.

A seagull outside, peered through the window bars.

Was it the seagull that screamed?

One eye staring.

A hollowed scar had put down roots where the other eye should have been.

Reacting to his audience, the gull leaned forward, lifted his wings and took what could only be described as a bow. Then the gull threw his head back, opened his beak, and issued an encore to his opening scream.

Her throat was suddenly dry, unable to swallow, let

alone speak.

'You!' Archie hissed at the seagull. 'I know you.'

Archie wasn't the only one. A one-eyed seagull made a regular appearance in her dreams, in the gull-drawn carriage that always delivered her to the same destination: this castle, this room, this floor and beyond. But this was no time to brood over this latest coincidence, no time to hope a crab might come along dig an escape route with his pincers; for now she needed to consign the connection of one-eyed gulls to the great big dog pile of all other imponderables. If Archie had found a key in the first gate, there might be a key on the outer side of the second; she just needed to fish her hand through the bars. Archie was still in conversation with the seagull.

'You were there outside the church when me and Marge got married.'

Seagulls only live a few years, of that she was sure, almost sure. Her hand slipped through to the other side.

'You spoiled a perfect picture. Me and Marge on the church steps.'

Patting wildly, her fingers wandered across the rusted lock.

'You were perched on that statue, on the shoulder of Our Lady. The Cyclops Gull we called you.'

An empty keyhole.

'And the other day. Tuesday. You were there when the ambulance arrived.'

'I need you to think back to that event,' said another voice.

She swung back round. It was the seagull. The seagull was talking. Actually talking. The same resonant voice of her dreams.

Her arms stiffened.

Archie visibly paled. 'The plane.' He threaded his

fingers through his sparse hair. 'Marge didn't want to go. She was worried about the fog.'

The seagull nodded.

'Stu, our son, told her she was being silly, said he was experienced enough to handle a bit of fog, that he wouldn't even dream of flying, let alone bring family along, if he thought there was the slightest danger. We nearly lost the slot; the grandson, Stu's son, and his mate took a lifetime to get ready, busy applying their eyeliner. Used to be just girls in my day did that.' Archie scratched his chin. 'Call themselves emos or goths or something. The labels keep changing. Now is it hoverboards or skateboards they've got?'

'What about you, sweetie?' The gull arched his wing towards his beak. 'Ring any bells?'

She nodded wearily.

'Bravo,' said the one-eyed seagull.

Her heart was beating so hard, she felt nauseous.

'Archie,' the seagull said, 'do me a favour and grab that tin outta your pocket.'

Archie reached into his pocket and fished out a small tin. The sort of tin that would hold mints. Gazing down with rheumy eyes, his wrists balancing against the stick, Archie unscrewed the lid and then he shuffled towards her.

'Now Brighid,' said the seagull. 'Take the tin and dip your thumb in.'

With numb curiosity she did as the seagull told her – the tin looked just like Tessy's tin in France; the label even bore the same sketching of acorns.

She dipped her thumb in. The wax was warm.

She had been hanging out with the old man for at least half an hour; it wasn't exactly summer either; any melted wax he happened to have in his pocket should have solidified by now.

'Who gave you this?' she asked, looking back up.

Archie was no longer there.

Her thumb pressed deeper into the wax, her gaze sweeping the dungeon.

'We've kept him long enough,' said the seagull.

It would have been impossible for Archie to shamble out of the dungeon so quickly and so silently. Both dungeon doors were still closed.

'Now,' said the seagull. 'How about you?'

'What about me?' Her voice sounded tiny. Her thumb felt sticky. She removed her thumb from the wax.

'Take a look at the tin.'

The wax was smooth and flat.

She had practically rammed her thumb in, had held it there for over a minute, but there were no indentations. No whorls. No thumb print.

It was as if she was a ghost.

The thought hit her like a diesel train going full throttle. Wind coursed through her very being.

'At last,' said the seagull. 'You're a tough nut to crack. Sorry about all the upheaval, but we had to get your attention somehow. Hector's done his best, but he's in and out like a cormorant and could only do so much.'

Unable to breathe. Unable to swallow. Brighid focused on her feet. Her boots were still there; black stitching and glue still holding leather and soles together. If she had vanished just like Archie, then surely she wouldn't be able to see her boots? Waterproof boots that always let the water in when it rained. She wriggled her toes, tried to push the tingling sensation she could feel in her limbs into some kind of movement. She managed a small hobble, forward and then back.

'Panicking will get you nowhere,' said the seagull.

Something vibrated.

The mobile.

Pocket and coat. Still there.

Her fingers plunged into the pocket, grazed across the top of the phone. Her hands were shaking; she could barely hold the mobile.

THANK THE SEAGULL AND CATCH THE BUS. X

'He's very eager to see you,' said the seagull. 'He's been waiting quite some time.'

What bus? That and the myriad other questions clogging her brain needed a release, but when she tried to open her mouth, her facial muscles no longer worked. She breathed in deeply, or thought she breathed in deeply. Her lungs felt heavy, as though she'd been holding her breath underwater. The intake of air, or possible intake of air, made the roof of her mouth itch, her nose tickle, her eyes water. She paused to sneeze, but the sneeze failed to arrive.

'Bless you,' said the one-eyed gull. Then he hurled himself away from the window, a flurried flap of feathers and wings swooping out over Peel Bay.

A stray white feather blew in through the bars.

The feather drifted to the dungeon floor, landing in the exact same spot Archie had stood the moment he had vanished. There on the ground, next to the feather, was a key. The key to the dungeon door.

If she really was a ghost, she'd be able to float through the door, all ethereal buoyancy. She felt too heavy to be a ghost. Everything felt dense: the air, gravity, smells, taste, her tongue – her tongue was like a bloated turd making her want to gag. She breathed in hard, thirsty for air. All she could smell was vanilla, wreathing her nostrils.

When she breathed out again her knees buckled; then she hit the ground.

It didn't hurt.

And she could now at least move, stretch her hand and grab the key.

She could just about haul herself up too.

Back up on her feet, she swayed, but managed to stay upright. The not-quite-a sneeze had somehow released the strange paralysis she'd experienced during conversation with the seagull. She shambled forward, boots still visible. Her hands were trembling so much, she was struggling to get the key into the lock.

There. It was in.

If she was a ghost, someone else would just see the key floating in the air, inserting itself into the lock, turning.

Dungeon gate open, she scrambled up the narrow steps, gripping the sandstone walls. Her hands sank into the stone as though it was something glutinous. She whipped her hands away, leaving no imprint, no sign she'd ever been there. Like all the others scaling these steps over the centuries. Where were they now? Where had Archie gone?

How long had she been dead?

Pockets still there. Boots still there. She emerged from the gloom to the bright open space of the cathedral's ruins.

EXIT.

She followed the sign and lumbered down the castle's main steps, legs like jelly and vanilla ice cream.

Pavement.

No sightseers bustling towards the castle thirsty for a spot of Viking and Celtic history.

No families grabbing an autumn afternoon bag of chips.

No reluctant teenager serving in the hot food kiosk.

No-one taking their dog for a walk.

No-one out on their bike.

No-one out on their unicycle.

No-one driving their car.

Stumbling across the pier, she glimpsed across the buckled bridge to the promenade; even the Cyclops gull had vacated the area, no longer available to offer directions.

The fishing trawlers were all tied up on the harbour side, bobbing on the incoming waves.

No fishermen.

No fish auctions.

One of the trawlers had been painted yellow. Yellow. Just like the fishing boat in that possible sighting of Algo. She had spent so long looking for him. But that was years ago. He'd be long dead now.

Her phone vibrated. She slid her fingers into her pocket, plucked out her mobile. A message from 14B. Hector.

MALE WHITE COLLIE URGENTLY SEEKS HOME OR RESCUE. HIS TIME IS UP.

Attached was the exact same screenshot Kate had sent; the same photo of the same dog in the same pound. Why was Hector sending it as well? She slipped the mobile back into her pocket. Too numb to fathom anything out, she shifted her gaze back to the quay side.

That fishing boat berthed up in Peel Harbour was bright yellow. So bright it shone like sunshine, made her eyes sting. She turned away, squinted at the beach, to the large mound of acorns washing up on the shoreline.

Scrunch. Scrunch. Scrunch.

That wasn't the acorns making that sound.

S-C-R-U-N-C-H.

Her heart.

S-C-R-U-N-C-H.

It was as though it was beating in her ears.

S-C-R-U-N-C-H.

Pulsating in her brain.

Every beat slower than the last. Pounding. Crushing. Scrunching. Her blood pressure was plummeting – she could feel it, as though her blood was thickening, clotting, coming to a standstill.

Her throat. So fiercely dry.

She grabbed the wing mirror of the nearest car parked up, a Ford Mondeo. And as she battled to stay vertical, tremors racked through every morsel of her being. Her limbs were getting heavier. She rolled up the sleeve of her coat. Her arm, the arm clinging to the Ford Mondeo, was turning grey; like that other time, in the swimming pool when Nuala Nicholls nearly drowned her. All she had to do was swim to the surface then, follow the lights. But there was no surface to swim to this time. Was she crying? She couldn't feel the tears. She couldn't even blink.

But she could hear the bus behind her.

She could hear the engine rumbling, the changing of gears.

A horn sounded.

She swung round.

A red and green double-decker.

Bus number 14B.

All she had to do was hop onboard.

Chapter 26

The current length of the New Lounge Age remained a mystery.

The days were now stretching. Daylight was creeping in beneath the closed lounge curtains earlier and earlier each day, lingering into what was probably late evening. Lowell no longer had time to check watches, never mind almanacs.

The last of the light was seeping away now, flattening the embossed fleur-de-lys pattern on the painted wallpaper. This was the moment he always looked forward to; the light from the radio's tuning window became more pronounced, a full moon in a darkening world.

The electricity had been cut off months ago; an oversight that could have had unthinkable consequences. Thankfully the radio turned out to be self-charging. So far anyway. No ordinary battery, even if there was one, could maintain all that crackling effervescence without some sort of drain on energy levels. There wasn't enough sunlight coming in to the room for it to be solar recharging; besides the radio was too old for that type of technology. So just how it was recharging was completely confounding. Ordering anything online was out of the question what with the electricity being down, so purchasing a back up set of batteries, or even better a generator, wasn't an option. Nor was a spot of the non-virtual, in-your-face-having-to deal-with-real-people sort of shopping. That would entail dangerous amounts of time away from the radio. No, he just had to keep listening and hoping. Perhaps it was the very power of his vigil, the sheer longing, the dogged determination to never give up that kept the radio hissing. That was the chief distinguishing feature of the new era, the radio's constant gush of untuned static, and he spent every waking hour trying to decipher it.

For some peculiar reason, he now knew the gush of untuned static was actually much more important than he had previously realised. It was a sense of certainty he felt in every bone in his body, an ache, an ache of old, arthritic bones; an ache that ran all the way through the marrow in his bones.

If that ache was anything to go by, it would seem he'd been studying the static hiss an awfully long time, much longer than the few months he'd witnessed the sunlight ebbing and returning, and in all that time, two things had persistently played on his mind: Nell, of course, or whatever her real name was; and his chances of survival should he ever find a way of entering the radio.

He had briefly contemplated taking the radio apart, finding a screwdriver or knife, and prising the radio open, but the thought alone had made him so nauseous, he'd had to grab BOFO and vomit bile and foam. He didn't eat much these days; in fact he couldn't remember the last time he'd eaten. There was no time for that.

He was an armchair captain now, exploring unchartered territories, navigating waves of static, searching for a way in.

Into Nell's world.

That's how he saw it. The space inside the radio. A world of endless oceans. Fizzing, sputtering, and hissing.

Any islets of celestial choirs were lost to the rising sea

levels.

The whistlers had fallen silent.

And so had Nell.

In his darker, more hopeless moments, he feared Nell had drowned in the deep Static Sea. He imagined her lying on the ocean bed, anchored down by the red line, white noise gnawing at her lifeless limbs.

Her scent had levelled off; that special blend of vanilla and honey was now ubiquitous throughout the room. Sure, there were the occasional peaks, when his nostrils would go into overdrive, but it was mostly when there was a draught in the room, when a gale was blowing outside and was slipping in through the gaps around the sash windows, rolling up dust made up of microscopic dead skin fragments Nell must have shed, bundling them all up, making Lowell sniff and hope.

Sometimes, though, it wasn't a draught, sometimes he swore he could feel her breath. The red line would twitch, as though her breath were coaxing a pulse into the radio.

Those lighter moments when, despite the cold, calm day outside and the central heating not working, a warm breeze blew across the lounge with a ghost of sunshine hair, he would find himself whispering one of the few things he remembered Nell ever saying.

'No-one really goes.'

And if he closed his eyes, immersed himself in the static, he would see her. She was floating about amongst the stars he imagined made up the Static Sea, his parents drifting alongside. Scents of honey, vanilla, and chips, intertwining. Mum and Dad didn't really smell of chips; it was just how he remembered them, thanks to the documentary.

Memories, occasional breezes, and nose hairs, that's all he had to cling to.

And the radio.

Not that he would ever actually *physically* cling to the radio; no, the radio had to remain the exact position it had always been when Nell used to talk to him. Even without electricity, he kept it plugged into the mains; not just because the motion of pulling the plug out may knock the radio the tiniest degree. Who's to say there wasn't some sort of separate electrical source spewing out from that socket? Or maybe it worked the other way around; maybe the plug was holding everything in; if he removed that plug the Static Sea might just drain away, escape down the holes in the wall socket.

With the plug in, the sea remained at high tide. Fizzing.

Exhaustion tugged at his senses, sharpening perception; he could almost feel the waves rolling as he sank further into the captain's armchair. The faux leather of the left-hand armrest, the one nearest to the radio, was worn and peeling. Burrowing his cheek there, he found comfort in its sand like texture. Gathering his knees into his chest, shutting his heavy eyes, he imagined himself curled up on a beach, the hiss and gush of the Static Sea lapping at his ankles. The armchair's buttons digging into his ribs were barnacles. On impulse, he licked the sand, tasted apples, bitten and gone bad, tasted his own breath; he hadn't brushed his teeth for a very long time. The banality of this thought soothed him, got him running his tongue along his teeth, counting. On the twenty-first tooth, he was already drooling on apple sand.

On twenty-three he heard a voice. A familiar voice.

'You're back just in time,' Algo said.

Lowell was back in the pound, floating about in the aisle between kennels.

Algo was standing at the door of his kennel cell, his

cataract eyes staring. 'The vet's just had his cup of tea. He was telling the warden his plans for the weekend. It's going to be cracking weather apparently. Not a single spot of rain. A touch cold, but ideal for walking.'

Lowell slipped in between the bars of Algo's cell, manoeuvring his invisible self to squat down on his haunches next to the talking collie.

Algo turned his head, gazed right back up at him and blinked. 'Black Labrador's up first. Petal was surrendered into the pound. Her humans no longer had any time for her. One of the volunteers who takes us out for walks called Petal an absolute dote. She's certainly that. Plus a whole lot more. She loves every human and every dog she meets. An angel on earth, that's what she is. The volunteer said she heard Petal's family were planning on buying another lab puppy. Now Petal's turned three, they don't think she's cute enough anymore. She's only been in a day, but as you can see the pound is full. All the rescues are full too, full to capacity and beyond. Rescue lady was here yesterday, blinking back the tears. Warden's beside himself as well, fretting about us, hasn't slept a wink. Soon as Petal's family signed that paper, she became property of the state. Aww, Jeez, look at poor Petal. Her legs are shaking. She knows where she's heading.'

Algo's head lowered.

'We all smelt it the moment we arrived. It's in the small outbuilding with the office and WC. I'm not talking about the coffee machine. Nor the synthetic lavender air freshener. Nor the citric disinfectant wipes they use on the table. *The* table. The empty table. It's the carpet tiles; they stink of it.'

Lowell swallowed, still tasted apples gone bad. 'Stink of what?'

'The terror. The panic. The loneliness. The despair. The

countless summer days stolen from us.' Algo cocked his head to one side. 'Can you hear that?'

'I can't hear anything.' There was no barking. No scratching. No whining. No lapping at the water bowl. Silence had fallen upon the pound. All he could hear was the faint hum beyond the EXIT sign.

'It's the electric razor. The vet is shaving Petal's front leg. Getting her ready.'

Hummmm.

Hummmm.

Like the radio.

Eyes wide open.

Lowell sprang from the armrest.

The tuning widow was still shining like the moon.

The radio was still hissing. The red line was still on zero.

He settled back into the armrest, lifted his head, checked the radio one more time. Closed his eyes again. Let the sand stroke his chin. Let the barnacles poke his ribs.

Algo was lying on a stainless steel table.

Panting.

A man with round glasses, syringe in hand, stepped over a bin bag the shape of a dead Labrador.

A Labrador with wings.

'He has no idea who he's killing,' Algo gasped.

'Is there anything I can do?' Lowell heard himself ask.

'Do you know what I dreamt last night? I dreamt I was in a lounge, curled up in an armchair. Listening to the radio. Funny, it was so real. I almost thought I was you. Lowell.'

Lowell woke with a jolt, his heart pounding, the hairs on his arm prickling.

'Lowell?'

A voice in the room.

'Lowell?'

Mum's voice.

He had given up on this moment ever happening.

The red line was twitching on five.

He blinked, shook his head. He wasn't dreaming. He was sure of it. 'Shall I call the lifeboat? Emergency services?' he spluttered.

'Oh, it's much too late for that.'

Her body had already been found.

There must have been a mix up with the dental records, DNA, whatever they'd used to identify her. The police liaison officer had simply said the records matched. Lowell hadn't thought to question it. The woman he'd presumed to be his mother lying there in the mortuary had part of her face missing; the rest of her head was bloated, features lost. She looked more like a jellyfish. All but one of her fingers had been gnawed away. It was the chipped red nail varnish on that one remaining finger that had convinced him it was her.

'Are you alright?' he breathed.

'I'm more than alright. It's blissfully calm here.'

He swallowed hard, feeling almost seasick. 'What about Dad?'

'He's here too. About time you joined us.'

'How?'

'Open the door.'

His gaze shot to the lounge door. Was that where they were? In the hall. Waiting.

'Not that door,' she exclaimed.

He swung back round, faced the radio. 'Can you see

me?'

'What do you think?' she said, batting back his question with another question, using the same tone she had used helping him to learn his times tables years before.

He scratched his arm. 'I don't know.'

'You have to work out the answers yourself.'

He dug his fingernails into the arm rest. His nails were like claws these days. Now, he had stopped biting them, they had grown so long they curled. 'Do you mean the door down in the basement.'

'That's the one. Obviously you have to open the lounge door to get there, so you weren't completely wrong. You were on the right track. Top of the class, Love. Top of the class.'

'I don't have the key code. For the door downstairs.'

'Don't you?'

He shook his head. 'No.'

'It's simple, Algo.'

The dog's name.

'You just need to work out the rhythm of the numbers.'

'What numbers?'

'The numbers will guide you. They've always guided you. Everyone has to have a rhythm of something to follow. That's how you got your name. Algo Rhythm.'

He rubbed his eyes. He was awake he was sure of it.

'How about I give you the first parts of the equation?'

She wasn't making any sense. 'Will you put Dad on?'

'You need to finish your homework first.'

His claw picked at one of the barnacle buttons on the armrest.

'Breeze blocks,' Mum said.

'What?'

'How many?'

'Fifty-seven.' Fifty-seven breeze blocks in Algo's

kennel.

'Correct. Bed?'

He dug his claw deeper into the armrest. What bed was she talking about?

'The number of claw marks on the pound's plastic bed,' she said patiently.

'Seventy-nine.'

'Pound name?'

'Number 4274.'

'Good boy. Days?'

'Five.'

'Bravo. My goodness there's going to be some treats in store for you.'

'What about the radio?'

He couldn't just leave the radio behind. Anyway, what was even behind that door in the basement? It could just turn out to be a storage cupboard.

Mum was taking an awfully long time to answer. He glanced back up at the radio. The moonlight was gone.

'Mum?'

No answer.

'Dad?'

No answer.

No crackling. No hissing.

The radio was dead.

◎ ◎ ◎

Nothing left to lose, Lowell stumbled down the steps to the edit suite.

His socks had holes; his toenails had torn through the wool. They clicked against the marble floor as he crossed the edit suite. On the thirty-first *clickity-clack* he arrived at the arched door.

The keypad lock, fitted to the heavy oak door just above the silver ball handle, was a mass-produced amalgamation of plastic and cheap metal parts, and probably a line available in most DIY and security stores. Although it boasted none of the intricate craftsmanship of the door or silver ball handle, whenever Lowell had tried to imagine what might be behind the door – smugglers' tunnels, intergalactic space – his mind always conjured up the keypad as the mystical gatekeeper.

Grazing his fingernail claws over the keypad's satin nickel veneer, careful not to touch the keys, he breathed in and swallowed; his heart was racing; his head was like an air balloon, full to bursting, ready to lift off. This was the first time he had ever touched the keypad.

His cheeks hurt. He was grinning, grinning inanely, the widest grin he could possibly manage. And he was crying too. He could feel the tears rolling down his face, into his beard.

The cheap metal casing gleamed back at him.

Nell said it was the door to the Garden. He remembered now.

He tapped the code into the keypad.

57-79-4274-5.

Something clicked.

The handle turned by itself.

The door swung open.

He breathed in.

The door had opened to a pitch-black space without any fragrant breeze, without any birds, without any chirping in the hedgerows, without any hint of grass, bedded flowers, crazy paving or even plain loose gravel. There was no Garden. Not even a garden with a lower-case g. And no stars. No planets.

He had stood here before. Hector had dragged him

away. He remembered that too.

Now though, there didn't seem to be anything beyond the door at all. Not Nell. Not his parents. He was sure he would hear them moving about, breathing.

He sniffed the air. Nothing. Just that smell of dank stone. Refusing to believe that's all there was, refusing to give up after everything he'd been through, he breathed in so hard he swore it produced sparks.

The sparks lingered.

Then it dawned on him. These were no self-induced sparks, but lights in the distance.

Pinholes of luminosity began pouring out like water out of a colander; a deluge, rinsing away the darkness for at least a hundred or so metres. And those hundred or so metres displayed the same pixellated fuzz, the same shredded monochrome chaos, as an untuned TV, digital signal removed.

He was looking at the Great Static Sea.

He was staring into the belly of the radio.

He edged closer, longing to hurl himself through the door to go slipping, sputtering and spattering, into that deep, deep, static frying pan sea all the way to Nell's electrical embrace. Sheer, absolute terror kept him standing at the threshold, toes curling, nails digging into the floor.

Biting his lip, gathering any courage he had left, he slowly and tentatively dipped his hand into the Static Sea. Shimmering luminescence trailed his fingernails; filaments of what could almost be faint, far-flung stars glinted then clouded back over again. The sting of electrostatic beneath his fingernails was uncomfortable, but not painful, more irritating, similar to someone tickling the souls of your feet and not quitting.

The whistle, he was hearing now, came right out of the blue, right out of the monochrome to be precise.

A high pitched whistle.

A whistle erupting from the very depths of the Static Sea itself.

A farmer's whistle. Sharp, precise. A language all of its own.

Here.

Here.

Here.

Driven by an uncontrollable impulse to follow the whistle, he glimpsed into the sea. The pull of the call quashed all fears. Refocused his mind. It was just him, the whistle and the sea. The Static Sea was certainly deep enough to dive in without any worries of hitting his head. So that's exactly what he did.

Fizzling through the waves, his arms, hands, and all his other bits, splintered and diffused into tumultuous, grey-scale speckles. It didn't hurt, it didn't even tickle.

When everything defragmented not so back together again he was no longer swimming but padding through a meadow on four, furry legs. He paused to take stock of himself and found he could stand, not only on the four paws but also on his hind legs and quite comfortably too. He was a dog, a white border collie if he wasn't mistaken. He looked a lot like Algo in fact, but peering down as much as he could, there was no sign of any bracket-shaped patch.

Something was in his mouth; he couldn't quite see what. The snout and whiskers were getting in the way, so he removed the ball-like object with his two front paws.

An apple. A red and green apple.

He took a bite. Tasted yellow. In the Garden every colour had its own distinct flavour. He remembered that now. He had lived here before. Yellow was famous for its distinct tang of vanilla; so too were the fruits of the ceirtduir tree. It's a scent that sometimes lingers on visitors from the Garden.

'Red and green make yellow,' he said, immediately impressed with his ability to talk. 'Woof.' That just came out; all the excitement.

The three suns in the sky were also pretty woof-inspiring, as was the cloud hanging over just one corner of the meadow precipitating not rain, but a waterfall. A waterfall maintaining a constant flow of 790 cubic metres per average blink. And he could smell, boy, could he smell, the aromas emerging from that waterfall. Chips, honey and oceans of vanilla.

0

Some follow the light, others the music. For Lowell it's numbers. It's always the numbers.

Anne M. Curtis was born and brought up on a small rock in the middle of the Irish Sea. She has worked as an editor and graphic artist for the television industry and has lived in London, Dublin, Northern Spain and France. She has travelled extensively around South America and India but now lives back on that little rock, the Isle of Man, with Pedro and their two dogs, Maggie and Alf.

Printed in Great Britain
by Amazon

47547461R00206